THE DRAGON TREE LEGACY

Acclaim for the Cain Casey Saga

The Devil Inside

"Vali's fluid writing style quickly puts the reader at ease, which makes the story and its characters equally easy to get to know and care about. When you find yourself talking out loud to the characters in a book, you know the work is polished and professional, as well as entertaining."—*Family and Friends*

"Not only is *The Devil Inside* a ripping mystery, it's also an intimate character study."—*L-Word Literature*

"*The Devil Inside* is the first of what promises to be a very exciting series…While telling an exciting story that grips the reader, Vali has also fully fleshed out her heroes and villains. *The Devil Inside* is that rarity: a fascinating crime novel which includes a tender love story and leaves the reader with a cliffhanger ending."—*MegaScene*

The Devil Unleashed

"Fast-paced action scenes, intriguing character revelations, and a refreshing approach to the romance thriller genre all make for an enjoyable reading experience in the Big Easy…*The Devil Unleashed* is an engrossing reading experience."—*Midwest Book Review*

Deal With the Devil

"Ali Vali has given her fans another thick, rich thriller…*Deal With the Devil* has wonderful love stories, great sex, and an ample supply of humor. It is an exciting, page turning read that leaves her readers eagerly awaiting the next book in the series."—*Just About Write*

The Devil Be Damned

"Ali Vali excels at creating strong, romantic characters along with her fast paced, sophisticated plots. Her setting, New Orleans, provides just the right blend of immigrants from Mexico, South America and Cuba, along with a city steeped in traditions."—*Just About Write*

Praise for Ali Vali

Carly's Sound

"Vali paints vivid pictures with her words...*Carly's Sound* is a great romance, with some wonderfully hot sex."—*Midwest Book Review*

"It's no surprise that passion is indeed possible a second time around"—*Q Syndicate*

Calling the Dead

"So many writers set stories in New Orleans, but Ali Vali's mystery novels have the authenticity that only a real Big Easy resident could bring...makes for a classic lesbian murder yarn."—*Curve*

Blue Skies

"Vali is skilled at building sexual tension and the sex in this novel flies as high as Berkley's jets. Look for this fast-paced read."—*Just About Write*

Balance of Forces: Toujours Ici

"A stunning addition to the vampire legend, *Balance of Forces: Toujour Ici,* is one that stands apart from the rest."—*Bibliophilic Book Blog*

By the Author

Carly's Sound

Second Season

Calling the Dead

Blue Skies

Balance of Forces: Toujours Ici

Love Match

The Dragon Tree Legacy

<u>The Cain Casey Saga</u>

The Devil Inside

The Devil Unleashed

Deal with the Devil

The Devil Be Damned

Visit us at www.boldstrokesbooks.com

THE DRAGON TREE LEGACY

by

Ali Vali

2012

THE DRAGON TREE LEGACY

ISBN 13: 978-1-60282-765-3

THIS TRADE PAPERBACK ORIGINAL IS PUBLISHED BY
BOLD STROKES BOOKS, INC.
P.O. BOX 249
VALLEY FALLS, NY 12185

FIRST EDITION: DECEMBER 2012

CREDITS

EDITOR: SHELLEY THRASHER
PRODUCTION DESIGN: STACIA SEAMAN
COVER ART BY BARB KIWAK
COVER DESIGN BY SHERI (GRAPHICARTIST2020@HOTMAIL.COM)

Acknowledgments

Stories sometimes come from the strangest places. This one started with a tree on my route into the city, and it inspired me to a new set of characters and a great adventure.

Thank you to Radclyffe for your guidance, advice, for giving me a home at BSB and allowing my imagination free rein to tell my stories. To be part of such a special family is an honor I'm truly grateful for.

Thank you to my editor, Shelley Thrasher. You teach me something new with every book, and you do it with patience and grace. The most valuable lesson I've learned on my own is that the ability of a good editor to make a book shine is a blessing. You're the best, and your red pen is legendary.

Thank you to Stacia Seaman for the final polish you give every book, and for always taking them to the next level.

The cover of this book is a piece painted by the amazing Barb Kiwak. Barb, you took my tree and made it beautiful, I can't take my eyes off it. When the Dragon Tree is mentioned in the book, please go back to the cover and enjoy Barb's work. Thank you, Barb, for the gift of your talent, and that it's on my book is lagniappe. In south Louisiana, that means it makes it a little bit more special.

Thank you to my first readers, Connie Ward, Kathi Isserman, and Tina Cerami. Your insights and comments are always invaluable, but your greatest gift is friendship. A special thanks to fellow author and friend Carsen Taite for all her advice and vlogs. All you guys are the best, and I really appreciated your help on this one.

Thanks to every single reader for your notes, e-mails, and encouraging words. Believe me, they go a long way toward keeping me at the keyboard. Every story is written with you in mind.

Thank you to my partner and love, C. You make me laugh, and you make me believe there is beauty in the world no matter what. You are my joy, my best friend, and I love you. *Verdad!*

For C
All my love

CHAPTER ONE

Wiley Gremillion softly sang the first few words of the song from Disney's *Pinocchio*, about wishing on a star, as she sat in the luxury sedan with her head resting against the window. The street where she was parked had two burned-out streetlights, making it almost impossible to see her until someone actually stood next to the driver's side of the car.

It was a gamble to sit alone in the dark in the neighborhood along the Mississippi River, but the only two men who'd ventured close to her car had quickly departed when she stared at them. She'd long ago perfected the fuck-with-me-at-your-own-risk facial expression.

The run-down neighborhood that cusped the river was in reality close enough to the grand homes of Uptown New Orleans to walk. The distance, though, could have been as wide as the Grand Canyon when you compared the dwellings.

She continued to sing, keeping her attention on the peeling red paint of the door on the small shotgun house third from the corner. This was her third trip to the street Katrina's floodwaters had spared, but it appeared devastated nonetheless, because of poverty and neglect.

She finished the first verse of Harline and Washington's song about desires coming true and smiled. Finally Jerry Dupre walked toward her on the other side of the street, wearing such dark clothing she would've missed him if she hadn't memorized everything about his stride.

Jerry hadn't been hard to find. She had detected the pattern of rapes Jerry had committed from the police reports, after hacking their system. Evidently, three brutal attacks committed in different precincts weren't enough to signal that a repeat offender was loose. But the details were too similar to ignore, so she'd hunted where people such as Jerry liked to brag. The idiot had posted pictures on a member-restricted Internet site that catered to sexual predators. From their comments, his fellow sickos had gotten off on the fear etched on the faces of the three young women he had chosen to inflict his special type of pain on.

Stripping away the security layers of the site had led her to the office of Dr. Jerry Dupre, a recognized cardiologist practicing across Lake Pontchartrain in Mandeville. At least he'd been smart enough not to play in his own backyard. But his cooling-off period was shrinking, so she spotted his urge to revel in the other side of his controlled and knowledgeable physician persona.

His audacity surprised her when he stopped at the front door of the shotgun house and tried the knob. Until now he'd just stopped on the sidewalk and stared as if he could see through the cypress slats covering the outside. On his knees it took him two minutes to work the lock, and he glanced back one more time before he stepped inside and closed the door quietly enough that no lights came on.

The girl on the bed was sleeping on her stomach, her sheets pooled along her waist with her legs bare, and Jerry was so focused on studying her like a slide under a microscope that he never noticed Wiley standing outside the bedroom door. He quietly unbuckled his belt, and from what she could see in the limited light coming from the large red display of the alarm clock, he was pleasuring himself, obviously wanting to be ready when he pounced.

"You teasing little bitch," he whispered, as if working himself into the frenzy that would justify the rape and beating he thought she deserved. At least that's how he'd explained himself to his fellow online buddies.

Wiley fanned her fingers out and waited for him to take one step toward the bed.

"You walk around half-naked and you wonder why shit like this happens to you." Jerry rocked his head from side to side, the bones in his neck cracking like a gunshot. His willingness to make noise was Wiley's clue that he was ready; his MO was for the girl to wake and see him. Then he'd get what he really wanted—panic and fear. Wiley was familiar with assholes like Jerry and knew what motivated him.

But he didn't know that this was his target's third night of peaceful sleep, thanks to Wiley's visits with a syringe full of sedative. Not leaving witnesses was something she and Jerry had in common.

"You're going to pay for your whoring ways tonight, bitch," he said, loud enough to wake the neighbors.

"You couldn't have said it any better, Dr. Dupre." She stood right behind him, jammed her Taser to the back of his neck, and zapped him with a high voltage. He dropped like a rock at her feet. The *thunk* of his head impacting the floor sent a rush of satisfaction through her chest.

He was heavier than she imagined, but she lifted him over her shoulder with no trouble. He'd be out for a while. She checked to make sure she had a clear shot to the car and left the double-cylinder lock she'd bought as a gift for the young woman on a small table near the door, next to her house keys and purse. Someone could still kick the door in, but someone like Jerry would have a harder time, if there was a next time.

Wiley locked the door, strode to the car, and dumped Jerry in the trunk. She bound his wrists and ankles with zip ties and duct tape. "You might've been in the mood to get fucked, but fucked up is what's on the menu tonight."

She slowly drove through the mostly deserted streets, smiling as she reviewed the next stage of her plan. The area in City Park she'd picked for their first stop stayed locked until the workers arrived at six, so she made no attempt to hide her identity. If someone glimpsed her shoulder-length blond hair or got close enough to see her oddly colored blue eyes, she wouldn't be concerned. However, the storage facility where the park personnel left their tree-trimming equipment was usually quiet and empty of the homeless who resided on the grounds no matter the time.

The heavy air hinted at rain. The early morning was hot as midday, making her hands slide inside her leather gloves. Weather-related discomforts didn't bother her after what seemed like a lifetime of training to ignore them, along with a lot of other things that bothered most people, like what she was preparing to do. Very few had the stomach to do what was necessary in such situations. Those who had trained her would remember her for her talent for killing. That was nothing to rejoice over, but when she could utilize it on a savage like Jerry, it salved any guilt that crept up.

She opened the trunk and Jerry blinked up at her, looking dazed and confused. She smiled. Before he could rally any courage and try to intimidate her, as often happened when idiots realized a woman had gotten to them so easily, she took a picture of him, the flash making him blink worse. She'd post his picture on his favorite website so his other so-called masters of pain would see how easily the tables could be turned.

"Hello, Dr. Dupre." She grabbed him by his collar and pulled him into a sitting position. "I'm sure you're pissed that I ruined your night of fun, but three young women were enough. At least that's all my employer knows about."

His cheeks inflated almost comically when he tried to talk despite the tape over his mouth, and he predictably glared up at her and tried to struggle out of the zip ties. He fully displayed the anger that'd fueled his new hobby until she pressed her hunting knife to his neck hard enough to draw a droplet of blood. Jerry went from predator to scared little boy in less time than it took for him to start blinking again. An image of his victims flashed through her mind and fury blurred her vision. Her hand trembled and she ached to hear him cry out in fear and pain. Taking a deep breath, she forced her rage back into its cage and steadied her hand on the knife.

"You've been a bad boy, Doctor, and tonight you have to pay for your crimes." She pressed the blade tighter against his skin. The sweat pouring off him in fat droplets seemed more to do with terror than with the heat. "But before we get to that I'm going to remove this," she tapped on the tape, "if you promise to behave."

He nodded so fast she had a hard time getting a grip to rip it off. "Who are you and what do you want?"

"Lower your voice or I'll make the decision for you, and I don't want to do that." A little of his blood ran down the knife when she silenced him with another small cut. "Shut up and let me explain the rules."

"Who are you?" he asked, this time quieter.

"I'm from the Hippocratic Oath Discipline Committee, here to remind you that you promised to first do no harm."

"What are you talking about?"

"You're a doctor, Jerry. You were supposed to help those who trusted you with their lives. That you did, but I know of three women who saw a different side of that bedside manner you're known for."

"They asked for it." His voice got louder again. When she hauled him out of the car to the ground and cut the ties to his feet, he went willingly to the young oak tree that Katrina hadn't uprooted. With his back to it, she ran a rope around his chest and pulled hard enough to pin him in place.

"They asked for it?" She showed him a picture of each of his victims, beaten so badly their mothers had barely recognized them. "Do you want me to call them and tell them you're here, and they can do whatever they like?"

"You don't understand the pressure I'm under. I didn't mean anything. They simply served as a release valve to keep me fresh so I can do good. Their willingness to take punishment made me a better doctor." His fast, desperate, tinny speech signaled that he could sense what it was like when someone else was in charge of his fate. Wiley was ready to pour more fuel on the flames that would burn away his self-confidence.

She slipped the pictures back into her pocket and laughed. Why were guys like this so pathetically the same? "That's the excuse you're going with? Really? If the cops had caught you, your jury would've had a hard time sitting in the deliberation room long enough to make it look like they gave you a fair shake."

"You think a jury will ever hear any of this?" He laughed and appeared momentarily cool, as if he'd gained the upper hand. "If you're a cop it won't matter if you can prove anything. No judge will allow a case to be built against me now. I have rights, goddammit."

"You've already been found guilty, Doctor." She cut his belt, an icy stillness spreading through her. She had no problem being judge and jury. "Tonight isn't about building a case against you, but sentencing you for your guilt."

"You can't do that." His voice carried in the stillness.

"Remember your promise to be quiet. If you don't, I'll decide for you."

"Decide what?" He fought against his bindings as if he'd only just realized the danger he was in.

"Decide on what price you'll pay for what you've done." She resheathed her knife and grabbed his jaw, forcing him to look at her. He smelled sour, like the evil inside him was starting to ooze out of his pores. "You may choose to lose either something you care greatly for, or your life. You have a minute to decide. If not, I will."

"Is this some kind of joke?"

"You have fifty-five seconds left." She calmly cut another piece of tape from the roll.

"Something I care greatly for," he blurted out before she could gag him. "How much do you want?" He cocked his head back, away from her advance.

"Money is what you care greatly for?" He'd lost his opportunity to answer, and she stepped back to take another picture of his wide eyes and gag. "How tragic for your wife and children."

He looked relieved when she unzipped his pants. He probably believed this was a joke and she was about to get him off. "If you rethink your answer, I bet something matters to you more than money." She cut his underwear away and stood back, studying his penis. He'd left his hard-on back at the girl's house, along with his old life. She'd give him back neither. "Oh, what difference an hour makes, huh?"

She took another picture before putting her hand on him. "Something that defines the sexual god you think yourself to be." He stayed shriveled in her hand, moaning through his gag and shaking his head as he tried to kick her away.

"Your choice, remember." She hesitated, letting him grasp fully what was about to happen, then cut away his testicles and held them up for him to see before she started the wood chipper and dropped them in. The grinding gears created a rough baseline to the blasts of air coming through his nose. The horror and pain in his expression left her unmoved. After all, he'd asked for it.

"Court's adjourned."

❖

Jerry sat next to her with his legs tightly pressed together and his hands squeezed between them as Wiley drove to the nearest hospital. After he'd watched her let go of what she'd deemed one of his most valuable possessions, he'd passed out long enough for her to swab the inside of his mouth with the large Q-tip-looking sticks the police used. She'd dropped those in a specimen bag from his hospital, along with the confession letter written on his letterhead. No matter how skilled the handwriting expert, they'd never be able to prove it was a forgery.

"Before I leave you, let's review a few more things." She glanced at him briefly as she turned into the visitors' parking lot. "You chose to live tonight, so if you think about taking out what happened to you on any of the women you hurt, *I* get to make your decision about your punishment next time. No matter how smart you think you are, *I* will find you, and *I* will kill you."

"Why did you do this to me?"

"To get justice for someone else since it's eluded me for years. I can't do anything about my situation, but I could do something about what you were doing."

She parked illegally in front of the hospital entrance on the second floor, not worried about being recorded by any surveillance. The hospital's cameras were on a loop that kept the same picture of the entrance starting at midnight, when any foot traffic through the area was close to nonexistent.

"It's been a pleasure, Dr. Dupre."

"Fuck you," he said, as if to prove he wasn't defeated.

"That's only going to be a figure of speech for you now." She laughed, glad to be out of the car. She pressed the car keys into Jerry's hand to get them bloody, then threw them close to the door. Her last look at Jerry made her laugh again. His anger burned brightly in his eyes, but he didn't take his hands from between his legs.

Wiley took the stairs and walked two blocks toward downtown before she pulled the prepaid cell phone she'd purchased for Jerry's job out of her back pocket.

"I had to go out to get something and some guy's blocking the door with his car. Could you send someone down to get him to move?" she asked the security officer. "Yeah, he's just sitting there. It's really strange." The rent-a-cop sounded more interested when she injected the right amount of worry in her voice. "Thanks."

She turned the phone off. Even if he told the story of what she'd done to him, he was sitting in his wife's sedan, so it'd sound like his sudden bout of conscience was short-lived.

It wouldn't matter much, though, since next to him they'd find the evidence to convict him neatly packaged, missing only the bow. It spelled out how Jerry had suddenly confessed because he'd decided to bleed to death. However, he'd make it to see his trial and the inside of a jail cell after all. If he'd chosen to die that night she wouldn't have hesitated to feed the rest of him through that chipper. It was what he deserved, but she'd honored her word to let him pick his fate.

The sky was losing the deep-violet shade she loved as she got into the old Dodge minivan with peeling green paint and unhurriedly drove to the warehouse district. Considering her love of vintage cars, this one was an odd choice, but no one would remember it because it blended in so well, like she did, no matter the situation. A half mile before her building she glided in front of one of the only occupied homes on the block and locked the van, leaving the wires in their original condition. The next time the owner cleaned it out he'd find the two crisp new hundred-dollar bills she'd left as renter's fee.

She had only one thing left to do, but it could wait, she thought, as she entered the four-story building with the name *Fleming* barely visible along the top. Like many of the surrounding places, the structure had first been the site of a textile industry, then a garment factory, and eventually high-priced real estate for young urbanites who transformed them into luxury condos.

The Fleming building was different from most that surrounded it. Wiley owned the entire space and didn't care for the modern chrome-and-leather worlds her neighbors had built, leaving exposed brick walls as the only hints of age. In contrast, she'd had only the wood floors on the first two levels refurbished and little else added, including the counters along the walls of the first floor for the tools and parts that it took to maintain her fleet of sixteen cars parked on the spotless green-terrazzo floor.

The cargo elevator rose slowly past the second level, and she glanced out at the large canvas that needed a few more days' work. As she stood in the center of the elevator and waited to reach the top floor, she started to shed the persona of the Black Dragon as easily as she did the blond wig and blue contacts. She took a deep breath when the car jerked a little and stopped before one of the largest canvases she'd created. It welcomed her home and helped her forget the bloody acts.

She stood and stared at the piece she'd titled *The Dragon Tree Legacy*, studying the tree at its center. Each stoke of heavy oil paint wove the story that defined the part of her life that her parents and the military hadn't had a hand in. It personified not only her first love, but also the empty coldness of that time. She'd found perfection in another person, but the woman and the life she'd wanted with her were gone—or, to be more precise, stolen from both of them.

This wasn't the time to get caught up in the past, so she took the spiral staircase to the roof. The fire pit she'd arranged the previous afternoon roared to life, one match consuming the identity of the woman

Jerry Dupre would never forget. She sat naked until it disappeared, gaining a bit of self-forgiveness because what she'd done didn't deserve her concern or guilt. She'd killed for the military and now she'd do it to rid the world of guys like Jerry, even if he only went to jail. For someone like him, prison would be more torturous than death. She'd do some jobs pro bono, but this one would pay the bills for quite a while.

She waited until the fire died completely, wanting to clean away the ashes. In the shower she stood under the hot water, the only thing on her mind the canvas she needed to finish. She'd captured only the image of the coastline along Big Sur, California, when she'd visited after getting the commission. The new manager of the Saints football team, a transplant from Los Angeles, had spent his summers in that area and wanted a reminder of happy childhood memories. No one understood needing a talisman like that more than her, so she'd agreed after he didn't blink when she told him her fee.

Clean, she headed down to the third-floor kitchen barefooted, wearing a pair of jeans and T-shirt. It'd been hours since her late lunch out, but she found nothing but a loaf of bread in the refrigerator and peanut butter in the pantry. Eventually she'd have to have the place stocked, but she'd had no time in the month since the contractor's men had finished renovations. She'd paid him a bonus for completing them ahead of schedule and not asking too many questions about the room that spanned the length of the kitchen on the windowless side of the building. The wall she'd had him construct out of old brick looked exactly like the exterior, with the only opening through the extra freezer she'd outfitted herself.

The place still lacked the small nuances that made it feel cozy, but after a long absence from the city, she'd come home, and that's what she planned to make this place. To ensure that she could keep the Black Dragon's lair she'd planned while she completed missions around the world, she couldn't accept too many jobs like Jerry's. If she did, even with a depleted police force, she'd leave a pattern if they didn't choose death.

She took her sandwich and glass of milk through the freezer door to her workroom or, more precisely, the Black Dragon's workroom. She'd always thought of herself as two parts of one whole. That was the only way she could complete jobs without hesitation. Jerry hadn't spent time that night with Wiley the artist. He'd met black ops Major Wiley

Gremillion, code name Black Dragon. And once this job was done, that's who she'd leave in this room. She didn't deny herself her dark side, but after tonight she didn't need it. Not until the next call.

The bank of computers along one wall featured a dragon flying from screen to screen in a random pattern, and along the other wall stretched her desk—the top empty except for the eight-by-ten framed picture to one side.

A much-younger version of herself stared back with her arm around Aubrey. Both smiling, they stood in front of the dragon tree. Those three short adolescent years had left an imprint on her heart as the happiest of her life. Right after her thirteenth birthday, her father had been transferred again, and she and Aubrey had communicated only through a multitude of letters and the occasional phone call. The stack of correspondence between them lay in the desk's bottom drawer, a testament to a friendship she thought of often. Five years after they'd left New Orleans, Wiley had entered West Point, wanting to follow her dad's path into a nomad's existence, but his dark, almost-black eyes and hair weren't the only things she'd inherited from him.

West Point Graduation 1995

Wiley glanced at the symbols of her new rank as she made her way toward her family once the West Point graduation ceremonies ended. Not only had her parents made the trip, but Aubrey and her parents were there to see her finish four of the hardest years of her life.

"You look fabulous," Aubrey said after running up and hugging her. "I'm so proud of you, Second Lieutenant Gremillion."

The way they looked at each other surely telegraphed the fact that they had cemented their mutual commitment early, and no amount of time apart had changed their feelings. Even with the crowd she didn't care. "Thank you." Aubrey's perfume made her heart rate go up and her hands itch to wander. Time alone couldn't come soon enough.

"You made it, kid," Colonel Peter Tarver said after giving her a casual salute. Aubrey had inherited his smile and his disposition toward life. Also, the marine colonel seemed to love Wiley as much as his daughter. "Top of your class too. Damn impressive."

Her father Buckston stood back and let the others finish what they had to say, but his face and smile were relaxed. He looked handsome in his dress uniform, the silver star of his new rank gleaming in the sunlight. She was his legacy, and she was clearly making him proud.

"Thanks, Colonel." She shook Peter's hand, then held hers out to Karen, Aubrey's mother. "Thank you for making the trip, Mrs. Tarver. I appreciate you being here."

"You're welcome, Wiley. My husband's right, though. This was pretty impressive."

"It's the Gremillion warrior gene," said Danielle Gremillion, her mother. "Congratulations, baby." Danielle hugged her before leading all of the Tarvers away so Wiley and her father could have a minute alone in the sea of people.

"General Greenwald called me yesterday," he said, his hand on her shoulder.

Every serious conversation they'd ever had started like this. Most people she'd known claimed their father was their hero, but she'd never uttered those words out loud. She simply accepted his greatness in every cell of her body, so those words weren't necessary between them. Her dad had given her not only an ideal to live up to, but a sense of herself that came from the certainty of having a safety net. No matter what she tried, how high she climbed, or how dangerous the situation—he'd always been a step behind her, ready to catch her if she failed.

"I know you might've had a different commission in mind, but I had to try."

"Wiley." He lowered his head and looked her in the eye. "If this is what you really want I'm not going to quash it, but talk to Aubrey first. You've been accepted, so if you decide against it, walk away knowing you're good enough. Carl Greenwald wouldn't have considered your application, much less green-lighted you, if you weren't. Going forward, though, will change you, and you'll have to live with your choices. More importantly, so will Aubrey."

"I want to show how good I am by actually doing the job, Dad."

"You realize I'm so proud of you that I'm about to pop all these brass buttons, right?"

"That made the day worth it."

"Nah, that's what will stand out more than anything today." Her dad turned her around and pointed to Aubrey. "I'm proud of you for more than just today."

They all had dinner together before Wiley left with Aubrey for a weekend in New York. The hotel and the restaurant reservations were her parents' graduation gift, but the real gift was their acceptance of what Aubrey meant to her.

"Do you think you'll be stationed in Washington near your dad?" Aubrey asked as they rode the elevator up to their room. "If you do, maybe I can get a job with Senator Breaux's office."

Nothing they'd thrown at her in her years at the academy scared her as much as this conversation. She glanced around the room before she concentrated on Aubrey. Every time she had her alone like this, every moment of their history flashed through her brain like someone had dumped a box of pictures into her head: the first time they'd made love after Aubrey's sixteenth birthday, their first kiss, their first fight. Their shared memories of the past were important, but not as much as the future she wanted.

"Are you okay, honey?" Aubrey put her hands on her chest when she stayed quiet.

"I need to talk to you about something important." Aubrey sat on the bed and listened. She didn't close her eyes and pinch the bridge of her nose until she heard her say, "I've been accepted into General Greenwald's special-operations unit."

"You want to be a sniper? All that work and studying, and you want to kill people and nothing else? Please tell me you're joking."

"If I give Greenwald a few years, we can go anywhere you want once my time's up. He promised me my pick of assignments."

Aubrey laughed, but she didn't appear amused. At least she hadn't left. "Tell me why you want to do this."

"I've known you since you were twelve, and I know the things you want. Your dreams are as clear to me as my own." She knelt in front of Aubrey and placed her hands on the bed next to her. "If one day you want to have a child who follows this path, I want to have macheted it clear. Especially if it's a girl."

"Not *if we* want to have a child. *When we* want to have a child." Aubrey kissed her. "And I'm putting in my order for a kid without the Gremillion warrior gene. I want one with the Gremillion doodling gene."

"I'll see what I can do." She got off her knees and crawled into bed until she was over Aubrey. "If you're really against this I'll try for a Pentagon post."

"Promise me you won't forget me and I'll give you my blessing."

"I swear it." The need to touch Aubrey overwhelmed her and she lowered her head for a kiss. When their lips met she slipped down a little so their bodies would come into contact as well and almost physically heard their connection click into place. To her, what they had together was like two puzzle pieces snapping together, each of them a unique fit that they'd find with no other person. "The only thing that'd make me forget you is a bullet to the head."

"Not funny, and if you manage to get shot for any reason, you'd better start running because I'm not taking it well." Aubrey put her hands on her chest again and flipped her over so she could start on the buttons of her uniform jacket. "I may not always love your choices, but I always love you."

Wiley gave up control as Aubrey undressed her, biting her bottom lip when Aubrey stood and let her dress fall to her ankles. The sight of all those curves made her even harder, and the pounding between her legs defined true anticipation. With Aubrey like this she felt no iota of discipline. Aubrey simply shredded the order and control the military demanded of her, and she welcomed it. No rules or fear of breaking any could make her deny this sensation.

"You looked so handsome today on that podium I cried." Aubrey knelt between her legs and made her bend them at the knee. The cold air of the room hit her wet sex, and she flinched. She didn't just want Aubrey to touch her, she needed her to. "The best part of seeing you was knowing you belong to me."

Aubrey followed the declaration by putting her mouth on her, and the relief of having her tongue pressed hard to her clit made her desperation climb until she was close to pain. She dug her heels into the mattress and clenched her jaws as Aubrey sucked her in. The orgasm hit so hard she cried out, and the only sensation left was her need to touch Aubrey in return.

After a deep breath she brought Aubrey up so they could trade places. When she saw how wet and ready Aubrey was, the sheer craving to consume Aubrey's passion swamped her, but first she slipped her fingers into the one place in the world that belonged solely to her. This was truly her home, and she'd fight whatever and whoever to keep it.

❖

From her first day at West Point her father's peers soon noticed Buckston Gremillion's kid and how she could shoot the wings off a fly from what seemed like miles away. More important, they never saw her coming. At graduation she entered a different army from the majority of her classmates, and she worked hard to make sure she was the best at her trade. As the old saying went, killing was her business, and with the missions she'd been deployed on, business was good.

For ten years that was all she'd concentrated on, and she was a master at eliminating targets however it needed to be done. Some targets served as examples to those who needed to learn a lesson, so she sat in her perch for hours waiting for the right shot. She had to make others look like accidents. Those left the biggest impression on her since human skin and bone weren't as fragile as people thought. It wasn't easy to slice through someone, and it took fortitude to shut off the instinctive horror she believed everyone was born with. How many more times could she detach her emotions during the job, then return from that dark, lonely place? How long before she would become only the Black Dragon?

Training and discipline only got you so far. They couldn't serve as a roadmap to help you find your soul. Every time she stepped into this secret place, that map got fuzzier, and she got closer to forgetting the upper ranges of emotion like happiness and joy. She hadn't felt them since Aubrey. The night of her graduation she had experienced the first cracks in the one thing she thought the most solid in her life. Ambition had made her the best, but it had also cursed her to this existence.

She placed her knife back in the empty slot on the wall, glancing briefly at the picture again. Raised by wanderers, she'd felt at home only in New Orleans, so she'd chosen it to work out of now that her commission had officially ended. "A home, but no girl." She spoke out loud, needing to hear some sound to stanch the loneliness.

The animated dragon landed and breathed out a long funnel of fire before receding to another screen when she brought the one in the middle out of hibernation. It displayed Jerry's private numbered accounts, and she opened the withdrawal icon. It didn't take long before she had transferred all the funds into two different but equally secure accounts. She had to give Jerry credit. He'd thought of everything in case his hobby threatened his freedom. Ten million would've gone a long way if he'd had to run, and he'd kept the cash from everyone, including his wife and the IRS.

The antique mariner's clock that was her grandmother's chimed ten times as she finished printing the account numbers and codes to access one of the accounts. Using the prepaid phone, she dialed the number to finish the job.

"Thank you." The woman on the other end sounded rougher and more gravelly than the other times they'd talked.

"You're welcome." What did the woman think of the computer-sounding voice answering her? Her first rule as she entered this aspect of her career was to never speak to clients without a filter. "I take it the police have come by to speak to you."

"They executed a search warrant after my kids left for school, thank God. The computer guy they brought with them was able to retrieve a ton of information despite the security measures my loving husband put in place. The first ones he found were the pictures I told you about. All together there were eighteen different women."

She knew that, but hadn't shared it so Jerry's wife would have an appropriate response when the police told her. "He won't be a problem anymore, and you'll get everything in the divorce, so your plan to move shouldn't take very long."

"About your fee," the woman said quietly.

"It's been taken care of." Jerry's stash was missing five hundred thousand. "When you arrive at your parents' house to settle your children, I'll send you the information you need to access the account. Move it if you want, but I'd suggest keeping it in the offshore bank I picked."

"I trust you, so send the information as is, and thank you for that as well. I feel like I've had my head in the sand to have missed all this, but I don't have time to think about that now. I'm on my way to pick up my children and head to the airport. Once they're okay with my parents I'll come back to deal with the fallout, but at least they won't have to face the embarrassment. It would've been easier if he'd chosen your other option."

After they first made contact Wiley had investigated Jerry's wife and her information, then explained what would happen. The woman had sounded hesitant at first, but their conversations always returned to the pictures she'd found. Those three women—tied, beaten, humiliated—and all the work of her loving husband of fifteen years. All the points of information that had made this woman lose any feeling for the man she thought she knew better than herself fulfilled Wiley's criteria for taking the job. She wouldn't spend her retirement taking jobs like some common assassin, but for a deeper reason. Whoever she took on would have to convince her that the world and the place they lived would be better off if the target lost either their freedom or their life. Her life had to have some code of conduct or she'd find no reason to live it.

"He's the father of your children, but I understand your position. I seldom give advice, ma'am, but your son is young enough to forget his father if you find someone else soon. Don't succumb to guilt at any point and give him or your daughter access. Your husband might've been able to hide this part of himself from you for a very long time, but he'll never give up the feeling it gave him."

During a long span of silence Wiley could picture the attractive brunette clutching the phone. "What does that mean?"

"His hunting days are over, and he'll never be a free man again, but I know the type. Memories of the power he held over those women will feed him for years. The day will come, though, when he'll need new conquests to quell that desire." She'd finished the computer search she'd started a few days earlier, and the thirty-three open cases she scrolled through had every element of Jerry's signature, starting back when he had graduated from high school.

"I still don't know what that has to do with my son."

"The time will come when he'll begin the process again, but with a surrogate. Who better to continue his work than his son? Considering that he won't be getting out, he'll satisfy himself by guiding a puppet to commit the same types of acts. The stories will be all he'll have left as he rots in a cell." Wiley ran through the files, wanting to see if any of the investigators had recovered DNA from the victim or the scene. "Do not give him the opportunity or satisfaction."

"Thank you. I can't tell you that enough."

"Good bye, ma'am, and good luck."

As soon as the phone powered off, Wiley dropped it into the shredder next to her chair. After she finished the search on Jerry and read his pathetic accomplishments as a serial rapist, she released a worm into her system that would root out any mention of him and destroy it. The job was finished as far as she was concerned, and nothing physical, forensic, or electronic existed to connect her to it.

Now she could return to her canvases and bury her emotions in the art that consumed her as much as the targets in her sights did.

CHAPTER TWO

W hat exactly does that mean?"
     Aubrey Tarver stared at her partner of six years, Maria Ross, sitting so calmly in their kitchen, and felt like the room was closing in on her. The pale-gray walls she'd taken three weeks to decide on suddenly appeared too dull against the black-granite countertops. The walls as well as her life were closing in on her, and she had to concentrate on her breathing to avoid panicking.

She'd met Maria, who owned a bar where she'd joined friends for drinks inside the Hilton Riverside in New Orleans, and after a few free rounds she'd given in and handed over her number. The dinner she'd agreed to as a thank-you for the bar tab turned into something comfortable, then permanent, but she hadn't planned to end up with Maria.

"I had to agree to a meeting, Aubrey," Maria said. "I don't fucking know how to make it any simpler for you to understand." She twirled her glass of lemonade in small circles between her hands. "I'm in no position to say no."

"Stop trying to make yourself feel better by trying to make me look stupid." Arguing was the only thing Aubrey would ever describe as passionate about their relationship. Maria took every possible opportunity to touch her, but she'd never really *touched* her in a way that made her want to share not only her life, but her dreams with her. "What exactly does that mean to me and Tanith? You promised this crap wouldn't touch our lives." Her chest constricted and bile lurked at the back of her throat.

"It won't, but don't pretend you don't like the money. This whole place is a shrine to how well you know how to spend it."

The job Aubrey used to have in the mayor's office now belonged to someone else, but she should have tried harder after it disappeared following the election. A new administration meant a new media manager. She had made enough connections to land a new job, but she was eight months pregnant when they'd handed her a pink slip. After Tanith came so had Maria, and she'd put off a new search month after month, always at Maria's urging. Her stupidity wasn't Maria's fault, though, but all hers.

"I didn't realize it bothered you." She didn't speak in anger or use sarcasm, and mentally she was already packing.

"Come on, baby, you know it doesn't. I'm just jacked because of this meeting. After it's over we'll laugh about how it was nothing."

Aubrey stood and pulled her shoulder-length black hair into a ponytail with the hair tie that had been around her wrist. It was time to go, but it would take a few days of planning to keep off Maria's radar. "Mention something once and I'd let it pass, but that's been a common theme with you lately. You don't have to worry about anything. It's all in your name, after all. The house, cars, and bank accounts—all of it."

"We can change that. I keep telling you I will, but you never accept my offer," Maria shot back, spilling a bit of her lemonade when she jerked her hands.

"You don't have to change anything, and I'm sure you're right about this meeting being nothing. Let me know if you need anything." She picked up her purse and keys, putting her hand on the doorknob before Maria's voice stopped her.

"I love you, you know that, so don't take this as a threat, Aubrey, but you owe me." Maria wouldn't look at her as she spoke. "Don't think about leaving me now."

They'd been through this before, and she placed another mark against herself on her tally of mistakes due to laziness. Fuckups happened to everyone she knew, but doing nothing to change her life meant she couldn't get upset with the past, only work to move on.

She walked out without adding anything to their conversation, letting Maria have the last word. The BMW sedan Maria leased for her sat gleaming in its usual spot, but she walked by it to the ten-year-old Accord she'd insisted on keeping. After a trip to the shop it was running like the day she bought it. Until she found a job, the little luxuries she was used to would be a memory.

"Fort Hood, how can I help you?" the man who answered her call asked.

"The personnel office, please." She parked in one of the visitor spots of the private school six blocks from the house and kept the engine running to stay cool. The greeting from the person who answered brought her attention into focus and away from childhood memories. "I need the contact information for Major Wiley Gremillion, please," she said, spelling the last name.

"Can I have your name, please?"

"Aubrey Tarver." It had been years since she'd made this call, and it'd be a miracle if Wiley was still stationed at Fort Hood, and a bigger miracle if her name was still on Wiley's contact list. After Wiley had left that last time, she'd warned her about calling unless it was a real emergency.

"I'm sorry, ma'am, but you're going to have to leave a message."

"Did you check the list? I said my name is Aubrey Tarver."

"The contact orders have been changed, ma'am. I'm sorry, but you're going to have to leave a message and wait for a call."

She panicked and almost turned off the car to let the heat rush in because of the chill. Had something happened to Wiley? "Is she okay?"

"Major Gremillion is fine, ma'am. Just retired. The contact orders were changed to protect her privacy. I'll send your request out immediately, so she should call you in the next few days, depending on her availability."

Retired? Wiley had retired. She kept repeating the statement in her head and it still sounded wrong. That had been their biggest disagreement from the day Wiley returned from her first assignment. Aubrey had seen the fire in her when she walked into the hotel room she'd rented for the weekend. The excitement had hooked Wiley and would own her forever.

That's why Wiley had severed their relationship. She'd cut all communications without much explanation, leaving only a sliver of an opening between them. "Call me if your life depends on it," Wiley had said. She hadn't left room for her to call and talk about Tanith, Maria, and the million other things that had shaped her life in the years since they'd last seen each other.

"Thanks, and could you tell her it's important," Aubrey said before leaving her cell number.

The recess bell rang, and the mob of kids in the playground meant she had to leave her air-conditioned cocoon. Before she did she waited for Tanith to make it outside. The tall eight-year-old was hard to miss with her shoulder-length black hair and smooth stride.

For so long Aubrey's life had been about the next cocktail party, the next contact that would help her career, and the next time she'd see Wiley. One afternoon, though, sitting in a staff meeting in the mayor's conference room trying to pay attention and not show the emptiness she felt after Wiley had ended their relationship, she made a decision. One that for her, who prided herself on order in all aspects of her life, was completely irrational.

It had taken three trips to the fertility specialist before the home-pregnancy test showed a positive result. Staring at the blue plus sign she'd doubted her choice at first, but as her waistline grew bigger, so did her excitement. When the doctor put the large squirming kid on her chest she fell instantly in love, and not even her parents could talk her out of the name she'd decided on, no matter what the sex turned out to be.

Tanith Wiley Tarver was her daughter and had been the center of her world from that first moment. So as bad as she felt about herself for falling for Maria's bullshit, it had been worth it, since she'd had the time to concentrate exclusively on Tanith.

"It's your day?" Tanith asked, her fingers looped through the chain-link fence that surrounded the playground.

"No, I'm the classroom helper tomorrow," she said, touching the tips of Tanith's fingers. "I came to ask if you wanted to take the afternoon off."

"You serious?"

"I want to talk to you about some things, and I don't want to wait until you get out of school."

"You okay?" Aubrey nodded and pointed toward the office. "I'll meet you there, Mom, as soon as I get my stuff."

When she finished signing the form to take Tanith with her, her daughter arrived, out of breath, as if she'd run from her classroom. She threw her backpack into the backseat and made no comment about the change in vehicles. To lessen the blow of what she had to say, Aubrey headed to the Camellia Grill for a couple of chocolate freezes. It was one of Tanith's favorite places and had recently reopened after the storm.

"What's up?" Tanith asked after they'd ordered.

"How would you feel about it being just the two of us for a while?" She studied Tanith's face for reactions.

"Did Maria hurt you?"

She smiled at the protective tone. "You and I have always been honest with one another, and I want it to always be that way." She brushed back the stubborn lock of hair that obscured Tanith's eyes and kissed her forehead. "Maria didn't hurt me, but it's time to go. Unless I love someone like I love you, it's not fair to stay." The pang of telling the lie made her nausea return, but she didn't want to make Tanith carry the load of what she knew about Maria. The woman hadn't hurt her, but she was positive that wouldn't be the case if they stayed with her much longer.

"You need me to do something?"

Tanith was young, but to Aubrey, she was wise beyond her years. Aubrey cherished all these talks and their time together because she was certain that when her little bird flew from the nest, she would most probably never look back. Tanith had been born with an adventurer's heart. She had looked for that quality in the list of possible sperm donors. Her exacting list had made the search for the perfect donor three times as long as actually getting pregnant.

An adventurer's heart was in the top three things she wanted, but she realized that also translated to a wandering spirit. She'd always believed, though, that for every gift God gave, he required a sacrifice. Tanith would have a solid foundation, but she had to build on it when her time came. If she did it right some lucky soul would pine away for her like she had for Wiley.

"I want you to keep this between the two of us until I make some arrangements, but I hate to put you in that position."

"I can keep a secret, Mom." Tanith pushed the fries they'd ordered between them. "It's not like we're that tight, since Maria likes you way better than me."

That was another reason to go. When she'd agreed to Maria's arrangement, Maria was thrilled but warned her that kids weren't her thing. Considering she was holding a six-month-old Tanith at the time, she should've walked right then. "We might have to start out at Grandma and Grandpa's, and they love you way more than me, so it'll balance out."

"Waking up to Grandma's biscuits every morning won't be hard to get used to."

"I'm sorry, honey," she said, dragging her fry through the ketchup so much it made a valley.

"For what?"

"For making you stay somewhere you didn't feel welcome. I know Maria wasn't the best to you, but I stayed because I could be home with you. It would've killed me to put you in daycare right off."

"Don't sweat the small stuff, like Grandpa says. You're my mom and I love you. I just want you to be happy."

"Thanks, sweetheart, and no matter what, I love you more than life."

❖

Wiley stood back from the canvas and studied the early-morning mist she'd added to the Big Sur landscape. When she'd made the trip she'd walked along the coastline and seen it in every possible light. Of all her choices, the mornings shrouded in wet fog and quiet made her appreciate the beauty of the area the most. At the moment the fog dissipated and all that was left was the slight mist, the steep inclines and water didn't have to compete with anything.

She looked at every inch of the canvas slowly and found nothing else to add, so she dropped her brush into the jar of fresh mineral spirits to clean after she hung the painting on one of the hooks along the wall to dry. That would take a few weeks, but she'd call her client to let him know she'd finished ahead of schedule.

As she stepped away from the wet painting, the front-door buzzer rang and the screen in the studio came on. She'd configured the security herself during the construction phase. Every room in the house had a screen large enough to display every space in the building.

Wiping her hands, she stared at the two men who stood at her door looking up at the camera above their heads. She recognized the guy on the right but had never seen the pale blond man with him. Colonel Don Smith was part of the deal she'd made with the military when she'd decided to retire, and he was casually dressed, as she'd requested when he came to meet with her. People tended to notice a guy in uniform with a chest full of medals. The army had invested a lot in her, so walking away had come with strings, or at least a handler, which was Don. The slew of psychological tests had been extensive, but the U.S. government felt reasonably comfortable that they hadn't released a WMD into society. She wasn't about to remind them they had trained her to pass those as well, even if she was swimming at the deep end of the crazy pool.

"Come on, Wiley, it's hot as shit out here," Don said through the intercom. The man with him wore a white linen suit and Panama straw hat that made him resemble a bad character from a spy movie.

She lifted her hand slowly and pressed the lock release, buzzing them in. This was the first time Don had visited her here, but from her description of the place he wouldn't have a problem finding her in the building. The pocket doors to the studio closed quietly behind her, and she took the stairs up to the third level and the large den across from the dining room.

"You couldn't have picked someplace cooler?" Don asked, stepping off the elevator. "It's like a fucking sauna out there."

"Heat's good for the skin, haven't you ever heard that?" She waved both of them toward a seat. "But you said you weren't going to call on me very often, so why would you care?"

"You also agreed not to be a hard-ass when I did, so smile."

"Are you going to introduce me to your friend?"

Don's smile faded a bit when she asked, and from their history she guessed his shadow hadn't been his idea. "Wiley, this is Walter Robinson."

"Are you subcontracting me to the spooks, Don?" she asked, locking eyes with Walter.

"Very perceptive, Major Gremillion, or may I call you Wiley?"

"It depends on why you're here, Walter." She put up her hand even though he didn't appear ready to interrupt her. "And we both know you're here to ask a favor, so let's not get lost on the path to telling me what it is."

"Where would you like me to begin?" Walter sat back on her couch like he was there for a social visit.

"As a test of your ability to tell the truth, let's start with what agency you represent."

"Currently I'm working in Mexico and South America with the CIA." Walter took a pack of cigarettes out of his coat pocket and held it up.

"Please wait until you're back in the sauna to light that, if you don't mind." She tapped the bottom of the leather driving moccasins she'd put on before coming up and almost laughed at Walter's sweat-stained suit. He must've fit into the South American landscape as well as a king cobra at a two-year-old's birthday party. "And your favor?"

"May I?" He took the jump drive from his other pocket and pointed to the laptop on the coffee table. She nodded and turned on the large flat-screen television that hung over the fireplace so Don could see as well.

The first images showed those killed in the drug war happening in Mexico, or at least that's what Wiley guessed as Walter flipped through a multitude of shots without speaking. The most horrific displayed rows of decapitated bodies. If they were meant to intimidate or terrify her, he would have to go some. So far she just wanted her lazy afternoon back.

"Anyone who watches television or reads a paper has some idea of how bad this drug shit has gotten." Walter stopped at a picture of a nice-looking blond man smiling from between two larger men, who appeared to be his security detail. "We usually try to control situations like this from within the country we're assigned to, but the level of violence surprised everyone. The worst part was the overflow into the U.S. border towns."

"You're right, Walter, I read the paper, so this is old news. I'm sure something in this slick presentation will get to the point of why you're here. Or are you an old Southerner who likes to take the scenic route when it comes to storytelling?"

Walter glanced at Don before he scrolled to the next picture of the same blond man, but didn't say anything else. She sat back and concentrated on her breathing. Patience was the foundation of her training, and she never begged, so Walter could sit there and play his mind games until Christmas and he wouldn't break her.

"I already told you she has top security clearance, so get on with it," Don said, letting his anger bleed into his voice. "Stop wasting time since my superiors already have agreed to this meeting."

"If you've got clearance, then I don't need to remind you that we're not having this conversation, right?" Walter asked.

"Trust me. I'll forget you before you make it to the elevator." She also prided herself for perfecting her sarcasm.

"This is Roth Pombo." Walter flipped through a variety of pictures, all seemingly shot in Mexico. "He's an American from the Phoenix area who moved to Cancun in his junior year of college, in early 2002. In four years he's gone from small-time hustler getting by to a major player in the Mexican cartel, with his own crew."

"Wasn't Mr. Pombo arrested last week in Mexico City?" Wiley asked.

"He's been on their most-wanted list for about a year. Remember when two U.S. State Department employees were gunned down accidentally on their way home over the border after attending a family member's birthday party in Nogales? Pombo started the mutilations that have been front-page news to scare off competitors, and we believe his crew shot our people."

"Good for the Mexican federales for catching this guy, then," Wiley said.

"We weren't expecting it, considering the number of police working for the cartels."

The "we" Walter had used was her first clue as to what she was dealing with, and why Walter was here. "What's Pombo doing for you?"

Walter smiled widely before shaking his head. "You were right, Don, she is bright."

"I'm also busy, so answer the question."

"We got someone in early enough that he came up with Roth." The change in name made Wiley think she was talking to the agent who was close to Pombo. "With time, the agency decided to have someone we could let work unhindered in the business as long as he helped us control the traffic coming in."

"Did he deliver?" From the number of photos of Pombo, and the settings where'd they been taken, he had done well on the working "unhindered" part of the equation.

"When we pitched him we backed ourselves up with enough evidence that he either cooperated or landed in jail as the best-case scenario. With his cruelty the other bosses would've killed him slowly once we turned him over. He accepted our offer and was smart enough to benefit as much as we did by taking out a lot of the small-to-medium players."

"Sounds smart, since going after anyone with more muscle would've started a war he couldn't have easily won or calmed down, even with your resources. By removing competition, though, he helps not only you, but himself with the higher-ups."

"Roth certainly knows how to work things to his advantage, but he's under the delusion he's untouchable." Walter stopped at the picture of Pombo in cuffs surrounded by masked police in a Mexican hangar. "After his arrest he immediately called the embassy for a ride and bail."

"He wasn't caught without some help," Wiley said, looking at how relaxed Roth appeared despite the deep shit he was in. "What'd he do?"

"He was under the delusion he was untouchable. Did you miss that part?"

"I haven't missed much so far, but that's not important since I'm not in your den asking you for a favor. You gained his trust, you worked him, and *you* gave him the illusion he was untouchable so he'd be successful in helping *you*." She hadn't met many company men, but they all brought paranoia to a new level. "If he'd acted any differently you'd be looking for his head to bury along with the body someone would've thrown out like an old newspaper. So what did he do?"

"After a long stretch of arrests based on Roth's tips, he took a vacation." Walter's slideshow continued. "At first my team and I didn't question it, and we relaxed when all the surveillance showed was him spending the money we helped him make. Then the shootout in St. Luis, Arizona, happened, and in two days twenty-five people were killed. Thankfully no civilians were caught in the crossfire, but we had a hard time covering that many dead on our side of the border. In the aftermath we lost sight of Roth."

"Did the Mexican authorities suspect his dealings with you and use Arizona as an excuse to move in?"

Walter laughed. "See, you don't know everything." He clicked to a new picture, and the Middle Eastern–looking man sitting with Roth on a yacht with his shirt off made her blink a few times. Not that she recognized him, but she couldn't miss the tattoo over his heart. It featured a *khanda* sword, or the wide double-edged blades used for centuries, at the center. Two curved swords called *kirpans* flanked the khanda and a closed circle drawn through it at the top portion of the blade, which represented a weapon called a *chakkar*. An old religious symbol, the curved blade on the left stood for truth, the one on the right for a willingness to fight for the right. The chakkar stood for the one God, never beginning and never ending.

"Arizona was Roth doing some housecleaning, along with keeping us busy."

"Who is that?" Wiley asked when a better picture of the meeting came up.

"We don't know his name, or where in Mexico he is, but Roth thought he would free him from our arrangement."

"What's a member of Tajr doing on Roth's boat?" Don asked.

"Coke and the rest of what this asshole Roth sells doesn't interest them. Their business is heroin."

"Getting product into the U.S. over a common border is easier than trying through the ports, like they've been doing." Walter let them study the picture a few more moments before he shut the system down. "This would've been a big payday for Roth, and a new venture-capital stream for the Trader sect or Tajr. When I saw the proof I had Roth picked up."

"What would you like from me?" Wiley asked, since she knew why Walter needed her.

"Roth knows he screwed up, and his new friends have vanished into Mexico, so he's facing this alone. His only way out of a death sentence is to trade the last chip he has for a get-out-of-jail-free card."

"What lesson are you trying to teach?" she asked.

"That his head is no match for a bullet. Considering he gets only ten minutes alone in the best maximum-security prison in the country, this will take talent. It's a distance shot that you'll get only one crack at, but Roth needs to be neutralized."

"Understood," Wiley said, accepting his file and his handshake.

She and Don watched Walter through the screens until he stepped outside. "You sure about this?" Don asked.

"He's still not being completely honest, so I have to try to find what he's hiding before I say yes, but I do need to consider it. If I don't accept this time, someone like Walter could make my life interesting." She stood up and headed for the kitchen. The peanut butter sandwich had left her hungry. "Interesting, I could do without for a while."

"You know that's why I'm here, right?"

She picked up the Lebanese-restaurant menu and held it up for Don to see before placing an order. "What, to make my life interesting?"

"No." Don twisted off the top of the beer she slid his way. "To keep it from getting too complicated. I feel funny about this, which means you must be getting some vibe from this guy."

"I am, but I haven't narrowed it down yet. Until I start, though, I won't know which of my theories is correct."

"Aside from Mr. Spooky, how's it going?"

The label on his beer bottle became the center of his attention, and unlike Walter, she knew what it meant when Don got nervous. Granted, his sense of paranoia had been helpful in the past, but it didn't make sense to her now. "It's an adjustment, but I'm coping."

"Not to sound repetitive, but did you watch the news today?" Wiley nodded and stood across from him on the other side of the island. "Dr. Jerry Dupre had an interesting story to tell after his arrest this morning." He opened his bag and put a copy of the police report on the counter, not rushing her as she slowly perused every line.

"The only story he should concentrate on concerns rape and torture. I believe that's why he was arrested, all other interesting things aside. The rest is theater meant to create a diversion from his crimes." He'd have to wait for her to say anything else when she went downstairs to accept the food delivery. When she made it back they were silent as she put out plates and utensils.

"What happened to him sounds far-fetched to the police, but it carries the Dragon's markings." She nodded as she took a bite of her chicken *shawarma*. "If I'm wrong I apologize, but if I'm not, I have to warn you about freelancing more than your artistic talents."

"What exactly are you warning me about?"

"Wiley, the brass let you go easily because you passed all the shrink's tests and didn't present a problem. If six months out they find out you're killing people, they'll put you somewhere I can't help you." He didn't elevate his voice, but Wiley could tell he was upset.

"Don't worry. I agreed to the consultant gig, and that's where I plan to showcase my talents," she said, smiling. "Anything else I do with my time is my business and won't interfere with my responsibilities to you." She stretched out the fingers of her right hand, since they were stiff from holding her brush for so long, and relaxed it into a loose fist. "I'm not a puppet that needs constant handling or surveillance, and I'll never go anywhere quietly."

"I'm telling you this because I care about you."

"I know, and I hope you understand I wanted to retire because I was ready for some peace. I'm trying to find that here, but my search won't blind me totally to things that need to be done." She got up and grabbed them another beer. "The doctor on the news this morning needed to be caught, and it's a good thing he was, since he probably wouldn't have given up his true passion."

"Good for the police, then, and I'm sure the courts will work out the story he told after he received medical attention. Not finding any evidence of his balls in the shredder he described makes the authorities think he's setting up an insanity defense."

"Back to Walter, then."

Instead of giving her the details of the job, Don started pushing his food around his plate. "There's more."

"About the rapist?" She was aggravated now.

"Dr. Dupre's not my concern, so no." Don reached behind him and removed his wallet. The card he took out was blank on the back, and he held it to keep her from flipping it over.

"Is today intended to test my patience?" Wiley didn't move. "I enjoy your company, but don't push it."

"Aubrey called."

She closed her eyes, and for a long minute she didn't breathe. It had taken five years and all of her discipline not to think of Aubrey Tarver as soon as she woke up each morning, but she'd managed it. At least that was the lie she told herself constantly to soothe the ache. She allowed the past to completely run free in her mind only when she sat at her desk and looked at the picture of them together under their tree. That was the anchor she used to keep the darkness the Dragon thrived in from sweeping her away.

Aubrey was simply a mix of happy and painful memories she'd learned to live with and accept, nothing more. She'd had no fantasies of what could be when she drove back to New Orleans to stay, and in almost nine years she'd never picked up the phone to get in touch, knowing the possible consequences if she allowed herself that luxury. When she'd had to let Aubrey go she felt like she imagined her targets did when her bullets hit them center chest. Only Aubrey's hit hadn't been a kill shot. She'd left herself lingering from the self-inflicted wound, and time had only made it fester.

❖

Army Installation outside Miami, Florida, 1997

"Thanks for your help, Wiley. It was a pleasure having you along," Major Billy Ewart said as the transport plane they were sharing prepared for landing. The marine was shorter than Wiley, but his bulk dwarfed her. She'd been his team's spotter as they carried out a covert operation in South America. Her face still itched from the camouflage paint she'd used to blend into the tree she'd climbed.

"Thanks for the invite." She stretched her legs out and closed her eyes. After an eight-mile hike through dense vegetation, they'd been picked up by helo and dropped at the airstrip. She was beyond ready to get to New Orleans and spend about four hours in the shower with Aubrey.

"We'll keep you in mind. With you covering our ass I felt as safe as a baby with his mama. You live up to your hype, Wiley."

The plane landed at an army installation outside Miami, and she'd already booked her commercial flight for that afternoon. Her assignments had been steady, but this last one had kept her away from Aubrey for three months without any contact.

"You taking some time off?" Billy asked as she shouldered her pack.

"I'm scheduled for a few weeks, so I'm going to New Orleans. How about you?"

"My wife's meeting me here so we can take our boys to the beach." Dutifully he took some pictures from his top pocket, and from the black smudges at the bottom corners, it was obvious he gazed at them often. "My youngest just turned five and can't wait to show off his moves in the water without floaties."

"Cute," she said as she flipped through the four he'd handed over. "They look like their mom," she said, and laughed. A year more and maybe she'd be doing the same thing in a grocery line. Aubrey always talked about kids.

"Smart-ass." Billy punched her in the shoulder. "Try to stay sober and out of trouble until we see each other again."

She nodded and smiled as she watched him jog toward the small group waiting on the other side of the fence. Judging by the three boys' haircuts, she figured Billy was raising some future marines.

The barracks where she'd stowed her gear was a block away, so she adjusted the weight on her back and started walking. With a few hours before her flight, she had time to shower and change into a fresh uniform. A hundred yards from the tarmac she was blown down by a catastrophic explosion. She elbowed her way to cover on her belly. Behind her a minivan was in flames, and unless she was wrong it was the vehicle Billy had loaded his family into. None of them could have survived.

She was numb by the time they mustered for a briefing. Their operation had been successful, so successful it'd warranted payback. At least that's what the base commander said.

"You think this was random?" she asked.

"A group has taken responsibility for today's actions. It wasn't random because they had the names of everyone we deployed, as well as their personal information. We've started our inquiry, but obviously we have a leak." The man spoke softly, but all the guys with her heard him clearly. Their actions had put not only themselves in danger, but their loved ones as well. "We've found two more devices so far and are reviewing surveillance of the area where your plane landed. Whoever did this was close enough to detonate it."

"Excuse me, sir." Outside the room she dialed Aubrey's number. No one here knew she existed or what their relationship was, but she had to be sure. "Aubrey, where are you?"

"Hey, what took you so long to call? I thought I'd hear from you hours ago."

"I know, baby, I apologize, but tell me where you are."

"We're headed to the ninth ward. The mayor is cutting the ribbon on a children's center this afternoon. Don't worry, I'll be waiting with tassels on." Aubrey whispered the last part and she came close to laughing.

"Isn't that bells?"

"It's New Orleans, lover. Tassels are a bit more titillating."

"Are you traveling with your boss?"

"You're sure interested in my position today, Lieutenant. What's up?"

The smell of that burning death trap seemed to be trapped in her nose. She couldn't think of anything but Billy's little boy swimming without floaties. That would never happen again now, and for once her confidence was blown as effectively as the minivan.

"Nothing, I wanted to hear your voice. I'll see you tonight."

On the flight home she thought only about the case the base

commanders had laid out. They had gone into the bowels of that hot hell and eliminated the rebels that were giving the government huge problems. The United Ways needed the strong alliance between their countries, but she'd always left the battle on the field. Having it follow her home was giving her a hard time. It had snapped a fundamental belief and left her afloat.

She'd tried to dismiss it since she wasn't a part of Billy's team, but that had fallen to hell too when the commander gave her the list and the pictures that'd been e-mailed before the fire had been extinguished. The rebels' contact had been kind enough to include her information. Thankfully only she and her parents had been listed. Not that she wished them ill, but the military probably had them in a bunker by now.

Aubrey didn't understand why she wanted to rent a car, but had promised to wait at home. During the drive into the city Wiley experienced a sense of dread, but she stopped at the hotel she'd booked for the night to try to control the panic. If something happened to Aubrey because of her need to prove herself, her life would hold no more meaning.

She stripped off her uniform and changed into a dark shirt and jeans. The airline had changed her outgoing flight to the morning, and she left through the service entrance as a precaution. She couldn't take the chance she'd been followed because she'd kept her personal life private.

Aubrey flew into her arms when she answered her door, and she didn't let go for a long moment. She wanted Aubrey's touch, scent, and essence tattooed on her heart before she made the break. To keep her whole she had to let her go. Even without the threat, the life she'd subjected Aubrey to wasn't fair to her. She deserved better than waiting for those few moments together, even if that situation wouldn't last forever.

"God, I love the way you hold me," Aubrey said as she kissed the side of her neck. "I missed you, honey."

"I missed you too." She held on tighter as the ramifications of a life without Aubrey hit her full-on. The bleakness made tears swim in her eyes, but she couldn't and wouldn't back down. "I have to talk to you."

"Can't it wait?" Aubrey clung to her so she could wrap her legs around her waist. "I want to prove how much I missed you."

The temptation made her wet. Wasn't this what she'd fantasized about when she wasn't on post in the trees? "Aubrey, really, we need to talk," she said, not having it in her to make love to Aubrey and then leave.

In her mind her argument was sound, and she tried her best to explain without a lot of emotion. Her leave was canceled and she was being deployed for perhaps a year or more. She didn't expect Aubrey to wait, didn't want her to, in fact, so she was giving her the freedom to go on without her. Her words caused pain so visible her chest constricted.

"You don't get to decide that for me," Aubrey choked out. The tears that turned to sobs were full of agony, and Wiley cursed her training not to break, because she didn't.

The echoes of Aubrey screaming, "Please, Wiley," were seared into her brain, and she'd never forgiven herself for inflicting that kind of pain on the one who owned her.

Her morning flight took her to Nashville and the Ewart funeral. Only one coffin held the remains of an entire happy family lowered next to Billy's grandparents. With it Wiley buried the future she'd planned on since she was fifteen.

❖

With Aubrey's pain ringing in her head, Wiley reached for the card and dragged it toward her without turning it over. "What does she want?" She had no reason to hide anything from Don since he knew enough about their relationship to have had her court-martialed but understood the consequences of doing so. Giving her up for being gay would've also meant giving up the perfect killing machine.

"If you want to know, you're going to have to call her because she only left her number. She understands that you might not be reachable."

"Fort Hood told her that?"

Don shook his head. "I told her that as a warning in case you decide against it."

"Thanks," she said, put the card in her back pocket, and went back to eating. She'd repaired the temporary crack in her composure. Don did the same and didn't say much else until he left with promises to regroup in a couple of days to plan her trip to Mexico.

Alone, Wiley lay on the sofa and stared out the window. Eight years was a long time to go without the one person she wanted and needed, and she hoped Aubrey didn't hate her for her choices.

She'd never been curious about the life Aubrey had made for herself, and strangely she wasn't now as she closed her eyes and went to sleep. Curiosity led to searching and searching led others to make the same discoveries, only they didn't have happy reunions in mind. As soon as her eyes closed, Roth Pombo dominated her dreamscape. She'd willed it so.

CHAPTER THREE

D id you get your homework assignment before we left school?" Aubrey asked Tanith as she grabbed the grocery bags from the backseat. This was her usual shopping day, and for now she wanted everything to appear normal. One glance at Maria's car, though, and a sense of dread spread over her head as if someone had cracked an egg on it. "How did my life get so screwed up?" she muttered to herself.

"I got it right here," Tanith said, holding up her bag. "You need help with that?"

"It's only a couple of bags, honey, so go up and get started, and maybe later we'll order pizza." She relaxed her smile as she faced Tanith, but seeing Maria standing at the door was making it difficult.

"You sure you don't need help?" Tanith asked again as she followed her line of sight. "I don't have that much homework so I can do it later."

Aubrey almost laughed at how perceptive an eight-year-old could be, though she'd missed so many things. "Don't forget what we talked about," she said softly, "so go up to your room like usual."

"Problem?" Maria asked Tanith when she stepped aside to let them in.

"No, you?" Tanith shot back, and kept walking.

"It's like she forces herself not to tag 'asshole' to the end of whatever she says to me. That kid needs an attitude adjustment," Maria said when Tanith was out of earshot.

"She has a great attitude, but she's eight. At that age they're like a mirror of emotion."

"What's that supposed to mean?"

Aubrey started putting groceries away, surprised at how ordinarily domestic the scene was despite how out of whack it really was. "They reflect whatever you show them. If you want her to be nicer, then put out a little effort."

"I would but it's a waste of time. That kid hates me."

"Her name is Tanith, and that's how she thinks you feel about her." She enjoyed the cold air from the refrigerator as she put away the milk and cheese, glancing at her watch when she put her hand on the handle to close it. Maria was usually on her way to the bar by now. "Are you taking the night off?"

"I own the place, so I can be late," Maria said, rolling down her sleeves to button the cuffs. "I wanted to talk to you before I left and apologize for earlier. Like I said, we'll be fine, and I'll do everything I can to take care of this fast so it doesn't become a problem."

"Thanks, I appreciate that. If it was only you and me I wouldn't freak, but you know Tanith comes first."

"With you, yeah, that's more than apparent." Maria hesitated after she grabbed her jacket from a kitchen chair but didn't come near her. "I'll see you later tonight."

As soon as Maria put her car in reverse, Aubrey ran upstairs and pulled the cord to bring down the folding ladder to the attic. Her luggage was stored up there, along with some of the mementos she'd collected throughout her life that were worth more to her than anything else in this house, aside from Tanith. When she put her foot on the first rung to head up, she heard the back door slam open.

"Where you going in such a hurry?"

The man who asked the question had a deep voice Aubrey didn't recognize, and she almost panicked when she heard a crash from the kitchen, as if someone had knocked the furniture over.

"Come on, Ralph, not here," Maria said loudly.

Aubrey put her finger calmly to her lips when Tanith appeared in the door of her bedroom, but the sudden onslaught of fear made her freeze.

"The kind of talk we need to have is going to be tough at the bar, so I decided to make a house call, since you aren't too good at returning phone calls." More breaking noises followed the man's words. The air conditioner came on and muffled whatever he said next.

With her finger still to her lips, Aubrey waved Tanith up the ladder, and she followed closely. From the edge of the opening they worked together to fold the ladder back up and hopefully keep whoever was downstairs from finding their hiding spot.

"Let's move back there," Aubrey whispered in Tanith's ear, pointing to the air-conditioning unit at the other side of the open space. They carefully navigated the rafters when the plywood flooring ended and sat with their backs to it. She put her arm around Tanith and closed her eyes to concentrate on any noise from downstairs. The heat made the sweat seep out of every pore of her body, and Tanith's forehead already felt wet, but the real pressure cooker was steaming downstairs and she wanted no part of it.

She'd missed her opportunity to leave by one night.

When the air unit cycled off she covered Tanith's mouth when they heard slamming doors from what seemed to be right under them.

"Nothing," Aubrey heard a man yell, which meant that more than one man was down there with Maria. She glanced at her watch again—a few minutes before eight. It was almost dark outside, and they'd probably have to stay put until the next morning. No matter how long it took, she wasn't moving.

"This is my house, Ralph, anywhere but here," Maria said, her voice much clearer now.

"Don't worry. We'll try to be as neat as possible."

Aubrey couldn't be sure, but the man's voice was different from the first one she'd heard, making it three men. The conversations became muffled again as the intruders moved away from below where they were sitting. The attic opening was ten feet from the top of the stairs, then came the vent for the air intake, followed by the master bedroom at the end of the hall. From their footsteps it sounded like they'd taken Maria there.

"No matter what, we have to stay quiet, okay?" Aubrey whispered to Tanith, who nodded. But she came close to screaming when she heard what sounded like a chain saw start. She pressed her hand to Tanith's ear and held her to her chest to try to keep her from hearing whatever came next. When the engine revved up to a whine she prayed they'd live to see the end of this nightmare.

❖

The chime of the clock over the fireplace woke Wiley to hear the last three of the eight. Her three-hour nap wasn't enough to make her feel rested, but she got up and went to clean the kitchen as a way to clear the fog from her head.

She'd planned to start another painting for the show one of the local galleries had booked for November, but the message in her back pocket had burned away the urge. She placed it on the countertop like Don had, blank side up, but the white square didn't give her a hint as to why, after so much time, Aubrey had reached out to her.

"I did say life or death, didn't I?" she said out loud. "I stayed away, so you should be safe."

Typed on the other side were Aubrey's name, number, and the short message to contact her as soon as possible because it was important for them to speak. The area code was local, which meant Aubrey had to have been content to stay close to home all this time. Wiley picked up the card and ran her thumb over the writing.

Before she could talk herself out of it, she dialed the number and exhaled when it started to ring. After the fifth time she took the receiver away from her ear to hang up, intending to throw the card away.

"Oh, God," a woman who she assumed was Aubrey whispered harshly, making her whip the phone back.

"Aubrey?"

"Wiley, we're in trouble," she said, still whispering and barely audible.

"Where are you?" She pressed the phone harder to her ear and searched for a pen. Aubrey gave her an address and a small explanation as to what she thought was happening. "How many?"

"I think three." Aubrey paused, then said, "Oh, my God."

"Hang up and call nine-one-one, if you haven't already."

"I didn't remember having my phone with me."

"Aubrey, make the call. Whatever's happening isn't worth your life." She slipped her shoes back on and opened the freezer door to step into the room behind it. She quickly keyed in the codes to unlock the gun cabinet near the desk that housed her collection of pistols. The two nine-millimeter semiautomatic weapons with silencers should be enough firepower. "Did you hear me?" she asked when Aubrey stayed quiet.

"If these guys hear sirens, they're going to come looking—"

"Aubrey?" Wiley flew down the stairs when Aubrey abruptly stopped talking and all she heard was faint breathing. "Stay on the line and tell me if anything changes."

"Please, Wiley, help us."

"I'm close, so hang on." The van from the night before was the best vehicle for this, but she didn't have time, so she chose the black motorcycle she'd had since her first days at West Point. After wondering about Aubrey for so long, she found it strange that they'd ended up about ten minutes from each other.

Uptown, where huge mansions sometimes sat next door to small shotguns in need of major repair, the address Aubrey had given her led to a fairly large home with beautiful landscaping. She'd always imagined Aubrey living in this type of home, but the phone call and the reason for it didn't fit the picture she was looking at.

She passed the house and parked her cycle, then took a shortcut through the neighbor's yard to reach the back without being seen. In the dark the separate garage building provided good cover as she looked through the windows for any sign of life and, through the small earpiece she wore, listened to Aubrey breathe.

Four cars sat in the drive, all of them empty, as was the outside of the house, so Wiley moved toward the back door. It had been ages since she'd entered a situation without knowing what and who she was up against, and the scars along her left shoulder were proof as to why she seldom did. She'd been shot more than once, but that old injury was the only one she chalked up to a stupid necessity. Answering the call meant she could drop the word *stupid* from the description if something happened to her. She'd accepted leaving Aubrey only because she knew her absence would ensure Aubrey's safety and happiness. A future alone was better than a repeat of what had happened to Billy Ewart's family.

Sweating under the jacket she'd grabbed to hide her guns, she slipped on a pair of gloves anyway. The door was locked but opened easily with the use of her tools, and she stood at the threshold listening for where anyone in the house was located. After she quietly stepped inside and locked the door behind her, she tried to ignore the overturned and broken furniture.

Shit, she thought, when she heard the distinctive sound of a chain saw revving up. The noise made her imagination skitter off into a dark place.

On the first floor the only light on was the one over the stove, giving Wiley enough to make out where the stairs were. She unholstered both guns and started up the stairs to the landing, which was halfway up and headed in the opposite direction. The next flight over her head made it impossible to see if someone was waiting to ambush her at the top. Even if that was the case, the saw revving up again and the screams that accompanied it gave her no choice but to move.

She started up with both guns pointed ahead, confident the custom clips that held fourteen rounds apiece would neutralize any problem. At the landing she saw that the upstairs was dark, so she gave her eyes time to adjust before she climbed the last few steps.

The stairs led to a hallway evenly divided in both directions as far as space, but on the side to the left, light spilled into it from the end room. Closer, she could make out where the noise was emanating from, and when the accelerator stopped she heard moaning. Whoever was in there was close to the breaking point, since the screams had stopped. Whatever Aubrey had gotten involved with since their last contact was seriously illegal to cause this kind of action on someone's part. No one showed up at your house and threatened dismemberment with garden tools for cheating on your taxes, or for parking tickets. Could her sacrifice have been in vain?

"Where is it?" a man asked in a loud voice.

A long runner on the hardwood floors in the hallway helped muffle her steps as she moved closer. The room had a large four-poster bed against the opposite wall, neatly made and undisturbed. Whoever was conducting the motivated conversation was in the master bathroom, along with his helpers.

"Tell me where it is and all this stops," the man said, in an almost soothing voice. The person's answer was too muffled for Wiley to make out. "That's your choice. Peanut, how about some more incentive?"

"Aubrey," Wiley whispered into her headset, confident the noise of the saw would cover her voice.

"Please, Wiley, I don't think we have much time."

"I'm going to disconnect for a few minutes, but don't panic, okay? Stay calm and I'll call you right back." She hung up and waited when she heard Peanut release the throttle.

"You think I like doing this shit?" The man's question was clear, but so was the mixture of someone's moans and crying. "I don't, but I'm not leaving until you tell me what I want to know."

"I can't tell you what I don't know." A woman, Wiley guessed, gave the answer, stuttering through the words so badly it was hard to understand her. The person sounded hoarse from crying, though, making their voice deep and raspy, so it could've been a man. Whoever the poor bastard was, they'd pissed off the wrong people.

"There's no way out, you know that, right? And if you don't tell me in the time you have left, I'm going to ask the pretty lady you live with when she gets home."

"No!"

"Marko, go downstairs and wait for the missing members of the family. Peanut, we're ready for another round."

Wiley stepped back farther into the dark hallway and waited. It didn't take long before Marko appeared, his white T-shirt covered in blood, as were his face and arms. She waited until he made it to the threshold before she put a shot in the middle of his forehead. As soon as the bullet left the chamber she ran forward, hoping to catch him before he hit the ground, but his weight and height worked against her. The short, chunky Marko fell on his back like someone had pulled a rug from under his feet, unfortunately in the part of the bedroom not covered by the tasteful Persian carpet.

"Marko, what the shit?"

She didn't have anywhere to hide now that she was in the room, and the man who asked the question sounded closer, as if he was walking out of the bathroom to investigate. The instincts Wiley attributed to the Black Dragon took over, and she kept moving toward the bathroom door. The first man she encountered died with his mouth in a tight *O*, as if he was poised to utter the word *who*, and the guy by the tub went down quickly, his final reflex pressing the chain saw throttle to the maximum until it died when it skittered along the enamel tub.

A woman cuffed to the shower head was dead from the large, gruesome gash that'd almost severed her head from her shoulders. With so much blood and gore covering her and the shower walls, it would've been impossible to determine the person's sex, but the torturers had cut away every bit of clothing.

The next step would take some planning, but Aubrey was her priority now. She pressed Redial on her phone, which barely rang once before Aubrey answered. "Are you in the attic?" she asked in a normal tone.

"Yes." Aubrey still whispered.

She walked down the hall searching for the light switch that would make it easier to navigate the area. "I'm going to open the ladder, so don't be scared."

"You're here?"

"Right below you." Wiley gripped the cord that would bring Aubrey back into her life, at least for the night. "Can you make it to the opening?" The sounds of movement made her holster one gun and tuck the other into the waistband of her jeans. As she rested her hands on the step at chest level, she looked up and saw Aubrey standing at the edge.

The years had changed Aubrey some, but not much. She was still tall and slim, but her face appeared more angular and mature in a way that reminded her of Aubrey's mom. The older Tarver had been a classic beauty whom Aubrey had resembled from childhood in every way except personality. Both of them would stop conversation when they entered a room and made whoever was on the receiving end of those ice-crystal-blue eyes feel like lady luck had landed in their back pocket.

"It's okay to come down," she said, stepping back.

"I don't know why you're in town, but thank God," Aubrey said, her back to her as she climbed down. "It's okay, honey. Wiley's a friend."

The comment made her look up, since she'd assumed that the *we* Aubrey kept referring to was the dead woman in pieces in the shower. A kid stood there peering back at her, so why the hell had what appeared to be a drug-ordered hit taken place in a house where Aubrey lived with a child?

"What happened to those guys?" the kid asked, not budging.

"They're gone." Technically she wasn't lying, but the girl didn't need to see the first guy she'd dealt with lying in plain view of the open master-bedroom doorway. "Hang on a minute, though," she said, walking over and kicking the guy's legs out of the way to close the door. "Bring her down, Aubrey."

Aubrey stared at her as if she should be afraid of trading three dangerous strangers for one old friend, but she blinked and the trepidation was gone. "Thanks for that." The young girl came down and put her arms around Aubrey's waist, acting as if Wiley was wearing an outfit made of live rattlesnakes that'd strike if she got too close.

"You can't stay here, so grab some stuff for her. You can stay with me tonight."

"Tanith, pack some clothes and your books, and I'll be in to help in a second." Aubrey had to break the hold the kid had on her to get her to move. "It's really okay, I promise."

Tanith walked to the first room on the other side of the stairs, glancing back every few steps. "There are two guys in your bedroom, and two more bodies in the bath. I realize you might need to pack a bag, but it's going to have to wait."

"For what? I don't want to be here ever again."

"It's not pretty in there, and we'll have to discuss the whys of what happened, but you're going to have to report this tonight."

"Why?"

"Aubrey, you live here, right?" She nodded. "You can't erase yourself from this house in the time the neighbors figure out four dead people are in here," she whispered, since Tanith was hovering around her door.

"Four, you said?" Aubrey asked, as if she'd just started paying attention. "No one's alive?"

"There were three men and a woman, and yes, they're all gone. Who was the woman to you? She was the reason those guys were here."

"Maria Ross." Aubrey blinked rapidly with her head cocked back as she said the name. "We lived together."

"I'm sorry, but I got here too late." By years, but it wasn't the time to get into that. The façade of a happy family living in the perfect house bought with drug money made Wiley think she was an asshole for crying over Aubrey from the moment she walked away from her. She'd accepted what'd happened and that Aubrey would move on, but this wasn't the direction she had in mind.

"What happened? What did they do to her?" The tears pooled in Aubrey's eyes until they fell in fat drops down her high cheekbones.

"Not now," Wiley said, pointing toward Tanith, who stood in the hall with two bags. "Which car is yours?"

"The old Accord," Aubrey said, she and Tanith following Wiley down the stairs and stopping to stare at the mess in the kitchen.

"My bike is around the corner, so take Tanith and drive to the drugstore a few blocks down, but don't pull into the parking lot. I'll meet you there in a few minutes and you can follow me the rest of the way." She wanted to drive them since Aubrey looked like she was in shock, but if Aubrey wanted a clean break from this, there were things to do. "Take your time, and try like hell to not get pulled over for any reason."

"Where are you going?"

"To make sure none of this follows you out of here."

CHAPTER FOUR

The bar Maria owned was starting to fill with businesspeople staying at the Hilton. Through the glass wall, the view of the Mississippi River from the third-floor location was spectacular. A three-man band was playing close to the entrance, but not so loud that conversation was impossible. The crowd of men in white shirts with their ties loosened sat in clusters with martini glasses in hand, telling stories of their conquests that day.

"What time is it?" Nunzio Luca tapped his feet impatiently. This was his first time back in New Orleans after a disastrous trip a year and a half before had ended with him watching his lover Kim Stegal get her throat cut.

Kim's death had left him unsure how to save the strides he'd made from Biloxi to New Orleans to establish a drug pipeline to the north. He'd succeeded thanks to a partnership with Big Gino Bracato, but he'd stupidly messed with the existing power structure in New Orleans, with devastating consequences.

The loss of Kim, who had been not only his lover but his best advisor, had rocked him, but the pain continued two days later. Before he could get home to face the wrath of his father, Junior, the assassin he'd hired turned on him and put a bullet through Junior's head.

His father hadn't kept quiet about his opinion of him, so at Junior's death a few of his captains had challenged Nunzio for control. The backing of his grandfather had kept him on top, but the old man expected results. Nunzio had to not only regain the business they'd lost, but also avenge Junior's death.

He'd used the time to find new suppliers and try to form new alliances to move product without much help from the men who'd worked for Junior. Progress had been slow, but moving too fast had been his mistake before.

"He's ten minutes late," Tracy Stegal said, nodding when the waitress pointed to them.

Nunzio probably wouldn't have bothered with Kim's sister, but he owed it to his lover to provide for Tracy like Kim had. Paying Tracy's way through school wasn't all Kim did for her, and after spending some obligatory time with Tracy, he offered her a job when she displayed a good head for strategy. It would take more experience to get Tracy to the same level as Kim, but she should become a great advisor.

"Is he bringing his mystery boss with him?" Nunzio asked, his gaze on the entrance. So far he saw no sign of Mitch Surpass, the point man for the new supply chain for uncut cocaine into the country. Mitch was always willing to provide whatever they asked for, but would never finalize a decision without checking with his boss first. Nunzio still had no clue who that was, and Mitch wasn't forthcoming.

"He just said he had an answer for you about the supply available for sale, and how he plans to get it to you."

"He isn't the only one we can deal with, so he better ditch the cloak-and-dagger shit." Another group of businesspeople walked in, took a table close to theirs, and immediately yelled at the waitress, making Nunzio lose the last of his patience. "Five more minutes and that's it."

As if realizing his opportunity to do business with him was about to evaporate, Mitch Surpass stopped at the door and scanned the room. Considering Mitch had picked the location, Nunzio figured if anyone was watching they'd be easy to spot because of the way Mitch was dressed. The tall blond was rail thin and appeared more so in his baggy cargo shorts and T-shirt with the sleeves cut off.

"Is this guy kidding?"

Mitch smiled toward the bar before he joined them, prompting one of the waitresses to deliver a beer without him having to order. Nunzio became even more nervous since too much regularity in their business wasn't a good thing, especially when they used places like this to conduct deals.

"My apologies, Mr. Luca, but some shit came up I couldn't get out of," Mitch said, his wide smile still in place.

"Was it election night at your skateboarding club?" Nunzio asked, still irked at the long wait.

"I was working and figured you didn't want to spend another hour here while I was changing clothes," Mitch said, his smile disappearing. "If you can't let it go that's fine, but good luck trying to get another meeting."

"You have that many people lined up willing to buy in the quantities we discussed?" He drained the last of his drink and slammed the glass on the table. Beside him Tracy shook her head at the approaching server to keep him from ordering another one. He made a mental note to remind her he already had a mother, since he didn't want to call her down in front of this asshole. "If you do, then give them a call. If not, stop talking to me like I'm new to this game."

"This isn't the best way to begin our relationship, so why don't we start over," Mitch said, smiling again. "I can't ignore problems in my business, like I know you can't when shit arises, but we'll have a profitable partnership if you're willing to forgive me this time. In the future I'll give Tracy a call if I plan to be late."

"Fine." Nunzio scanned the room again for anyone too interested in their conversation.

"The bar belongs to a friend, Mr. Luca. Believe me, it's safe from nosy patrons," Mitch said, obviously noticing his every action.

"If you know so much, then tell me when I'll be meeting with your boss. You have to realize nothing will go down until that happens."

"I made it clear to Tracy, since she arranged all this. You'll be dealing with me, and strictly with me." Mitch took a sip of his beer, keeping eye contact with him over the rim of the glass. "We'd love to do business with you, but our terms are nonnegotiable."

"Then you really must think I'm new to this, Mr. Surpass," he said, trying to make his name sound like a curse word. "I walk away from this and we're done. Good luck to you getting me back to the table." He threw the threat back at him. "After I do walk I'll put word on the street that anyone doing business with you is buying from confiscated shit the DEA is using for their sting operation. You and your secretive boss can take turns dipping your dicks into all that product, since you'll be waist-high in it. No one's going to be interested."

"No one likes to be reminded of their mistakes, but this is a good time for a history lesson." Mitch had lowered his voice but he appeared as tense as a guitar string about to snap when he leaned forward. "Your clout on the street lost some punch when someone shot your father and Junior told anyone who'd sit long enough what a cruel joke from fate you were. Fuckup was his favorite nickname for you, but there were others. You've gained some ground since then, but not enough to sit here and threaten me. My being here at all is a gift, so why don't you cut the shit."

Nunzio stared at Mitch the entire time he was talking and was ready to shoot him between the eyes when he finished, consequences be damned. The feel of Tracy's hand on his thigh made him bite off the response he had ready, and for that he was grateful to her. This guy wasn't worth throwing away what he'd worked hard to build for himself without his father's shadow tainting any of it. Patience now, though, wouldn't save this son of a bitch. Mitch and his smug smile weren't long for this world.

"Shut up before you fuck up any more than you have already," Tracy said, squeezing Nunzio's leg gently as she spoke to Mitch. "Junior's dead, so whatever opinion he had about anyone, especially my boss, isn't important to anyone of consequence. Forgive my disrespect, Mr. Luca, but your father, for as much as he talked about you, is the one who ended up with a bullet in the head. That should clear up any misconceptions you and your boss have on that subject, Mitch. You aren't our only option, and you're the one who fucked this up. That's all the reputation on the street we'll need because, according to you, we're desperate. Who passes on that kind of deal unless you're the cops?"

If he'd closed his eyes, Nunzio wouldn't have a problem imagining Kim sitting next to him. Tracy sounded powerful enough for him to believe she'd shoot Mitch for his honesty, and from Mitch's expression, so did he.

"How about we start over one more time?" Mitch said after another sip of his beer. His smile was back in place, but the way he opened and closed his hands made Nunzio think he was suddenly nervous.

"How about you fuck off?" Tracy said, glancing quickly at him as if checking to see if she'd overstepped herself. He almost laughed at the puckering Mitch's asshole had to be doing, but only nodded. "Tell your boss we'll be taking our money and our chances elsewhere."

"Mr. Luca," Mitch said, turning away from Tracy, "no one else's going to give you the guarantee we can."

"Take the lady's advice and fuck off, asshole," Nunzio said as he stood and threw thirty bucks on the table. "You can play games with somebody else, and I'm going to take my fifteen million somewhere else."

He gladly followed Tracy out of the bar to the elevators not far from the entrance. Their suite was midway up, facing the river, and they didn't start talking again until Nunzio closed the door. He'd brought only two other guys with him, both new to his crew, and they were a few rooms down. The meeting with Mitch had been the first time he'd been out since their arrival because he didn't want anyone to recognize them.

"Get Mike and Phil in here," he said to Tracy as he stripped off his jacket. Mike Walker and Phil King were both over six feet tall, with such blond hair they appeared to be twins. Unlike his father, he hired for killing skill instead of who their Italian grandmothers were.

"How'd it go, boss?" Mike asked a few minutes later.

"Like shit," he said, pouring himself another drink. "Phil, head down and see if the wannabe surfer is still down there. If he is, try to keep an eye on him." He took a swallow. "Tracy, go with him and point the bastard out, but don't hang around too long."

"Anything you want from me?" Mike asked when they were alone.

"Yeah." He paused to finish the Scotch he'd poured. "Pack a bag and head to Mississippi. The damn place is still rebuilding, but there's enough open for you to make some contacts. Start anywhere but the Gemini and put feelers out about a big buy."

"Think any of the guys you dealt with before are still around?" Mike asked, sitting at the edge of the sofa. "Might be a good place to start."

"I'll give you all the contacts I had, but there's something else." He unscrewed the bottle again but decided against a fourth drink. After Kim and Junior's deaths the bottle was the only place he found peace, but it was time to regain control. "Ask around about this Mitch Surpass and his shy boss."

"Anything in particular you want to know?"

"Whatever you find, call me, but the most important thing is what the fallout will be when I rip out Surpass's heart."

❖

"What's going on, Mom?" Tanith sat next to Aubrey, clutching her school bag to her chest like it would stop the bullets she seemed sure were imminent.

They were parked across the street from the drugstore Wiley had told her to go to, and Aubrey hadn't lifted her forehead off the steering wheel since she put the car in park and shut off the ignition. The paralyzing fear from listening to Maria get killed made her feel like she'd sat for hours with every muscle in her body clenched. She was exhausted and should be consoling Tanith, but she couldn't find the energy to move.

"Please answer me." Tanith's voice cracked from what she recognized was the beginning of tears. Tanith didn't cry often.

"I'm so sorry." She took a deep breath and turned her head so she could at least look at Tanith as she spoke. "What happened didn't have anything to do with us."

"Maria's dead, isn't she?"

She nodded and started to cry. Their partnership might not have been a fairy-tale romance, but Maria hadn't deserved to die that way. The sound of the chain saw, or whatever it was, would haunt her the rest of her life. Maria had suffered, her screams had confirmed that, but through it all she hadn't given them up. Their time together was over, and she'd been so angry, but this wasn't how she'd imagined it would end.

Hearing Maria die was almost as surreal as seeing Wiley standing at the bottom of her attic ladder, assuring them it was okay to come down and leave the house.

"Who were those people?" Tanith seemed to have a ready list of questions.

"I think the less you know about that, the better off you'll be, baby."

"That's all you're going to say?" Tanith raised her voice enough to make her close her eyes. Because she had, the knock on the window made her jump. She whipped her head around, expecting another group of assassins, but seeing Wiley made her heart rate slow.

"Leave some space between us and follow me," Wiley said before heading back to the bike that held as many memories for her as Wiley did.

They headed toward downtown, and Tanith sat silently next to her as Wiley led them into the French Quarter and the parking lot next to the shopping center that had once been the Jax Brewery. She pulled in and parked after Wiley motioned for her to do so, and got out with only her wallet and Tanith.

"You want me to leave my car here?" she asked once Wiley approached them. "I will, but it won't be safe for all three of us to ride on your bike."

"Where were you today?" Wiley asked, walking toward the most crowded section of the lot until she found two vans parked side by side. Aubrey gave her a rundown of her itinerary, keeping her arm around Tanith. "We're going to keep this simple so when it comes to facing a police interrogation you won't have problems."

"My mom didn't do anything wrong," Tanith said, with venom.

"She was involved in something to land up at the other end of that talk those guys wanted to have, kid. Sorry to be blunt, but we don't have time for sugarcoating."

"She meant me, Wiley," Aubrey said, kissing Tanith on the head. "Maria wasn't into parenting, as she put it."

"Sorry." Wiley looked at Tanith again. "What happened to you tonight isn't an anomaly. Those guys wanted something, and Maria either had it or knew who does."

Aubrey smiled at the patience Wiley showed, and how Tanith listened and nodded. The lines of respect had been drawn without her input or help. "Wiley isn't our enemy, and I called her because I trust her."

"The two of you went for a chocolate freeze to discuss leaving Maria, you went home to put away groceries, and Maria was still there," Wiley said, giving her a CliffsNotes version of her explanation.

"That's what happened before she left, and Mom got us in the attic before those guys got upstairs," Tanith said.

"The end of your explanation is," Wiley looked at both of them, but Aubrey knew this was her story for the cops, "you and Maria argued, so you took Tanith out for a sandwich. After that you took Tanith home to your parents', where you planned to join her later. You took her there in case Maria was still in a fighting mood when you went back to pack."

"I have to go back?" Aubrey was terrified at the thought.

"Ask your dad to go with you, and I'll be there watching. You'll be fine, but the truth of the night stays with the three of us. Peter's reaction has to be as genuine as yours when you call nine-one-one," Wiley said. "Understood?"

She and Tanith nodded and didn't look back at Wiley when she told them to head to Maespero's for dinner. It would take a miracle to keep food down, but Wiley said it was important for the waitress to remember them for the drink she'd asked Tanith to accidentally spill. They couldn't be nervous, or cry, only look relieved that they were putting a bad relationship behind them.

The line for the popular restaurant wasn't too long and they scored a table by an open French door. Wiley's presence four tables over helped calm any jitters Aubrey felt.

"That's her, isn't it?" Tanith asked, after she put her menu down. "You used to talk about her when I was little, but you stopped when you thought I'd start understanding."

"Understanding what?" She decided on the same burger Tanith had picked.

"How much you loved her. That part I got even though I was five, but Maria never did."

"I explained to Maria often enough that she understood where I stood on the subject of our being together. A relationship of convenience isn't the example I wanted to give you, but I wanted you to have the same foundation my parents provided me. Since I'd decided to raise you alone, I thought I'd have to work twice as hard to do a halfway decent job." Tanith's question made her smile, and when she did a bit of the horrid night faded.

"But it doesn't explain the stuff you gave up." Tanith leaned forward and whispered. "You know, her."

To Aubrey's relief, Tanith didn't point in Wiley's direction. She came close to laughing, wondering what Wiley would've done if Tanith had, because even though Wiley didn't appear to be watching, she knew better. When they dated, it often bothered her that she never truly had one hundred percent of Wiley's attention, but pushing her on the subject was like asking her to stop her heart from beating. The training was too engrained, but while annoying, it'd also kept Wiley alive, which was her other reason to not complain.

"Don't think I'm putting you off, but this isn't the place to talk about my past and the people in it," she said as she watched the waiter approach with their food. The burger looked good and she took some deep breaths, trying to prepare her stomach for at least some of it. "When we're alone, I'll answer whatever you want."

Tanith seemed appeased by her promise, so they lapsed into silence as they ate. The quiet allowed her to study Wiley as well as she could from her peripheral vision. All the things she'd admired about Wiley were still there, as far as she could see: the straight posture that always made her uniform look so good, the short, shiny jet hair, and the gentle calm no matter the situation. The rest, like she'd told Tanith, would have to wait until they were alone, but her heart clenched. She'd never stopped loving or wanting Wiley, but no plea had brought Wiley back from her self-imposed banishment.

❖

The muffaletta sandwich Wiley always ordered when she ate here tasted like sawdust, but she forced herself to eat it. All those fantasies she'd had while she and Aubrey were apart had shattered like a bullet hitting a target when she saw that kid staring down at her from the attic opening. She'd wanted Aubrey to have a chance at happiness, but she couldn't bring herself to think of Aubrey with someone else. Honor had made her leave, but it hadn't made her forget.

She'd tried for months afterward and had taken as many assignments as she could complete. Losing Aubrey had ripped holes in her that'd been as painful as if a weapon had inflicted them. Walking into that house, though, had made her doubt herself and the Aubrey she'd known.

Had Aubrey even given her a thought when she replaced her and moved into the storybook house and decorated a nursery?

She'd called Aubrey back, so she was stuck until this situation played out. Only an asshole would leave Aubrey and the kid in the open to be finished off, and she wasn't an asshole. She, along with everyone close by, looked toward Aubrey's table when her daughter spilled her drink into Aubrey's plate. She had to give the kid credit for executing it perfectly. When the cops came asking questions, and they would, someone here would remember Aubrey and Tanith. After Aubrey called in the crime scene, the police would have to clear her before they widened the scope of their investigation.

"The number I called you on is registered to an employment agency," she told Aubrey after they'd finished dinner and were back in the parking lot. "In this case that'll fit the rest of your story tonight, but remember to keep it simple. You want the cops to put you under the microscope, then move on."

"What about the rest?" Aubrey asked.

"Worry about what's important right now. If you try to get ahead of yourself, the police will take their time clearing you, especially if they think you're either hiding something or involved." They stood between the vans again, but Wiley still felt too exposed. "Nothing's going to happen to you, but don't let your guard down. Don't trust anyone until you know all there is to know about tonight."

"Thanks, Wiley." Aubrey took her hand. "This isn't how I imagined seeing you again, but I'm glad you came."

"No stops until you get to your parents'." Wiley took a step back. She wanted Aubrey's touch still, but now wasn't the time to indulge. "Are they still in the same place?" Aubrey nodded. "Warn them you're coming, and let your dad know you want company when you go back for your stuff."

"When will I see you again?" Aubrey closed the gap between them but didn't touch her this time. She still smelled the same.

"I'll never be too far away."

"You said we were going to your place tonight," Tanith said.

"Eventually you might have to, but your grandparents' place makes more sense."

"What if those guys go after us again?"

Wiley could hear and see the fear in Tanith. Living through something so horrific at this age could damage the kid's future. "They'll have to get past me, and that's not going to happen."

"You'll be there?"

"As soon as I'm done with your mom and grandfather, I'll be there."

Her explanation seemed enough to make Tanith nod, so Wiley left it there. The rest of the night and how it played out was up to Aubrey, and she couldn't help her with that. Their ride across the lake was uneventful, and Wiley followed them back only after she was convinced no one was tailing them.

She wasn't ready to call Don for help. The situation was complicated enough without adding to it, but depending on how motivated these people were, he'd remain her first choice for backup. For the moment she had no choice but to leave Karen and Tanith vulnerable while she watched over Aubrey and Peter. Not that Karen Tarver couldn't take care of herself and her granddaughter, but this was beyond the scope of her usual threatening, mother-hen, protective streak.

The traffic was light on the return trip, and she almost enjoyed the twenty-four-mile stretch over the lake. She'd meant what she'd said to Tanith about being okay, and in a way she'd also promised herself to take care of Aubrey and her child to the best of her ability so she could finally make peace with what she'd had to do.

As horrific as the night had been, it presented her with the key to freedom from her past, and she planned to take it.

❖

Mitch waited until Nunzio and his bitch were in the elevator before he made the call that would get his ass handed to him. His boss Emray Gillis was a man of few words until you fucked with his plan, and Mitch had managed a huge deviation from it.

It had taken three months of negotiation for both Emray and Nunzio to agree to all the terms, and it had been a problem for the impatient Nunzio. Emray loved moving slow, with Mitch serving as his middleman, but Mitch had just cut the line of the biggest fish they had hooked so far. Now they might not get Nunzio's money but might have to waste another three or so months on meetings. That wasn't what Emray had expected.

"When's the exchange?" he asked, and Mitch could hear a car horn blaring in the background. He'd ridden with Emray a few times and tried to avoid it if he could.

"We hit a snag tonight, but with a little finesse we'll be back on track." He got the confession out as quick as he could manage, and a slew of protesting horns close to Emray indicated his reaction.

"What the fuck?"

"He insisted that you two meet before he committed to the deal, and I gave him some lip about it. The greaser got pissed and walked."

"Get with the times, Mitch," Emray said, obviously having arrived at his destination since Mitch heard him slam his door. "Nobody says 'greaser' anymore, and you'd better have some idea about how to get Nunzio back that you're dying to share. Did you think we had a lot of free time when you gave Nunzio lip?"

"I told you everything else's being taken care of," he said, blowing the waitress a kiss when she delivered another beer. "You'll not only have all the pieces in place from this deal, but later on I'll deliver what you're missing."

"I didn't misplace anything, I was fucking robbed."

Mitch rolled his eyes. His plans for the night were about to derail. The waitress who'd been pouring his beers had promised an unforgettable midnight swim in the hotel's pool if he brought enough blow.

"The guys are recovering your property, and I'd give Luca the night to think about it. His need to do business with us is bigger than his ego, so he'll call."

"You'd fucking better hope so," Emray said, laughing, "because if you screw up my schedule, I'll take you out myself."

CHAPTER FIVE

The house was quiet and still when Aubrey and Peter Tarver turned into the driveway. All the cars that had been there earlier were still there, so whoever they had to report to wasn't missing them yet. Everything and everyone inside was exactly like they'd left it, and Wiley had waited until she heard the Tarvers open the back door to scale down the side of the house.

She'd been too concerned with getting Aubrey and Tanith away from the carnage to do a proper sweep, so she'd lost Aubrey as soon as they were in the vicinity of her house. She hadn't done her usual neat cleanup, but every bullet casing her guns had ejected and every slug was in the plastic baggie in her pocket. The coroner wouldn't have a hard time reporting what the causes of deaths were, but would only be able to speculate what type of weapon was used.

Lights were starting to come on as she imagined Aubrey making her way through the house, so she quickly scaled the magnolia tree growing in the across-the-street neighbor's yard. The small earpiece she'd inserted allowed her to hear the conversation Aubrey and Peter were having as they moved about. She'd planted enough low-tech listening devices to monitor not only for any surprise visits before the police arrived, but also to hear Aubrey's police interrogation. Keeping it simple sounded easy until you faced the detectives who'd assume this was a better, faster, and cheaper alternative to a nasty breakup. Division of assets wasn't a problem when the person you had to share with was dead.

Wiley wanted to hear firsthand every answer Aubrey gave, since nerves would make any recap either Tarver gave useless. They'd deal with any deviation Aubrey made, but knowing what they were would make it easier.

"The argument got this out of control with Tanith in the house?" Wiley heard Peter ask, along with some shuffling noises as if he was straightening furniture.

Aubrey watched her dad try to put everything in order. They'd never discussed the decisions she'd made after Wiley again because, as he put it, he'd said his piece and didn't see any reason to rehash the mistakes he felt she'd made. He treated Tanith like the center of his universe, but Maria was at the top of the list of things he'd never agree with.

"No, we had words, but the furniture stayed put during our talk," she said, technically not lying. "I know you don't like her, and it's time to move on if you and Mom don't mind helping us out for a while. Tanith deserves better than this."

"So do you, baby girl," Peter said, and finally came closer and hugged her. "Your mom and I'll be happy to have you with us until you're ready for whatever comes next."

She leaned against him, trying to act like there weren't a bunch of dead people upstairs. "Thanks, Daddy. That's Maria's car out there, so try to stay calm."

"You got it."

"Come on," she kept hold of his hand, "let's go grab some stuff and leave." Following Wiley's instructions, she called for Maria a few times as they climbed the steps.

"What the hell?" Peter said when he opened the door to the master bedroom. "Stay here but in sight."

He walked ahead, calling for Maria like she had, but gave way to retching, caused, she knew, by whatever he'd found in the bathroom. "Aubrey, stay there. Don't come in here." He came out wiping his mouth with his handkerchief with a haunted expression that made Aubrey feel guilty. "We need to call the police."

"Is Maria in there?" she asked, walking into the bedroom and stopping when her dad held her back. The two men who lay dead on the floor appeared so surreal with the rug as their backdrop she wanted to close her eyes and will them gone.

"Aubrey, let's get downstairs," Peter said, standing behind her with his arm wrapped around her waist. "I don't know what's going on, or what happened, but we need to get the hell out of here."

She couldn't stop staring at the two bodies. The kill shots had landed, from what she could tell, in exactly the same spot on their foreheads. Wiley might've been retired, but her skill set was still intact, and for once she was thrilled that Wiley took her job so seriously. These killers had never stood a chance and barely saw it coming, from what she'd heard in the attic. They were dead by Wiley's hand at her urging, and she didn't feel bad about it.

"Come on, we'll call from the car." She let herself be led away. "It's not safe to be here."

In the car Aubrey allowed all the feelings she'd bottled up to come out, and her dad had to finish the emergency call since the operator was having trouble understanding her because she was sobbing. The more she reviewed all the things she should've done to avoid this, the harder she cried. Maria never wanted to make changes in her personal or business life, so she should've left months ago. She'd put it off, and now she'd endangered Tanith's life by exposing them to the people who'd killed Maria.

Peter gave the operator the address and summary of what they'd found. He was still on the phone, but Aubrey could hear the sirens getting closer. She held her hand out and felt better when her father immediately took it and squeezed her fingers. His presence comforted her, but she'd have true peace of mind only if Wiley was sitting next to her. Only Wiley could keep her and Tanith safe from the goons Maria had invited into their lives. These guys would keep coming until they got what they were after.

"They're on their way," Peter said, putting his phone against his chest.

"Oh, God, Daddy," she said, leaning back until her head fell against the seat back. "How did they kill her?"

"Not now." He squeezed her fingers again and placed his phone against his ear. "Yeah, we're still here. Tell them I parked on the street and have my engine running. If anyone but the police show up, I'll have no choice but to get my daughter to safety."

A few minutes later the driveway was full of squad cars, and the rest boxed them in place. They were as trapped as she and Tanith had been in the attic.

"Mr. Tarver." A middle-aged man tapped on the driver-side window lightly with his badge. Aubrey studied his face to make sure she hadn't seen him with Maria. He and the woman standing behind him didn't match any face in her memory. "Sir, could you please step out?"

"We'll be okay," her dad said, waiting for her to open her door before getting out and introducing them.

"I'm Detective Barry Smith and this is my partner Detective Glenda Mazerac," Barry said, holding out his hand in greeting. "Do you live here, Ms. Tarver?" he asked when she shook his hand.

"Yes," she said softly.

"Do we have your permission to go in?" Glenda asked gently, but Aubrey could see the anticipation in her face. Both detectives were half turned in the direction of the house, poised as if waiting for someone to fire a starter pistol that would kick off the race to try to convict her for what they found inside.

"Yes," Aubrey said as she wiped her face.

"Mr. Tarver, would you show us what you found?" Barry asked.

"Ms. Tarver." Glenda swept her arm toward the house. "If you think you can, we'd like for you to come too. That way you can point out anything that's missing."

"Is that really necessary?" Peter asked. "From what I saw, robbery wasn't the motive."

Glenda hesitated, but gave in after directing one of the uniformed officers to keep an eye on Aubrey, as if to make sure she was all right. *That's wishful thinking, Glenda*, Aubrey thought as she watched the three of them walk away. *I won't be okay until this nightmare is over.*

❖

"How long has your daughter lived here?" Barry asked as he stepped ahead of Peter.

"Her partner Maria owns the house, Detective," Peter said, and stopped walking. "Look, what you're going to find is pretty goddamn horrible, but my daughter didn't have anything to do with it. The truth is I don't know who's capable of doing something like what's up there."

"No one's accusing anyone of anything, sir," Glenda said. "Let's go in and assess what we have."

Peter stayed by the back door as directed while Glenda and Barry walked through the first floor with their guns drawn. It was a waste of time, but cops didn't appreciate advice on how to do their jobs. The danger that had visited the house was dead, alongside Maria. He was sure of that when he saw the dead guy with the chain saw clutched in his hand.

But who had killed the pack of wolves? He kept that thought to himself as he looked around the kitchen. This was his daughter's home, but they had seldom come to see her here. When they got together to enjoy time with their granddaughter, it was mostly at their house across the lake.

They'd had only one conversation about Maria, and he'd been totally honest about the woman who'd help raise Tanith. After that long talk he hadn't seen any reason to belabor the point of how neither he nor Karen liked Maria. The decision had been Aubrey's, and it'd be up to her to change it. It didn't look good that Aubrey had made up her mind on the day Maria received a dramatic visit from the thugs she was involved with.

"It seems clear," Glenda said, and waved him in. "Let's go upstairs."

Peter pointed them toward the stairs and allowed them to go ahead of him. He'd left all the lights on, so the first guy was easy to spot. Seeing him again made Peter realize he'd never checked out the other side of the upstairs, which was what Barry was doing now, his gun pointed and ready.

"It's clear," Barry said, loud enough for Peter and Glenda to hear him.

"Are you okay to do this?" Barry asked Peter with his hand on his shoulder.

"Just so you know, the fresh pool of vomit on the floor is mine. I don't recognize those guys, but what they did in there was inhuman."

They didn't linger, and Peter sat with Aubrey in the den while the forensics team started processing the scene. Barry and Glenda did a good job of limiting the people in the house and had left them alone to supervise.

"Ms. Tarver, we'd like you to come downtown after we're done so you can answer some questions," Barry said, bringing them a couple bottles of water.

"Can't we do it here?" Aubrey took his hand along with the water. "I don't want to be away from my daughter too long."

"Where is she?" Glenda asked, sitting next to Aubrey.

"I left her at my parents' house since I was coming back here to pack."

Barry wrote in a notebook as she spoke. "Where were you going?"

"Maria owns the bar in the Hilton Riverside, but she makes most of her money selling drugs. From what she told me recently, she was acting as the middleman between suppliers and sellers. After finding out, I wanted to leave so my daughter, Tanith, and I would be safe." The answer wasn't as simple as Wiley probably wanted, but it was basically the truth. The only white lie was how long she'd known. Three months was an eternity to live with the situation, and she hadn't moved fast enough to leave, but she'd add that failure to her list of mistakes once she cleared the police's radar.

"Maria was into drugs?" Glenda asked, and Aubrey could tell she was trying not to laugh. "How'd you find out? Did she suddenly blurt it out over dinner one night?"

"I dropped an earring in my closet last month and it rolled under Maria's shirt rack. After getting on my hands and knees I found a large, packed duffel."

Since Aubrey stopped there, Barry stopped writing and looked up at her. "Did you look in it?"

"I did only because I was curious about being suddenly single. Our relationship hasn't been great, and I thought she was leaving long enough to allow me to find a new place."

"You didn't want the house?" Glenda sounded as if she were asking more about a personal matter rather than trying to advance their investigation.

"I watch enough television to know right now I'm the prime suspect," she said, and Barry and Glenda nodded. "This house and all the bank accounts except for a household account are in Maria's name. I own none of it, I will inherit none of it, and I don't have any large insurance settlement in my future."

"What about your daughter?" Glenda asked.

"I already had Tanith, and she was the compromise Maria had to make to get me to agree to move in with her. Our relationship failed not only because of what she was hiding from me, but primarily because of the way she treated my child. She was interested in me only, but my daughter comes before anything or anyone. Since neither of us was willing to bend, it was time for me to move on."

"Understandable," Barry said as he started to jot again. "Back to the duffel. If it wasn't a weekend bag, what was in it?"

"This was more of a full-size bag you'd use on a long vacation, Detective, and it was packed to the top with bundles of hundreds. Each pack contained ten thousand dollars, and that's as far as I counted."

Barry held his hands out about three feet apart. "Was it this big?" Aubrey nodded. "How much total, if you had to guess?"

"Three and a quarter million."

"That's an interesting guess," Glenda said.

"It's not an estimate. When I confronted Maria with it, that's how much she said was in there and the two others she had. The bar has always been successful, but not that much. Except for the month she was closed after Katrina, the place cleared about fifteen thousand after expenses."

"Three million plus is a lot of motive," Barry said.

"The money was only in the house overnight. I don't know where she took it or where it is now. If you want, search the house, my parents' place—anywhere you want." Aubrey stopped and covered her face with her hands. "I was desperate to get out of here, and Maria was threatening me to make me stay. I picked today out of panic. A large supplier had a problem and requested a meeting with her. When I saw how nervous she was, I wanted to put as much distance between us as possible."

"So you think this is drug-related?" Glenda asked, and Aubrey wanted to scream at how stupid she found the question.

"I was scared, but I never imagined this. My dad wouldn't let me in the bathroom, but marines don't have reactions like he did. Whatever happened isn't something I could do under any circumstances, and I don't know anyone who could."

❖

Aubrey was being too long-winded, but she sounded believable. At least until that last line, Wiley thought. You do know someone capable of that, and worse.

The call had gone out describing what the responding officers had found, so police cars lined the street. Aubrey's neighbors were also standing in small groups talking and keeping a vigil. All the extra police weren't necessary, but everyone was eternally curious about the macabre.

So far, though, they'd been barred from the house, but they weren't leaving, which gave whoever ordered this the perfect opportunity to come back and observe. They'd have to, since Maria hadn't given up her secrets, and even if she had, the interrogation squad was dead.

From her perch in the tree, Wiley watched the crowd through the night scope she'd brought. "I know you're here," she whispered, searching for the anomaly in the group gathered.

She'd bypassed him twice in her constant sweeps, but even the cops milling around hadn't noticed the one thing wrong with his uniform. The guy standing alone in Aubrey's front yard was about five-ten; judging from his eyebrows the light-blond hair was his natural color, and the scar along his right cheek that reached his jaw was recent.

Everything about his uniform was perfect except for the badge. It appeared authentic but was pinned on the wrong side of his chest. Not even a rookie would've made that mistake.

Whoever he was, he'd been turned away from the door twice and hadn't started a conversation with anyone since Wiley had noticed him. As the coroner arrived the guy took out his cell phone and made a call, but kept his phone to his ear long enough to make her think he'd gotten no answer.

"Can you think of any names of people Maria mentioned doing business with?" Barry asked.

"The only employees I know are those working at the bar. She kept all the rest of this to herself. She didn't even mention who she was supposed to have a meeting with, and I didn't ask."

From the questions it seemed Aubrey's interview was almost over. The police wouldn't have any reason to detain her longer so they'd let her go for the night, right into the arms of the fake cop waiting for her outside.

More vehicles marked *Coroner's Office* arrived, and the people in them started carrying out gurneys. The cop stood straighter at the sight, staring and seeming close to panic. The man made another call. Still no answer.

"I realize how difficult this was, Ms. Tarver, but thank you for answering our questions while all this was still fresh in your mind."

Wiley heard Barry as well as some background noise, probably meaning that everyone was starting to stand. It was time to go, but she wanted to see fake cop's reaction when Aubrey and Peter walked out. His panic probably stemmed from the police pressure that would come from the hit-team killings more than their intended targets. That was a rule Wiley broke only when she didn't have a chance of getting out alive. Even if there were witnesses, they were so scared that ninety-nine percent of the time they couldn't identify you if their lives depended on an accurate account.

"If you need anything else, I'll be staying with my parents," Aubrey said right before the back door opened. When it did, the cop moved closer, took a look, then retreated to his tree.

Peter opened the passenger-side door and helped Aubrey inside as Barry and Glenda watched. The fake cop spared them some attention, as if to notice what car they were driving, before he continued his surveillance of the house.

Wiley waited to make sure Peter didn't pick up a tail before he turned to drive out of the neighborhood and stayed put when he didn't. Aubrey and Tanith weren't safe yet, but until she had the chance to sit with Aubrey and ask her for the truth, she had to follow what few bread crumbs she had.

"And this asshole is getting ready to drop bucketloads of them," she said, meaning the fake cop.

Chapter Six

Freddie Buhle was starting to get that twitch in his stomach that would ruin his night. It had begun when he'd had to put on the fucking police uniform to track down the idiots Mitch had insisted on for this.

The only slight relief had come when he saw Maria's girlfriend walk out of the house. He didn't know what had happened and what Maria's story was, since Peanut wasn't answering his phone. If they'd killed the girlfriend and her kid as well as Maria, it'd be months before they could get back in there to find the missing cash. A splash across the headlines like that and the police would have no choice but to devote some serious time to the case.

If Maria's bitch was alive, though, what was with the multiple body bags and wagons? He was tired of waiting but Mitch would want an answer, so he leaned against the tree again, trying to appear busy by scrolling through his phone to keep the other cops away from him.

He tried Peanut's number again and turned to leave when it finally connected. "Where in the hell are you?"

"Could I ask who's calling?"

"Cut the shit and tell me," he said.

"This is Detective Smith. Can you identify yourself?"

"Fuck." The word exploded in his head as he disconnected. No sooner had he done so when the phone started ringing, registering Peanut's number.

He broke his phone in two, dropped the battery in a drain on the way to his car, and removed the SIM card before tossing the phone too. The pain in his gut was excruciating now, but he'd have to ignore it.

Not only had he dialed a cop from the front yard of a crime scene, but Peanut and his morons were dead.

"And there's no way that piece of ass did that," he said about Aubrey.

He had another prepaid cell in the car and took a deep breath before making his call. "We got problems," he told Mitch when he answered. "And they're fixing to get a whole lot more fucked up."

❖

Wiley was already on the ground and moving when the cop started walking and ripping his phone up. Her fake cop was most likely in charge of the guys she'd eliminated, but what would he do now that he knew they were dead?

The bike started on the first try, but as she quickly pulled away from the curb, she wished again for the old van. She loved the vintage ride, but it was definitely more noticeable. She couldn't take any chances now, since nothing about the entire night made sense to her.

Could Aubrey have changed so dramatically in the time they'd been apart that she would've hooked up with a dealer? She couldn't wrap her brain around the answer, so she wasn't even wasting energy wondering about Tanith.

The guy she was following didn't go far, stopping at the valet section of Harrah's Casino downtown. The guy threw his keys at the attendant who'd run up, and from the greeting, he was a regular. The valet who stepped up to help her never took his eyes off the hundred she held between her fingers.

"You think you can leave it parked up here ready to go in case I have shitty luck in there?" She held the money at his eye level.

"No problem."

She took a right after entering, hoping to spot the uniformed man since she'd lost sight of him. He was walking fast enough to make her sure he was there to meet someone. "Either that or he's got a bad gambling jones," she said softly as she scanned the room.

She skipped the slot machines and headed to the tables. Because of his clothes he instantly stood out at the craps table, but he wasn't interested in the action. He was standing behind a guy she was sure was carded on the way in because he was the only player dressed like he'd finished his paper route before heading to the casino.

Whoever he was, he'd had a good run, judging by the number of chips in the tray in front of him and the way the crowd was cheering him on. The guy appeared young, but fake cop waited patiently to be addressed. That took ten minutes, as if his being there had changed the guy's luck since he rolled a seven after only three more tosses. The seven cooled the crowd, but the dealers looked relieved.

The heated conversation she watched take place close to the cages was short, and the younger man couldn't seem to stop saying the word *fuck*. They were both upset, and from what Aubrey had said to the police, these guys had three and a quarter million reasons to worry if it had been their responsibility to get that duffel full of money back. From the tall blond paperboy's reaction he was higher up the food chain than fake cop but wasn't the boss.

"Did you stay to make sure?" the younger man asked.

"The fucking cops answered Peanut's phone, so no, I didn't, but I saw enough black Hefty bags to carry away Maria and your gang of mental giants."

It was the only part of their conversation Wiley overheard when she went to the cage to get a couple of hundred dollars in chips. To stand there after the cashier counted them out would've made her, so she pocketed them and put a twenty in the nearest slot machine with a good view of the two men.

They talked with their heads together a few minutes more before heading to the front entrance that led out to the valet stand. Wiley pressed the maximum-bet button and kept her eyes on the reels as the two walked past her in a hurry.

"Hey, look, you won," the woman next to her said, and pointed to the triple bars with two three-times symbols lined up. Six hundred bucks on her first try made the woman smile on her behalf. She was casually dressed and had a convention nametag with *LISA* written in big block letters.

"Must be your lucky day," Wiley said, waiting for the two men to walk out of her line of sight.

"Don't you mean *your* lucky day?"

"I've got someone to meet, so play it out for me," Wiley said as she stood. "If you hit the big one you can buy me a drink."

The cop's car was all ready to go and Wiley saw both guys get in, making her job easier, but the relief was short-lived when they drove a half block and got out at the Hilton. The valet this time paid more attention to the paperboy.

"We're in for the night, Jimmy, so park it," the cop said, leaving his engine running.

Wiley didn't bother with the parking service and left her bike on the street so she could catch up. Inside she saw them at the top of the escalator that opened to the lobby and entertainment area. The bar facing the river was still open, but only a few stragglers sat there nursing drinks.

Her two leads were standing at the guest elevator bank waiting. Her only clue from the chase was that these guys who'd hired the dead men in Aubrey's house were on the twelfth floor. She'd hack the system but doubted she'd find their real names on the registry. They weren't the two smartest-looking players, but what they'd tried to pull off had taken some skill and connections to accomplish.

Tomorrow she'd have to face two likely scenarios to keep Aubrey and Tanith safe, but that would remain a mystery until she got to know these guys better. Depending on who they worked for and how badly they wanted their money back, she started planning for option one. That consisted of another pack of goons showing up at the Tarver home, grabbing Aubrey and Tanith, and killing Peter and Karen. These people couldn't afford witnesses after tonight.

Had it been her, she'd be at the Tarvers' house already, making sure the police were still in New Orleans putting together their case. If they were, she'd have been in and out by now with whatever information she needed. That had been her training when something went wrong. You struck when the target didn't expect you, and the best time for that was right after you fucked up the first plan.

I bet these aren't the types who like to get their hands dirty, Wiley thought as she headed for her bike. She was tired, but she had to move all the Tarvers tonight. "I'm sure Karen can't wait to see me." Wiley laughed at the way Aubrey's mom always turned into a shepherd trying to lead her one little lamb away from the career-military wolf. "If you approved of Maria more than you did me, I hope you're happy with the death and destruction she brought to your door."

❖

"She didn't say anything on the way home?" Karen said to Peter as they watched from the kitchen while Aubrey and Tanith talked in their den.

"You had to see that bathroom," Peter said as he poured himself a whiskey. He couldn't get the smell of vomit out of his nose, but didn't want to take his eyes off his family to shower and change. "That bitch was into drugs, and now the scum she was doing business with knows who Aubrey and Tanith are."

"Aubrey told you she was involved in this?" Karen took a sip out of his glass. "There's no way I believe Aubrey has that in her."

"She said that's why she was leaving, because she found out that's what Maria was up to."

Karen finally met his eyes and put her hands up. "What? You're talking in that tone of yours. What aren't you saying?"

"It's what she's not saying." He pointed at Aubrey with the hand he held the glass in. "Don't you think this is odd?" Peter shook his head. "I'm not judging her, only making an observation."

"She didn't have anything to do with this, and we don't need her to bolt. And if she thinks we don't have faith in her, that's exactly what she'll do."

"Karen, I'm telling you what I think, not planning to turn Aubrey in." He kept his voice down, but the nerves that had tied themselves in a bundle were unraveling in his stomach. Instead of relaxed, though, he was agitated.

The knock on the back door stopped their discussion, and even Aubrey pulled her head away from Tanith and stood. Peter put his finger to his lips and smiled at them, trying to ease their obvious terror.

Whoever it was knocked again. How had the visitor gotten over the fifteen-foot fence circling the entire back without triggering the alarm and motion sensors? By the third knock he opened the kitchen drawer closest to the door, took out the .357 he'd placed there earlier, and removed the trigger lock he'd attached to it because of Tanith.

"Take the girls to my study and lock the door," he whispered to Karen. "You hear me fire, you arm everyone and call the cops. No matter what, don't open the door."

"Mr. Tarver," someone said through the door. "You can stand down, sir. It's Wiley Gremillion."

"I should've known she'd eventually show up in all this," Karen said as she yanked the door open.

"Hello, ma'am," Wiley said with a smile that made her appear as if she were there for a root canal on every tooth in her mouth. "May I come in?"

Karen's concerns about Wiley were hers alone, but Peter felt confident that whatever came next would be that much easier to handle. Wiley was the exact opposite of Maria, but he'd given up hope that Wiley would find her way back to Aubrey.

"Just happened to be in the neighborhood?" Peter asked as he embraced Wiley, then closed the door.

"Saw the lights on so I figured the coffee would be on as well," Wiley told him, and laughed.

It wasn't until Peter laid eyes on Wiley that he realized how much he missed her. Of anyone in Aubrey's life, Wiley had been the only partner good enough for his little girl, and he loved her enough to forgive her the stupidity of leaving.

"Did you have anything to do with this?" Karen asked.

"With what exactly?" Wiley answered in the same forceful tone Karen had used. Karen's mouth twisted in a way that looked like she'd suddenly sucked on a lemon.

"This mess with Maria and the police—don't act coy."

"Mrs. Tarver, I answered a call from an old friend in trouble," Wiley said, and her easy manner made Peter think of those dead guys in Maria's house. The shots were identical and the only reason Aubrey and Tanith were fine.

"If she tells me the trouble is over, I'll disappear as quickly and effectively as I did the first time. You don't have anything to worry about. I won't ruin Aubrey's life." Wiley was sure Aubrey had shed tears of suffering because she'd left, but Karen's had most likely been tears of joy.

Aubrey had come into the room. "She's right. I've done a great job of that all by myself."

"I need to talk to all of you," Wiley said.

"We can handle it from here," Karen said, and stepped between her and Aubrey.

"Tonight you walked within ten feet of the man those guys worked for." She glanced at Aubrey first over Karen's shoulder, then Peter. Until she'd found and eliminated every target, they didn't have time to spin stories, even if Tanith was within earshot. "He was dressed like a cop and he saw the two of you leave. After you headed back here, this guy met another man, who's either his boss or partner, to let him know everyone but Aubrey and Tanith were dead. The three dead guys and Maria can't tell them where the missing money is, so no later than tomorrow they'll come looking for the next breathing target who might know. If you can handle the same scenario that played out earlier on your own, that's great. If you can't, then drop the attitude, Mrs. Tarver, and this won't be as painful to get through."

"Are you getting thin-skinned, Lieutenant?" Karen waved her farther into the room. "You were always so polite, no matter what kind of mood I was in."

"I'm retired *Major* Gremillion, and age has taught me that it's a waste of time to butt your head against immovable objects." She thought of the time she'd wasted trying to win this woman over and never come close. "You won, ma'am, I concede that fact, and I'm only here because your family's going to need my help, starting now."

"That was you, Wiley?" Peter asked as if Wiley would understand the question. "Can I talk to you?"

"Daddy," Aubrey said softly. "Could both of you back off? I didn't call Wiley because I needed help, but she was nice enough to show up even after I told her what was going on. She's right that this is beyond what we can handle."

"Listen." Wiley was about to laugh at what bullshit they were concentrating on. "I wasn't kidding about the guy outside the house. You've got until maybe tomorrow morning before they send someone else to ask you what your partner didn't answer. You need to get out of here."

"Whatever you say," Aubrey said. "If you want out, though, you can go. You've done more than I have a right to ask." It sounded like she was still stinging from being deserted.

"You'd leave us?" Tanith asked Wiley.

"No." She looked Tanith in the eye. "What happened to you is weird, isn't it?"

"I thought my mom and me were going to die."

Even Karen stopped breathing. As the adults in Tanith's life for the duration of this nightmare, they needed to draw the terror out of her. If they couldn't, the horror would grow and fester in the dark corners of her mind. Once the ghouls set up shop there, they sucked away pieces of your soul.

"Come on, let's you and me talk," Wiley said.

Tanith led her back into the den and sat next to her on the sofa. "Thanks," Tanith said as an opener.

"How old are you?"

"Almost nine, why?"

She held her hand out to Tanith and saw that Tanith noticed her shoulder holster. Tanith didn't hesitate to take her hand, and she felt a surge of jealousy and anger toward a dead woman. Here was someone too precious to sacrifice to a quick buck.

"Only a liar wouldn't admit they were scared, so it's good that you told me the truth. Whenever you ask me something I promise to do the same, no matter what." She shook Tanith's hand to seal her vow. "And I'll listen whenever you need to talk."

"What are you going to do?"

Tanith's question was a good opening to lay out her plan. Not that she'd had a lot of time to put an acceptable one together. Those types, where every contingency was accounted for, took months, weeks if she pushed it, but she couldn't come up with anything even half-assed in a few hours.

"Hopefully you haven't unpacked," she said, but she looked at Aubrey as she spoke. "I want you and your mom to come with me."

"And my mom and dad?" Aubrey asked.

"Does your sister still live near Natchez, Mrs. Tarver?" Karen nodded. "For tonight do you have somewhere you both can stay and watch the house?"

"Like a neighbor?" Peter asked.

"Whoever ordered this knows where Aubrey and Tanith are, and they'll be back. We need to remove them from any place familiar and not make anyone think that Aubrey's fleeing. Right now she's the police's only credible suspect. If she disappears, she seals her guilt."

"So why do you want us to stay behind?" Karen asked.

"If I'm right, they'll leave a message when they come looking, and you'll need to tell the police about it. Let them know you're going wherever you decide, and that Aubrey and Tanith are off-limits until they arrest whoever's responsible."

"How will we keep in touch with you, Wiley?" Peter pointed toward the kitchen, probably in an effort to talk to her alone. "Why don't you two get ready to go?" he told Aubrey. That was all Wiley needed to hear—he agreed with her.

Aubrey looked back at them a few times but did leave them alone.

As she moved away, Wiley followed her with her eyes and had to control her breathing to not tear up at the sudden swell of emotion. It was unbelievable to be here only a night after dealing with Dr. Jerry.

"Do you really think these sons of bitches will come here?"

"They want their bag of money back," she said softly, "and Aubrey is their next logical step. It's best if you're not here when they arrive."

"The three dead assholes—that was you?"

"Aubrey called and I came. If I was a storyteller, you would've stopped listening to my fish tale when I got to the part about what I found when I got there."

"So the story Aubrey told the cops was bullshit?"

"Where's your gun cabinet?" she asked when she saw Aubrey coming back. "Don't go outside, okay?" she said to Aubrey and Tanith. "They were both in the house when Maria was being chopped to pieces. What she told the cops is what I told her to, because she needs to clear their radar first. If the cops know where your family is, believe me, so will the people oiling their chain saws. If these assholes don't show up here by tomorrow, they'll expand their search until Aubrey and Tanith are found. What in that cabinet isn't registered?"

"More than enough to do the kind of damage that'll convince the police and whoever else is watching that I'm not fucking around." Two pistols in the bottom left corner caught her attention, since they'd be the envy of any collection. "That's what you had in mind, right?"

Peter removed the pistols and placed them in a bag with four new boxes of ammunition. "Think these are enough?"

He reached in the bag and held up one of the Colt .45s. "These belonged to my great-grandfather. They've been handed down since then, and will be after I'm dead. I don't believe they'll ever be in an auction, so they aren't registered. I keep them in perfect working condition and they're the only forty-fives I own. Don't worry about me, Wiley. I'll do what needs to be done, even if it's burning my own house to the ground. Concentrate on my daughter and granddaughter. I'm glad you answered her call, and I know you'll do whatever it takes to keep them safe."

"Wiley," Karen said when they rejoined the group. "Don't make the same mistakes twice. Don't take your eyes off them."

"Don't worry." She hugged Karen and smiled when she clung to her. "Before you go, take what's most important to you. Don't give them the satisfaction of destroying your memories or treasures."

"My memories are safe in here," Karen tapped over her heart, "and I'm entrusting my greatest treasures to you."

"They'll have to kill me, you know that, right?"

"Try to avoid that, Major," Karen said as she placed her palm against Wiley's cheek. "We have plenty of sparring to do before you're firmly in my good graces."

CHAPTER SEVEN

D on," Walter Robinson said after Don answered on the second ring. "I'm not disturbing you, am I?"

The ten o'clock news had headlined the crime scene in one of the large homes in Uptown New Orleans, and even though Don was back home, his satellite service was set up to show the news from New Orleans. It hadn't fazed him at first, but then he saw Aubrey and Peter Tarver walk out of the house. The sight of her sent him into a panic that spiked when he called Wiley and the phone went right to voice mail. That meant the phone that was supposed to be turned on at all times wasn't, which in turn meant the GPS tracker was also off. If Wiley had been responsible for the headlines yet again, there was no way to prove it.

"Not at all," Don said, after muting the set and freezing the picture on Aubrey and her father. "What can I do for you?"

"I need an answer in a few hours, if possible. My folks tell me our problem is about to be moved, which would only escalate the fallout from all this."

"Before I can utilize any solution, I need clearance. This isn't like calling Terminix for a bug problem." He advanced the recording a frame at a time but still saw nothing out of the ordinary that would require a call to his commanding officer. Even if he'd seen Wiley holding Aubrey's other hand on the way out, he'd talk to her before deciding on the next step. "You also have to realize that a go from my superiors doesn't mean instant gratification. A job like this takes planning, and that takes weeks for perfection."

"I called you because you control perfection, and she's usually ready to go when called, from what I've read about her." From Walter's tone he could tell he was talking with a clenched jaw. "Don't make the mistake of dragging your feet, Colonel. Reliable assets get reassigned all the time, and I'm an expert in how to do it. Work with me, or you'll spend the rest of your career shuffling paperwork at a recruiting office and trying to talk pimple-faced boys into enlisting. You can spend the rest of your days trying to find another Wiley, though I highly doubt you'll be that lucky."

"Go ahead and make your calls, then. You'll find that assets also are retired all the time, and if I'm reassigned that's exactly what will happen. After years of service I'm sure she'd appreciate you activating the release clause in her contract."

"Are you two delusional? This is a time in our country's history when you get to go when you're done, and people like me make that decision for you."

"People like you?" Don had to laugh. "You've never put in the kind of time my friend has, and that combined with a perfect completion rate earned the exit contract that the president signed. Force the issue and not even the total power of the Oval Office can stop her bill from getting stamped *Paid in Full* when it comes to any commitment. Do it and I'll send you a thank-you note for doing *her* a favor."

"No one's that important."

"If you're a gambler, Mr. Robinson, then make your call. Before you do, think of only one thing."

Walter laughed this time. "What, how pathetic your threats are? Or how much pleasure it will give me to bring you down?"

"Both good suggestions, but no. After you finish banging your head into the brick wall of the exit clause, think that there's no asset that equals the one you'll be responsible for cutting loose." Don didn't see any other news on Aubrey's case, so he turned the television off and powered on his computer. "Good luck getting any cooperation from the Pentagon after that."

It was satisfying to end the call on the asshole, but this wouldn't be the last they heard from him. Don knew the type well, and so did Wiley. They'd eventually win the war but not before a few intense battles.

His bags were still packed from his morning trip to New Orleans, so he booked himself on the next transport headed south. Hopefully he'd hear from Wiley in the next few hours before his flight, if only to warn her about Walter. As he touched his car-door handle, his phone rang and he fumbled to get it, relieved since he thought it was Wiley.

"Where the hell are you?" he asked, without checking the ID screen.

"I'm guessing you were expecting someone else," General Carl Greenwald said.

"Sir." Don lifted the phone away from his mouth to take a deep breath without his superior officer hearing him. "My apologies."

"Problems?"

"Nothing a new girlfriend couldn't help."

Carl laughed. "If that's how you answer the phone, I'd be bitchy too." As Carl spoke in his usual slow pace, Don's phone buzzed, showing he was missing a call from Wiley. "I don't like to intrude on your evening, but I just got off the phone with some asshole from the CIA."

"Walter Robinson?" He was trying to stay calm but was mentally cursing.

"Actually his name was Craig Orvik, Mr. Robinson's boss. There's nothing I love more than having some egotistical airbag ream me over something I don't have a clue about."

"Walter is determined to get us to share the Black Dragon, but I haven't finished vetting the facts."

"Is she stable and settling in?"

"Beautifully, sir." Wiley was important, but Don needed to get back to what Carl and this guy Orvik had talked about. "Did you and Orvik come to an understanding?"

"If you hear from Walter again, call me. Company assets will have to solve the problem these guys are having if our friend decides this isn't something she wants to do. I explained that if either you or our friend says no, they need to move on."

"Thank you, sir." The call ended painlessly, but once Carl heard about the crime scene in the house inhabited by Aubrey Tarver, he'd be calling back. Once that happened he'd have to have a great explanation ready so he could keep his job as Wiley's contact. Without him as a middleman, and if the brass thought Wiley wasn't stable, Carl would reshuffle assets, as they were referred to. In military speak, that meant that another asset would retire the Black Dragon permanently.

"Running a few errands," Wiley said on the message she left. "Give me a few hours and I'll give you a call."

"I hope you're taking deep breaths, kid. If you leave a death trail, this isn't South America or Iraq, and people like Carl are going to notice."

❖

The ride back to New Orleans had taken forty minutes longer since Wiley had bypassed the twenty-four-mile bridge, not wanting any record of her SUV on the traffic cameras. Tinted windows and the early hour had been their only two bonuses so far, and she was glad she'd returned home to pick up the vehicle.

The long ride hadn't produced any other excitement, so Tanith had fallen asleep in the backseat. Wiley could feel Aubrey's eyes on her, but she concentrated on the road, not wanting to get into a conversation she was too tired to intelligently participate in. She wasn't looking forward to one even after forty hours of sleep.

Once they were in the warehouse district she circled the block before she opened the garage door and drove in. With a flip of a switch the alarm was disarmed and she was free to turn the ignition off. Not even that woke Tanith, and Wiley envied the deep, peaceful sleep that she hadn't enjoyed in years.

"Is this your place?" Aubrey asked, turning away from her and looking at the neatly lined toolboxes and workbenches. "I hope it is. You must be in heaven here."

"I haven't experienced heaven in years," she said, not being able to hold back the honest response. "The living quarters are on the top floor." She got out and walked to the back for their bags. Tanith's head popped up when she gently closed the door, which changed her assessment of the peaceful part of that sleep equation. "There are three guest rooms, so pick the ones you like best."

"Thanks again for all this," Aubrey told her as she guided Tanith toward the elevator.

"I hope you haven't forgotten what you mean…what you meant to me." Wiley corrected herself, but from Aubrey's expression she'd caught her lie. "You don't have to thank me for something I offered to do a long time ago."

The second and third floors were dark, but a dim pocket light over *The Dragon Tree Legacy* painting made it easy to navigate to the light switches on the fourth floor. Wiley illuminated the space and didn't disturb Aubrey as she stood in front of the painting and stared.

"This is beautiful," she finally said, her cheeks wet. "Who did you get to paint it?"

"It's mine. I decided to see where the doodling took me and tried oil instead of a pencil." She waved toward the hallway on the side opposite her room and home office. "You both must be tired, so follow me." Since she'd activated the lights the rest came on automatically as they moved through the space. "The alarms are armed again, but feel free to move around. You'll be okay as long as you don't open an exterior door. The kitchen is on the third floor, but I don't have much in the way of food." Aubrey opened her mouth to say something, but Wiley simply said "Good night" before she walked away.

The morning would be soon enough to start their lines of communication, so she turned her cell phone back on and headed to the office next to her bedroom. When she sat in her chair, the exhaustion she'd been trying to ignore almost swamped her, but she dialed Don's number.

"I only have a few minutes," he said when he answered.

"Big plans this early in the morning?" A glance at the grandfather clock across from her and a quick calculation meant it was now half past five in Washington.

"I was able to get on a transport headed back your way. Walter's raising hell, and I watched the news from your hometown. I saw an interesting picture of Aubrey and Peter leaving a house where four people were found dead."

"You were the one who handed me the message. I called and caught her at a bad time."

"How do you define 'bad time'?"

"Her partner was handcuffed to her shower massager while some guy practiced his chain-saw skills on her limbs. Aubrey and her daughter were in the attic at the time."

"Jesus," Don said, exhaling loud enough for Wiley to hear him despite the engine noise in the background.

"God wasn't anywhere near that bathroom, believe me. If you aren't on the plane, don't board. I'm not saying I won't eventually need you here, but I have to figure out why this happened and how I can prevent it from happening to Aubrey and her child."

"She has a child?" Don asked as if he hadn't understood or heard her before.

"Smart girl who sounds like she's wiser than her eight years. Don't worry, Don, I'm not freaking out over this and I don't need you here. I'm going to get them out of this tight spot and go back to my canvases."

There was a long pause, as if Don was debating whether to take her advice. "I want updates, and call me the minute you hear from Walter, because I know the dick is going to try to go around me to get to you."

"Thanks, and you got it. Like I said, I might need you here soon, but there's no reason to crowd up the place if it isn't necessary. And to keep your ass out of the crack it's in, call Carl if you haven't already. You want him hearing all this from you."

"How about those dead guys?"

"The only drug-related thing we've been asked to intercede on is what Walter's harping about, but what happened to Aubrey's partner is definitely drug-related."

"You're taking this well."

She laughed and pried her body out of the chair before she fell asleep in it. "Yeah, it's always great to hear the woman you assumed was the love of your life took up with a cokehead who's dealing on the side."

"Love fucking hurts," Don said, and the background noise had faded away.

"Yeah, fuck you too, buddy. I'll call tomorrow after I get some sleep."

She took the phone with her and dropped it on her nightstand before heading to the bathroom to strip for a quick shower. She put on a pair of pajama pants and a T-shirt, in case she had to deal with any unwanted visitors. Before closing her eyes she brought up the different surveillance cameras located throughout the property and left them on the big-screen television hanging on the wall across from her bed. For now all was quiet.

"Let's hope it stays that way, but it won't. I know a lot more about that than about love," she said, and laughed before closing her eyes and falling asleep instantly.

❖

"Sometimes people sure make this too fucking easy for us," Mitch said. He and Freddie were parked a block from the Tarver home, staring at Aubrey's old Honda.

"This is the kind of neighborhood where everyone wakes up at four to run a marathon before work." Freddie divided his time between studying the house and the rearview mirror. "That ain't gonna be cool if things don't go well."

"Relax," Mitch said, as he touched the butt of his gun tucked into his waistband. "Emray told me this guy's retired, so no one's going to miss him if he doesn't show up for work. All we need to do is go in there and ask his daughter where our money is. The fastest way to have that conversation is to use the kid. Are you up for that?"

"That bitch ain't so fragile. She killed all our guys, so watch your back."

They quietly shut the doors to the luxury sedan they'd borrowed from the hotel parking garage and kept to the street as they moved closer to the house. Everything was quiet and dark, which made Mitch relax and take his time with the lock. The house would stay dark since Freddie had cut the main power source, effectively knocking out the alarm system as well. It was funny to him that people put their safety in the hands of companies who paid their technicians a little more than minimum wage. They installed systems that might've told them if a moron was breaking in, but they were better off with a dog if you took a little extra time to cut the juice.

"Start in the master bedroom and take care of the parents while I look for Aubrey and her kid. Do not let that old guy get the jump on you. We've had enough fuckups for tonight, and I don't have the balls to tell Emray we botched this too."

It took less than five minutes to see that the house was empty. All the cars were parked outside, but the entire Tarver family had disappeared and left nothing behind to clue Mitch into where they'd gone. The quiet left him cold, since for the third time in less than twenty-four hours he'd have to call Emray and tell him he'd failed. His boss wasn't the forgiving kind, and this was strike three.

"If they came here they took all their stuff, because the other three bedrooms are clean," Freddie said after they'd met back in the kitchen. "What now?"

"Hopefully wherever they are, they'll have access to the local news." Mitch opened the oven, disabled the pilot light, and turned the knob as far as it would go. He did the same to the gourmet stove with the six burners before he pushed Freddie to leave. "Give it a good ten minutes," he said as they walked quickly back to the car.

None of the neighbors had stirred twenty minutes later, so Mitch was confident there would be no witnesses to report what happened. No one would be able to describe the man who'd set up his shot by using the roof of his car to steady his hands, but he kept his eyes on the house as Freddie did just that. The three bullets that pierced the den windows in rapid succession set off the explosion that rocked everything in a two-block radius. Even if the Tarvers wanted to stop running, they wouldn't have a place to run home to. Destruction on this scale caused fear, and that's what he wanted most—Aubrey and her daughter to be afraid of what would happen if they didn't cooperate. If Emray gave him free rein, Aubrey would think what happened to Maria had been a blessing compared to his plans for her.

❖

"Holy hell, she was right." Karen Tarver sat in the backseat of Peter's Suburban and watched the house they'd built after Peter's retirement from the military get blown to bits. The sight made her angry, but she was relieved she'd listened to Wiley about taking the things that were important to her. All the family photos and other treasured mementos were safely boxed in the back of the large vehicle.

"I don't think Wiley told us what could happen to simply gain points with Aubrey. She's not the fabricating kind—never was."

"Your views on the subject have always been a bit biased, honey." Karen watched as her neighbors came running out, robes flapping open, with stunned expressions. She had a strong urge to open the door and yell that they were all right, but she stayed in Peter's embrace since the two morons who'd done this were still parked close by. "Do you remember she gutted Aubrey and walked away without a bit of remorse?"

"I was pissed then, and I'm still pissed, but I've always thought you were biased too when it came to Wiley." Peter spoke softly, his mouth close to her ear.

"What do you mean?"

"You let your feelings about your experiences when we were first married bleed into your attitudes when Aubrey and Wiley started to get close." He held her in place when she tried to move away. "I can apologize forever and it won't be enough to make up for all the moves and lonely nights."

Wiley resembled this part of Peter the most. They never argued about anything, not really. Instead they explained their side rationally, and no matter how angry she got with him, Peter never raised his voice or loosened the reins on his control. When Aubrey had told her what happened she saw history repeating itself and wanted better for her.

"It was hard, but we made it through."

"That's because you gave us a chance. You never gave Wiley that, and—"

"All this is my fault, then?" she asked with heat.

"I don't blame you for anything." Peter turned her so they were facing each other. "I just want you to lay aside the old hurts and give the kid a chance. I may not have liked why Wiley left, but I understand it. Look out there," he said, and turned toward their burning house. "This isn't over, and it won't be until these people either get what they want at any cost, or someone stops them."

"It's up to the 'kid' to do that, then?"

"If you've got a slew of better ideas, now's the time to share them."

She laughed at his attempt at sarcasm as she reached for the phone Wiley had left with them. Wiley answered before the third ring. "Two guys broke into our house, then blew it up."

"Where are you?" Despite the early hour, she sounded completely alert.

"In the park nearby. Peter didn't want to endanger any of our neighbors, just in case. Take care of my girls," she said, before handing Peter the phone.

It took less than ten minutes for the tactical conversation between the two. The sun was starting to rise and the area had filled with emergency responders and the flashing lights of their vehicles. Before Wiley and Peter finished, Peter's personal cell rang.

"Good morning, Detective Smith," Peter said as he handed Karen back the other phone. "We're all fine, why do you ask? Since you obviously didn't believe my daughter and didn't offer protection, I had to do whatever it took to keep my family safe. If I hadn't, you and your partner could've scratched us off your suspect list when the fire department handed you a shot glass of our remains."

"Where are you?" Barry Smith asked.

"Staking out my house and watching what's left of it burn to ash."

"You've been there all night?"

"Stop playing games, Detective, and write this down." He gave Barry a description of the two men and the license number of their car.

"Where's your daughter?" Barry asked after repeating the information back to him for accuracy.

"Aubrey and Tanith are safe, that's all I'm saying. You got everything from Aubrey last night, so until you find whoever's responsible, they're off-limits."

"She's a witness in a murder investigation, Mr. Tarver."

"She's in danger, and you and Glenda got it wrong, so back off. You want information from her, you'll come through me, and that's how we'll work it until all these guys are caught."

"That might not be up to you, sir."

"I'm not asking permission, I'm telling you, Detective. If that's not good enough, then do what you need to, but be careful about getting the district attorney's office to file charges only to keep Aubrey close and in danger."

Barry laughed. "Is that a threat?"

"You don't know me well, but I don't threaten anyone about anything. I'm just keeping my family out of danger and telling you how I'm going to do that. Aubrey and Tanith are safe, and to assure that not even my wife and I know exactly where they are."

"I'll be in touch."

"Did it go like you thought?" Wiley asked once Peter finished the other call.

"Exactly, so what now?" The two men who'd blown up the house drove away slowly. "We head north?"

"No, knowing Mrs. Tarver, that'll lead to a string of sleepless nights, so I've got something else in mind." Wiley explained her plan and he didn't interrupt. "Take the long route and call me when you're close to your final destination."

After he hung up he crawled over the seat to the front before helping Karen do the same. He turned away from the destruction and neither of them glanced back, as if realizing it wouldn't do any good to grieve over a place they'd never return to.

"Have you never questioned if Wiley was the right choice for Aubrey?" Karen asked, but didn't look at him.

"Wiley isn't perfect, sweetheart, and no one will ever be completely worthy of Aubrey."

"But?" Karen took his right hand in both of hers.

"The heart wants what it wants, and if you deny it you'll never truly be happy. They met young and the bond was cemented, and it didn't make a difference what anyone else thought about it. I like Wiley not because she's perfect, but because she loves Aubrey the way I love you."

"Don't you mean she *loved* Aubrey?"

"I saw how she looked at Aubrey and Tanith. She not only feels remorse for leaving, but after seeing her with our granddaughter, I can tell she's sorry for all the things she missed out on. The sentimental part of me is praying they both remember what they found in each other when they were kids. If they do, the real winner will be Tanith."

"She did seem taken with Wiley."

Peter glanced away from the road for a moment and smiled at Karen. "She did because she's finally found the reason Aubrey brought her into the world. Wiley didn't father her, but Tanith is hers, even if they only found each other yesterday. Wiley's going to give her the piece of herself she'll never find from us or Aubrey."

CHAPTER EIGHT

After the Tarvers' call, Wiley knew she wouldn't sleep, so she got up and dressed for a workout in the gym next to her studio. She didn't turn on any lights and moved silently down the stairs after pausing at the hall that led to the guest rooms.

When she'd planned this place, guest rooms seemed wasteful. The only visitors she'd ever trusted before last night were her parents and possibly Don. No way would she have imagined Aubrey here where parts of her soul hung on the walls.

It was too late to worry about that now as she worked the circuit of machines. She slipped on the gloves she used on the punching bag hanging in the center of the room. Eventually she'd have to find a sparring partner, but for now kicking and hitting the bag would have to suffice.

Halfway through a roundhouse kick she saw Tanith standing outside the door. She put her hand up to stop the bag from hitting her as it swung back from the kick's force. The hour spent in here had darkened her gray T-shirt, and sweat dripped from her head.

"Good morning," she said, and waved Tanith in. "Did you get some sleep?"

"Yeah." Tanith came closer and hit the bag with her fist softly. "You really can whale on this thing." She pushed it this time as if to make it swing and test the weight.

"It's a good stress reliever." She stripped her gloves off and dropped them on the small refrigerator full of water and juice. "Want one?"

"My mom's still sleeping," Tanith said after pointing to an orange-juice bottle.

"That's good. I'm sure yesterday had to have been hard for her."

"Did you know Maria?" The kid spoke hesitantly, probably from shyness and not a communication problem.

"No, but because of your mom's relationship to her, I'm sure you'll miss her."

"You think Maria was like a mom to me?" Tanith finally raised her head and made eye contact. "Do you?" Tanith's eyes were glassy, but she sounded angry.

"Your mom and I were friends, but we haven't spoken in years, so I don't know what kind of relationships you have with anyone." Having Aubrey and Tanith here wouldn't be easy since she had no experience with children and talking to them. "You were as big a surprise to me as I'm sure yesterday was to you, but no matter what, you're safe with me."

"That's cool." Tanith dropped her eyes again. "And Maria wasn't like my mom. My mom and me were leaving there, and leaving her. Did my mom tell you that? She's not like Maria at all. You don't have to worry about that, or us being here." Tanith was talking so fast Wiley thought of Jerry's speech pattern when he was explaining himself and his actions. It signaled true desperation, knowing if you didn't get everything out something bad would happen. "I promise we won't be any trouble."

Wiley wished an instruction manual would drop from the ceiling. Their conversation had gone from mundane to what sounded like Tanith begging not to be thrown to the curb.

"Do you like peanut butter?" Tanith nodded but still kept her eyes averted. Something had spooked Tanith and she was starting to understand what that was, or at least she hoped she'd guessed right. "Good, since it's the only thing in my kitchen right now." She moved closer and put her arm around Tanith's shoulder, but kept some distance between them for comfort.

In the kitchen she made two peanut butter sandwiches and poured two glasses of milk before she sat across from Tanith. The upstairs was still quiet, so if Aubrey had a problem with her talking to her kid, she'd have some fence mending to do later.

"Maria and you weren't close?" she asked, as a way to start.

"No." Tanith shook her head vehemently, as if to show her the word wasn't enough.

"She's gone, though, and you don't have to share how that makes you feel if you don't want to, but I'd like it if you would."

"I'm sorry she's dead, but not real sorry." The way Tanith peeked up through the hair that'd fallen on her forehead made Wiley want to laugh. She'd tried that look on her mother on more than enough occasions. "Do you get me?"

"Whatever you feel isn't wrong, but I've found it's not necessarily a good thing to wish someone dead. Karma's a wicked mistress at times and repays those kinds of thoughts ten times over. But yeah, I get you."

The half sandwich Tanith had left stayed in her hand as Wiley listened. "I hoped we'd never see her again when Mom said we were leaving, but not because she'd be dead. Her and Mom argued a lot, and now I kinda know why." She took a small bite and swallowed. "Why'd you break up with my mom?"

"Is that what she told you?" Wiley poured herself another glass of milk and put the carton between them. Behind her the coffeepot started by first grinding the right amount of beans.

"No," Tanith said, as if this had somehow become an interrogation and giving short, noncommittal answers was important to her survival.

"Your mom was special to me, but being with me was holding her back."

"What's that mean?"

"I was stationed in Texas, and she was here. I had a few years to go with the army, and that's hard, waiting when you're in a relationship, so we thought the best thing was to stop seeing each other."

"That's not exactly true, Major," Aubrey said, as she descended the stairs in her jeans and T-shirt. "I'm still kind of mad at you for not giving me much choice in the matter. Anger must've clouded my judgment, because after that it seems I became an idiot. After one mistake the pile of others got easier to make, I guess." Aubrey kissed Tanith's temple, then smiled at Wiley. "My first call yesterday was to force your hand. You've shirked your responsibilities long enough," Aubrey said, but from her smile Wiley could tell she was taking it easy on her, perhaps because of Tanith. "It's time to stop running and coming up with excuses."

Wiley kept her eyes on Tanith. "You have a lot more good things to show for your time than I do."

"Don't be too sure about that. You might've been off fighting the good fight, but you're going to have plenty of good things to show in your future." Aubrey put her arms around Tanith from behind and sighed. "Aren't you as tired as I am?"

"I'm actually exhausted."

"You loved me—I never questioned that." Aubrey had tears in her eyes as she spoke. "I hope you never questioned how I felt about you, but the time's come for you to come clean, Major."

"You want to get into that now?" She stood and picked up her empty plate as an excuse to turn around and gather herself. "I'm still the same old Wiley. My reasons haven't changed." The rational part of her brain screamed that this wasn't an appropriate conversation to have in front of a child, but nothing had made her forget. Not the assignments that made Maria's death seem tame, and not the women who took care of a physical need, though never a deep emotional one. She'd wanted Aubrey from the time she was thirteen, and having her, every bit of her, had made her crazy when she'd had to let her go.

"I'm not giving you the option of walking this time." Aubrey held Tanith tighter when Wiley faced her again. "I called you because it was time Tanith knew the truth of who you are to me, and the truth of who she is in my heart."

"What do you want from me?"

Aubrey glanced up toward where *The Dragon Tree Legacy* painting hung, then back to her. "Show her."

❖

Wiley saw the way Tanith looked between them when she stood stiffly at Aubrey's request. If she'd had any questions about this kid from the moment she saw her, the name Tanith had answered them all. It was why she hadn't needed the kid to tell her what kind of relationship she and Aubrey had with Maria.

No matter how hard you tried, you couldn't build a relationship on the wreckage of another one, especially if you weren't willing to let go. Tanith was like a living, breathing reminder of how badly she'd fucked up.

"Please, Wiley, show her," Aubrey repeated.

She peeled her shirt off and turned so her left shoulder was visible. The tattoo started at the center of her bicep, circling her arm until it reached the top of her shoulder. The dragon's wings were folded against its body, as if it was asleep, but its blue eyes were open. It was a work of art since it looked like it had perched on her and wrapped itself around her arm to rest. The head, though, which dipped below the slope of her shoulder back onto her arm, appeared forever vigilant.

Aubrey led Tanith closer so she stood motionless as Aubrey traced her finger along the tip of the tail. There, along the dragon's body, was the name *Tanith*, followed by *Aubrey*. It would have been easy to write over them without damaging the tattoo much, but she'd been superstitious about changing it. Not that she'd wanted to. Erasing Aubrey's name would've been like erasing her from her life. In her mind and heart, only death would do that.

"That's my name," Tanith said, her face inches from Wiley's arm.

"Actually, it's the dragon's name," Wiley said. The room was cool enough to raise goose bumps along her skin. "Tanith is the pagan goddess of war and protection, who takes many forms, one of them being the dragon." She turned to show them another dragon inked on the other arm and shoulder. This one was smaller, but its mouth as well as black eyes was open, and a small tendril of fire shot past the visible fangs. "And her sister, Tanit. Legend says they were the two sides of the same coin, with Tanit being the goddess of justice and vengeance. Tanith is the protector of life, and Tanit is the black dragon who takes it away when it's necessary."

"That's why you named me Tanith, Mom?"

"Wiley and I read the story of Tanith together when we were younger, after we found our tree. When I got pregnant, it was the only name I wanted to give you because it was special to me, and to Wiley."

The front door buzzer made Aubrey and Tanith jump, and gave Wiley an excuse to put her shirt back on. Markings and scars of any kind weren't a great idea in her line of business, since they were easy to remember, so she seldom wore anything that displayed her yin and yang, as she referred to them. The Tanith tattoo had come first, and Aubrey had sat next to her as it came to life, and Tanit second. She'd gotten it after she had to let Aubrey go, to remind her why. The Black Dragon and its place in her life had cost her.

"Who is that?" Tanith asked, her hand on Wiley's side.

Wiley pressed her fingers to her lips when the monitor in the kitchen came to life, displaying the image of the front door. Walter was back, impatiently pressing the buzzer.

"I need you both to go upstairs and stay in your rooms. Try to stay quiet until I tell you when it's okay to come down. This guy doesn't need to know I have company."

"Will you be okay?" Tanith asked.

"Are you?" Aubrey said.

"He doesn't have anything to do with Maria and last night. Walter's trying to force me out of retirement to clean up a mess."

"Can he, if you don't want to?" Aubrey asked.

"Freedom is never free," she said seriously, locking eyes with Aubrey's. "That isn't just a recruiting poster, so think about that before you ask or talk about anything other than me helping you out of this mess. I have my freedom, but guys like Walter show it won't be without costs. Why I ran won't change until I'm dead."

Aubrey nodded and led Tanith upstairs. Alone, Wiley bundled her anger in her fists before moving to the intercom. Walter was forgetting the rules Don had explained.

"Can I help you?" she asked, opening the mike.

"We need to talk," Walter said, not lifting his head. "We don't have a lot of fucking time left."

"I work for Don, Mr. Robinson. Any timeline or orders I agree to obey come from him, so if you're worried, call him."

"Do you really want to force my hand?" Walter whipped his head up and glared at the camera. "I scream national security, and Don's superiors will shit all over themselves to fuck him and you over for not cooperating."

"What exactly do you want?"

"Open the fucking door first, then I'll be happy to give you a list."

She buzzed him in and watched to make sure he didn't wander away from the elevator. Once the doors opened he barely glanced at her as he headed for the seat he'd occupied the last time. He was wearing jeans and athletic shoes today, which didn't make him appear as cheesy as the first time they'd met.

"Have you started planning yet? Pombo's being moved sooner than we thought, so don't screw this up," Walter said as soon as his ass hit the seat. "Are you ready to go?"

"Would you like to share anything else with me?"

"Like what?"

"Putting this guy's brains on the wall seems important to you. Why is that?"

"In the past, did your superiors have to give you a long explanation?" Walter's voice kept getting louder. "I don't fucking think so, so this won't be any different. Pombo has to go, and you need to get going."

"I'll be ready, but I'll need a contact to collect my shopping list before I get there." She stayed on her feet and leaned against the back of the couch. "That'll take me a few days. If you want anything more, call Don, and he'll pass along the information."

"I'll set up whatever you need, and your contact will be one of my people." He leaned forward and reached behind him as he spoke, his gun lying across his lap when he was done. "Do we understand each other?"

"Display a gun in my home, Walter, and you'd better be sure you have the stones to use it."

"You sound like a cartoon character," he said, and laughed.

"I'm not threatening you." She wasn't armed, so she widened her stance in case she had to run for cover. "But just like I know you and what you're capable of, you have to have some idea of how this will end if you don't back down."

"You're telling me you're not scared?"

"You should be asking yourself what kind of life I think this will be if an asshole is knocking on my door less than three months out. There are worse things than death." She felt naked, but it wasn't the time to back down. "Do we understand each other?"

"I thought you military types were brimming over with respect." Walter laid his hand over the barrel but didn't move to put it away.

"I'm retired."

He laughed again and slowly holstered the weapon, then raised his hands. "I'm only trying to explain how urgent this is, and that the job isn't voluntary."

"I haven't turned you down, so back off and stop telling me how to do my job. And don't show up here again unless Don's with you." She moved to the elevator with him and walked him out, not trusting him alone anywhere in the building. Walter had a problem, and it was big enough that he could barely contain his desperation. Pombo was a badass, but Walter's hounding meant that whatever the jailed drug lord hadn't said yet was his trump card.

Her cell rang as she rode back to the fourth floor, but she was expecting this interruption. "Take the shuttle to the Delta terminal, then the escalator down to baggage claim. Once you're there, walk down the long hallway past the main carousels to the third set of doors. That route should shake off any ticks you might've picked up. If you did, call me back so we can fumigate before you infest all of us."

Only one door was shut down the hall to the guest rooms, but the second room she passed had an open suitcase on the bed. "You both can come out now," she said after she tapped on the door.

"Everything okay?" Aubrey asked.

"Some things are easier to take care of with a high-powered rifle, but I have to have more willpower than that." She looked past Aubrey to Tanith, who sat playing some sort of gaming device. "I have to go out for a couple of hours, so I'm setting the alarm. Please stay inside and don't use any phone."

"When you come back, do you think we can talk? There's so much I want to tell you."

"You don't owe me any explanations. I didn't give you much of a choice but to find a new life. Who and what you did with that freedom isn't my business, and I'll never judge you."

Aubrey nodded and wrapped her fingers around Wiley's arm. "I was so angry for so long about so many things I didn't understand, but I tried to make peace with it. I'd like for you to listen while I talk, and while you don't in any way owe me, when we talk I want you to pretend none of this happened. Do you think you can do that?"

"We were good at pretend games when we were children under that tree, but we're all grown-up now."

"I just want to talk to you without you thinking I'm doing it so you'll keep us from getting killed."

"Fair enough." She took a step back in a need to put distance between them. History was a fucking bitch that taught lessons like an abusive parent who beat the shit out of you until you snapped or bent to their will. Aubrey was teaching her that she couldn't have everything she wanted, even if the heavens opened up and showed her who and what would make her life complete.

Wiley still feared the reasons she'd had to leave Aubrey behind, but at night when she slept, her dreams didn't replay the painful memories. Unconsciousness only revealed the times she'd put her hands on Aubrey because she'd been desperate for her touch, and how hard she'd worked to make her smile. Those moments were as seared into her brain as the lessons the army had taught, different as night and day, but both an integral part of her.

"We have plenty of time for that before you go back to your life," Wiley said, and turned to leave before she dropped to her knees and begged Aubrey's forgiveness.

She'd been an excellent soldier because she could always adapt and change her plan in real time in the field. That talent was rooted in experience and knowing her limitations. None of that had mattered when she'd shared time with Aubrey. Those were the only times in her life that she'd set herself adrift and floated on the feelings Aubrey intensified in her. She'd been able to drag herself through a life without that and without Aubrey. No way could she repeat the process and keep her sanity.

There was no going back. Not willingly. Not for any promise of reward. Not to heal. Not ever. The price was too great.

CHAPTER NINE

Nunzio lay on his back and scrubbed his face with his hand, trying to wipe away the lethargy that never truly disappeared after he watched Kim drop to the floor dead. He'd stayed long enough after the mob boss, Cain Casey, had run out the door like the devil himself was chasing her, to watch the blood pool spread around Kim like a death halo.

He'd fled alone and run to his grandfather when Remi and Ramon Jatibon, the heads of one of the other families, left the scene. After everything Kim had meant to him, that he hadn't buried her still brought him a sense of shame, but he wasn't about to ask either Casey or the Jatibons what happened to her body. The time for vengeance, not only for Kim but for his father, was coming, but he wasn't ready yet.

The actions of that day and the battle he faced afterward gave his wife her excuse to leave. She demanded only two things when she told him to get out, and he'd given in, over the objections of his grandfather and mother. He wrote her a large check and agreed to stay away from their daughters. Had they had to hash it out in court, his ex-wife would have negotiated the amount of the check, but not the children. In her opinion they were still young enough for the Luca name not to taint them. Casey and the Jatibons had to make up for that loss also.

Tracy and infrequent updates on his two little girls were all he had of the life before he watched Kim bleed out. Unlike then, he kept the most recent picture he'd gotten of his daughters in a frame next to his bed, to remind him of everything Casey had taken away from him. Everything he'd built from that day took him one step closer to getting it all back, with the exception of his ex-wife. Like Cain, the day would come for her to pay for the humiliation they'd piled on him.

"Are you awake?" Tracy asked softly from the other side of the closed door.

She was young, but she'd kept him sane and provided him with the sense that he mattered to someone. Once everything was on track he'd set her up somewhere doing whatever she wanted for the loyalty she'd given him.

He got up and put his pants on before answering the door. Tracy was dressed and ready to go out, but waited to have breakfast with him. That never changed no matter what was happening. She handed him a cup of coffee before she went to uncover the room-service dishes.

"Mitch called an hour ago and said there might be movement on what you wanted," Tracy said as she poured raisins and nuts into the bowl of oatmeal she'd ordered.

"What'd you tell him?"

"That you still weren't interested, even if the first shipment was free." That was exactly what he'd said the night before.

"When did Mitch's supposed boss want to meet?" The steak she'd ordered him was almost tender enough to cut with his fork and made him smile. Tracy delivered everything he liked.

"He said he was working on it, but his guy doesn't see a need. Mitch told him you wouldn't move ahead without a meeting and asked if you'd be patient until tonight."

"What's tonight?"

"He'll have an answer one way or the other." Tracy stopped to take a bite and a deep breath. That was the giveaway that she had more, and whatever it was, he might not like it. "While I was waiting I made some calls on your behalf."

"Did I ask you to do that?" He cut up the rest of his meat and mixed it with his eggs and hash browns.

"No, but I know what's coming." She pushed her bowl away and picked up the large glass of juice. She held it like she was trying to hide behind it.

"I don't like playing twenty questions right after I open my eyes, so tell me what the hell you're talking about."

"These last few months have been charity for what happened to Kim, but you didn't need to take care of me because of that."

Nunzio slammed his utensils down and pointed at her so fast she flinched as if he might hit her. "You should be thanking me for keeping you alive, not giving me shit." His anger had risen so quickly he could hear his heartbeat in his ears.

"I don't blame you for what happened, and I'm doing my best to prove to you that I belong here. Please see that I'm not some little kid before you dump me somewhere for what you think is my own good." She had gotten up and knelt next to his chair. "Last night should've proved it to you, but if you need to hear it—I want to stay."

"Tracy," he said, his voice raspy. "You're young and smart. You don't need this. You have a choice, and that's what Kim wanted for you. I've got plenty of scores to settle before I head off to Florida to play golf with Papa."

"That's what Kim wanted, but I want to stay with you." She moved one hand up his thigh and placed the other at the center of his naked chest. "She was my sister, and I want to help you avenge her death."

He'd been dead inside for months, only moments of fear and indecision breaking the cycle, but Tracy's touch was like an electric shock to his system. She must've seen something in his eyes since her hand went even higher on his leg. "You can't want this."

"I know what I want." She rubbed her palm over his erection through his pants. "I got us another meeting with someone else for tonight." Her touch became firmer and faster. "But right now I want to show you what an asset I can be."

It had been so long, but this was not a good idea. Tracy was Kim's sister, and he'd made a promise to watch out for her, not fuck her.

"You're all I have, Nunzio," she said as she stood and started shedding her clothes. "And I want to be with you even if you send me away."

She reached to open his pants when he stood, but stopped when he placed his hands over hers. The expression on her face undid him and he released his hold. It was time for him to start over, and with Tracy he'd finally get it right. She'd be a partner who'd embrace every aspect of his life and watch his back.

"Come on," he said, and held out his hand. When Tracy accepted it, he led her toward his bedroom.

The rest could wait, especially Mitch, since the closer they got to the bed, the lighter he felt. It was time to have something to be happy about, and Tracy was the quickest and most convenient way of achieving that.

❖

Wiley cranked the old bike, wanting to exit without having to open the large garage door. She didn't worry about anyone following her as she headed for her first stop. The grocery was not only a necessity if they didn't want to live on peanut butter, but that's where she'd flush out the people Walter would most likely have sent. She was willing to bet on it.

Walter had assigned her a target that, up to that point, he was the only one pushing to terminate. So, until Don and his superiors gave the go-ahead, Walter had to shift his priorities in a new direction. If she gave him an opening to trap her, he wouldn't hesitate to bypass the brass to get her to do his bidding. Once she did, she'd belong to Walter until one of them was dead.

She found a parking spot close to the door, wore her helmet inside, then placed it in a cart and moved quickly to the back. Anyone following her was probably laughing at her amateurish attempt to ditch them. At the end of the aisle she took a left and headed to the end of the meat display, which was well out of sight from the row she'd picked.

The two men in the aisle she'd come down, and the other guy one over, came close to having their shoes screech when they abruptly stopped. They split up and, the second they saw her standing there, seemed desperate to find something to focus on. Her back was to them, but the mirrored panels that separated the refrigerated section from the butcher's work area were perfect for the initial trap she'd had in mind.

Once she'd made brief eye contact without turning around, she started placing items in her cart like she'd noticed them but didn't realize why they were there. It was humorous to see how much they seemed to relax when she didn't glance at them again.

For the next hour she walked through the store, mentally filling her pantry with everything from staples to bottles of wine for the cooler she'd installed in the kitchen. When she was done she'd filled almost three carts, the third—which wasn't stacked as high as the others—she left almost in the spot where she'd started. The moment she lifted her helmet out of the space built to carry a child, her three shadows tensed. She'd had the choice of three markets close to her building to pick from, but this one had one difference that made it perfect.

The aluminum swinging doors led not only to the section of the warehouse used to store produce and bakery items, but to where the bathrooms were located. She didn't know if these guys had done the same reconnaissance she had, and even if they had, they couldn't take the chance to let her disappear.

The warehouse was cool, but ten degrees warmer than the store, and dim from the few overhead lights and lack of windows. Boxes were piled on large, tall, sturdy shelves, and the smell of cardboard made her nose tingle. If any of the employees were back here they were being extremely quiet, which was great since she wanted these guys out of commission for at least an hour. She climbed the second shelf stacked with boxes of toilet paper.

"Spread out," the tallest of the men said, and pointed to his left and right as soon as they cleared the door. Each of them took out a gun. Use of force told her that Walter had taken off the gloves. When someone did, he was either stupid or desperate. After spending more than twenty minutes with him, she hadn't ruled out that Walter could win a contest on both counts.

She waited until the smallest of the three passed her position before she moved. With one last fan of her fingers to get a better grip on her helmet, she jumped down and connected with the bottom of his jaw when she swung her headgear like she was fast-pitching a softball. When the guy dropped she was already running toward the back of the row. The silence in the place would work against her now, but most people in this situation never expected her to come right at them. The sudden adrenaline rush was small, part fear and mostly excitement. This part of her job never got old.

The second guy toward the back got his gun about a fourth of the way up before she hit his hand first, then came back up with the helmet again. When he went down she moved to the top of the shelf next to her and waited. She needed to center herself and figure out where the team leader was.

He seemed to be the most experienced of the three since he didn't make a sound. But suddenly a kid walked through the door with a dolly.

"Get lost," the guy screamed, and she saw his gun come up when he pointed at the stock boy. The crash of the dolly echoed through the space and then the doors swung closed. Unless the kid ran all the way home with a damp pair of jeans, he was alerting someone about the armed maniac in the back. She had only a small window to finish this without shooting an agent of the federal government.

Don had taught her to use whatever was available to come out on top. She smiled as she took a can of peas out of one of the boxes on the shelf under her. With about twenty feet between them she tried for his hand, hoping that even if she missed she could distract him. She started moving when the can left her hand and was on him before he could reach his gun, which had slid under the bottom of the shelf closest to them.

She landed on his back and put him in a sleeper hold, even though he was swinging back at her, landing a few blows. It didn't take long for him to be out cold, and she rushed to drag him toward a dark corner and zip-tie him to one of the pipes coming from the ceiling. She emptied his pockets, interested in the leather box inside his jacket. The vial with no markings and the syringe moved Walter to the top of her list, and he wouldn't like the attention. Whatever was in the bottle would've been her ticket to Mexico, where not even a case of tequila would've helped her hangover.

"Thanks for the head start, asshole. And, Walter, I'm going to teach you the meaning of 'voluntary assignment.' After you went to so much trouble I'm almost curious now to hear what Mr. Pombo's side of the story is." She filled the syringe and injected his neck. Before company arrived, she repeated the process with the other two. As she walked to the swinging doors she dismantled their guns, spreading the pieces throughout the space, and threw their wallets into the toilet and flushed. Once she finished her housekeeping, she strolled back into the store to pay for her purchases and arrange for a delivery to the building.

She didn't know if anyone was waiting outside, so she left out of the back loading bay and strode to the business next door. The rental car she'd ordered was waiting with the keys under the back passenger tire. She took her time driving to the airport, staying on River Road as long as possible before she cut over a major thoroughfare to the interstate.

During all the days and nights she'd spent in nests around the world holding a high-powered rifle and waiting for the order to pull the trigger, she'd tried her best to keep her mind clear. Aubrey had always been the crack in her discipline, and she'd thought about her often as she kept her target in sight. No amount of imagining what happened next could've come close to this. Any hope of a quiet retirement, accepting the commissions she wanted both in art and for her other skill set, had disappeared. These assholes and Aubrey showing up like this held her peace of mind like she'd held Jerry's balls and dropped them into a shredder, but perhaps she deserved it after what she'd put Aubrey through.

After twenty minutes of evasive moves to ensure no one was following her, she drove into the airport and headed to the baggage area. She stopped in an empty parking space and kept the engine running. If she didn't have any other surprises, she could complete the rest of the first phase of taking the Tarvers out of the line of fire.

Peter came out first, rolling two bags, Karen following him closely. They didn't look too upset, considering what had happened to them that morning. The sight of them, though, made a piano drop to her shoulders and a headache bloom in the base of her skull. She'd spent her life trying to plan the next move, and this time would be no different. But with the group she'd collected in the last twenty-four hours it'd be like planning for every contingency while juggling a hundred tennis balls.

"Are you both okay?"

"My house got blown up," Karen said as she climbed into the backseat.

"You should talk to your daughter-in-law about that. If you want, once we get to my place I'll set up a séance and you can ask her why this happened. While you have her on the line you can ask her where the money is so we can ditch these guys." She smiled when Karen laughed, but she never stopped scanning the area for anything out of the ordinary.

"Let's get something straight." Karen pushed over so she was in her line of sight in the rearview mirror once Peter joined her in the back. "Maria, the asshole, was not my daughter-in-law. I don't mean to speak ill of the dead, but that woman was a problem from the moment Aubrey met her. I said it then and no one listened to me except Peter, but all Aubrey had eyes for was Tanith. And you lost your right to be flip a *long* time ago, so cool it."

"I'm sorry. I didn't mean to give you a hard time. It's been a long day so far." When Peter closed the door she took off and headed back toward the city.

"Has anything else happened since we saw you last?" Peter put his arm around Karen and looked at her in the rearview mirror. His cologne, still the same, reminded her of her father. Both of them never changed the little things about themselves they were comfortable with.

Seeing him again made her realize everything she'd missed when she'd lost Aubrey, including Peter.

"No, sir." She had to concentrate to take her eyes off him and pay attention to the road ahead and behind them. "Aubrey and Tanith are fine." She told them about the visit from Walter that morning, not wanting them to think she was keeping anything from them and to prepare them in case he showed up again.

"I thought you said you were retired?" Karen asked.

"I am, but Mr. Tarver will tell you, sometimes it's easier to shake an octopus with a crush than the military when they don't want to completely let you go."

"Can I ask you something personal?"

She glanced back at Karen again and laughed. "I have a feeling you're going to ask even if I say no, so don't let me stop you."

"I know it was you who broke it off, and even though you made my daughter miserable, she tried to defend your decision by telling us she agreed with you because of the years you gave to your assigned unit. She would never come out on top in your life, so it was a good thing you beat her to the punch. Then and now I thought that was all bullshit." Karen's sigh sounded to Wiley like part exhaustion and part disgust. "I thought she should've put more thought into an excuse that sounded so lame, but you re-upped. Why didn't you ever consider her and what she wanted? We could've avoided all this mess."

"Because I didn't have a choice." It was all she could say to keep the truth from coming out.

"Everyone always has a choice, Wiley." Karen didn't sound as harsh as she had from the moment they'd come together again.

The traffic picked up as she got closer to her exit, and she was glad to be out from under Karen's microscope. "If I'd become an accountant, then you're right, I would've, but from the time I started my assignment the world became a different place. I tried, but I became a victim of my own success, as they say."

"You gave them over ten years," Karen said, and put her hand on her shoulder. "Other people can share the responsibility or wear the cape, superhero. I know exactly what your purpose was while you served. It's like the SEALs, I guess. People think they're invisible, cool, and totally badass, but there's always a toll, and those you leave behind always pay it."

The red light prolonged her agony, and Peter was choosing to stay quiet. "I volunteered for two years. Year three wasn't my wish, and whether you believe me or not, it wasn't a choice. In that time I saw what the waiting was doing to her, and I wanted to save her from the life I'd chosen." She'd never forget the expression of delight on the commander's face when she saved him the speech of why they needed her to stay. He couldn't give a crap why she wanted back in the field. Her pain, her issues, her life didn't matter as much as what she could do for them. "The other seven came as a bonus for the guys who wanted me in the field."

"You had a death wish?" Peter finally said.

"I had a need to keep busy, and I still do. If we're going to be spending time together until I can get you somewhere safe, we'll have to leave it at that." She turned onto her street and made the block twice before she felt it safe enough to turn in. As the garage door came down she called the phone she'd given Aubrey and told her not to worry.

She would take care of that for all of them.

❖

Wiley disappeared into her office as the Tarvers had their family reunion. Once her computer came out of hibernation she started her search of Almoloya de Juárez prison. When the drug war had become the cluster fuck it had, the Mexican authorities had built it to house the worst of the drug lords. It was their version of a supermax facility, where all the cells were wired with closed-circuit television to reduce the number of guards that came in contact with the population. That in turn cut down the influence these guys had with the outside. This would be Pombo's final home, if he lived to make it to trial and conviction.

"How high is the level of your stomach acid?" she asked Don when he answered his office phone on the first ring.

"High enough, and when I get an ulcer I'm naming it after you." She heard his door close and let her head drop to the back of her chair. The air-conditioning was set to the high sixties, and she took a deep breath through her nose, trying to relax. She wanted to check Roth Pombo off her to-do list. "What's going on?"

"Walter was back today, and I ran into a few of his guys at the grocery. They came with their own pharmacy, so I'm sending you what was left for analysis. I want to know what these goons had in mind, especially since I had to disarm all three of them."

"Where exactly are they?"

"Either they're working off a bad hangover, or they're still sleeping it off with the paper goods and cans."

"Anything else you need?"

"I want the specs on Almoloya de Juárez prison, and a layout of the town."

She waited for Don to gather his thoughts. "You're doing this? You have to know Carl's going to stonewall them as long as possible."

"The general's always been fair with me, but I'm going to Mexico to check out the viability of this operation. If I'm going to end up next to Pombo in a shitty cell eating beans for the rest of my life because this is impossible, I'll just work on my tan." She sealed the vial in a plastic box, then put it in a FedEx box with Don's address on it. "Tell me when you get your hands on the information I asked for."

"Anything new on the other front you were working on?"

"The painting you saw the first day you were here? I finished it that morning, but so far I haven't started anything else."

"Wiley, don't fuck with me."

"I'm not ready to talk about that yet, but you're my first call when I am." She picked up the brass block she used as a paperweight and pressed it to her lips as she waited to see if another lecture was coming. The top of the heavy object had one of her father's dog tags embedded in it, and her mom had the twin. When Buckston retired he gave them to the two people he credited for his success. No one went so far in the military without the help and support of his family.

"Make sure you do, and I'll get that stuff for you by this afternoon. Depending on what we find we'll set the plan and the assets you'll need to finish." He didn't linger on the line and she pressed the disconnect button before she dialed another number.

"Are you calling to invite us to your new place? I can't wait to see it."

"I knew that talking you into caller ID was a bad idea." She laughed and could mentally smell the cookies her mom was known for. While she'd spent a lot of time with her father learning the nuances of every weapon and their pros and cons, she'd spent as much time with her mother sitting on a stool talking about life in general as cinnamon cookies baked in the oven. All her life the smell of the spice had sent a wave of warmth through her.

"It was the best idea you ever had, since I haven't had to talk to any of those loathsome telemarketers, but I'll tell you all about it when I check out that awesome kitchen of yours in person."

"Am I going to hurt your feelings if I tell Dad something before you?"

"Depends," Danielle said, and Wiley knew the wheels in her mom's head were spinning. "Is it work-related or personal?"

"For right now we're sticking to work-related."

"Does that mean something personal's on the horizon?"

Even with the air-conditioner running she could hear someone outside the door. She couldn't tell which of the Tarvers it was, but her tension went up. None of them was the enemy but they were out of place here, and because of the life she'd led, she didn't know how to distinguish the difference. She couldn't control her heightened sense of vigilance.

"It's not what you think, but I promise to tell you about it once I'm done with Dad."

Her mother had also learned not to ask too many questions, and Wiley heard her put the phone down and walk away. After her dad's retirement they'd stayed outside Washington, her mom saying it'd be permanent only while she was still serving. Now that she'd settled, Danielle was ready to put up a For Sale sign and move south.

"Wiley, you there?" Her mom's voice startled her from her daydreams.

"Is he not in?"

"Hang up and he'll call you back as soon as he's in his office."

That took less than five minutes, and she picked up her landline in the middle of the first ring. "Hey, Dad."

"You okay, kid?"

"Nothing that climbing out of this rabbit hole I've fallen in won't fix." She told him what Walter wanted, not concerned with sharing the information since her father still enjoyed top-secret security clearance despite his retirement. She wasn't the only Gremillion the army was interested in keeping around. If the military and the country kept their secrets in a cemetery, her father not only had the key, but a mental map of who and what was in every plot.

"That's all he shared with you?"

"He said that's all I needed. I surmised that Roth Pombo has a secret and Walter wants him to die with it."

"What do you need from me?"

"How'd you like to take a trip to Mexico with me under an assumed name?" Whoever was outside her door was frantically pacing, so she tried to tune them out. "It'll be easier to do the recon together and get back before we become obvious. If I return I want to be in and out before the shit flies."

"What's your rush, and why not get it over with in one trip?"

She paused, not wanting to ignite another argument with him. The seven extra years she'd given Carl and Don weren't only a problem for Peter and Karen Tarver. Her father had her flown to Washington when he'd received word she'd agreed to stay on. It was one of the only moments in her life she'd seen him truly angry and direct his fury at her. Peter had said "death wish." That had been his starting point, and he'd piled on until he'd ended his rant by sharing his unvarnished opinion of what she was doing.

"I received a message from an old friend yesterday." She stopped to shore up her defenses. "Before I say anything else, I promised Mom she could hear the rest."

"I've got a feeling I know where this is headed." He didn't sound angry, but she sensed his fury like an approaching tornado. "Go ahead."

She could tell he'd engaged the speakerphone, even if her mother hadn't said anything. "I got a message from Aubrey yesterday afternoon."

"And you called her back?"

"Buck, let her finish."

She smiled at hearing the true disciplinarian in the family. "This involves a little more than calling her back." She tried to keep what she'd walked into at Aubrey's house short and sweet.

"Wiley, I'm your mother, and I love you." Her sigh was prominent. "But I'm fucking tired of being lied to, so it's time to spill your guts. You said it was over, but not why, and you said you'd leave her to live her life. Though since you know she picked a deadbeat pushing dope, maybe you should've left her in the attic to rot. You do not under any goddamn circumstances put your life in danger for what is essentially trash."

She laughed at the profanity. Danielle Gremillion had lived her entire life fussing at anyone who used bad language, as she put it, until she hit menopause. The hot flashes had in a way melted away her rigidity on the subject, and at fifty-eight she'd learned to use the word *fuck* in any sentence.

"You're right, Mom, I didn't tell you the truth. The truth affected all of us and was why I changed security regarding not only Dad but you."

"Between the two of you and your secrets it's a miracle I haven't run naked into the night screaming from insanity. I'd swear you both think I'm a member of Al-Qaeda."

"It wasn't that we didn't trust you, sweetheart," Buckston said. "We didn't want you to worry." He told her in his customary straightforward way about what had happened when she'd returned from South America. "Since then only Wiley and two other members of that team are still alive, but one of the men had his wife and son killed. You might not have agreed with what Wiley did, but in essence, by giving Aubrey her freedom, she saved her life. I'm damn proud of that."

"There's more," she said, after her dad's great defense.

"Of course there is, but don't think we're done talking about this," Danielle said.

"Her daughter Tanith was up there with her."

"Tanith?" Judging by the creaking of leather, her father must've sat up. When she served he wasn't only her father, but also the man Carl Greenwald answered to. Brigadier General Gremillion knew exactly who the Black Dragon was, what she was capable of, and what was tattooed on her arms. "She named the kid Tanith?"

"How old is she?" her mom asked.

"My math puts her conception about two months after we parted company, so don't read too much into the kid's name. They're all here, and they'll have to stay until I put Walter at ease with some movement."

"Then what?"

"Mom, that's a great question I have no answer for. Until I have a better idea who the players are, I don't feel right about putting them out."

"Hang tight and we'll be there by tonight," her mom said.

"Should I be afraid?"

"Not yet." Her mom laughed and Wiley hung up, looking forward to seeing them.

The pacing outside had stopped so she opened the door, expecting to see someone nonetheless. The sight of Aubrey made her stomach clench with what she remembered was need. Touching Aubrey was the one thing she ever admitted to herself that she excelled at. Neither her art with the brush nor a gun came close.

Her sex didn't care about the past, Maria, or the reasons she'd left. It was like a starving lion clutching a gazelle in its claws. Aubrey was that instinctual thing in her life—her nature.

CHAPTER TEN

The news better be good, Mitch, or you're gonna be on the street. You feel me?" Emray Gillis sat at the table in his kitchen and stared at Mitch in a way that made him tense.

Mitch had met Emray when he stopped his car on his corner a year before. He'd been reluctant to get in until Emray put a stack of hundreds and a bag of pure Mexican white on the seat for him to see. For a kid who'd grown up in the worst housing project in New Orleans, working as a runner for the dealers that worked the city, he knew when life threw you not a bone, but a steak dinner.

He was always looking for the next big score that'd get him that much closer to putting the shit pile he'd grown up in another step behind him, but he hadn't gotten his own crew by being a fucking idiot. He could make money, but every chance he got gave the cops an opportunity to take him down, and that was who he was afraid Emray was. Only the cops didn't bait with as much product and weren't as fucked up as Emray, who always seemed a second away from losing control. When he did there was always a pile of bodies after the coke haze cleared, and Mitch was smart enough to know no matter how good a job he did, he wasn't indispensible to Emray. No one was.

"We lost Maria's bitch, but we left a message at the first place she's gonna run to."

"So you don't have my money?" Emray had a pile of blow in front of him and was putting it in dime bags, wearing a pair of thick rubber gloves. Mitch didn't understand why he did such a menial task.

The house puzzled him too. Instead of some mansion, Emray lived in a small shotgun at the cusp of Uptown, with steel bars on every window and door. No one keeping him under surveillance would ever guess the size of Emray's business if they concentrated on the peeling paint and weed-riddled yard. He was worth a fortune but sat at this old worn table and divided up his piles of blow because he didn't trust anyone else to do it. He knew the exact amount of his inventory, each guy at the corners he had working, and how much money had to come in. Any deviation and Emray came down hard. No one got a second chance.

"Not yet." Mitch looked Emray in the eye but couldn't help lowering his gaze to the gun next to the hill of white powder. "Freddie stood outside as the body bags came out, but no one brought out the duffels. The money wasn't in the house, and with the trouble there we don't know if Maria told the guys we sent in where it was."

"We sent in?" Emray could've been staring at him, but with the sunglasses he couldn't tell. "You sent them, Mitch, and my patience's running out. Do I need to explain again how important it is for us to find that cash? Did the gravity of our situation not sink in the first time I told you all this shit?"

"No, I'm still working on it, and I won't let you down." The smell of burnt coffee made his stomach hurt, but he made no move to leave. Nothing about this place had changed, ever, from the first time he came here, like Emray himself. The guy gave him the willies, but the size of his bank account and what it had gotten him forgave a multitude of sins. "We need to talk about Nunzio."

"What's to talk about? I sent you to finish something and you fucked it up. That's like your new way of doing business." Emray pulled away from the table suddenly and punched the top of the counter behind him, as if not wanting to lose a speck of the drugs. "How the hell am I supposed to pay the suppliers? What's going to keep the pack of killers those assholes are going to send from putting a bullet in our skulls?"

"You told me to try to improve our deals when I could and keep you out of the day-to-day stuff." Emray kept the place cold, not wanting to let the air stagnate, he said, but sweat was pooling in the crack of Mitch's ass, and he wanted to stick his finger in the hill of coke and shove it up his nose. If he was going to take a bullet to the head, he wanted to take the trip to hell flying on his own steam. "He wasn't going to make the deal without face time."

"Forget about that and find my cash. I should've gone and talked to Maria myself. I might not have gotten my money back, but I would've had the satisfaction of killing that fucking cunt myself."

"How about I tell him he's getting a discount if he forgets meeting you, and once we get his cash we squeeze him for whatever you need?" Mitch tried to change the subject before he became a stress reliever for Emray's anger, now that Maria was dead.

"I don't give a fuck how you get it, moron. Fucking get it."

"Don't worry," he said, but his asshole puckered. He didn't know a good way out of this situation. "I'll call you tonight."

Mitch didn't turn his back on Emray as he left. They weren't partners and he didn't trust Emray not to shoot him. Freddie was sitting on the hood of the car waiting for him, and the temperature difference was so great the humidity made his sinuses flare.

"Where to?"

"Let's start at the hotel and Nunzio again. You okay with only collecting half of what I promised you?" His head was clearer after leaving the dark hellhole Emray called home. "If you are, drop me off and I'll handle the rest."

"Tell me why first." Freddie rubbed the scar on his face and Mitch had to look away. The way Freddie fooled with it made him think he might wear the pink, puffy skin away.

"Emray's moving shit for the Delarosa family and he's skimming. That shit's okay when you're making money, but Maria took a ton of it and fucking died. If Emray don't find that stash before them Colombians come looking, a world of hurt ain't going to begin to explain what's going to happen to him."

"The Delarosa family? That's some people you don't fuck with."

"No shit." He glanced behind them out of paranoid habit, but nothing stood out as a problem. "Of the money Maria took, only five hundred large belonged to Emray, and he hasn't said it, but I'm sure Hector Delarosa wants his three mil or his coke back."

"Only we don't have either."

"There's no *we*. Emray trusted Maria and the bitch fucked him, only Emray's not the kind to go down alone."

"So what?"

"We talk Nunzio into investing and cut our ties once we do."

Freddie parked a few blocks from the Hilton and put his hand on his bicep. "You screwing Emray over? He finds out and we both dead."

"Don't worry about having to go back to the corner, or Emray chasing you down. We'll work our own deals after this and leave his ass to find somebody else to do the shit work for him. If you don't think I can handle it, run back to Emray and wait for him to cut you in. Only you better pray he don't cut you up."

Freddie went back to stroking his scar. The new souvenir to his profile had come courtesy of Emray after he was late picking up a shipment. Emray had cut so deep his knife had traversed Freddie's cheek and cut his tongue as well.

"I follow you, Mitch."

"Good to know." They got out and reached the front of the hotel in time to see Nunzio and Tracy pull away. Maybe she hadn't been shitting him about having other meetings. "Let's see where they're headed." He needed to know if Nunzio had found another supplier. If he did, he was taking his stash and his little brother somewhere quiet until the Colombians finished dealing with Emray. He didn't want any part of that.

❖

"You said we could talk," Aubrey said when Wiley opened the door to her home office and simply stared at her. Wiley's expression made her think Wiley believed she'd disappear if she took her eyes off her. "Do you have time now?"

"Sure, come in." Wiley waved her in and led her to the two leather chairs next to a wall of windows. "This might sound trite, but I want you to know how sorry I am for the way I handled things. What I did hurt you, and I showed you very little consideration."

The way Wiley's gaze caressed her made her overwhelmingly sad. She looked like she hadn't come to terms with their history and had survived the hellishness of it alone. "If you need me to forgive you, I did a long time ago. I knew you didn't leave to simply hurt me. You had to have had a reason even if you never shared it with me."

"I knew better than to feed you a pile of crap feel-good lines."

Aubrey laughed at Wiley's straightforward approach. When they'd started dating she'd loved Wiley but had been under the impression that

Wiley didn't possess a romantic thought. That notion died the first time Wiley handed her a doodle, as she called them. The sketch of her made her consider herself beautiful for the first time.

"You aren't capable of that, but it's time for the truth."

"What are you hoping for here, aside from not getting killed?" Wiley leaned forward and rested her elbows on her knees. "The reasons I left haven't changed." She told the story of the Ewart family and the ensuing investigation. "That team made a few more trips back and has effectively neutralized all but two members. They're highly motivated, and I don't think that'll change now that I'm retired. Whoever the leak is, we've never found him."

It sucked to be right. Wiley had thrown herself on a grenade to save her. She'd sacrificed everything to keep her safe. "Do you think you can sit and listen? I have a lot to say."

"Take your time."

"I forgave you, but I'm still pissed. What gave you the right to decide what chances I'm willing to take? I understood what you were doing. I always accepted everything about your job, but not you walking out on me."

"Do you think it was easy?" Wiley's misery was so clear in her voice. "You're an incredible woman and I knew you wouldn't go through life alone. I'm being selfish, considering what I did, but the thought of someone else touching you, loving you…it made me wish whoever was hunting me down would finally find me and end it." Wiley covered her face with her hands and Aubrey came close to taking her into her arms, but they had to finish. "That you were alive and free to live your life however you wanted kept me going, so I wouldn't change anything if I got a do-over."

"Oh, Wiley." The cliff Wiley had left her hanging from was still jagged from regret, and the easiest and fastest way to release them both from their mistakes was to let go. From the sound of it, what she wanted was perhaps too high a climb, but if she had to, she'd start from the bottom to get back what she needed most. "I want you to understand something. Why you decided what you did doesn't change the fallout from it. I've been waiting for you to change your mind and come back to me, and I'm not—I can't change that in my heart."

"What about Maria?"

Wiley's question made Aubrey think of something her father had told her about himself and Wiley. They were good at their jobs because they could shut down every emotion under extreme situations. Most people's brains short-circuited in reaction to panic, making it nearly impossible to escape dangerous positions. Wiley, he'd said, was a master since she seldom showed fear. She never flinched, not until she'd asked about Maria, and Aubrey thought it was a major victory.

"I'm not avoiding the question, okay," she said, taking a chance by placing her hand on Wiley's bicep. "And I'm not blaming you."

"You have the right to say whatever you like, including, 'Go to hell, Wiley.'"

"That might still be an option, so don't tempt me yet." She laughed, and Wiley swamped her momentarily when she smiled. "I'm sure you'll never believe me, but my call yesterday had nothing to do with Maria and her problems."

"I'm not leaving you to the wolves, Aubrey. Until this is over I *will* protect you."

"Wiley, shut up, okay. I said I wasn't lying. When you walked out on me you broke something inside that was key to my happiness. It finally occurred to me weeks later that you had to have had some reason. I knew with certainty that you've never quit anything in your life, and you loved me. Breaking your promises was probably as hard for you to do as it was for me to hear you do it."

"Thank you for that."

"Then believe that Maria didn't replace you and what you mean to me. I didn't have you here to share the life we'd planned, so I went ahead without you. I filled the gigantic holes you left with a baby, the child *we'd* always talked about, until I got you back. Maria came after Tanith, but she fell a mountain short of substituting for you."

"I spent a lot of time daydreaming about you," Wiley said, her eyes now on the view. "What job you had, what lucky bastard you shared your life with, and all the other little things that make up a person's life. That's as close as I could get. Those fantasies were all I allowed myself."

"I'm still not finished, but don't think I'm accepting that going forward, Major."

"Think of Tanith before you say anything else. She shouldn't have to live constantly looking over her shoulder." Wilcy's expression was now clear, calm, and almost detached. Wiley had fully repaired whatever cracks she'd managed. If she didn't hurry, the Black Dragon would pull the trigger and their future would be dead.

"Tanith is all I think about, Wiley. Raising her alone while still licking my wounds has been like running down a steep hill. Eventually I'm going to lose my footing and the momentum will land me either on my ass or on my head."

"You're not being rational."

"Rational," she screamed, "to hell with rational. Why do you think I picked the name? It's time to step up, soldier. You've shirked your duty to her and me long enough."

"If you need money—"

"Do not insult me. I'm not here for a handout, I'm here for what's mine—you. I'm tired of being alone."

"You haven't been alone."

The sound of the slap and the sting in her fingers made her regret doing it the second she connected with Wiley's cheek. "I'm sorry."

"No harm done. I deserve it."

"Have you been celibate since we saw each other last?"

Wiley hesitated but answered truthfully. "No."

"Did it feel the same?"

"No," Wiley said in a hoarse whisper.

"That's how it was with Maria." She stood and shook her head when Wiley started to do the same. "Tanith is yours, Wiley, so even if you don't want me, it's time for you to get to know her. She's waited her whole life for you even if she doesn't realize it yet. Don't you dare disappoint her."

Aubrey walked out knowing they hadn't made an inch of progress. If Wiley held firm, she and Tanith would be in exile forever, and that scared her more than sitting in the attic waiting to die.

❖

"How did you manage this?" Nunzio asked, his eyes fixed on the devastation visible from the interstate in New Orleans east. It looked like every building had sustained both major wind damage and flooding. "Even your sister tried but couldn't get to him. That's why we had to deal with that motherfucker Bracato."

"We don't have a meeting with Mr. Delarosa yet." Tracy put

her hand on his knee and squeezed. One morning in bed and she was already acting possessive, he thought. "According to everyone I talked to, he never takes meetings with anyone he hasn't done business with before."

"Then how the hell did he take over the cartel?"

"His paranoia came with success."

Tracy moved her hand higher up his leg and he stopped her before it became a distraction. "Kim would've taught you business requires a clear head. If you're serious about staying, then don't act like a whore anywhere but the bedroom."

"You talked to Kim like that?" Tracy asked, moving away from him.

"I didn't need to." For the first time since Tracy had come to him, the aggravation that stemmed from impatience made him want to hit something. He'd already lost so much, so how much more could life fuck with him? "And if you're going to act like a spoiled brat I'll leave you here and get you a ride back to the hotel."

"Why are you acting like this? If you regretted giving in to me, then say so."

"You're already way ahead of anyone with no experience, so let's be clear about a few things. I need someone to help me rebuild what was stolen from me. To do that you need to know when to concentrate on business and when to get my dick hard. If you don't get it, this isn't the time for whatever fantasy you have spinning in your head."

Tracy hesitated, as if knowing there was only one correct response to the situation. He wouldn't give ground or another chance if she fucked up. "We're meeting with Miguel Gonzalez today, Mr. Delarosa's business manager. From what I could find out, Gonzalez took what Hector made and expanded his fortune. The capital from both legitimate and drug money fueled Hector's rise to true power. He trusts Gonzalez implicitly, so if we can convince Gonzalez we're a good bet, he'll get you the meeting with Delarosa."

"What are they doing here, after this storm plowed through the Mississippi coast?" When they reached the bridge over the lake he closed his eyes. Tracy really was a fast learner, or something else entirely.

"Hector bought a house in New Orleans a few months before Katrina, planning to move his operations and his daughter here. Part of that plan, like Rodolfo Luis's, was to use both New Orleans and the Gulf Coast to expand his operations. The storm was both a setback and a plus, so he divides his time between both places."

"How'd you find out so much so fast?" She'd mentioned Hector's paranoia, but that was how you stayed alive and free. No green little girl walked into his life and got the book on someone so high up like Hector without either government help or by spreading her legs. If either was true, then he would cut her budding career into little pieces and feed it to the crabs along with her cute ass.

"I spent some time with the midlevel dealers while I was waiting for you to get into town. Hector's the guy everyone wants to work with, and they'll use anyone or any means to get to him and his safe, endless supply." She crossed her legs and kept her face turned away from him. "If they can't jump on that train, Emray's a good second bet."

"But?" There had to be more, and it fascinated him how much Tracy knew.

"Hardly anyone except Mitch has met this guy. If Mitch hadn't earned his street creds, Emray would be sitting on a mountain of coke snorting it himself. With the amount of product he wants to move, not showing his face has *cop* written all over him."

"Good work," he said, and laughed. "You impress this Miguel guy like this and you might get a job offer."

"Eventually you'll figure out it's in your best interest to keep me around, whore or not."

He seldom tolerated lip from anyone but stayed quiet when Tracy tried to stretch her limits a bit. She'd caught him in a weak moment that morning, but he still wasn't completely sure about her future with him. Outside the bedroom his gut told him not to go full in and share all his secrets.

Tracy was Kim's sister, but she was still an unknown.

CHAPTER ELEVEN

Wiley watched the sunset from her rooftop patio, trying to ignore the heat. The talk with Aubrey had unsettled her, and with the Tarvers here, she didn't have anywhere to release her pent-up feelings. The sketchbook next to her had taken some of the edge off, but her hands were too sweaty to improve the landscape she'd already finished.

She'd thought back again to the day she'd broken it off with Aubrey. No matter what she put in her mouth for weeks after, it tasted like sawdust, and she was cold all the time. She found a sense of herself only with her unit until she tired of the government's urgency. Then she figured the days were an eternity with nothing to do but paint and think. Before the phone call, she'd been on the verge of trying to venture out to try to find someone to at least spend time with.

"Are you armed?" Peter asked from the door.

His humor broke her pity party and she waved him over. "When I told Carl I wanted out, they put me through two months of tests and observations."

He sat across from her and put his feet up on the rim of the spotless fire pit. "That sounds about right, considering your length of service. Since you're here, either you proved you're not crazy or you bluff well."

"I'm not crazy," she said, and smiled as she took the pistol from the back of her waistband and laid it on the sketchbook. "You don't have to worry about me killing you while in the throes of a flashback, but I'm almost always armed."

"You need new friends if anyone thinks you capable of that."

"I was working on it." Soft solar-powered lights now lit the space, but despite the sun setting, the heat hadn't broken. At this time of the year it never would, no matter how late it got, but Peter seemed unaffected.

"And we came in here and fucked it up for you?"

"You're welcome to stay as long as you like." She laughed as she stood to turn the ceiling fans on. She didn't mind heat, but mosquitoes drove her insane. "Isn't that what people say when they're trying to be polite?"

"We're way beyond polite, kid." He stretched out on the sofa and accepted a beer from her. "I know that's what you're thinking but you'd never admit it."

"Did Aubrey send you up here?"

The way he looked at her made her believe that Aubrey's problems embarrassed him. "No, but her mother's been providing a shoulder all afternoon."

"Ah, more reasons for Karen to demonize me."

Peter shook his head and sat back up. "Let me explain a few things to you that'll rip up those ideas in your head."

"Aubrey's already given me the long list of why I'm an asshole."

"You think that's the only reason I'm up here? To pile on?" He kept eye contact, a rarity for anyone she dealt with. "We could pull out of here tomorrow and I'd still want to clear the air. I'd want that because of how I feel about you, Wiley."

"I'm sorry," she said, and she was. "It's been a long day."

"I'm sure it has, and it'll probably go downhill from here." She tapped her bottle against his. "I don't want to know what you and Aubrey talked about, but hear me out."

"You can tell me whatever's on your mind, sir, but let me go first. When I was done at Aubrey's and got her out of there, I was confused and pissed, really more pissed. The kind of pissed that dropping the assholes in there didn't help alleviate." She took a long swig of her beer. Peter Tarver didn't deserve her disrespect. "But it's not my place to get pissed. I let her go and she moved on. What and who she moved on to was her prerogative. She didn't owe me anything, and she won't no matter what it takes to get you all out of this cluster you're in. It wasn't like she went behind my back."

"What she wanted, Wiley, was you. That's all she's wanted since she was too young to know any better. The happy memories she's made since you walked all revolve around Tanith."

"If you were in her place, you'd open your arms and welcome me back? Remember that I have a gun before you lie and say yes."

He laughed, then drained his bottle. "You know me better than that. You fucked up and broke the most precious thing in your life. No one can take that back, but I'm not here just because of Aubrey. My daughter's an adult, and she'll have to find a way to come to terms with whatever you two decide. If she accepts, good, but if she doesn't, she doesn't. I'll kick your ass from here to Sunday if you fuck up and hurt her like that again, but I want to talk to you about my granddaughter. Tanith has been my concern from the day she was born."

"She's a good kid—smart, protective, and strong."

"Stop me if Aubrey's told you this already." She got two more beers from the outdoor kitchen fridge and waved him on. "She took forever finding the right donor before she considered trying, and she got everything she wanted. As Tanith grew she reminded me more and more of you. When she was old enough to form her own opinions, Maria's fantasy life with Aubrey started to unravel. Tanith didn't like her and made no attempt to hide it."

Maria's not my mother, Tanith had told her that morning. She'd desperately wanted her to know how she felt. "She explained that to me today."

"Tanith wants to know you, Wiley. I believe she needs, more than anything, to know you."

"And you're afraid I'll shoot her down?" If this was a new strategy to get around her defenses, it was working. "I won't, in case you need to hear me say it."

"Thanks, and while you're in a reasonable mood, can I put in a word for my kid? We haven't agreed on a whole lot in years, but I love her. I'd like to see her happy again."

"That's what I want too." She wished she smoked, if only to have something to do with her hands. "I need you to know that what I did, it wasn't easy for me. No matter what you've thought of me, and how many times you've cursed me to hell and back, it wasn't easy. If I'd had a choice I never would have left Aubrey."

"Have those circumstances changed? Can you give her what she wants? Fuck, I should ask if that's what you want first."

"I'll give you the file to read later, but no, nothing's changed."

"Aubrey isn't going to wait forever, kid. Don't fuck this up twice in a lifetime. No one's that lucky."

"Did you miss the part where I said nothing's changed?"

"Let me explain something to you, as plain as I can make it. Aubrey and Karen are never going to understand our choices. Your mom's been an army wife for years and she loves you, but I doubt even she understands you and your dad completely."

She was paying attention but couldn't stop scanning the rooftops nearby. One glimpse of Peter by the wrong people and she'd have no choice but to move them. "That's probably true."

"Then learn from me and Buck. Don't punish the people in your life who haven't drunk the army's Kool-Aid by making strategic maneuvers without them. I have faith in you to figure out a way to napalm the landscape if whatever threat has kept you away is still out there. If you want it bad enough you'll find a way."

"Aren't you the insightful one?" She stood and put the pistol back in the hidden compartment near the door. "Let's take all our problems one at a time."

"Let's," Peter said as the landline rang.

It was her parents. They were either at the airport or downstairs. It didn't matter where. With her mother's arrival, Peter wasn't all she had to worry about.

❖

"What's it take to get a drink in here?" Roth Pombo screamed at the camera bolted into the ceiling in the corner by the door with one small glass square at the top and a slit at the bottom. The assholes who'd locked him in here were going to pay for the twenty-four-hour-a-day fluorescent lighting. The hum and the brightness never went out, and it was driving him slowly up the wall.

"Stand back," the guard said in a heavy accent. Pombo had learned the hard way what he meant and had the bruised kidneys to prove it. He stood and pressed his hands and face into the wall, his back to the door. "You have a visitor."

Finally, he thought, hoping the cameras were privy to their meeting. Walter Robinson had kept him waiting long enough. If Walter had done it to fuck with him, it was time to teach him a lesson. Once he got out of here the first thing he might do was shove a fluorescent tube up his ass.

He smiled as they cuffed his hands to his waist and shackled his feet. After they let him out he'd hunt down every guy in here who'd gotten his rocks off by using him as baton practice. Every badge he collected would be found in the mouths of the decapitated heads.

"It's about fucking time," he said when the guard opened the door. The chill of fear made his hair stand on end when he didn't see Walter.

"I tried for days to get in, Señor Pombo," said his attorney, Antonio Hernandez.

The guy could work miracles sometimes, but he couldn't possibly cut him loose with the number of charges he'd compiled. He was going to sit in his cell until his trial or they beat him to death.

"Are you okay?" Antonio asked, moving his chair to the other side of the stainless-steel table.

Pombo was panicking, so he was grateful Antonio was thinking straight. The federales had to be watching and listening. This wasn't the U.S. judicial system.

"Where's Walter? Did you deliver my message?" The coldness of the chains around his waist and his shackles seeped through the rough material of his prison uniform. For the first time since he'd been brought here, he felt confined.

"Señor, keep your voice quiet." Antonio placed his briefcase on the table and came close to hiding behind it. "I sent everyone to look for Walter, but he gone. His partner say he leave for U.S."

He wasn't surprised that Walter had double-crossed him, not really. The story he thought would save him wasn't a trump card here. The guys in charge would see it as a pathetic try for freedom. "Smart move, Walter."

"What?"

He knew the game now, and he had a small window of opportunity. "Listen carefully." He probably wasn't getting out, but Walter wasn't free of him yet. Before he ran out of time he repeated his instructions again. "Do you understand?"

"I will not fail you, señor. You have my word."

"Spend what you need, but get it done. The rest you already know."

"I no let you down. I swear it on my mama."

❖

Wiley laughed at the silence they came down to. Her parents had all the codes to get into her home. They always had, as a precaution if she either got hurt or eliminated in the field. If that ever happened, they had accepted the responsibility of erasing the Black Dragon's existence. The conversation had happened only once, and considering everything she'd done, it had been one of the hardest things she'd ever experienced. Now was the time to enjoy that her mother was probably in a staring competition with Karen.

That wasn't the case. "Hey," she said, prying her mother's eyes off Tanith, who was acting as if the girl were the only thing in the room. "You made good time."

"Are you kidding?" Danielle said, her arms open. "I thought we'd never get here, and your father gave his standard lecture when we went through security, which didn't help at all."

She hugged her mom and halfway expected either ninjas or a stripper to waltz in and add to the bizarre dream she was sleepwalking through. "Hey, Dad. You should've called. I would've picked you up."

"You've got enough on your head, kid." Buckston slapped her on the back and laughed. "Why not make introductions so this nice young lady can relax," he said, referring to Tanith.

Wiley did as he asked, and her heart opened to Tanith when she saw how she looked at her father. Tanith had grown up with three important people in her life, but it was clear she thirsted for more. Aubrey had obviously given her a taste of information and now she wanted answers.

"It's nice to meet you, Tanith," Danielle said, holding Tanith's hands. Aubrey had found a way to make her mother relentless, and after seeing Tanith that's what she'd become. The thought made her shake her head. The scene was too surreal with her father standing behind her mom, his hand on her shoulders. To Wiley it appeared as if she'd robbed them of the opportunity to stand at the nursery window in the hospital.

"Dad," she said, ready to get back to something familiar. "Do you want to talk now or wait until morning?"

"I'll start dinner," Danielle said, not letting Tanith go. "When you're done I'd like a tour."

Buckston followed her quietly until they reached her office. He chose the chair Aubrey had sat in earlier and steepled his fingers in front of his chest. "If I thought it was possible, I'd be cursing you for getting that girl pregnant and leaving her behind. That kid is like a ghost of you at that age. How'd she do it?"

"Wishful thinking, Pop. They're leaving once this is over, so don't get attached."

"A bout of wishful thinking's going on, but it ain't mine." He laughed and crossed his legs at the ankles. "You're right to take things slow. Slow will give you the opportunity to see that walking away this time will be the coward's way out. If Aubrey hasn't proved herself to you yet, then I'll personally kick you in the ass to get you to open your eyes."

"Why is it that no one seems to understand the stakes of a happy reunion?"

He laughed along with her before taking two passports and airline tickets out of his back pocket. "I'm mellowing in my silver years, but blindness isn't one of my ailments yet. We've got a lot to get to, so I'll leave you alone for now, but I'm not sure about your mother." He put his hands up to stall anything she had to say. "I know, 'Shut up, Dad.' These and an overnight bag are all you and I'll need, so go eat your mother's feast and give her that tour before you turn in. We leave tomorrow at zero-six-hundred hours to complete your reconnaissance. Carl hasn't given his okay yet, but if he does, I want you to be as ready as you can be."

"Are you sure you want to?"

"We'll be gone two days. This place will still be standing, and while you're finding nests, I'll make sure your head's screwed on straight."

She leaned back, pressing her toes into the hardwood floor. "You think it's not?"

"You've got a lot on your mind, Wiley. It's only natural to be out of whack some. All that," he pointed toward the kitchen, "could make you sloppy out in the field. If someone has to have your back, I'm glad it's me."

"You're right, so thanks for answering my call."

"I'm glad you trusted me enough to ask, and I hope you know how I feel about you all the time, but I'm proud of you for getting them out of harm's way. Damn proud."

"It's funny how things turn out."

Buckston looked at her with a smile that softened his face. "Not really. You've been angry a long time and the army's reaped the reward of that. When you came back here, I knew you needed to lay those feelings to rest. I love you, Wiley, and I've always been proud you're my kid. All I want, all your mother wants, is for you to be happy. It's time for you to want that too."

"You'd take that chance?"

"It don't matter none what any old goat tells you, but I know you want an answer."

"I already heard Peter's, but I'd like you to share whatever's on your mind."

"The girl didn't call me, kid, so my feelings don't count. I'm asking you to be honest with yourself. Do what'll make you happy and bring you peace." His chair creaked when he stood and hugged her. "You're too special to be alone. It's time for you to rejoin the living, and I have every faith in you to keep what's yours whole and safe. I'm not knocking the others who went into that jungle with you, but no one alive is better at what they do than you. If you run this time, it'll be because you're too afraid to take the chance."

"I'm going to have to put a whole lot of people down before I get to think about happily-ever-afters."

"What's the problem, then? Not enough bullets?"

❖

Wiley stepped into the kitchen and smiled at Tanith before going to stand next to her mother. Danielle had rummaged through the bags of groceries that had been delivered and was making as quick a meal as she could from the ingredients. They didn't exchange a word as Wiley took the knife away from her to chop her onions to add to the stir-fry Danielle had well under way.

"Do you know how to cook anything, Tanith?" she asked.

"Mom taught me how to make her famous brownies, but that's all."

"You'll have to make me a batch. I miss them."

"Maybe tonight," Tanith said, smiling and acting more relaxed than Wiley had ever seen her.

The rest of her company was sitting in the den listening to Buck and Peter catch up. The ringing phone was the only thing that broke the calm, since it was Peter's cell. "It's a local number," he said to Wiley, holding up the phone.

"Let it go to voice mail if you don't recognize it."

Peter held the device as it rang three more times, then went silent. "I can't stand this much longer," Karen said, pressing her hands together. The phone dinged once about a minute later. Whoever it was had left a message.

"Let's see, but call your voice mail from the phone in my office," Wiley said.

Tanith's good humor looked to have evaporated and Wiley took a chance to make it better. Before she walked away she opened her arms and kissed Tanith's forehead when she quickly stepped into them. "You okay?"

"I'm glad I'm here." That was all Tanith said as she clung to her.

"Me too."

Tanith stayed with Danielle while everyone else followed Wiley to her office, where they listened to the message Detective Barry Smith had left. "The second line in here will register as a business outside Detroit, Michigan," Wiley said, when the short order to call him back had played. "Tell him you left your phone in Louisiana by accident, so you'll have to call him whenever you can without giving away your position. Unless there's something I'm not seeing, they should've cleared Aubrey by now and he's just following up. If that's the case, tell him you expect another call once they have someone in custody."

"What if he traces the call?" Peter asked.

"Like I said, he'll think you're in Michigan. He won't be able to break through my firewall unless you keep him on the phone for an hour."

Peter dialed the number and put it on speaker so Wiley and Aubrey could listen in. "Detective Smith, Peter Tarver."

"Mr. Tarver, where are you?"

"We've been over this already. I'm not telling you something that could endanger my family. We've lost enough in the last few days, so what can I do for you?"

"We checked out your daughter's story and it seems to have panned out, and in the amount of time she had I don't think she could've dug out every bullet that hit those guys in the house."

"Do you have any idea who did?"

"We're working on it. You'll be the first to know if we have anything."

"Thanks for the call, then." Peter hung up and Wiley smiled at him.

"Good," she said as she brought her computer to life. She changed the address the number was attached to in a few keystrokes. "I doubt they would've found you here anyway, but by clearing you they've given me a few days to work on something else I have going on. My dad and I will be flying out in the morning. I need your word that you won't leave the building until we get back. The only way this gets blown now is if anyone spots one of you in town."

"Where are you going?" Karen asked.

"Unfortunately that's classified, but it has nothing to do with this. The guy who asked me for a favor does know where I live, so I have no choice but to go. I don't want him coming here while we have a house full."

"Don't worry, Wiley, we'll stay put," Aubrey said. "Can we do anything to help?"

"Stay inside."

❖

"I was beginning to think you don't like me," Walter said. The Whiskey Blue Bar in the W Hotel was close enough to Wiley's place not to be suspicious, but far enough away to draw Walter's minions from her doorstep. "You don't call, you don't write." He twirled the amber liquid and a few cubes of ice in his glass.

"This isn't like you're asking me to pick up your dry cleaning." The bartender stopped in front of them and she ordered a club soda. "But now that you mention it, I did think hard about calling you back."

"Did I hurt your feelings?" Walter laughed, and the sound grated on her.

"The people you work with might find your sense of humor hilarious, but I don't have the patience for it. I do have a joke for you, though."

He pointed to his glass again and winked at the bartender. "Am I going to find it funny?"

"I don't know you well, so you tell me. How funny is having your brains splattered by a specially made hollow-point bullet fired from a semiautomatic sniper's rifle?"

"You're right, that's a joke. If we're going to work together you're going to have to do better than that to threaten me."

Walter stared at his new drink as if unaware of her eyes on the side of his head. "This is a one-time thing, so I don't give a crap what you think about my technique. Have any of your people come after me again with any kind of needle, and I will hunt you down. You're never going to see it coming, and I'm not going to lose a bit of sleep over it."

"Sounds like you're dying to spend the rest of your life in a mental facility."

She placed the fifty-one-millimeter bullet next to his drink and grabbed him by the wrist when he tried to touch it. "I don't like you, Walter, not at all. If you'd ever had to do my job, you'd realize the targets we're ordered to take down have nothing to do with dislike, hate, or revenge. They're merely a target like those at the range, but I'll make an exception for you. I'll pull the trigger and feel good about it. The real satisfaction, though, will be that there'll be no consequences to killing you. Trust me about that."

"Stop fucking with me and tell me when you're leaving," he squeezed out through his teeth since he couldn't break her hold.

"I should finish my recon by tomorrow night. If it's doable, I'll stay and take care of the problem. If your information is accurate, it shouldn't be too difficult to find a perch high enough to get you out of my life."

"What if there isn't?"

The bullet seemed to fascinate him since he couldn't stop staring at it. "The type of facility we're talking about shouldn't have higher-than-standard walls. Their security would stop anyone long before they reach them, so if he's still enjoying his moments in the sun, I shouldn't have a problem."

"I'll have my partner waiting with anything you need."

"All I need is for you to stay the hell away from me here and in Mexico. My contacts will take care of my shopping list." She pocketed the bullet and left a ten on the bar. "Don will give you a call once I'm done."

Walter kept his eyes front as she left, but he'd been predictable from the beginning, so it didn't take much to find the two guys he'd sent to tail her. Since he'd gone to so much trouble, she led them through the French Quarter toward New Orleans east and its miles of deserted streets. A little practice before she left wasn't a bad idea.

When she exited off the interstate she sped up at the bottom of the ramp, not worried about traffic. It was nonexistent here. Her bike sounded out of place in the silence, but she could still hear the car behind her. She drove a block, kicked the stand down, but didn't kill the engine. The car's lights made it impossible to see what color it was or if anyone else had joined the two who'd followed her out of the bar.

Once the nine millimeter was in her hand she tuned out everything but the oncoming vehicle. The calm around her might've been shattered, but as she emptied the clip the only tenseness she experienced was in her finger and shoulders. When the last bullet left the barrel the two front tires were flat and the radiator was hissing steam.

The two front doors opened but the guys wisely stayed put. She changed the clip, holstered the weapon, and drove off. Most likely there was another car, but she didn't spot it as she doubled back to the highway. She guessed they'd wait outside her place.

"I'm going shopping, so don't wait up," she told her father when he answered his phone.

"Be careful, and remember it's an early flight."

"I'll be there." She disconnected and turned toward the city again. "Whether I want to or not." Her words echoed inside her helmet, but they made no emotional impact. This job wasn't her idea, but like all the others it quieted everything in her head, including the ghosts from her past that were haunting her home.

CHAPTER TWELVE

W iley, good to see you, man," Dante Guzman said when he opened the door to the South American antiquities shop he co-owned with his sister on Magazine Street. The long street that started in downtown New Orleans cut through both Uptown and the Garden District, and was home to hundreds of small businesses. The Guzmans had opened the place fifteen years before with the help of their father and were sandwiched between a specialty jewelry store and an Indonesian furniture store.

"Good to see you, and I'm glad you were still here." She glanced around the space full of statues, paintings, and jewelry they imported from Mexico and South America, but didn't spot Juliana, Dante's sister.

"Even we have to do inventory, and Juli doesn't trust the staff not to break something. Now that you're here, I'll make a run for it before she notices the stuff in the back hasn't been counted." She laughed and followed him toward the back of the building. "She's waiting for you upstairs, and the last time I checked, she had almost everything you need. Take care, and I'm still waiting for the series of paintings you promised me."

"I'm halfway through your list, but I haven't had much time in the studio lately." The painting she'd done of their childhood home in the mountains of Colombia hung on the wall behind his desk. She looked at it as he locked the antique mahogany desk that had been his father's. The small pistol he'd removed from the middle drawer went into his suit pocket, and she smiled at him when he hugged her.

"Your art is your greatest talent, my friend. I don't care what people like Don say. Things like that," he pointed to the large canvas, "will mark your legacy."

"Let's hope so, but I doubt pretty pictures will keep me out of hell."

He embraced her again and kissed both her cheeks. "Then we'll both sit in the heat and drink eternity away. Take care of yourself."

Their store was in an old house, but the siblings conducted business strictly on the first floor. The top floor was an apartment Juliana used when she was too tired to drive to the old plantation she'd refurbished thirty miles outside New Orleans.

"You're late," Juliana said when Wiley reached the bedroom in the back of the house. "Maybe you weren't looking forward to this as much as I am."

Her friendship with the Guzman siblings had started when she'd been separated from her team in Bogota five years earlier. She'd been serving on her fourth joint mission put together by the army and the Colombian government. After months of meetings, ten high-profile targets had been identified, and she'd been assigned two of the last to be eliminated. By the time she arrived, the cartels had heightened security and flooded the streets with money for information. If Juliana hadn't helped her with supplies and a place to stay, she would've been dead in less than a day.

There'd been only one way to celebrate the relief of getting to live, as Juliana had put it, and that's where their true relationship had started.

Like the first time, Wiley stood and admired the beauty of Juliana's naked body. Her brown skin, jet hair, and black eyes were mesmerizing. She looked for such a long time that the caress of her eyes made the dark nipples pucker and Juliana spread her legs slightly.

"You know me better than that," she said as she leaned against the doorjamb even though she wanted badly to run her hands along the swell of Juliana's stomach. Her desire this time, though, was tempered with guilt. Aubrey was only a few miles away, still hoping for all the things she'd promised so long ago. "I had a few ticks to burn off before I got here."

"Business should never come before pleasure." Juliana crooked her finger, beckoning her forward. "I've been wet since you called."

Wiley could almost hear her own heartbeat when Juliana slapped her hands away and slowly unbuttoned her shirt so she could get to her pants. Everything that'd happened to her that day melted away when Juliana pulled her jeans down before she urged her to sit at the edge of her bed. When she did, Juliana took her shoes and pants off so she could kneel between her legs.

"It's been too long."

"You're right, but don't think you have to do this," Wiley said, before she framed Juliana's face with her hands. Their last meeting had been two years ago in the house in the painting downstairs. Juliana had been nothing but kind to her, so she couldn't tell her that the flames of want burning through her guts hadn't started because of her.

"You'll have to beg me *not* to touch you. Have I suddenly become hideous to you?"

"No. I have a lot going on." She'd never considered what was between them love, but it was more than sex. They'd spent a week naked in that remote place, surrounded by coffee plants and colorful birds, when she painted that canvas for Dante.

"So don't waste time talking about things outside this room if I only have a few hours." She leaned back when Juliana put her mouth on her. Not until Juliana's lips encircled her hardness did she realize she'd been turned on since Aubrey had come to talk to her. Maybe she was getting too good at denial, but at the moment she didn't care. The release had become paramount.

Juliana sucked harder when Wiley grabbed the back of her head and wrapped the shoulder-length silky hair around her fist. She didn't close her eyes. The last time she'd been safe enough to do that it had been with Aubrey, but she was losing control nonetheless. She took a deep breath and tightened her hold when Juliana stopped and laid her head on her thigh.

"That's for keeping me waiting up here and getting wet at the thought of you." Juliana opened the drawer of the nightstand slowly, obviously remembering how she felt and reacted to sudden movements. "Want to prove to me what great shape you're in and how badly you want to make things up to me?"

The harness appeared to be the same one Juliana had brought with her when they'd met in the mountains, and she stood as she strapped it on her. "You left me craving this since the last time."

When the belt was fastened, Juliana swirled her tongue around the head of the dildo before sucking it in and out. The motion made the small attachment next to her rub against Wiley's clit. She didn't need a reminder of how badly she wanted to come. The torture ended when Juliana lay back and spread her legs after bending them at the knees.

"Are you going to keep me waiting some more?" Juliana asked, spreading her sex to prove how wet she was.

Wiley knelt and held the cock by the base to better guide it in. Juliana had chosen a shorter, thick one that matched Wiley's skin tone, her artistic side emerging in strange ways. Wiley tipped her hips forward slowly, making sure Juliana took the thickness all right.

"Show me you missed me," Juliana said, running her hands down her back to her ass. It was all the permission she needed. She pumped her hips, driving deeper and enjoying the sound of skin slapping against skin. With her eyes on Juliana's face, she stopped when the orgasm gave her no other choice. Juliana had dug her nails into her ass hard enough to break the skin.

"Still so, so good." Juliana drew her legs up so she could put her feet on the backs of her thighs. "Now that I'm almost comatose, how are you?"

Juliana took a deep breath and let it out in a slow, strong stream when Wiley pulled out and rolled next to her. "I was fine until an active fly landed in my web."

"Always the puzzler, aren't you?" Juliana turned and rested her chin on her shoulder. "Let's move to safer subjects you can actually talk about. How's the house? Did the frame for the *Dragon Tree* portrait come out to your liking?"

"You and Dante did a masterful job finding the perfect wood for that painting."

"That one seems special to you, so Dante made it himself from wood our grandfather carved years ago."

The gift was generous, considering the small amount of time they'd spent together. Juliana, though, understood her and her need to not get attached. "You know I'll treasure it as much as the both of you would've."

Juliana lifted her head and rested it on her hand as she placed her other hand on Wiley's abdomen. "Are you ever going to tell me the story of that piece? If you don't have time now, then I'll wait until you come back."

"It's a long one I'm not sure I know how to tell."

Juliana smiled, but her expression seemed melancholy. "I'll never own your heart, but I'd like to hear about the woman who does."

"How do you know I painted it because of a woman?"

"Am I wrong?" Juliana asked, sitting up so she could light a cigarette.

"It's a historical work," she said as she removed the harness. "I'm not trying to put you off, but I really don't have time."

"Then put your pants on so I can concentrate." Juliana pulled on the silk robe draped across the end of the bed and took long drags of her smoke as she dressed. "You're leaving tomorrow?"

"In the morning, so I need my list in place by noon, if you can manage it."

"I'm not even going to ask because I know better, but where you're going—it's not a nice place." Juliana led her to the office at the front of the house where she took a small envelope off the desk. She sat on the love seat against the opposite wall and ground out her cigarette. "Everything you asked for is in place and ready for pickup. I made sure my most trusted courier is there to greet you."

"I'm in your debt again," Wiley said, joining Juliana and taking her hand.

"I billed enough since I figured this job isn't something you picked. The government cries, but their pockets are still deep." The robe opened enough for Wiley to see Juliana's breasts when she leaned forward to light another cigarette. "Remember to be careful. You are always the hunter, but the men who serve time there control all the jackals in Mexico. The guns you asked for don't have enough rounds if the pack turns against you."

"I'll do my best, but thanks for the advice."

"And remember that you owe me a story." Juliana kissed her cheek and she took it as a signal that it was time to go. She'd never kissed Juliana on the lips. That intimacy had nothing to do with their relationship, but she did wonder if Juliana's husband enjoyed that act with her.

The much-older gentleman Juliana had chosen rarely left Colombia and had been a concession to Juliana's father. Wiley didn't know his name but felt a bit of sympathy for the guy. In the eyes of the law, Juliana was his wife, but he'd never own her. Juliana, she figured, gave only glimpses of her true self to very few people, and only Dante knew her completely. Her brother and closest friend would never betray her trusts or her secrets.

"Take care and I'll see you soon."

She put the envelope in her front pocket and left by the back door. The street was still busy because of the numerous restaurants in the area, but she didn't spot any more of Walter's men. If they were there watching, they were doing a better job of blending. As she headed back to her place, the thoughts of Aubrey that Juliana had drained from her head returned.

Even if she'd had time to tell Juliana the story she'd asked for, she wasn't sure she'd know how. The beginning was clear to her, but the end was still unknown. The only certainty was that there'd be one, and it'd come as soon as she could assure the Tarvers' safety.

❖

"When are you coming back?" Levi Evans asked, turning away from the crowded town square in Mexico City to be able to hear Walter's answer. His supposed partner had left for the States without calling him or providing any updates on the case they'd been working.

"I need a few more weeks. Then if things go well I'm getting us transferred stateside for a while. Arizona or California has to be better than some of the hellholes we've been stuck in, huh?"

His waiter put the can of Coke and the honey bun he'd ordered down while barely looking at him. He'd be damned if he'd eat or drink anything not in a wrapper until he was back in Florida. "You gonna tell me why you bugged out of here so fast?"

"Look," Walter said, and from his tone Levi knew he was about to get the brush-off. "I don't have a lot of time so listen carefully. I need you in Almoloya de Juárez before morning. The brass ordered a cleaner, and I want to make sure the job's done right."

"When's this supposedly happening?" Would it fucking kill these people to put a soda in the fridge? The hot drink fizzed up all over his hand and sleeve. "Pombo's the Mexican government's problem now. The well of information is dry."

"Levi, I don't need your goddamn opinion or insight. I need you to be at the airport in the morning. The place has one runway, so it should be easy to spot any arriving American."

"Calm down, Wally, I'll be there. I figure it's not worth the effort, but if the boss wants this done I'll send you pictures of the show." Levi ripped open his honey bun and put some money under the glass filled with melting ice. He'd been here for three years, but his stomach refused to acclimate to the food or water, and he was fucking tired of having diarrhea. If the heat didn't kill him, the chafing on his ass cheeks from the frequent bathroom trips would.

"What's up?" Kevin Marshal asked.

Kevin was a new kid who looked like he'd won a contest from the back of a cereal box and the prize was a job with the CIA. His enthusiasm was starting to work on Levi's nerves more than his red ass.

"Go pack a bag. We get to babysit Pombo again." He shoved the rest of his pastry into his mouth and put his hands up. "Not the time for questions," he said as a shower of crumbs fell out of his mouth.

❖

The building was quiet when Wiley got home, so she made it into the shower without having to talk to anyone. She took her time to make sure everyone was asleep. Though Juliana was supplying her weapons, she wanted something from the dragon's lair and didn't need anyone to see her going in to get it.

She leaned forward with her hands against the tile of the shower and let the hot water hit the back of her neck. All the stress from both her guests and Walter had made the muscles in her neck and shoulders knot up, but she still had things to do before she could get some sleep.

The labs hadn't finished analyzing whatever drug Walter's men had tried on her, but Don had come through with the specs of the prison where Roth was being held, as well as pictures of the town. The best place to shoot from was the bell tower of the Catholic church, but that'd be the easiest, most obvious place to get caught. The town wasn't huge, so this one would take more thought.

She dried off and put on a pair of sleep pants and a T-shirt. If the house was still quiet she could retrieve the scope she always used for distance shots. She wouldn't have either time or opportunity to calibrate a new one.

She used the steps to the third floor and stopped when she heard the soft crying. With only the kitchen lights on dim, she tried to locate the person in the den.

"Aubrey?" It had been a while, but she hadn't forgotten that night when she walked away. Aubrey didn't cry often, and she could remember every occasion. "Are you okay?"

"Compared to what?" Aubrey laughed as she sat up. She was still dressed, so Wiley guessed she had been sitting here when she'd gotten back.

"The last few days couldn't have been easy to get through."

"I don't really measure my life in days, more like in moments, and some have been much harder than others." Aubrey rubbed her eyes with the back of her hands. "You don't need to stay up with me. I know you're leaving early."

"You probably think I'm heartless for what I did, but all the sacrifices haven't completely killed my humanity." After turning the lamp on the side table on, she understood the meaning of regret. Her chest hurt from the what-ifs she associated with this woman. Wiley wasn't sad often. Fear and exhilaration she knew, but her mood was different now.

"I've never thought of you as heartless." Aubrey looked at her and combed her hair behind her ears. "And I'm not trying to get rid of you. I want you well rested since whatever you're doing tomorrow needs your full attention. Your errands seldom had anything to do with picking up loaves of bread from the market."

She nodded, trying her best to return Aubrey's weak smile. "Why the tears?"

"It's still my pressure valve." Aubrey wiped impatiently at her face and tried to widen her smile. It held for only a moment.

"You haven't had time to decompress, so don't beat yourself up like this. What happened isn't your fault."

"You don't have to be so nice. I wanted so much for us, for Tanith, but this situation never crossed my mind, and it should've. I planned to get out before Tanith knew the truth I'd discovered a few months ago. She's young but probably already thinks I'm an idiot."

"I'm not in any position to give advice, but you have to take care of yourself. Whatever happens, Tanith's going to need you."

"Do you know what's wonderful?" Aubrey drew her legs up and rested her head on her raised knees. "You haven't changed all that much. Not really."

"You're wrong." She sat a few cushions over and leaned back. "I've changed as much as you have."

"You've become a brain-dead mother with no ambition except taking care of your child?" Aubrey moved slowly and reached over to take her hand. "You're the same where it counts." Wiley moved closer so Aubrey wouldn't have to stretch, but the touch made her body temperature rise. "The core of that kid I met all those years ago is still intact."

Aubrey's touch suddenly turned cold, but it wasn't Aubrey's hand that'd become frigid. Wiley's body was like ice as the realities she'd tried to bury stormed up, refusing to be ignored. Her life had been so empty, and it was too late for any kind of happiness. This safe existence she'd share with the Black Dragon would be all she'd ever have.

Perhaps her father was right and she could decide to get back something she thought she'd lost forever. Only that trail still ended at the same dangerous place for Aubrey. "Why do you think so?" she couldn't help but ask.

"You returned my call and didn't hesitate to come when I told you where I was." Aubrey put her other hand on her bicep. "The way you treat Tanith makes a huge difference as well."

"To you?" This close, with Aubrey's perfume and her warmth, Wiley's brain became an active beehive. Her shattered discipline allowed a logjam of thoughts to flood in and dull her into forgetting the things she had to do.

"Yes." Aubrey moved her hand higher. "But more importantly, it made a difference to her. You'll never believe me, but I knew from her first breath that the two of you would like each other."

"Tell me about her."

"I'll tell you whatever you want to know." Aubrey brushed her fingers through the hair at the base of Wiley's neck. The first time she'd done that, Wiley had found the courage to kiss her. "But you have to know the answer lies with the same reason I fell in love with you. The reason I gave you my heart."

"Tell me," she said, sounding winded. Aubrey's smile, like now, had always drawn her in and captivated her.

"It was the goodness that's at the core of you. Not one time from the moment I fell in love did I worry about you hurting me or lying to me. And you didn't, not until that split second when you left me. We both knew you were lying, and losing you almost killed me."

"That wasn't easy," she said, and closed her eyes as Aubrey caressed her neck. "Surely you know that."

"I tried to hate you, Wiley, I tried for a really long time, but I kept thinking about that kid under the dragon tree. She grew up to slay monsters that are all too real, but you didn't lose yourself to the horror.

Eventually I figured out that you were too damn noble to put me in any type of danger, so you left me instead. That's what I chose to believe, anyway. It's nice to know I was right, but it's not much consolation." Aubrey moved closer and placed her head on Wiley's shoulder, moving so tentatively she seemed to fear Wiley might push her away.

"Those monsters are still lurking, waiting to take what's most precious to me. If I allow that to happen, I'll give them what they want most by putting a gun to my head." She put her arm around Aubrey and drew her closer, wanting to remember the feel of her. "I can live with the pain as long as you're whole."

Aubrey stayed quiet, but from the way she was shaking, she was crying again. "That's why Tanith reminds me so much of you. She's selfless when it comes to the people she loves. Maria wasn't good with her, but she stood it for me, so how lucky I've been to have you both looking out for me."

"I'm happy you have her."

"Wiley, can I ask you something even if it totally wears out my welcome?" Aubrey said in a voice slightly above a whisper.

"Sure." She pressed her cheek to the top of Aubrey's head.

"These people who killed Maria and want their money, they aren't going to stop. If you have to make a choice in all of this between me or Tanith…let me go." Aubrey still had tears in her eyes but her smile hadn't failed.

"If I haven't changed that much, then you have to know I'll never accept that as a viable option."

"That's a given, but life holds no guarantees, so if something happens to me I want Tanith to stay with you."

"On the off chance something does go wrong, your mother's never going to agree to that." The back of her neck and the muscles in her entire body tightened again. That was her body's warning to leave or escape a perilous situation. Having this conversation was as dangerous as anything she'd ever done, and she had to stretch her fingers and fan them out before she reached for Aubrey's hand. "Tanith has a parent, and you have to trust me to keep you safe."

"I've questioned myself plenty but never you, Wiley."

"We have a chance to be friends again." She squeezed Aubrey's hand, recalling her younger self and how incredibly lucky she'd been to have shared herself with Aubrey. "So how about we're honest with each other?"

"I want your promise you'll do what I'm asking." Aubrey moved closer to her and Wiley held her breath. She'd stuffed her desire for Aubrey down as far as she could shove it without total amnesia, but having her this close would make it impossible to let her go. "If I'm not here, I want Tanith to have what I did. I want you to take care of her and love her. Maria was my mistake, but Tanith wasn't. If you really look at her, you have to know why I had her."

"Aubrey, please," she said, Aubrey's tears tearing at her heart.

"I'm so very tired of missing you."

"I've missed you too, and sometimes the memories of us back then completely swamp me. What happened was so unfair, but we can't go back…no matter how much I want to or how easy it would be. Especially now, because of Tanith. If something happens to you I wouldn't be much good to her." She opened her hand, but Aubrey didn't let go. "So you should reconsider your request. Tanith deserves better than me."

"She's yours, baby. I didn't think I had to say that out loud. Tanith is as close to you as I could manage, and the main reason I called for you." Aubrey pressed her hand to her cheek again. "It's a lot to take in, I know, but she's missed so much with you already. Don't rob her of the future as well."

"I'm so sorry," Wiley said, her voice raspy. Her eyes burned and she was nauseous from the massive amount of emotions that Aubrey's words conveyed. "You have every reason to hate me, but I didn't have a choice. I don't deserve everything you've given me after I ran."

"My heart made its choice so long ago, and that hasn't changed," Aubrey said as she now wiped Wiley's tears. "Right now we both have to bury the past. You're leaving in the morning and I need you to be sharp, not worrying about ancient history."

"I just wanted to keep you safe and alive."

"I know that," Aubrey said, before kissing her cheek, "and it's a given that's what you'll do until you clean up all this mess. I wanted to talk to you before anything else happened so you'd know how I felt and what I want."

"Did you remember something else? You can be honest even if you think it'll upset me."

"I told you everything, so I'm not cracking up on you. I just have a sense I'm going to be rewarded for all my sins and not even you'll be able to stop it."

"By leaving you I made you think you couldn't count on me." She pressed her fingers to Aubrey's lips when she tried to interrupt. "You don't have to pretend that's not true."

The memories of the men she'd killed from her perch in the trees came to her, as well as the satisfaction it'd given her. She didn't feel any emotion during an assignment, but those guys had killed so many innocents she didn't suffer a bit of guilt for carrying out her duty. Unfortunately the sense of honor lasted only a second compared to what it'd cost her.

"I can't change what I did and how much I hurt you, but you have my word I'll get you and your family through this."

"Go to bed." Aubrey pulled Wiley's fingers away to speak. "You need to rest and stay safe. You've got a lot to come home to."

"We can't go back."

"I'm not interested in going back," Aubrey said, kissing her palm. "I'm interested in moving forward."

This wasn't the moment to argue about it. "You still believe in fairy tales."

"Why wouldn't I?" Aubrey pressed her hand to Wiley's chest. "I know white knights really do exist. Mine is tall and strong, and she carries me and my daughter on her shoulder to remind her that when the fight is over, she's got a place to come home to." She slid her hand to Wiley's shoulder and moved her sleeve up so the bottom of her tattoo was visible. "A place that's been yours from the first time you accepted that I belonged with you and to you."

"Isn't that an overly simplified way of looking at it?"

"You have a beautiful place," Aubrey said, confusing her.

"Thanks."

"Would you trade it to be with me? To never have had to leave me?"

"Yes." No hesitation, no attempt to hide her exposed heart.

Aubrey touched her face gently, closing her eyes when she placed her fingers against her lips. "Then it's simple. You're mine, Wiley, and I want all the childhood dreams back. I refuse to let you go this time, so don't keep running from me. I'll keep coming unless you tell me you don't want me anymore." She pressed her hands to Wiley's cheeks, forcing eye contact. "Can you say that?"

"I could, but you know me well enough to realize when I'm trying to hide something."

"Thank you." Aubrey laid her head back on Wiley's shoulder. "I could spend the rest of my life here, but you need to go to bed."

"Remember to stay inside, and if you can, make a list of anyone Maria might've mentioned." She stood, pulling Aubrey up with her. "The amount of money that's missing will keep these guys coming until it turns up, so you either have to figure out where she hid it or develop a list I can work from to eliminate the threat."

"I'm so ashamed it'd have to go that far. You shouldn't have to kill for me."

"Persuasion doesn't always end in death. If you can think of any leads, I'll give them a choice." She thought of Dr. Dupre and his decision. Sitting in a cell was to him a fate a hundred times worse than death, but choices made in the heat of the moment were the worst. Dying was preferable to having to live in a hell of your own making.

Dr. Dupre was too weak to pick what in essence would've set him free. She hoped she had a stronger spine when her turn came.

CHAPTER THIRTEEN

Wiley stood in her kitchen with her eyes closed, listening for anomalies. She needed everyone asleep so she could get in to get the equipment she needed. Her skin was still highly sensitized from her time with Juliana and Aubrey, so she sat on the counter with her legs folded and took long, deep breaths. She let her mind wander as a way to relax.

The highlight reel of her mind flew back to her teens and the anticipation that always built when she got a letter from Aubrey. She opened her eyes and smiled at the romantic mush probably driving up her insulin levels. Being frivolous seemed so foreign to her now, that capacity rusted, frozen.

She didn't hear any sound except the hum of the refrigerator and the air conditioner, so she jumped down and quickly ducked into the dragon's lair. The room was dark except for the computer screens and the low lights in the gun cabinets near the desk. She moved the mouse, and the middle screen was the only one with a blinking message icon.

When she'd retired she'd researched the best way to take private contracts without too many complications. The wisest course, she'd decided, was to take out two ads in national publications for investigative services. That's how their connection, like the one with Jerry Dupre's soon-to-be ex-wife, had started. She hadn't decided Jerry's fate until she had definite proof he'd committed numerous rapes and that Mrs. Dupre was in no way involved with law enforcement.

The punishment provided Mrs. Dupre's clean break from the monster she'd lived with, and an appropriate ending for Jerry. All along he'd thought himself too good and smart to get caught. His arrogance had cost him, and he wouldn't be the last to make the same mistakes.

She'd never bothered with cheating spouses or other cases like that, so sometimes she had to cull through the list to find the Jerrys of the world. She really didn't have time for the blinking message icon, but she opened it anyway. With everything she had to do, she felt normal here at her computer and wanted to enjoy it as long as she could.

She deleted the first twenty e-mails, hoping the disgruntled wives and a few husbands found someone to follow around their disloyal spouses. The next two were from the same guy, and each word dripped with agony at the loss of his sixteen-year-old daughter. Tammy Culver was, according to her father, Sheriff Wilbert Culver, an honor student and cheerleader at her high school in Brownsville, Texas. Wilbert wrote that she'd been popular and happy until the last three months of her life. It had spiraled out of control until it ended in an overdose, and he blamed a guy named Mitch Surpass. Only Mitch would never pay in the legal system Wilbert was paid to uphold—he had obviously learned to navigate the system.

After reading both notes twice, she easily hacked into Sheriff Culver's system since he'd foolishly sent his e-mail from his office. There seemed to be a thriving drug business coming through Brownsville, but it was mostly a stopping point for northern destinations. The investigation into Tammy's death had been vigorous, resulting in numerous arrests, only most of the guys serving time were low-level. None of them had been stupid or brave enough to turn on anyone up the food chain.

The bigger minnow Wilbert had targeted was Mitch Surpass, but nothing came of it. On another screen she found a picture of this guy and stared at it. Mitch's jeans, cowboy boots, and collared shirt made him look different, but she recognized him right off. This was the guy from the casino that fake cop had rushed to talk to after Maria's death.

"What the hell?"

She looked at Mitch's surveillance photo and could only imagine the connections that'd led her to Maria's bathroom, which made her thoughts skitter off to a dark, dangerous place. Despite her promises to Aubrey to keep her safe, that'd be impossible if Maria was involved with a dealer big enough to operate in more than one state. If that was true, she could keep the Tarvers alive only by keeping them locked up in her home. That wouldn't be feasible long-term.

She placed a battery in a new cell phone and dialed the sheriff's number.

"Hello."

His voice was gruff, and there was plenty of background noise. "Sheriff Culver, I just finished reading the note you sent." Her voice and number were unrecognizable to him, but she didn't want to linger with him either. "What can I do for you?"

"I can't talk now. Can I call you back?"

"It's now or next week, sir." She searched for pay phones in the area, finding it humorous that it took longer to find them than Mitch's information in Wilbert's system.

"Wait," Wilbert said, and she could hear the grief and desperation in his voice.

"I'll give you ten minutes to get to..." She gave him the address of the truck stop. "Use that time to gather your thoughts. As an officer of the law you should know the ramifications of sending the note and taking my call."

"Okay."

She needed some sleep, but the morning flight would have to suffice. As she timed Wilbert she unlocked the cabinet that held the long-range rifle she'd used for years and detached the scope. It was calibrated to that weapon, but she didn't want to chance at least that part of her equipment. Without the mount she could explain her love of bird-watching if airport security was worried about it.

"What do I call you?" Wilbert asked when she called one of the phones lined up in front of the truck stop's restaurant.

"Whatever you like and feel comfortable with. Before we start, you have to know the consequences of where this conversation might lead. If I decide to help you, there'll be no turning back. So, having said that, what do you need from me?"

"My daughter Tammy was sixteen when she met this guy, and he encouraged her to experiment with drugs."

"Not to cut you off, sir, but I know the backstory, and I agree with your assessment of the situation. What kind of help do you need?"

"I tried to follow procedure, even though I wanted to kill every one of these sons of bitches, and I didn't get shit out of it. They killed my little girl and no one's going to pay for it."

"Why do you suspect Mitch Surpass?"

"Because all the scum we picked up we suspected worked for this guy, but I'm not stupid enough to think it stops with this bastard Surpass." He paused, and from the three thumps she heard she guessed he'd punched the side of the phone booth. "I'm not weak. I'd kill him and whoever else to avenge my Tammy, but I got three other kids to worry about. If they send me away they ain't going to have a soul that gives a crap about them."

"Mr. Culver, go home to them and erase every trace of our connection."

"You're not going to help me. Do you know how hard it was for me to contact you?"

"I didn't say that." The top of her head prickled at the possibility this was a trap, but she ran her hand through her hair to try to dispel the suspicion. Some things were worth fighting and sacrificing for, no matter what it cost you. "You wrote me, so there had to be something about me you trusted. Go back to your family and I'll eventually be in touch."

"So all this horseshit you're hiding behind is for nothing. I know why I called you and what I want out of it. There ain't no tiptoeing on my end."

"I'm not blowing you off, Mr. Culver. You laid out your problem and that's all I need from you. I'll just hope you won't do anything stupid now that we've talked. Bringing in anyone else is only going to complicate things."

"You swear this guy will pay."

"I give you my word." She started a new search on Mitch Surpass and did some other electronic housecleaning as she spoke. "Anything else?"

"I'll pay you whatever you ask, but it might take time."

"Promise me you'll be patient and we'll work that out. I'll call you when I have something."

She made sure everything was locked before she left, glancing briefly at the picture on her desk. In that one second in time, she and Aubrey were younger than Tammy Culver was when she died. They'd had the chance to screw up the possibilities of what could've been, but Tammy Culver had only had one chance to mess up and her game was over.

Aubrey's life had led her to the guy Wilbert blamed for his daughter's overdose, so if she needed a reminder of what the stakes were, Tammy was it. In any other circumstances she might have brushed this off as coincidence, but she couldn't. Tammy was only one casualty of Maria's dealings, and Wiley wanted the cycle to stop there.

"As soon as I get back we have a date, Mr. Surpass." The dragon screen saver ate his image away. Now that she had Mitch's name, fake cop wouldn't be difficult to find. "Your boss might be better camouflaged, though."

By helping Wilbert she might solve Aubrey's problems. It sounded like an easy fix, but those came along like easy shots. She'd never had one of those in all the ones she'd taken.

❖

Roth Pombo's attorney, Antonio Hernandez, sat as Muñoz and Ernesto Masurdo made a few calls. The brothers were set to inherit Pombo's business, but they were still indebted to him enough to do his bidding. Of all the guys on Pombo's payroll, the Masurdo brothers were as loyal as sharks, but they wanted Pombo's endorsement. One word from him and it'd be easier to take over once he was gone.

"Did you find him?" Antonio asked Muñoz. When Roth had moved up a few rungs, he'd immediately courted the Masurdo family. Rosa Masurdo had given birth to three boys who'd all grown to over six feet tall, and she'd raised them to fight their way to the top. It was the only way she saw to escape the poverty that'd plagued her family for generations. The loss of her husband and oldest son hadn't changed her mind. The promises Roth had made cemented not only the brothers' loyalty but Rosa's as well. With Rosa's blessing, her sons killed and served Roth with gusto, while she sat in her new house on the beach praying for their souls and safety.

"He left town for Almoloya de Juárez. You can tell Roth we've been watching this asshole from the day he got snatched," Ernesto said. He spoke softly and put this hand gently on Antonio's knee. For years he'd had to endure their violent ways, but they'd keep him alive in the coming shit storm. "You know Roth won't get out of this crack he's in, don't you?"

"I know as well as Roth that he's been betrayed, but he's my friend."

"He's our friend too," Muñoz said, sitting on the other side of him. "We'll do what we have to, but we hope you realize your friendship is as important to us."

With Roth in jail the water had been chummed and every predator for miles was swimming in for a share. If he hoped to survive with his bank account and his life, he needed someone else to stand behind. Since it was a necessity, he needed to go with the ones who wanted him.

"Do you think you can take care of our problem?"

"The first part of our plan is already in place," Muñoz said.

"Thank you." He gripped the strap of his briefcase. "It'd be my honor to stand with you at the next meeting. We could use the opportunity to share with the other bosses what Roth's wishes for his share of the business are."

"Then we're agreed," Ernesto said. "After all this is over, our family will enjoy having you as our advisor."

"It'll be my pleasure."

❖

Levi stepped out of the bathroom at the gas station they'd stopped at to kill some time and took a deep breath of fresh air. The only flight arriving from the U.S. was due at fifteen minutes after twelve, but he'd gotten Kevin out of bed at six after another terse call from Walter.

"You want something?" he asked Kevin, who was waiting to use the toilet that hadn't been cleaned since the sixties. "I'm grabbing a Coke."

"I'll take one."

The day was already getting hot, and Levi was glad he'd worn shorts and a lightweight shirt. He'd be cooler and they'd fit in better than some of the law enforcement who worked the area. He was still trying to figure out what a cleaner was doing here, and what Walter's angle in all this was.

He glanced around as he walked through the front door, making the bell tied there ring. This place looked like a movie set, with the fan with streamers tied to the grill and the antique cash register, but they had Twinkies. He got two packs and two sodas from the pan loaded with ice.

When he put his loot on the counter he stepped back and tried to quickly get to his gun, which he'd tucked in the back of his waistband. Of all the things he'd noticed on the way in, the one he missed was the guy behind the counter. As the sound of bullets came from the side of the building, he recognized the man pulling the trigger across from him.

The shot would take him out, and one of Roth's men would take credit for the kill. He'd stayed in the game too long. Sloppiness and laziness had killed him.

"Call Ernesto and tell him we're done here," the shooter told his partner in Spanish. "The other guy's dead?" he asked the group that joined them. One of the men who'd come from outside ripped open the package of Twinkies and shoved one in his mouth.

"He died in that shit hole," the guy said around the sponge cake, making everyone laugh.

"Load them both up. We have time for a drive before we have to meet Antonio." He took five hundred dollars U.S. from his shirt pocket and handed it to the woman hiding under the counter. "I don't have to come back, right?"

"You are welcome to return whenever you like, but not because I'll tell anybody about today."

He smiled briefly and handed over an extra hundred. Both Ernesto and Muñoz had wanted this done, but with no headlines. The two men they had killed would rot together in the hole they'd dug already, at least most of them.

"Wait at the airport, but don't look for trouble," Ernesto said. "If you see an American arrive, follow but don't get too close. Let me know where they're staying." The guy who'd been on the phone with Ernesto took both of the wallets his men had taken from the dead men.

The Florida and Texas driver's licenses didn't appear out of order, but etched into the back was a phone number—the same number on both. That wasn't normal and was worth another call to Ernesto.

"Is there a problem?" Ernesto said, obviously having recognized his number. The shooter explained what he'd found and read out the number. "Good job, hold on a minute."

He smiled, congratulating himself for being observant. When the guy next to him fumbled for his phone, having to put the old fat guy down, he pressed his phone closer so he wouldn't miss Ernesto when he came back on the line. When he turned his back on the crew, the noise and the pain were instant.

"Add him to the pile and get rid of all of them. Bring me the wallets, but keep the cash. If you decide to be nosy, I'll be happy to hand the job over to one of your friends," Ernesto said to the guy who'd just shot the would-be detective who'd killed Levi.

"I'll have it all there by this afternoon. I won't let you down."

"Good, you're promoted."

❖

"Are you here on business, Ms. Kelley?" the immigration agent asked Wiley when she presented the passport her father had given her.

"No. I'm with my dad for a long-overdue vacation." The guy stared at her, then Buckston one lane over, before he stamped the document. "Thanks," she said, shouldering her bag and following Buckston out of the building toward a car-rental lot full of vehicles that looked like they'd been used in a crash derby the night before.

"I've already reserved one, but don't worry. It has air-conditioning."

"Are you low on cash?" she asked, joking.

"Get in, wiseass."

The streets of Mexico City were as crowded as the last time she'd been here, so she closed her eyes as her dad navigated the traffic. She hadn't had a chance to check on any of the searches she had running, and the lack of information had left her a bit anxious. Information from reliable sources had kept her alive.

"When you see the Posada Cantina, pull in," she said when she felt her dad shift into fourth and pick up speed. "Where we're headed is about a two-hour drive if you go the speed limit, so the cantina should be an hour and fifteen minutes from here."

"Do you want to go the speed limit?"

"I do, so try your best. We want to get in and out of here with as little contact as possible, since I don't trust Walter one iota."

"Are you going to share what you have on Roth Pombo, or do you want to surprise me?" Buckston rested an elbow on the door ledge and drove with the other hand.

"Walter showed us what he had but wasn't willing to leave anything hard copy. If I had a short-term-memory problem I might shoot the wrong guy."

"Walter didn't pick you out of the phone book, so he knows what he's getting. No paper trail, though, means he'll disavow you quicker than your bullets if anything goes wrong."

"I'm not taking any chances, so don't start chewing your nails.

You'd never know it, but I thought my life would get less complicated when I retired."

Buckston laughed and turned the air conditioner up a notch. "What exactly is your plan?"

Her father knew who she'd been to the military, but she hadn't shared her new community-service work with him or anyone. She didn't think he'd feel differently about her or turn her in. She wanted to do this to atone for everyone she'd ever killed. Not that she needed God's forgiveness by killing more people, but for herself. Ridding the world of people like Jerry was better than volunteering at the local food bank.

"If I can't figure something out, I might send them home with you and Mom." He laughed again. "You think I'm kidding?"

"I'm sure you'll come up with something before that happens." His silence made her open her eyes and turn her head toward him. "You've talked to Aubrey, right? She doesn't know anything that'll get them out of this faster?"

"You think she's holding back so she can hang around? I've already thought about that."

"And?"

"This isn't about getting back at me for walking out. I believed her when she told me she didn't have any idea what Maria was up to until it was too late. The Aubrey I knew wouldn't have fallen for someone like that."

Buckston clasped her hand. "We agree on something, then. I still remember Aubrey as the idealistic young girl who was always in our house. I loved her because she loved my kid."

"That was a long time ago, and it's taken me a lot of years to not think of her that way, but I didn't have a plan B when it came to what happened." She closed her eyes again, and when the car stopped she didn't remember falling asleep. "I'll be right back."

Juliana's agent was a woman who led her to her car out back. The bag in her trunk held enough firepower to start a small war. After the quick stop, they were in their hotel room forty minutes later.

"I want to be out of here in three days tops, so let's split up," she said, putting her sunglasses around her neck. "I think we shouldn't go back more than four blocks."

"Meet you here at six."

"That might give me time to see how well-calibrated this thing is."

She put the sniper rifle between the mattress and its platform and gave her father a pistol and three extra clips. All the guns Juliana had gotten were clean and well-oiled, which alone was worth the steep price.

"See you then, but call if you run into any problems."

She opened the door to three men standing outside it. "You said something about a problem, Dad."

❖

"I'd like to invite you to have a drink with me," the older man said. "I realize you're probably tired from your flight and travel, but it's important we talk."

He spoke with a Spanish accent, but Wiley guessed he'd polished his cultured English while being educated in the States. The two apes behind him seemed out of place, but judging from the guns they had holstered under their jackets, the old guy's invitation would be hard to turn down.

"My parents taught me to never accept candy or invitations from strangers." She was naked without a gun or cover, but damn if she was going to show fear. Maybe this was Walter's man and he had a flair for the dramatic.

"My apologies." The man bowed slightly from the waist before offering his hand. "I am Antonio Hernandez."

"How can I help you, Mr. Hernandez?"

"Will you please share your name with me?" He threaded his fingers together at his waist and smiled.

"Anyone who knocks on my door usually knows my name."

"I don't mean to be rude, but I'd like your cooperation since you're intelligent enough to know our talk isn't voluntary." *It's a burden to always be right about this shit*, she thought. "Why make it more unpleasant than it has to be?"

"I'm Tanit Kelley and this is my father Jason," she said, using the names on the bogus passports her dad had gotten. "We were on our way to sightsee, so can you please tell us what this is about?"

"Sightseeing in Almoloya de Juárez?" one of the tall men behind Antonio asked, and laughed. His accent was thicker and sounded less educated.

"Please, Miss Kelley, could you tell me if the name Roth Pombo means anything to you?" Antonio asked.

She hesitated, her fingers twitching involuntarily. This was totally unexpected and not good if these guys weren't with Walter. "Not to be rude, but I'll need more from you, Mr. Hernandez."

"Señor Pombo knows it's a matter of time before someone from the States comes for a fatal visit. Before that time he'd like the opportunity to talk with whoever is assigned that task. Do we understand each other?"

"I'm not admitting to being whoever it is Mr. Pombo is waiting for, but what exactly does he want to talk about?" It was hot outside, and the room was musty from lack of use, but she was chilled. She was fast on the draw, but it was a gamble to reach for her gun. The clamminess of her skin stemmed from fear.

"Do you like stories, Miss Kelley?"

"I'm not a fan of fictional tales, but if it's educational then I'd love to hear it." She sensed her father moving closer behind her but never took her eyes off the two men with guns.

"Are you armed?"

"That's like asking my weight." She laughed. "It's impolite."

"We are all in a dangerous business, and in a dangerous place, but if we go to visit the jail they will not accept any weapon on your person."

"Let's head downstairs to the bar," Wiley suggested, and was surprised when all three men turned and headed for the stairs. If she'd wanted to, she could've taken all three of them out since she was now free to reach for a weapon. "What do you think?" she asked her father.

"I'm curious. Do you think these guys are with Walter?"

"Interesting way to go about this if they are. If they are, though, it's like he's torturing this guy before killing him."

When they entered the bar Antonio was sitting at a table alone, but his shadows hadn't gone far. Taking their cue, Buckston headed for the bar, leaving her to sit with Antonio.

"I'm sure this is a surprise perhaps," Antonio said when she sat next to him. "I do have the right person?" he asked, appearing unsure for the first time.

"Señor Hernandez, I'm not a nervous tourist who doesn't know how to shake you, but this isn't the way I usually do business." Eventually this would all make sense, but it was like a Rubik's cube. She'd put one side together only to screw up all the others. "Do you have any connection to Walter Robinson?"

"I warned Señor Pombo about that snake." Antonio hissed the word so vehemently, he had to wipe the spittle from his chin. "I would think you have a bigger connection to him."

"Touché," she said, signaling to her dad she was fine. "You want to give me a hint as to why you're here."

"Is Roth a dead man?"

Stalemates she understood, and Antonio had mastered the technique. "I don't want to be here, and it's not in my best interest to be seen with your boss. Thank you for the invitation, though."

"Do you know how many lawyers are in this country starving because they cannot make a living?" Antonio spoke like something haunted him. "There are fewer grains of sand on our beaches."

"I'm not here to judge you, sir. That job isn't one I'd ever volunteer for."

"You talk in circles and never answer a question, do you?"

"Talking isn't a great talent of mine, so I'm not as good at it as you. Whatever Mr. Roth's future may be, it won't have anything to do with me or my decisions."

"But if you're ordered to pull the trigger?"

"Good luck, Mr. Hernandez." She stood and saw the two men reflexively reach for their guns.

"Mr. Roth wishes to speak to you about Walter Robinson and their dealings. He knew this is how Walter would end things, so he's been waiting for you." Antonio's words stopped her, and when she turned around he was staring at the tabletop. "Our truce will end when you walk out."

Juliana's comment came back to tap her on the shoulder. She was in a place where she'd never have enough bullets. The only cool thing on her body was the Glock pressed against the small of her back, and it made her ignore the sweat that was making her clothes uncomfortable. One glance at her dad and she was ready for whatever came next.

"That sounds like a threat."

"It's not often I have to speak to someone in this manner," Antonio said, still not looking at her. "If this wasn't so important I wouldn't be here doing so now."

"If I am in Mexico at Walter's bidding, what kind of person do you think I am?"

"There's no skill in killing, but I'm sure Walter thinks you possess such talent."

"There's skill in everything, and for some, killing qualifies. Don't ever forget that." She fanned her fingers out and almost laughed when the two men brought their hands higher. It was too early in the game to kill three people in this public a setting. With a quick glance she saw both the men's pulses and the sweat dripping off their foreheads. No way in hell could they draw and pull off a kill shot.

"That's your answer, then?"

"Answer something for me first, then you're either going to let me go or shoot me." She walked back to the table and pressed her hands flat on the top. "If your boss knows so much about what his future holds, why are you here?"

"I trust you're a person who keeps her word. I gave Señor Pombo mine that he could tell you what he sees as important before his time is up. If you don't, I will try my best to kill you."

She thought back to her first meeting with Walter and her impression of him. His desperation was a red flag that she could dispel by one short conversation with the man he'd condemned. Not that she believed Antonio, but there was something she hadn't figured out about the situation. Maybe between Walter's tales and Pombo's vengefulness she'd find a bit of truth.

"What's the latest we can go?"

"I'll meet you here in four hours," Antonio said, smiling like his neck had been spared from the block.

"I can't wait."

CHAPTER FOURTEEN

How are you holding up?" Karen asked Aubrey when she joined her on a bar stool in the kitchen. From that spot they both had a clear view of *The Dragon Tree Legacy* painting.

"I feel like someone's around every corner waiting to rip me to shreds for something I know nothing about. Maybe I deserve it for not listening to you about Maria. Hell, if someone does kill me, all this would be over and Tanith will be okay." The painting was done so it could be sunrise or sunset. Your perception depended on your level of optimism, she guessed. She'd been staring at it for a while wondering how Wiley saw it.

"Think before you say things like that. Whatever happens, your goal is survival, especially because of Tanith," Karen said as she hugged her. "What good is having all these military types around if not to sleep better at night?"

"I don't think I have a battalion at my beck and call, Mom."

"Your father told me where you were when Wiley called you, so that's not exactly true." Karen moved close enough to put her arm around her. "I'm sorry if you don't want to talk about it, but I can't stop thinking about it. It terrifies me to think what could've happened."

"You know what Dad says about could've?"

Karen laughed. "Not worth the brain cells to worry about it. Still, that must have been terrifying. How are you doing with all that?"

"Honestly, it's so surreal I haven't really processed everything." Her eyes strayed back to the painting. All those memories, her first kiss, Wiley taking her first steps in becoming her lover, and the happiness she'd experienced in that one spot. When they'd found the courage to express their feelings for each other, Wiley had reminded her of a newborn colt. She'd been surprisingly timid at first but eventually she'd learned to run.

"Do you want to talk about it?"

"I called her a few hours before everything happened because I wanted back what was stolen from me. I was tired of being out in the cold. Everything I did after Wiley was my attempt to erase her and what she meant to me, but I just made mistake after mistake, and none of it touched how much I missed her."

Her mom kissed her temple. "Honey, you've got to let some of this stuff out, but don't you dare blame yourself. None of it is your fault."

"I can't say that." She moved slightly away from her mom and rested her elbows on the granite of the island. "Wiley's out there in danger because of me." Compounding her guilt was the fact that she hadn't really thought of Maria until now. She didn't miss her the way someone should miss a lost lover. She was relieved to be free of not only the flawed relationship, but the danger Maria had knowingly put them in. That sounded cold to her, but she longed for the touch of someone she wanted, someone she deserved. She wanted Wiley back and to get on with their lives.

"If you can say that, you don't understand Wiley at all."

She glanced up at her mom before she set her eyes on the painting again. "You don't have to pretend now, Mom. When Wiley left me you never gloated, but I could tell you wanted to."

"You never admitted what really happened, but you were both miserable. Well, I guess Wiley was miserable, considering she disappeared effectively. From what I can tell, though, the misery continues."

"What's to admit?" Had Wiley been sorry or upset they'd had to part? Or had it given her the freedom to take the chances she'd been afraid of losing her over? "There wasn't an explanation, she walked away."

"I'm not out to condemn her. You can be honest, and if you are I think it'll help with all this."

"It took me a long time to work out for myself that Wiley wouldn't have left for someone or something unless she couldn't protect me from it. She's always felt duty-bound to keep me safe, and while I can't fill in the blanks this time, I can only imagine what the penalty of staying would've been." She cocked her head back to keep the tears from falling. She was tired of being so emotional while Wiley was so strong.

"When you first called and told us, I was happy, relieved, really," Karen said softly. "I was convinced you'd be better off, and after your anger faded you were. To me you seemed lighter and happier without her. Then when you had Tanith I thought her name was the only link to the past you were keeping."

"I don't want to rehash this," she said, standing up.

"At least give me the chance to apologize for letting my mistakes and regrets taint your life." Karen put her arms around her waist and held tight. She had no option but to sit.

"When you met Wiley and started sneaking off to that tree to make out, your father and I were falling apart. Our move to Louisiana was the sixth in three years, so that and the military's all-boys club had hit my bullshit limit. He wasn't the guy I'd dated, and certainly not the man I'd committed myself to."

Aubrey didn't want the reminder of those nights when she hid in her room with her pillow wrapped around her head. The fights had never gotten anywhere near violent, but the screaming was relentless. In those hot and emotional moments she was terrified. It wasn't the history she'd wanted to repeat, and that she wouldn't have to was the only comfort she'd found in losing Wiley. She loved her, but the fear they'd turn into her parents had always haunted her. Of course that only lasted until she had a quiet moment to think. Then every second with Wiley confirmed the lie she was trying to live.

"You were so unhappy back then." The hurtful words her mom had flung at her father skipped through her mind like a stone over water. How had they survived all those things that could never be unsaid? Maybe it was no different than living with all the things she and Wiley had left unsaid.

"I was, and thinking back on it, that might be why I was so hard on Wiley and what she meant to you," her mom said, squeezing her hand before she went on. "I'm ashamed to admit that, but one look at those spit-polished shoes and buttons, and all I saw was a young Peter Tarver. I wanted to spare you the uncertain waters you were heading into."

"What happened had nothing to do with you, so you have nothing to be ashamed of, nothing to apologize for. In reality there's no one to blame." If she didn't get Wiley back she knew loneliness wasn't fatal, but the coldness of it would be insufferable. She'd lived with that even though she'd had someone in her bed for years.

"I've got plenty to atone for, believe me."

"How did you and Dad work it out?" she asked, trying to change the subject.

"At first I thought letting him go would've been the coward's way out. You know the SEALs' motto. 'The only easy day was yesterday.' If that was true for his job, then I figured all that hell we put each other through, all the blaming, screaming, and hurting, had to be worth something. No one fights over something unless it's of value to them. Your father's my piece of this world, aside from you and Tanith, that I'm willing to fight and die for. Once he realized it, and more importantly, *I* realized it, I set aside my anger and made it work."

"Thanks for sharing that with me."

"I didn't tell you to make myself feel better, but so you'll learn from my mistakes as well as what I did right."

She turned and made eye contact with her mom. "What's that?"

"I'm sure Danielle and every military spouse has a similar story. Who you picked and what she does means you must make concessions if you want a future with her. If you don't find you can, you owe it to both of you to stand up for what will make you happy, even if for you that means walking out."

She laughed, but her mom didn't crack a smile. "If you think I'd ever be happy without her, you don't understand me at all. I just need to figure out a way into that thick, beautiful head of hers to convince her of that."

"Wiley's not as hardheaded as her father, so that won't be as difficult as you think," Danielle said from behind them, obviously having heard some of their conversation. "I'm her mother, so I know Wiley and her understanding of kill shots. Those are second nature to her, but thank God it wasn't fatal when she turned the gun on herself and her future with you. You're right that she saw it as her duty to leave, but the wound of doing so was deep, and from what I saw, it came very close to breaking her." Danielle placed her hand on Aubrey's cheek and smiled. "I'm begging you not to let your anger finish what she's already been through."

"The only thing I want is for her to stop running away from me, Mrs. Gremillion. I swear it."

"We've known each other long enough, so call me Danielle. When it comes to Wiley, I believe you. After all this crap, I'm praying we all get what we want."

The sound of the buzzer from downstairs was like a stun gun that silenced everyone. Aubrey could sense the shock like a current that ran from Danielle's eyes to her chest. Whoever it was, they weren't expected, especially by the person Wiley had probably been the most up front with—her mother.

The visitor kept their finger on the buzzer, and the screen closest to them was filled with an FBI identification and federal warrant. She went numb from the thought of being found here and taken away somewhere beyond Wiley's grasp. Her limbs were leaden and all she wanted to do was hide as she heard Tanith run down the stairs. This was like being a hamster on a wheel. They could run as fast as they could but not get anywhere.

"We know you're in there," the man said, pulling the documents back far enough for them to see his face. "Open up, or we'll blow the door."

"Mom," Tanith said. "It's him."

❖

"Who's this guy?" Annabel Hicks, New Orleans FBI Bureau Chief, asked her assistant after she handed her an envelope with her name on it.

"He didn't say, ma'am. All he asked was for me to hand you that, and he'd wait. Whenever you're ready, he said to come and get him."

Annabel tapped her fingers on her desk, staring at the thick packet with the block letters on it spelling out her name. She didn't recognize the guy sitting in her waiting room, and from experience she knew there was no Santa. Anyone offering free gifts usually came back not only to bite you in the ass, but to rip it to shreds.

"Keep your eye on him, and stop him if he tries to leave."

"Yes, ma'am. Anything else?"

"Have Sean and Lauren meet me in the situation room, please." She put on a pair of gloves and dropped the yellow envelope into an evidence bag.

Her heels clicked on the terrazzo floor and the echo ricocheted off the walls like gunshots. Annabel had been stationed in New Orleans for three years, brought from Washington to tamp down organized crime and the growing drug business. Since her arrival she'd experienced one setback after another, so the sound of her shoes in the empty hallway reminded her that not only was her career as tattered as if someone had machine-gunned her résumé, but she was also alone.

"Something new, ma'am?" Agent Sean Porter asked as he entered with Agent Lauren Blaise. They headed the local bureau's terrorism division.

"We've got a live one in the lobby and he thinks this is his way in," she said, opening the evidence-bag seal after she and the others had placed masks over their faces as a precaution. "Depending on what's in here, I want you both on this case."

Sean accepted the job of dumping the contents onto the stainless-steel table. She'd read the paperwork later, but for now the pictures were the most interesting find. Not that she recognized the man's face, but the tattoo clearly visible marked him as a member of Tajr. She'd attended enough briefings on the growing terrorists cell that she didn't need to look anything up. She was sure.

"You don't have any clue who the man is who dropped these off?" Lauren asked as she flipped through the pictures.

"None." She picked up the phone. "Escort our guest in waiting into an interrogation room, please," she said to security.

"From the background this isn't anywhere local," Sean said, pointing out the blue water with rock formations close to the boat.

"I'll run both men through the system and see what pops up. While we're waiting, go introduce yourselves."

"I'm Special Agent Lauren Blaise and this is Special Agent Sean Porter," Lauren said, sitting and placing the folder containing copies of everything he'd brought in on the table. "What's the purpose of sharing your information, Mr. Robinson?"

"Your boss runs a tight ship." Walter leaned back, laughing and staring at the mirror. "I thought this would take much longer."

"And you wonder why our agencies don't cooperate better," she said with a tight smile, wanting to punch his face. "Now that we've proved ourselves adequate to talk to you, what's all this?"

"The pictures I included were taken in Mexico. The American is currently incarcerated in Mexico, but the Tajr member disappeared after the Mexican authority roundup."

"Fascinating," she said.

Walter explained Roth Pombo's progression from small-time dealer to major player, as well as his budding interest in outside investors. "Roth was about to cut a deal with these guys before he got picked up."

"If you need our help in Mexico I can direct you to the Washington Bureau for whatever intel is necessary, but our jurisdiction doesn't extend that far without a mandate from the Hoover Building."

"I realize that." Walter's expression became more serious. "I'm here because my partner and I have reason to believe Roth was further along in those plans than we knew from our investigation. We believe the man we photographed with him is in New Orleans."

"You believe a lot of things, sir, but what proof do you have?" Lauren asked.

"That's classified, so you're going to have to take my word for it."

Lauren stared at him for what seemed like ten minutes before getting up and leaving. If Walter's phone rang while he was in here he had his story ready for his superior, Craig Orvik. This meeting was a total gamble, but he needed leverage. Wiley was the best, but he knew now he'd never control her. Well, not without incentive.

Before he'd gone to Don he'd taken the locks off Wiley's information. He found two interesting things within that thick folder, aside from Don being right about her exit clause signed by the president. Don would always be Wiley's handler, and all her future assignments were voluntary unless they originated from the president or the secretary of defense. To Walter that was a dead end, so he'd concentrated on the second point.

The military's thorough investigation of Wiley's life interested Walter also. With all that digging, the Pentagon found Aubrey Tarver, but nothing had come of it. He concluded that the brass let it go since Wiley's relationship with Aubrey had kept her stable. When Aubrey left it had unbalanced her, but not in a way that made her nonviable in the field. By reading between the lines, it seemed as if command had welcomed the implosion of Wiley's personal life.

A large part of the file detailed the assignments she'd taken in Iraq at the beginning of the war. The number of kills had impressed him and he wanted Wiley under his thumb. He'd finally found a way to do that, but only if these people played ball.

Sean sat quietly until his earpiece obviously came to life. "Mr. Robinson, you're going to have to give up something."

"While we're in here talking about this," he slid a picture toward

Sean, "this guy is getting that much closer to what he wants." He sat back and tried for a disgusted expression. "Do you have any idea what the Tajr sect is capable of?"

"Yes, sir, I do. Even though we're in what I assume you think is the end of the earth, we do get briefings on all matters of national security."

"These are recent developments that arose from our ongoing investigation. If your agency can't help me track down these leads, I'll have to call for reinforcements. When we set up shop here, don't complain. I offered to make it a joint operation."

"Wait here, I'll be right back."

He checked his phone to make sure Annabel Hicks hadn't called his bluff. When it buzzed he flinched, but then felt almost giddy when he recognized the Mexican number.

"Robinson," he said, not believing he was having to take this call here.

"Walter, this is Carter Winslow. I'm in Mexico City."

The name sounded vaguely familiar. "Yes."

"I'm calling on behalf of Mr. Orvik's office. He's requesting your return to Mexico on the next available flight. If that's not possible in the next few hours, he'd like you to call and we'll arrange one for you."

"I'd like to talk to him before I go anywhere on the order of a flunky."

"He'll be unavailable for a while. Mr. Orvik and the director are both at the Pentagon after the latest developments from your team."

"Developments?" He was starting to get pissed. He remembered Winslow now. The guy was like a machine remembering facts and had the social graces of one with that monotone voice. "Spit it out or get me in touch with Orvik."

"Both Levi Evans and Kevin Marshal were reported missing and subsequently found. Their last communications with us were that they were on an assignment initiated by you stateside. Since I was already here for auditing purposes, we investigated, and Mr. Orvik wants answers before we respond."

"Why not ask them if something went wrong?"

"Both officers are dead. Their heads were dumped in front of the police station, their bodies haven't turned up yet. Their wallets and identification were gone, but both men had their cell phones shoved into their mouths. It's them, no doubt. You understand now why you're needed back here."

"You have to give me a day."

"This isn't up for negotiation. Mr. Orvik will be awaiting your itinerary."

The line went dead. His time was up, but he still had one thing left to do before he left. The door opened when he stood, and both Sean and Lauren blocked his exit.

"Going somewhere?" Sean asked.

He used the call to his advantage since he knew the agents had listened to both sides. "My team is dead, so I can't afford to waste any more time. I don't even have time to take back the information I shared with you, so I want your word you'll shred it."

"What lead were you following here?" Sean asked. "We can't help you if you don't release that information."

"A few days ago the sect leader from the photograph with Roth sent a death squad here to take out some of their operatives. They succeeded in taking out everyone but one. That person we believe is still in the city." He laid out the rest of his story with urgency. If they could get a warrant he could leave for Mexico with his plans still a go.

"Give us an hour and we'll be ready," Lauren said.

"I appreciate it."

CHAPTER FIFTEEN

A ntonio gripped his briefcase in a way that made Wiley think
someone would come and rip it away if he let go. The way the
leather was worn away there showed it was a habit.

The only prison she'd ever been in aside from this one was in
Kandahar, Afghanistan. That assignment was more to her liking since
they'd released political prisoners, who in turn had helped with the war
effort. As she'd watched those men and a few women take their first
tentative steps of freedom she'd wondered what that'd be like. Bars had
never imprisoned her, but she'd never been truly free of her past.

The killing had taken a little of her peace of mind, even though
she knew the people she'd eliminated were, like those prison guards
and their militia backup, truly evil. Humanity and her sense of it was at
times a fragile thing, but she couldn't change what she'd done.

"It usually takes forty-five minutes or so to walk him down,"
Antonio said.

She nodded and almost laughed at the thought that he was afraid
she'd leave out of boredom. Unfortunately she was stuck here until
Mr. Pombo got whatever was bothering him off his mind, while her
dad worried in their hotel room. Whoever the two guys Antonio had
brought with him were, they'd disappeared when she'd agreed to this.

"Señor Pombo," Antonio said when Roth was finally ushered in.
"You look well."

"That's why I never minded paying you the big money," Roth said
as he was led to his seat. Once there, the guards shackled him to the
table and said something gruffly in Spanish. "Antonio knows how to lie
well to not hurt my feelings."

"I brought the representative you asked to speak to," Antonio said.

"I'd shake hands, but touching of any kind unless it's to beat the shit out of me isn't allowed." Roth lifted his hands as high as they'd go, showing her what a tight leash they had him on.

If that was the sum of her existence, she'd knock one of her teeth out and use it to slit her wrists. "You know what they say about karma, Mr. Pombo."

"Please, I'm miserable enough. Take the bitchy remarks down a notch."

"What can I do for you?"

"Just listen. I've had a good run, and when I went into this, I wasn't drunk or high enough to know it wouldn't last forever."

"If you're looking for a book deal, I can't help you." The sterile smell of this place was starting to give her a headache. The combination of bleach and sweat was overpowering.

"You think I'm stupid?" The statement suggested anger but Roth showed no emotion as he spoke. "I know why you're here and who sent you. Our mutual friend can't afford for me to live, even if it's in this fucking place." A thick chunk of his hair fell in his face, and he whipped his head back to try to remove it. That made it worse, since it appeared as if he hadn't washed it since he'd arrived here. This somewhat broken man had replaced the carefree guy she'd seen in Walter's slideshow.

"Your friend and I've been dancing around this since we met. If you've got something to say, now's the time. If you can't, you can't, but I won't beg." Being here was a mistake. It'd be difficult to shoot this guy and make it through customs without them recognizing her as Pombo's visitor. Perhaps Walter was right about Roth, and all this was about playing her. "Nice meeting you," she said, standing.

"Promise me a reprieve and I'll trade you something for it." He tried blowing the greasy hair from his eyes. "Take this if you have just a sliver of doubt about Walter," he said, almost in a whisper, but he still didn't sound desperate.

She glanced at the guard before she raised her hands. The thick, muscular guy nodded and she combed Pombo's hair back. "I'll give you a week if you make it worth my while," she whispered back as she touched him. "Remember, though, if not me, someone will come back."

"That's good news." He smiled and she almost believed him. Death was the only way he'd be free again, unless his religious beliefs were engrained. All those decapitated bodies were his ticket to another sort of hell, if the preachers were right. "It was fucking fun while it lasted, so the memories will suffice."

"Which one in particular do you want to share with me?"

"There was this girl one night that brought me to my knees. Changed the game for me so I put her in the last place the fuckers would look. Sometimes when it's right under your fucking nose, you miss stuff. Understand me?"

It sounded like gibberish actually, but she thought she was following. "Sounds like someone worth remembering."

"Yeah," Roth said, his face softening. "Amber nights and willowy trees bought me a few months of peace where Lee ponders the north. You should try it, and let me know if you enjoyed it as much as I did. Especially the sunsets."

"I'll do that." She repeated the information in her head so she wouldn't forget a detail. "What memories do you think it'll hold for me?"

"If I'm right, you'll find a story that'll change your view of things. It's like finding religion in a cutthroat world." Roth winked and laughed. "Even if we don't talk again, give Walter what I didn't get a chance to."

"Will do," she said, anxious to go. "Try to hang in there. It sounds corny, but close your eyes and think of that place. Every nuance, curve, and the smell of it. If all you see is that, then you can't see or hear the fluorescents."

"Thanks, and if my memories aren't compelling enough, then I'll buy you a beer in hell."

It was funny that Roth didn't raise as many alarms as Walter had in their first meeting. The other side of the gate was jammed with traffic, with a group of women with children praying and holding lit candles. She walked slower so Antonio could keep pace with her, but as soon as they'd cleared the wall of the prison she stopped.

"Good luck, Mr. Hernandez. You have my word I'll be on the next plane north, so Roth's safe from me. I have no idea if there's a backup, so if something happens it wasn't me."

"Did you understand what he wants?"

"I have a general idea. Is he allowed any communications with anyone besides you?" Amber Willow was holding Roth's ammunition, but she needed to know it was time to share.

"Only me and anyone on my staff. That's how I got you in, but no phone or computer." Antonio's ride was waiting on the street, and one of the men who'd accompanied him leaned against the front passenger door.

"Have you made any calls for him?"

"Yes, but you must tell me what all that meant if you want the number."

"I don't need the number, and if he'd wanted you to understand he'd have made it plainer. If you want my opinion, he didn't tell you to keep you safe. It looks like you've got enough problems." She cocked her head toward the car. "Maybe if you've made enough, you should consider retirement."

"The only way out of this trap is to chew my leg off. I'm too old and don't have the strength for that, but thank you for the good wishes. I return them tenfold."

She dialed her dad's number as she started toward their hotel. "Pack," she said when he answered. "I'll be there in less than thirty."

"The last flight today is after ten."

"Plan to be on it. We've got enough to think about."

❖

"You've got two minutes," the man said again, banging his fists against the metal door.

"Who do you think that is, Tanith?" Danielle asked, having to force her eyes from the screen to look at her.

"He came to see Wiley and she made us hide so he wouldn't know we were here." Tanith grabbed for her hand and, from her expression, finally resembled a terrified eight-year-old. "We didn't hear much, but I could tell Wiley didn't like him."

"We'll have to discuss later about keeping secrets, but I don't think they'll let you hide in your room this time." She took a deep breath at the thought of having to tell Wiley about this when she got home, but opened the freezer door anyway. "It's soundproof, so don't think you have to play dead, but don't come out until I open this door again." Peter nodded and she shut them in.

"If you damage anything I'm sure the media would love to

hear about it, so calm down until I get down there," she said into the intercom.

She was tempted to take the stairs to delay them even more, but opted for the elevator. On the way down she stirred up her wife-of-a-general persona and prepared to not take shit from anyone.

"What's this about?" she asked, bracing her hands on the door frame to block their entry, and almost let go when she saw how many agents were standing outside with their guns drawn.

"Please step aside, ma'am," the young man standing farther back said, not touching her. "We have a warrant to search for persons wanted for questioning in an ongoing investigation."

"If you wanted me I'll happily comply and save you the trouble, since I'm the only one here."

"We're wasting time," the man who Tanith recognized spat out. "She's lying."

"I most certainly am not."

"Who are you going to believe, her or the scan? There are five distinct heat signatures in there."

"Your equipment must be malfunctioning. I assure you I'm the only one here. If you don't believe me, a couple of you can take a look." Her confidence came from Wiley's eye for detail. The dragon's lair was a true void from the world. "Not you," she said, pointing at the man holding the warrant.

"You're in no position to give orders."

"Take it down a bit, Walter," the young woman standing next to him said.

"The warrant is only for people, right?" she asked.

"Yes, ma'am. I'm Special Agent Sean Porter and this is my partner Special Agent Lauren Blaise. We do have a right to come in, but we don't want to make this hard on you. Is Wiley Gremillion at home?"

"*Major* Wiley Gremillion is my daughter, and she and her father, *General* Buckston Gremillion, are out of town for a few days on business. I'm here helping her finish unpacking, but if you don't believe me I'll allow you two to do a walkthrough."

Both agents glanced at the man they'd called Walter before following her through the door. "I realize I'm a scary old woman, but please don't point those at me," she said, motioning to their weapons. "And save it. I know more about protocol and procedure than the two of you."

She stood in every doorway as they looked in every possible hiding place, finding nothing. In the room Aubrey and Tanith were sharing, Lauren picked up the portable gaming device and held it up toward her.

"Whose is this?"

"Mine," she answered quickly, without blinking.

"Yours?" Sean asked, smiling.

"A silly gift from Wiley to hone my reflexes. Turned out to be pretty addictive."

"There were five heat signatures in here, ma'am," Lauren said.

"Call down and have them do it again. I'm positive you're mistaken."

They continued their search even after it was confirmed that the only people moving around were the three of them. Even though they were in the clear, Danielle insisted they finish what they came to do. It took a couple of hours but Sean and Lauren had been thorough, even opening the trunk of every car on the main level.

"Satisfied?" she asked when they reached the door.

"I know this is an inconvenience for you, but we had to search," Lauren said.

"It's not an inconvenience, young lady, it's an insult considering what my daughter has done and sacrificed for this country. I also know you're not about to share with me what this is about, but you're dead wrong if you think Wiley has done something unsavory."

"You have a right to read the search warrant, ma'am," Sean said. "The people we were looking for are part of an ongoing investigation with national-security concerns."

"You think Wiley's harboring terrorists? Who's your supervisor?"

"Special Agent Annabel Hicks," Sean said.

"Thank you, now get the hell out of Wiley's home, and if you come back you both will regret it."

"It's not wise to threaten government officials, ma'am," Lauren said.

"It's not as stupid as searching the home of a highly decorated veteran for terrorists. I'm not threatening you with physical harm, only promising you that my story will be much more interesting to the national news folks. If you're through wasting my time, get out." She slammed the door and leaned against it to calm the jumble of nerves running rampant through her stomach. The situation was getting truly bizarre.

"The real hissy fit will begin when she gets back and I tell her where I had to stash her terrorists," she said softly, and laughed.

❖

"This is fucking unbelievable," Nunzio Luca said as the driver took the road along the coast in Biloxi. "All those big houses, fucking gone. Are these guys sure this place is coming back? It looks like someone nuked all this."

"Our type of business is being rebuilt faster than the casinos. The state wants all of them open as soon as possible so the money will start flowing again." Tracy was still pressed up against the door with her face turned away from him toward the water. Maybe he'd been harsh, but setting strict rules from the beginning was important. Things wouldn't get confused if he kept to the promises he'd made himself.

"I don't see that happening, but then I don't give a fuck. We aren't here to live in this heat pit fighting off mosquitoes. I just need a steady product coming in so we can go to work."

The construction crews along the beach were knocking off for the day, so the traffic was at a crawl. Their driver finally turned at the lighthouse and headed inland. Miguel Gonzalez had picked a place called Jazzeppi's, and from the number of cars in the lot, it was one of the only open choices. Actually, from the look of it, the storm surge had stopped twenty feet from the building, sparing it and the railroad tracks behind it.

"Is this guy trying to butter me up?" he asked, seeing it was an Italian restaurant. "That'll be a leap since these rednecks know nothing about sauce."

"I'm sure it was either this or his apartment," Tracy said. She got out and waited so she could walk behind him to the door.

"Mr. Luca," the attractive blonde behind the desk said. "Welcome to Jazzeppi's. Mr. Gonzalez apologizes but he's running late. He insists you have a drink in the private room he's reserved. He'll be about ten minutes."

"Did he send a picture of me or something?"

"I'm sorry if you're not Mr. Luca, but our manager has a picture of him and your father. The resemblance is uncanny."

"Is your manager here?"

"He's out for two weeks, and I know he'll be sorry to have missed you." The woman led them to an intimate room and closed the door with a promise of drinks.

"Now we know why Gonzalez picked this place. Anyone who was a friend of my father's has his own heightened sense of paranoia."

Miguel took a few more than ten minutes to arrive, but this time Nunzio didn't mind as much. If given a preference, he'd do business with the Delarosa family instead of the mysterious Emray.

"My apologies, Mr. Luca," Miguel said, with a thick but understandable accent. "This town has become a hive of activity and confusion."

"No problem, and thanks for agreeing to meet."

"Tonight we will eat and you will tell me your problems," Miguel said as he poured himself a glass of wine.

"And what will you talk about?" This guy had a way and style about him that he found aggravating. He'd never been able to pull off that kind of ease with anyone.

"I am here because we," Miguel pointed between them and smiled, "or should I say you and my boss, have a common but different problem."

"What's that mean?"

"Our common interest is I believe the same. We both want to build a good business, as is our right, and we want to keep it safe."

"I'm listening."

"Our common problem is a man named Emray Gillis." Miguel made the name sound exotic. "He is causing problems for our shipments, and for you he hides behind the little men who work for him."

Nunzio leaned forward and put his elbow on the table. "You know this guy? I mean, you've met him?" His anger rose so quick he clenched his fists, making Miguel lean back.

"I personally have not, but he has sat down with Mr. Delarosa. We have never done business with him."

"May we know why?" Tracy asked, and Nunzio turned and stared at her as a warning to keep quiet.

"But of course, señorita." Miguel smiled at her. "My boss never does business with anyone who never allows him to speak during a meeting. His other sin was believing he was the smartest person in the room." Miguel seemed to relax again as he kept his eyes on Tracy.

"Does Delarosa know anything about this guy?" Nunzio asked.

"*Mr.* Delarosa knows so many things it is very hard to remember, and you are in no position to be disrespectful, Mr. Luca."

"Sorry, but this Emray has done nothing but yank my dick since we started our deal. His lapdog Mitch wants a shitload of my money without me laying eyes on his boss. I'm not stupid."

The way Miguel stared at him made him believe he did consider him more than stupid after all his mistakes. "Listen, Mr. Luca," Miguel said, pouring himself more wine. "You can thank a long-lost friend for my being here tonight, but loyalty will buy only so much of my time. I'm not here to listen to you cry like a child who wants the treat his mother will not give him."

"What old friend?" As much as he tried to curb the parts of himself that'd allowed his enemies to exploit him, casual comments like that shredded his ability to curb his response.

"When you were first here with your casino and your father's backing, I answered a call from Kim Stegal. We discussed a deal between your family and the Delarosas. Kim never felt comfortable with what you'd worked out."

"You met with Kim?" He shut his jaw and glared at Tracy again. If Kim had gone behind his back to get to this guy, it'd happened again. "Actually, never mind all that. Are you here to talk about the past or business?"

"How much product are you able to buy?"

"I've got fifteen large, and once we transport we can work out a regular delivery." He tried taking deep breaths to squelch the fire in his chest. "I've got the cash close, so it's not like you have to wait to get paid."

"You offered Emray the same deal?"

"Only with a meet. If he won't sit down with me, I'm not showing him a dollar."

"He turned down your money because of that?" Miguel asked before finishing his wine.

"Hell, yes." He poured Miguel's next glass, finishing the bottle. "Would you do business with a ghost?"

"If Mr. Delarosa had, we would not have climbed very high in this world." Miguel twirled his glass by the stem. "Thank you for coming tonight. I will talk with Mr. Delarosa about you and your needs."

"You're done?"

"The food here is good, so please enjoy, but yes, I am done for tonight. I will call you once I have something for you."

Miguel kissed Tracy's hand before he left, and Nunzio waited until he closed the door before he moved. He lashed out and grabbed that same hand and squeezed until Tracy grimaced. He knew if he pressed harder he'd break her fingers.

"What else have you done behind my back?"

"Please, you're hurting me." Tracy tried to pull her hand free by hitting his wrist. "I didn't do anything to betray you, and I had no idea Kim talked to these people before she died."

"I'm here practically begging because everyone fucked me over. My business was stolen from me, my father was murdered, and I was tossed aside like some bitch who didn't deserve any respect." He squeezed harder and enjoyed the tears that pooled in Tracy's eyes. "If you think I'm going to let that happen again, you're as crazy as you are stupid."

"You wanted another option aside from Emray, and I tried to give it to you." Tracy was crying in earnest and stopped trying to get away from him. "Maybe you're right—I should leave. Kim left me a little money, so I'll be okay on my own."

"Giving up already?" He let go and she turned away from him, cradling her hand against her body. "You have to understand where I'm coming from."

"I do, and I know you don't need or trust me. Whatever you felt you owed my sister, you've done enough." Tracy stood and walked out, but he guessed it was only to get herself together in the restroom. After thirty minutes, he cursed himself for his weakness but went looking. Tracy was gone, and she had a good head start.

❖

"You sure you don't need me to call someone to look at your hand?" Miguel said in Spanish. His head hurt from the wine he'd consumed and from the concentration it took to sound coherent in English. "It's swollen, so it might be broken."

"It's not," Tracy answered in decent Spanish. "He wasn't thrilled with your confession that Kim talked with you. If I ice it, it'll be okay. Thanks for waiting around outside."

"Nunzio is as predictable as the sun rising in the morning. He's a man with very little imagination." He packed a plastic bag with ice, wrapped it in a towel, and placed it on her hand when he sat next to her on his sofa. The condo he'd purchased a few years before when they'd started to expand in the U.S. markets was in one of the only buildings still standing along the shoreline. "It's one of the reasons I always thought your sister's brains and talent were wasted on him."

"Love has nothing to do with brains, Miguel, you know that."

"And sometimes it has everything to do with it." Kim had called on the pretense of doing business with their organization, but that wasn't her main reason. She'd figured out Nunzio would never come out of the war he'd started without major losses and casualties. Her only miscalculation was her death and not Nunzio's. She had, though, protected the one thing in her life she loved: Tracy. A raw talent he was confident would surpass Kim's accomplishments before too long.

"Why did you agree to protect me?" Tracy asked, leaning against him.

"My ambition will never lead me to want to break from Hector, but there are so many men with us who want my job." Tracy had been seventeen when they'd first met, and even then he knew she'd be as beautiful as her sister. At that age, he'd been able to influence every aspect of her life. "To protect what I have is tiring, so I need someone to watch my back. I want that to be you."

"Are you pleased with what I found out?"

"You always please me, but you did give me the answers I needed to an interesting development. That'll please Hector as well."

"A bonus, I guess, but you're the only one I'm interested in making happy." Tracy turned to face him and placed her injured hand on his chest. "Please don't send me away for so long again."

The thought of his wife and two daughters back in Colombia crossed his mind and just as quickly left it. At seventeen Tracy, he had figured, would be a body he could use to satisfy his need until he got to go home, but after one taste, he was hooked. He imagined this was what the addicts felt like when they raised their crack pipes to their lips. "No, beautiful one, you won't be leaving my side again."

He hoped Nunzio had enjoyed the little bit he'd allowed Tracy to share with him, because that wouldn't happen again. "You're home," he said, staring down at his hard dick in her swollen hand.

Tracy straddled him and he laughed when he realized she was naked under her skirt. He hissed when she mounted him, glad she insisted on not using any type of protection. If he was lucky, Tracy wouldn't only share his life, but she'd give him what his wife couldn't now—a son. If she did, he'd give her whatever she wanted in return, even if it was Nunzio Luca's head for what he'd allowed to happen to her sister.

CHAPTER SIXTEEN

W hat's this place?" Tanith asked, her eyes roaming the walls and computer screens in what Aubrey could tell was fascination.

"I'd guess this is Wiley's secret place," Aubrey said, almost closing her eyes, not wanting to intrude on Wiley's privacy more than they had already. From the first night here she'd enjoyed studying the paintings on the walls, getting a sense of who Wiley kept hidden from the world. How ironic that now she had those on display for everyone to see and kept this a secret. The reality of the Wiley she'd known seemed skewed and lost. "Don't touch anything."

"Not even this?" Karen asked, holding the frame on Wiley's desk.

She had a copy of that same photo, and in a bizarre way, it'd saved her and Tanith's lives. Before she walked out on Maria she'd wanted to make sure she took all her treasures with her. This picture and the hundreds they'd taken through the years were in boxes still in the attic where they'd hid. Aubrey ran her fingers over the glass when her mom handed it over and tried to swallow.

"Do you still love her, Mom?" Tanith stood right next to her so she could look at the picture as well.

"I never stopped." That was in so many ways the sad truth of her life. She'd found who she wanted as the young girl in this picture, which should've translated into a lifetime of bliss. Only finding Wiley so early had turned into a curse because no one else would ever measure up. Not really.

"I don't understand," Tanith said.

"That makes two of us, honey." She put the frame back and looked at the gun cabinets. "Something happened and Wiley had to leave to keep me safe. She did that because she loved me, but it was still hard."

"That sucks."

She had to laugh at Tanith's blunt assessment. "True."

"Is she some kind of commando like in the movies or something?" Tanith asked, obviously willing to forget the sentimental talk for the cool toys behind the glass.

"Wiley's actually one of the only female snipers ever to serve in the army's special forces," Peter said from the chair in front of the screens.

The word *sniper* made Tanith's expression light up, as if her grandfather had said Wiley was Wonder Woman, Supergirl, and Batgirl all rolled into one. "Do you think she'd tell me about it when she gets back?"

"I'm sure she would if you talk to her." Aubrey couldn't help but go back to the picture. Why here of all the places in the house?

"Do you think Wiley likes me?" Tanith didn't sound as confident.

She guided her to the other side of the desk and sat her in her lap. "See how this tree in the picture looks like a dragon," she said, and Tanith nodded. "We were a little older than you when we found it, but we'd go and sit there in the afternoons and talk. The Dragon Tree heard all our plans and dreams, and our one wish."

"What?"

"That we'd be together forever with a family of our own." She kissed Tanith's temple and tightened her hold on her. "So even though Wiley had to go away, she didn't stop wanting that."

"She told you that?"

Karen smiled, as if giving her permission to tell the lie. "Yeah, and she can't wait to get to know you. She's got your name tattooed on her arm, after all."

Thankfully the answer seemed to be enough and they all stayed quiet as the search continued outside. Aubrey thought about how Wiley had lived and functioned with no one but her parents. Or maybe that was being presumptuous of her. Maybe she didn't live with anyone, but had found someone to share a bit of her life. If that was true, whoever it was had to be extremely understanding, since Wiley's house didn't contain a trace of them.

Even if Wiley wanted to open herself to her and Tanith, this room meant her old friend the Black Dragon wasn't truly gone. Eventually

Tanith would lose her childish wonder and see Wiley for what she was and what the government expected of her. Hell, that most probably wasn't a good argument, since she doubted Tanith would ever not consider Wiley cool.

When the door opened she startled enough to jiggle Tanith in her lap. Danielle smiled and stepped in. "I don't think we need to discuss what a secret this room is, right?"

"Thanks for trusting us," Karen said.

"How do you think Wiley's going to take this?" she asked.

"Don't worry about that. It's not like we could help it." Danielle held her hand out to Tanith. "If you were the guy named Walter, you'd have a problem." They all stood in the kitchen and watched Danielle close the back of the freezer. "Let's go through the steps of how to access that room in case we need to use it again."

"Do you think they'll be back?" Karen asked.

"They didn't find what they came for, so I wouldn't discount it, but hopefully Wiley and Buck will be back before that happens," Peter said, and almost as if he'd conjured them up, the phone rang.

The explanation didn't take Danielle long, and she said the word *yes* about twenty times, obviously answering Wiley's questions. "She's right here, hold on," Danielle said before handing her the phone and escorting everyone into the den.

"Are you okay?" Wiley asked, their connection static-filled and noisy.

"Your mom made sure we were, and I'm sorry we had to barge into your space."

"It's not like you're going to put an ad in the paper." Wiley actually joked. "At least now you know they won't let go without a fight. You should think about that."

"You'll need a better line of attack, Major. Tanith is setting up a fan club now."

"We both know better than that, and I'm sorry you had to go through that when I wasn't there. Walter, if he was behind this, was out of bounds. I'm sure he and the rest of those guys won't be back, so you'll be fine." An announcement that sounded like it was coming from a speaker close by came over the line in Spanish. "That's our flight."

"Did something go wrong?"

"Not yet, so keep your fingers crossed it stays that way. I'll see you soon."

Those were the words Wiley always said right before they parted in their past. "Keep your head down, and try to get some sleep on the way home." She smiled at Danielle as she listened to Wiley's steady breathing on the line. "When you get back we'll figure something out."

"It's time for a little offense, so you bet."

❖

"What were Levi and Kevin doing outside Almoloya?" Carter Winslow asked Walter. The flight FBI Agent Annabel Hicks had escorted Walter onto had arrived ten minutes before at the private airstrip Carter had leased for the night. For nine minutes of that time he'd listened to Walter curse, since he'd had his men disarm him as soon as the plane's door opened.

"The last time they checked in, Levi said they were following a lead that initiated from you in New Orleans. I need the answer to that as well as the reason you were in New Orleans." Carter crossed his legs and ran his finger along the top edge of his diet-soda can. Walter could scream all he wanted, but it wouldn't rattle him. "Why you got the FBI involved is something we'll get to eventually, so relax."

"Carter, you don't ever get your hands dirty in the field, so let me explain a few simple concepts. With Levi's help, we brought down Pombo and let the retards from the federales take the credit."

He didn't glance up when Walter smashed the table top with his open hand. "You reported the Pombo case closed. According to you, no other involvement was needed, not without giving away our involvement." He flipped through the file his boss, Craig Orvik, had given him after he told him to take care of it. "Why press the Pentagon for a shooter? Is Pombo's case closed or not?"

"Don't you think he's going to throw all of us under the federale bus to save his ass?" Walter stood up and pressed his back into the nearest wall. "Isn't the objective of our job to not leave a friend behind?"

"We've already taken steps to make anything Pombo says not believable, so he's not your problem anymore."

Walter stepped closer to him. "Why has Orvik cut me off?"

"He's busy trying to explain your two dead team members to the director, as well as why you pressured Major Gremillion and, more precisely, why everything you told him to pressure the Pentagon with didn't pan out. Enough history, though. Tell me what happened with Levi and Kevin."

"We were following leads that Pombo was still conducting business from jail. His operation is an octopus with thousands of tentacles. Levi volunteered to stay in Mexico while I tried to pick up anything stateside that'd lead us to the Tajr group Pombo was working with."

"What were Levi and Kevin doing the day they died?" He aimed Walter's chair in his direction and pointed at him to sit. "Before you answer, you should know that Levi called Mr. Orvik, and he did take that call."

"What's this about, then? Careful with trying to burn me, Carter. I *will* make you sorry if you have the balls to do it."

"Mr. Orvik needs your side of things to close this, so take your paranoia down some."

"My paranoia is why I'm still alive." Walter was flip, but the sweat was pooling at the waist of his pants.

"If you need bluntness, then you're done. Pombo brought some arrests, but the death of two of our people wasn't worth it. You can walk with no pension, which Mr. Orvik will take into consideration, or you can stay. You know him well enough to know what steps he'll take." Carter picked up all his paperwork and placed it in his briefcase. "Let me know what you decide. I'll give you a few days to think it over."

"I don't need time," Walter said, moving uncomfortably close to him. "Tell Orvik he's a chickenshit for not coming himself, and if he tries to push me out he'll have his own lynch mob to deal with. You can fuck yourself."

Carter watched him leave and nodded at the guys with him to follow. "Sir," he said when Craig Orvik answered, "he refused and walked." He went on to tell him everything Walter had said, including the threats.

"Make sure you don't lose him."

"Anything else?"

"Pay Mr. Pombo a visit since you're already there, only go through his attorney. We're missing something and I need to know what that is. Once you're done, make New Orleans your next stop. Tell this shooter it's in his best interest to give up whatever Walter shared with him."

"Wiley's a woman, sir, but don't worry. I'll cut off all the loose ends."

"Don't miss any. Make double sure of that."

"Yes, sir." Carter hung up and pulled Wiley's file. He had his orders, so if it took a nuke to scorch the land Walter had made, he wanted to know what he was up against. From the first paragraph of the classified information he knew the mountain had gotten much steeper.

"You don't realize what you're asking," he said to himself about Orvik's order regarding Wiley. "Jesus."

❖

"What's first?" Buckston asked as their plane took off.

"If you're not too tired, I'd like to stop at the FBI office before we head home. I've already called and made an appointment with the agents responsible for the search." Wiley took out a notebook and started writing down everything that had happened since Walter showed up with Don. It was time to draw connections among all the players as well as the events.

"What do you need from me?"

"The hard-ass attitude you do so well. I'm not going to appreciate an audience if I've got to stretch my wings a little."

"No problem," Buck said, then reclined his seat and closed his eyes.

She had an idea of how to get Walter out of her life, but she didn't have an exact road map. Her only real clue was the woman Pombo had mentioned. She doubted Amber Willow was in the book, but it was a start.

Agents Lauren and Sean were waiting when they arrived at their offices from the airport. Wiley didn't care to be put in an interrogation room, but it was necessary.

"Can you explain why you showed up with a team to search my daughter's house?" Her father's voice sounded especially loud in the enclosed space. "And before you throw out the word *classified*, call this number and check my level of clearance."

"We had information of a Tajr sect setting up in New Orleans, so we had no choice but to follow up, sir," Sean said.

"You thought I'm branching out into terrorism?" she said, laughing. "Did you even ask about me before you scared my mother with the show of force?"

"The tip led us to your door, Major. You know we didn't have any choice but to go wherever it took us."

"Who was nice enough to deliver this gift?" she asked, concentrating on their expressions. "It had to be some generous guy, because I don't think I pinged your radar because a sect leader friended me on Facebook."

"We can't give those kinds of details," Lauren said, and her father took his phone out and pressed one of his contacts. He gave his tag number and asked for the secretary of defense. Lauren hesitated, but her dad motioned for her to continue. "Both of you would've done the same in that position."

"You might want to call your supervisor in," she said when her dad placed his phone on the table, the speaker feature on. The classical music always made her want to laugh. Considering that it was the Pentagon, she thought they should've played a snappy military march tune instead.

"Major Gremillion," the woman at the door said. "I'm Special Agent Annabel Hicks, and while I'd love to talk to the secretary, let's us straighten out a few things before we waste his time. General, it's a pleasure, sir," Annabel said when he disconnected the call.

"I need a name, ma'am," she said, once the niceties were done.

"Walter Robinson came and dropped this off as bait." Annabel placed a file on the table. Wiley flipped though it, not having to read anything since it was the same crap Walter had shown her the day they met. "Both of you know I couldn't ignore the Tajr connection, but we didn't go in blind. The courtesy I gave you was giving in to your mother's wishes to have only my two agents search your place. Before we got the warrant I made a few calls about Walter. His supervisor told us he was not sanctioned for his visit here and his talks with you were out of bounds. No one over Walter's pay grade had cleared whatever he asked for."

"Contact Colonel Don Smith in Washington. He was the first person Walter reached out to, and once he asked for his favor, Don, as well as his supervisor, General Carl Greenwald, received plenty of pressure from someone other than Walter. Both men wanted me to come out of retirement."

"Major Wiley Gremillion, code name Black Dragon, recently retired and hands off, according to General Greenwald and Colonel

Smith. From what wasn't redacted from the file they shared, you're almost mythical," Annabel said with a smile.

"You don't have to worry, ma'am. The army will vouch for my mental stability. My being here will not be an issue."

"I'm not your problem, Major."

"I'm retired, it's Wiley." She flipped through the file again until she got to the picture of the alleged terrorist. "Can I have a copy of this?"

"The entire file is yours."

"A gift?" she asked, knowing nothing in life was free.

"Yes, but if you're a stickler for thank-you notes, address it to Don. My gift is the call I received from Craig Orvik. After an incident in Mexico, Walter is now considered burned. He walked out of a meeting to explain how his team was killed in a way that suggested one of the cartels was responsible."

"Thank you for the information, and I'll return the favor by coming by and telling you this story's ending." She stuffed all the pictures into the file and shook Annabel's hand again. "I hate to be piggish about asking for anything else, but you and your team need to stand down."

"That's the orders we've gotten, so no worries. The only way you'll see us again is if you ask, or if the Tajr angle pans out."

"If Walter was right about that, you have my word you'll be my first call." She walked out, with her dad right behind her. Annabel had been extremely helpful but not exactly truthful. No way in hell would she make her agents back off, but that could be useful, especially when it came to keeping Aubrey and her family safe.

❖

The lights were low throughout the house when Wiley and Buckston got home, and she enjoyed the hug he gave her before he headed toward his bedroom. She wasn't tired, but a shower was necessary before bed. In the morning she had to find a way to visit General Lee without the world watching.

She flipped the bathroom light off and stopped before she reached the bed. It'd been a long time since she'd found Aubrey in her bed anywhere but in her dreams, but that's where she was, lying on her side waiting on her.

"Do you think for one night we can turn back the clock?"

"To what date?" she asked, her fingers twitching from the urge to paint Aubrey like this.

"To right after you kissed me for the first time. It was easier to get you to hold me after that."

"Letting go was the hardest thing I ever did," she said, sitting on the edge of the bed. "Holding you was always my privilege."

"I've always loved the way you express yourself." Aubrey sat up and scooted closer so she could take her hand. "It was one of so many things I missed, but the top of my list has to be the feel of you. I always loved how you held me, Wiley."

"Hopefully Maria gave you a little of that."

"If you want me to lie, I will, but that won't excuse me my sins. I'm still not sure who I'm angrier at, Maria or myself. After I moved in with her I allowed myself to become someone I would've readily criticized once upon a time."

"What do you mean?" She didn't hesitate when Aubrey pulled her down and pressed against her.

"I've been a kept woman whose only contribution in a long time was picking furniture pieces and paint colors. She paid the bills and touched me even when I really didn't want it." Aubrey wrapped her fist in her T-shirt and exhaled against her neck. "I was a great prostitute."

"You're a great mom, and the rest is crap. Maria's gone, and once I'm done you'll be free to do whatever makes you happy."

"Don't say things you don't mean," Aubrey said, lifting herself up a little so she was looking down on her. "And it's okay to be honest. If you'd met me for the first time a year ago, nothing about me would've been memorable."

"Problem is, with your theory anyway, I didn't meet you a year ago. I met you when I was young and impressionable," she said, smiling as she touched Aubrey's cheek. "They give you rose-colored glasses when that happens, so you'll always get a pass from me."

"Let's hope that's always true," Aubrey said before she leaned the rest of the way down and pressed her lips to Wiley's. "Are you mad your mom showed us your room?"

"Now that you know it's there, you should realize who the real whore in the room is. The army isn't the kind of pimp to let go easily, so don't make any decisions out of misplaced loyalties. How we got here hasn't changed."

"Right now what I want is for you to not kick me out of here." Aubrey kissed her again before she lay back down. "If we take baby steps maybe we won't screw up as badly."

Wiley's craving won out, so she put her arms around Aubrey and closed her eyes. The bed moved again a few hours later but she didn't budge, not wanting to scare Tanith off. In a way she came alive again, if only a little, when Tanith took her hand and whispered, "Thank you, Wiley."

She didn't know what Tanith was grateful for, but it didn't matter. She wanted to pretend for one night what her life could've been. It was a reward to herself for doing without for so long.

CHAPTER SEVENTEEN

D o you think that's smart?" Buckston said when Wiley described the next part of the plan.

"I don't think Roth would've gone to the trouble for kicks. At least I'd like to think so. Who tries to piss off the person sent to kill you?" She sat back in her office chair and held her coffee cup against her chest. Since she hadn't spotted Aubrey or Tanith, she assumed they were both still asleep in her bed. "Right now all I have is Roth and some other bad guys that have drugs in common. Maria might've given me some information, but she's dead."

"You talked to Don," Buck said, crossing his bare feet at the ankles. "Walter's own people have fucked him over, so he's certainly not your problem anymore."

"So I should leave a wounded, cornered animal alone? He's been here, he came back looking for something, and he's going to keep coming back until he gets what he wants." The air kicked on again, raising goose bumps along her sweat-slicked body. She'd worked out but didn't want to disturb Aubrey and Tanith by taking a shower.

"Which do you think it is?"

"You've memorized my file, what's your guess?" She had the answer already and so did her father, but sometimes saying it out loud shook something loose.

"He came for you, but when you didn't roll over, he came for Aubrey."

"The question is, how did he know to come for Aubrey? She's in Carl's file of me, but that section of the paperwork is closed. So—"

"He's either a really lucky guesser, or there's some other connection. Which do you think it is?"

"The only way to know for sure, if I'm right in my game of connect the dots, is to talk to Amber Willow. I believe she doesn't have all the answers, but enough of them to get us going in the general vicinity of the right direction."

"What do you need from me?"

"A ride later, then to stay out of sight until tonight."

"You aren't seriously thinking of walking around Lee Circle out in the open? If someone wants you eliminated from all this, you can't pick a better location for a drive-by with multiple exit points."

Lee Circle was in fact a traffic circle with a small park featuring a bronze statue of General Robert E. Lee on a tall marble column in the middle. She'd driven around it numerous times but had never actually gotten out and walked the perimeter. "No. I have a better idea."

"I'm all ears."

"If that's true, you'd know we aren't the only ones up anymore. You'll have to be happy being surprised when we move out later," she said, laughing as she stood up.

Aubrey was in the kitchen rolling out biscuits when Wiley got downstairs, Tanith standing next to her with flour-covered hands. "I might have to buy a treadmill if this keeps up," she said, putting her hand on Tanith's shoulder. "Did you drug my mother to keep her away?"

"She's not up yet," Tanith said. "Her door's still closed."

"We wanted to thank you for not kicking us out last night," Aubrey said.

The light coming from the top-floor windows highlighted the subtle differences in Aubrey's hair from the way she remembered it, even though it was pulled into a tight ponytail. She lifted her fingers but not her hand off the island, having to force herself not to touch Aubrey's head.

"Let me see what's keeping her," Buck said, a foot already on the stairs. "Tanith, you want to come with me?"

"That's one of the slick moves he learned from my mother," Wiley joked when Tanith ran to keep up with him.

"I'm surprised you noticed." Aubrey wiped her hands.

"Them leaving or that my dad was trying to be smooth?"

Aubrey shook her head and rolled her eyes hard enough that she figured it'd make her dizzy if she tried it. "You're one of the smartest people I've ever known, but sometimes you need a hard blow to the head, Gremillion. They left because they know what your next move should be."

Aubrey stepped around the island and waited. The rest she figured was up to her. "Tell me why first."

"Why what?"

"You may want to gloss over what happened to the team I went to Colombia with, and ignore the danger of starting over with me, but why put Tanith in that spot?" Aubrey exhaled at her question and pressed her fist to her forehead. "I'm not asking you to blow you off."

"I need to give her as full a life as I can. As her mother I owe her that. In my heart, if I show her even a sliver of such a treat, it'd be enough. If I decide to walk away from you, I'd be safe, but I'd have the questions that the what-ifs would raise." Aubrey took a small step toward her as if to encourage her to close the gap. "A day of happiness is worth an eternity of misery to me."

"You always were a little on the syrupy side," Wiley said, taking Aubrey's hand and kissing it. "I'm not saying no, but we have a ways to go before I say yes."

"You always were practical," Aubrey said, pressing her body to Wiley's. "Right this minute you don't need to be. We've been apart a long while, but I haven't forgotten that tactician's mind of yours. It's an important part, but not the sum of who you are."

She couldn't stand it anymore. Not the indecision in Aubrey's voice, not the need, and certainly not the desire. When she put her arms around Aubrey's waist and lowered her head to kiss her, Aubrey's arms flew up and wrapped around her shoulders. She came close to laughing at every single cliché that momentarily flitted through her head about coming home, but Aubrey's insistent lips quieted her thoughts.

"Promise me you'll fight for this, that you won't chicken out because you can't guarantee the outcome," Aubrey said as she framed her face with her hands. Aubrey was crying again, but this time she had a smile so wide it made her laugh. As if to make her not overthink the situation Aubrey kissed her again. This time, though, the kiss was full of the passion she'd always experienced with Aubrey. She opened her mouth slightly and Aubrey took the invitation. The last time she'd been in this position she'd fallen into an abyss alone right after.

"My God," Aubrey said when their lips parted.

She rested her forehead against Aubrey's and closed her eyes. "You make me crazy."

"Someone has to," Aubrey said as she laid her head on her shoulder. "You need some craziness, and someone to have fun with. Do you remember how?"

"We've got some stuff to get through before we can think about fun." Aubrey kissed her again, quickly. "I'm not pushing you away," she said, following Aubrey as she tried to retreat.

"I know, but I'm tired of losing out to what needs to be done. What I want is for you—" Aubrey stopped and lowered her head. "I'm sorry, I'm not being fair."

It was time to quit running. Slowly she slid her hand around the side of Aubrey's neck under her hair. Aubrey didn't raise her head so she bent until she could reach her lips, knowing full well the message she was sending and what Aubrey would think if she pulled back again.

"You don't get to leave again without consequences," Aubrey said, tugging on her hair. "Not again."

"I know, but you still have to be patient. I shoved my emotions in a closet after I had to go, so it might take a while to brush the dust and wrinkles out."

"No one paints like that," Aubrey cocked her head toward the large canvas, "being emotionally numb."

"The memories—the legacy of that time with you kept me sane. Thanks," she said, before enjoying one last kiss.

"No need for gratitude, Major, but I'm getting antsy already for this to be over, so do what you need to finish."

"We have to find a few people so we can fill in the blanks. Once we have answers it's a matter of lining up the tin cans so we can knock them down."

"Can you do that now that you're a civilian?"

"The Black Dragon might be hibernating, but she's not completely asleep," she said, picking up the phone. "We need permission to let me huff and puff a little." She dialed the number from memory and waited. "Don, how about a trip down South?"

"Will he mind that I'm here?" Aubrey asked, finishing her biscuits, her tone uncertain again.

"He gave me your message in person, and he called when he saw you and your dad on the news."

"Did you get a lecture?" Aubrey asked, laughing.

"No, Don's my friend and I trust him because he knows me." She held her hand out to Aubrey, smiling when she didn't hesitate to take it. "He not only knew I'd call, but that I'd help you."

"Did you have to think about it? Are you sorry?"

"I did think about it," she said, and Aubrey let her go. "Not because I didn't care, but because I knew I couldn't turn away from you twice in my life. Twice wasn't in me."

"And all your fears?"

"I'll have to learn to live with them."

"And if you don't?"

She kissed Aubrey's knuckles when she offered her hand again. "Then I'd have to let you go."

"Learn to accept them and remember what I said. A day of happiness is better than a life without you. If I get that day, and all of you, then all this time without you won't have been for nothing because now we know how precious this is." Aubrey smiled as she kissed her palm. "But I know you. You'll fight whoever and whatever to get what you want. A long time ago you forgot that, but I have faith you're smart enough to learn from your mistakes."

"I can't fight logic like that."

"No wonder you were promoted so much."

The chance that Walter still had the authority to have anyone watch her house was slim, but Wiley didn't take any chances when she pulled out late that afternoon. After breakfast, the day had been both familiar and bizarre. Sitting and spending time with Aubrey and her family had been familiar, but bizarre in that she'd figured she'd never do it again.

Aside from getting reacquainted with Aubrey she enjoyed her long conversation with Tanith the most. She'd taken Tanith into her studio and talked to her while she started a new piece. The exercise had calmed her, and Tanith had opened up since she wasn't staring at her. Tanith was incredibly bright, but after a few hours with her, she picked up on some of her fears and a subtle shyness that'd disappear one day when Tanith grasped how special she was.

"You sure about this?" Buckston asked when they turned toward St. Charles Avenue. "If anyone with a bit of talent is watching, you're an easy shot."

He was right, but what choice did she have? She'd thought Don would've gotten here in time to send someone who wouldn't be a known entity in this game, but that was out. The homeless guy with the WILL WORK FOR FOOD sign gave her an idea. He hustled over when she rolled her window down.

"How about an easy hundred?"

The guy looked at her, then Buck before he shook his head. "I'm not into anything kinky."

"Good to know since we want you to keep your pants on at all times. I need you to take this and head over to Lee Circle." She handed him a phone and the hundred. "If you take my call and hand the phone off to whoever I tell you to, I'll give you a couple more of those."

After he accepted, she drove to the World War II Museum to park and shouldered her backpack. She and Buck crossed the street to the Ogden Museum but walked through the tight space alongside the building to reach the hotel that overlooked the circle. A few minutes later after she'd picked the lock they were on the roof with a good view of a few city blocks.

Their friend had left his sign behind and grasped the cell she'd given him tightly in his hand. From what she could see through her scope, no one around him appeared to be waiting. Twelve other men were sitting around, so she widened her search.

"Call him and tell him to say he has a call for Roth. He doesn't need to shout," she said to her dad as she emptied her pack. The rifle it contained wasn't her favorite, but in such an open area she had no choice because the gun broke down into four pieces, fitting easily in the small pack. Its scope was much more powerful than her binoculars.

Three blocks down she spotted a familiar car, and after adjusting the scope for distance she saw fake cop sitting with his head reclined, smoking a cigarette. He lifted his head and scanned his mirrors and the area in front of him every few minutes. "What are you doing here?" she said softly, watching how he massaged the scar on his face.

"We got a taker, but if his name's Amber, he must have mommy issues," her father said.

"You know Roth?" the man in shorts and dark polo shirt said to her on the phone. The outfit was touristy, but the powerful scope let her see the logos. If he was Amber's stand-in, she didn't find him on a street corner.

"I spoke to him recently," she said to the guy in the polo shirt, but watched fake cop.

"Bullshit."

"You don't believe me, call his lawyer, Mr. Hernandez, and ask, but careful before you take the chance. Roth didn't sound like he wanted anyone but me to know about this meeting." Fake cop lifted binoculars and pointed them toward the circle. He was obviously looking for someone or had a real interest in Confederate military losers.

"What did he say?"

"In a roundabout way he gave me this location and Amber Willows's name. I'd like to know if you know how to get in touch with her. Roth wanted us to have a conversation."

"Nowhere in the open."

The binoculars were still up to fake cop's eyes, and his movements showed that he'd started his car. "Your friend on the phone is on the move," her dad said. If fake cop was ready to go, that meant he knew who Amber's friend was.

"Does anyone know you're here?" she asked as she released the safety. The shot, if she had to take it, was over five hundred yards.

"No, and I'm going to keep it that way by not meeting anywhere in public. If you can't agree to that we don't have anything else to talk about."

"Name the place, and I need you to stay calm. There's a guy close to the television-station building and he's made you. I need you to get going and keep the phone. Give my messenger a couple hundred, but that's the only person you should talk to on your way out."

"Where do you want to meet?" The guy sounded like he was trying to keep it together, but his breathing was starting to change.

"Walk away and wait for my call. I promise it'll be as soon as I make sure you leave alone."

She adjusted her angle to compensate for the slight breeze and moved her fingers to the side of the trigger. Fake cop glanced into his side mirror, getting ready to move, but before he merged into traffic, she took her shot. The expression of shock, then horror on fake cop's face was almost funny when his engine shot a line of steam from the hole she'd made in the hood. He went from gripping the steering wheel to diving under the dash in a heartbeat.

"You can't be dumb enough to think I missed, can you?" she said to fake cop, sweeping the area again to see if she could spot who she now knew was Mitch Surpass. "Anyone else look interesting?"

"No one stands out, and I don't see the guy whose picture you showed me."

The silencer did its job since she'd shot fake cop's car in front of the NBC affiliate and no one came rushing out, so after a few minutes, she dismantled the rifle and motioned her father to the door.

"I need you to drive back with one stop on the way. After this, whoever that guy was on the phone is spooked, so we don't need a crowd scaring him underground and taking Amber with him."

Buck didn't appear thrilled with her plan but relented, heading toward the shopping center next to the aquarium. He drove in and out, not stopping or phoning her until he reached her place. "Thanks, Dad, and I'll call you when I'm done."

"Hello." The man sounded out of breath.

"Where do you feel the most comfortable for a talk?" She rode the elevator up to the Westin lobby on the twelfth floor and walked into the bar. The man on the line was silent. "I know you said not public, but how about the Westin?"

"That's pretty crowded since it's packed with workers."

"You've obviously done a great job keeping Amber safe, but after having to take a shot at the location Roth gave me, someone else knows she's here. Someone who knows who you are too."

"Roth wouldn't have given us up, so why wouldn't I believe it's you laying the trap?"

"I can't convince you. The decision to talk to me is your choice, but I'm not out to hurt you." She pointed to the club soda as she picked a bar stool.

"Roth told us whoever showed up would be the person sent to kill him." The slam of a car door meant the mystery man had arrived somewhere. "He said to stop going to the meet point if the news reported him dead."

"He was more persuasive than the guy who sent me to put a bullet in his head. Roth Pombo was simply a job, and I didn't complete it. Now the guy who ordered the hit is no longer in a position to make anyone finish it, but that doesn't mean he won't end up dead." She looked intently but briefly at everyone sitting in the bar. "In my talk with Roth, I got the impression him giving up his secrets had to do with payback more than anything. I'll be here for thirty minutes if you want to give him that."

"How will I know you?"

"I'll know you, so be careful on the way over."

"Nothing?" Nunzio said when the new guards he'd flown in entered his suite. He'd stayed overnight in Biloxi searching for Tracy, but she'd disappeared so effectively he hadn't found any sign of her.

"We looked at every hotel and talked to the few cabs in the area, boss," the taller of the men said. "She either walked or caught a ride with someone to somewhere out of Biloxi. We spread around enough cash to flush her out if she was still here."

Her cell was also off and not accepting any other messages. The temper he'd displayed toward her had backfired, and he was the one learning a valuable lesson. He'd pushed away the one person aside from his grandfather who gave a fuck about him. All he could do was write her off or wait until she was ready to come back.

"Call the guys back," he said, dismissing everyone from the room. Not only had Tracy not called, but Miguel had vanished, not answering any of the three messages he'd left. His patience for this place and the supposed suppliers he was trying to cut a deal with was about to snap.

He wanted a deal so he could get back to New York and concentrate on building his business. The next time he came to Louisiana it'd be with an army of men who'd plow down anyone who'd fucked him over. There were plenty of names on that list, but to make sure no one escaped what he owed them, he'd bide his time to do it right.

The loud ring of his cell made him flinch, but he smiled when he saw the Mississippi area code. Tracy hadn't lasted on her own as long as he thought, so he gave his anger permission to bleed into his voice. "Where the fuck are you?"

"That's not important, Mr. Luca," Miguel Gonzalez, or who he assumed to be Miguel, said. "Do you have a problem?"

"Nothing important." He wiped his brow and stood, not knowing what to do with himself. "Do I get my meeting with Mr. Delarosa?"

"Even better, he offered to do business with you." Wherever Miguel was, it was windy. "All the product you can handle, delivered to New York, only the charge will be two thousand more a kilo."

"That's cutting a lot off the top."

"The offer is nonnegotiable and on the table for the length of this call."

"I don't get to meet with Mr. Delarosa either? That was the problem with Emray." He mouthed the word *fuck* three times, the sensation of having his short hairs and balls caught in a vise all too real. "The amount we're talking about isn't a few kilos."

"Your worry with Emray Gillis is understandable, but Mr. Delarosa should be known to you. His reputation is sound. If you do not know this, then perhaps you should return to the casino business." Miguel's breathing was steady and deep. "Do you wish to withdraw your request?"

Fuck, he mouthed again, not wanting to be rushed, so he took the chance. "I'd at least want his word he'll be willing to talk price after a few shipments."

"Our boss is a fair man, so we'll see how things progress."

"Yeah," he said, letting the word die away.

"Is there something else?"

"Have you spoken to Tracy again?" Asking hurt more than a shot to the gut.

"She has not phoned me again. Is there a problem I should know about?"

"Nothing that concerns any of this. I'll wait for your call so I can give you the money." He disconnected, then dialed Mitch Surpass and left a message. "You and your boss can go fuck yourselves on the mountain of powder I was going to buy."

He tried Tracy again, but just got constant ringing now. She was gone, and whatever debt he owed Kim was settled. He'd do this alone.

"So stay gone, you little bitch."

❖

The guy Wiley had been on the phone with walked in first, but he did little to hide the stunningly beautiful woman following a few steps behind him. If this was who Roth had on his mind while he rotted in prison, it wasn't the hum of the lights and the guards' batons driving him insane. Wiley stood and pointed to the table located behind a screen.

"You've seen him?" asked the blonde Wiley assumed was Amber Willows.

"I did." She turned her glass with her thumb and index finger. "Considering where he is, he looks okay. He talked as much as he could about you without causing you a problem."

"What's your name?" the woman asked.

"The best thing for both of us is to talk, then walk out of here knowing we aren't going to become coffee buddies or pen pals." She briefly took her eyes off Amber to make sure her friend was okay and that no one was overly interested in their conversation. "Roth wanted you to share something with me. That's all we have to talk about."

Wiley tensed when Amber reached for her purse and stuck her hand inside. The thick white envelope she retrieved stayed in her hand, so Wiley placed hers on her thighs to not present a threat.

"Roth knew it'd take more than talk for someone to believe what the assholes who helped bring him down promised him. The first of those lies was he'd never be in jail for any reason." She opened the flap and took out a sheet of paper. The letter, signed by Walter, basically said just that. "Everyone thought Roth was just a killer, but he's smart. He wrote it all down."

"What's your connection to him?"

Amber placed the envelope on the table and covered it with her hands. "I thought you didn't want to be friends?"

"If this is real," she handed the letter back, "I'll be happy to give it to the right people. To know it's real I need to know your connection to Roth and why he'd trust you with whatever else is in there."

"We were together for a year, then two months ago he got me out of the Baja and told me to come here. He has a place in the city." She closed her eyes, obviously upset having to talk about this. "We came once after we'd hooked up. It's safe and I have to stay until I hear from him."

"What happens if he gets killed?" Wiley took a sip of the watered-down soda. "I don't mean to be abrupt, but it's a real possibility."

"We have an out. Anything scares us and we walk." Amber placed her hand over mystery man's. "I'm staying because I owe it to Roth to try to help him."

"You don't have anything to fear from me unless you come after me or my family. I will, though, need to see this." She tapped the envelope slowly.

"I've been waiting for you." Amber pushed it away. "I'm free now."

"There was a man watching the circle today, and while I know who you are," she said to the guy with Amber, "he did too. Perhaps you've been safe and laid low, but someone knows you're here."

"Did you see this guy's face?" Amber asked.

"He has a scar from here to here," she said, running her finger along her cheek.

Both Amber and her companion stood at her description. "Are you sure?" Amber asked, and she nodded. "I've got to get out of here."

At the door the man hesitated and held up her phone, making her nod again. Whoever these two were and how they fit wouldn't be completely out of her reach if mystery guy kept the phone she'd given him. The secrets to unraveling what Walter was up to probably lay in Mexico, but she didn't want to fly south of the U.S. border unless she was on vacation or under order of the president. She didn't see either of those options in her future.

CHAPTER EIGHTEEN

Tell me why I shouldn't kill you?" Emray Gillis asked Mitch as they sat in the kitchen of Emray's house. The mound of coke was gone, replaced by kilo and dime bags.

"We sat on the guy you told us to watch. I used only Freddie and two other of our most trusted guys. No one's come close to this guy for two weeks, so when he got on the phone, Freddie went to check it out. The next thing we knew, some asshole shot his engine out."

"What's that mean?"

"There's a big fucking hole in the hood, and whatever bullet this douche bag used cracked the block." Mitch waved his hands around like a crazed maniac, but Emray barely noticed him.

A bullet placed precisely enough to take out the car but not cause enough of an issue that the cops flocked to the area. "Where was that moron parked?"

"In front of Channel Six," Mitch said.

Emray had to laugh. If you wanted to gamble and draw attention to yourself, taking the shot in front of a television news office was high stakes. "Did Freddie see anyone, or was he jerking off while he was supposed to be working?"

"You said to wait for the first guy who was out of place or acting weird. The guy he was watching was there every day so we thought he was a regular, until some homeless guy walked up and handed him a phone. When Freddie went to check it out, somebody took a potshot at him."

Emray got up and yanked open one of the decrepit kitchen drawers, making Mitch jump. "I want you to sit on this house until I tell you otherwise," he said as he wrote out the address. "Tell Freddie and the others to try not to talk to anyone and don't get made. Someone else takes a shot at him and misses, I'll finish the job. You understand me?"

"Yeah," Mitch said. The tic above Mitch's right eye that flared whenever he was nervous made him look like he was hooked to a live wire, and Emray wanted to keep it like that.

This wasn't the time for any of them to relax.

❖

Wiley sat at her desk in the dragon's lair since she didn't have a reason to hide it after her mother revealed every secret she had to her houseguests. The papers Amber had given her covered the wood surface, and from what she'd read, Roth had been a meticulous record keeper. If Walter had been as thorough, he'd have kept better control of his informant.

The picture that most interested her from the stack Amber included was shot at a different angle than the prize of Walter's collection. It was the supposed terrorist, his shirt still on, motoring up to Roth's boat. The man behind the wheel of the powerboat circled in red ink was Walter. That he'd been the one who'd delivered the sect member had slipped Walter's mind when they'd first met.

Roth had also kept a journal, and his and Walter's meetings were recorded almost verbatim, from what she could tell. From the beginning of their working relationship neither man trusted the other, but Roth had elevated his obsessive paranoia toward what Walter was capable of to a level that made Wiley wonder when he ever slept.

Obviously, not only had Walter delivered the Tajr member he had waved around as the reason Roth deserved to die, but he'd also been the driving force pushing Roth to do business with him. According to Roth, after an hour with the narcissistic asshole and Walter, he passed on what sounded like a lucrative relationship. Two weeks after Roth's refusal, the local police had raided his compound loaded with piles of proof of all his crimes, then turned him over to the federales.

Wiley took notes as she tried to make connections that'd help her formulate a plan, and she covered the wall next to her in pictures and index cards detailing her thoughts. The monitor by the computer bank clicked on and she saw Don standing at the door with his pack. She collected all the information from the folders and stepped out, wanting to have the room locked before he made it upstairs.

"Your mom went down," Aubrey said. Bowls of ingredients sat, cut and ready, on the island for whatever Aubrey was cooking.

"Tanith, could you put this in my office, please?" Wiley asked, making Tanith smile.

"Did you find anything?" Aubrey asked.

"Maybe," she said, listening for the whirl of the elevator. "Did Maria work with anyone who visited her at home a lot? I need a starting point, so even a minor thing could help."

"The only people she had over were her employees from the bar. She spent so much time there I can't believe she had the opportunity to be involved with anything else."

"Some bars are havens for products other than booze. Who made the most visits?"

"Her manager," Aubrey said as she stared at her so intently, Wiley swore Aubrey could read whatever was written across her heart. "Her name's Natalie Naquin, but she left after the storm. I remember Maria was pissed that she disappeared, but I didn't pay much attention. I figured she was upset because she'd lost her mistress, not because of business."

"You don't sound too mad about it."

Aubrey placed the lid on the pot closest to her and wiped her hands. "I'll explain this to you as many times as I have to. Maria wasn't you, no one has ever compared to you and, more importantly, how I feel about you. Betrayal only hurts when the act is committed by someone you've allowed inside so completely, you bleed from the disappointment." Wiley stood as Aubrey stepped closer and placed her arms around her waist. "I never let anyone in that much—only you."

"Do you consider what I did a betrayal?"

"That's why I called you," Aubrey said as she laid her head on her shoulder. "If I hadn't at least tried to stem the bleeding, it could have killed off a big part of who I want to be."

Aubrey clung to Wiley when she lowered her head and kissed her. "I've missed you." Aubrey nodded but didn't say anything. The elevator was getting closer, so she kissed Aubrey again and released her.

"Has Don changed much?" Aubrey asked.

"His hair's longer, but his fuse is shorter. He lost the patience to deal with assholes well after he turned fifty, so I try not to mess with him too much. Why do you ask?"

"I trusted him to watch your back whenever you were away from me. I'll tell you the rest later."

"It smells good in here," Don said as he dropped his bag. "A good change from the last time I was here and had to settle for takeout. Aubrey, how are you?" Don hugged Aubrey like they were old friends.

"Wiley's keeping us safe, so I'm okay. Did you have a good trip?"

"It was smooth enough for me to read some stuff before I got here. Wiley, you want to review now or after we eat whatever's on that stove?"

"It'll take us a few hours to finish, so go ahead," Aubrey said.

Danielle headed toward the bedrooms, Wiley assumed to get her father, so she led the way to her office. The envelope was sitting on her desk, and Tanith was still in the room playing a game.

"Is any of what you have classified?" Wiley asked.

"We can review the bland stuff first."

"Hey, Tanith," Wiley said when Tanith raised her head. "This is my friend Don Smith." She finished the introductions and almost laughed at the size of Don's smile.

"Do you want me to leave?" Tanith asked.

"Not if you don't want to, but if we bore you too much, feel free to take off." Tanith turned the game off and stayed on the chair by the windows. "What'd you find out?" Wiley asked Don.

"The agency has disavowed Walter, for now anyway. The to-do list he came to us with rattled too many cages in DC, and people started asking questions." Don handed over the intel sheets Carl had received and shared with him. "I haven't met with Walter's supervisor, Craig Orvik, yet, but from what I hear, the Pentagon is coming down hard, and Orvik is trying his best to contain the situation. Cutting Walter loose and screwing him over was his first step."

"Orvik didn't give any clues as to why Walter was here?"

"None, and the more he's questioned, the more adamant he gets that they'll deal with Walter themselves."

"What did you find?" Don asked, placing the closed folder back in his briefcase. Whatever else was in it wasn't appropriate for Tanith, she guessed.

"I found the clue Roth gave me." She told him about her meeting with Amber and showed him the picture of the boat with Walter and the Tajr member. "From what Roth wrote, Walter tried to cram this guy down his throat."

"Let's map it out," Buckston said as he came in with Peter, both men shaking hands with Don.

"Tanith, could you drop those blinds for me, please?" Wiley said as she got a box of tape strips from her desk. The only thing this room had in common with the studio and the dragon's lair was the wall of eraser board for situations like this.

From the notes she'd made from Amber's envelope, Wiley started taping pictures on the board and writing names under them, much like she had with the copies she'd made. Whenever she could make a connection, she drew lines between the photos.

"Walter came to us about Roth," she said, pointing to pictures of both men. "The crisis he dangled was this guy." She pointed to the supposed terrorist. "I know I'm retired, but I don't believe we've ever encouraged the courting of anyone set on destroying as much of the country as possible. From this picture," she pointed to the boat, "I don't think Walter was trying to infiltrate the Tajr."

"Not with that face," Peter said.

"If he was tight with Roth, I don't know why Walter's so anxious to get rid of him now," Wiley said, more for her own benefit. "There's something else weird." She put up the grainy photo she was able to get of Amber and her friend before they left the bar. "This is the woman Roth told me about, but while we were making contact, someone was watching."

"Who?" Don asked.

"The night I had to go to Aubrey's, I followed a guy dressed like a cop from her house to the casino downtown. He was in a rush to meet with a guy named Mitch Surpass." She hadn't found fake cop yet, but Sheriff Culver of Brownsville had included Mitch's picture with his e-mail. "It could be a coincidence, but I find it troubling that anything having to do with Roth can be tied back to whatever happened to Maria." She drew a line from Amber to the square she'd drawn and written *fake cop* in.

"Wiley," Tanith said as she slowly stood and walked to the board. "This lady worked for Maria and came to our house. I don't remember her name, but it wasn't Amber."

"Are you sure?" Wiley asked, and Tanith nodded. "Do you recognize anyone else?"

"Just her," Tanith said, and pointed to Amber's picture.

"Could you go get your mom for me?"

Tanith took off toward the kitchen, leaving them all looking at the picture of the beautiful woman. "Could all the crap be related?" Peter asked. "If Maria wasn't already dead, I'd kill the bitch."

"Can I do something for you?" Aubrey asked, and judging from the glance at her father, she and Tanith had heard what he'd said.

"Tanith recognized someone, so maybe you could provide a name," Wiley said.

"That's Natalie Naquin. Remember, we were talking about her earlier. She was Maria's manager."

"Her name's not Amber Willows?"

"Not unless that's her stage name if she took up exotic dancing or something. She certainly had the face and body for it." Aubrey stood with her hands on Tanith's shoulders but never lost eye contact with her. "What's she got to do with all this?"

"She was who I met with today." Since Wiley was no longer Roth Pombo's problem, she explained in broad strokes why she went to Mexico. "Natalie is who Roth is pining for and trusted enough to give his stash of information."

"This Roth Pombo guy is big into drugs?" Aubrey asked.

"He was, but he's in Mexico's version of supermax. If Maria was involved with these people, it might explain where she got that much money," she said, and sighed. "It would also explain why and how she died."

"Wiley, these people won't ever stop coming after us," Aubrey said, and from her expression she was sorry for blurting that out in front of Tanith.

"The more we know, the better off we are." Wiley couldn't stand to see Aubrey in so much pain so she opened her arms, and Aubrey and Tanith came forward. The men dropped their eyes, but Wiley noticed all three were smiling. "Think of it this way. I'm not shooting in the dark anymore." That might've been an old saying for anyone else, but she hoped Aubrey knew what she meant.

"Where do we start?" Buckston asked.

"With Mitch Surpass. His partner was outside Aubrey's and waiting for whoever was with Natalie at the park. Since he saw us together at the bar where I met Natalie, fake cop knows she's here. If Roth trusted her this much, it might take the heat off you and Tanith. It makes sense to me that she'd have the money since she was holding all this stuff." She pointed to the board.

"Do you have a clue how to find this guy?" Don asked.

"No, but I have a clue where to start."

"Are you going to clue us in?" her father asked.

"Don and I are going to the Hilton and take a look around. Fake cop and Mitch had a room there the night Maria died. They're probably gone, but it's a start if I don't find out anything."

"You sure you want to go out alone?" Buckston asked.

"Don was my spotter for years, and I'd feel better if you and Peter stay here in case something else comes up."

"I'm going to check in," Don said. "Is two hours good?"

"Stay for dinner," she offered.

"I think I'll change my hotel to the Hilton, so I'll take a rain check."

Once Don departed, her dad and Peter left her to run a few searches for Natalie Naquin and Mitch. While the computer ran the program, Wiley stared at the wall and the arrows she'd drawn. The connections almost made a circle. The middle was empty, though, and until she could fill it in with who was pulling the strings, she wouldn't find Maria's missing money. That was one way of buying Aubrey and Tanith's freedom. The other was finding and killing everyone involved.

"Wiley, are you sure you want to get involved in all this?" Aubrey came back and stood on the other side of Wiley's desk.

"It was bastards like this that stole my future with you, so don't ask me to stop. I may not get all that back, but I'll be damned if I'm going to let you and Tanith live with a target on your back."

"I appreciate that, but it's not fair to put you in danger for something Maria did."

"Were you lying about how you feel and what you want?"

"No," Aubrey said, her eyes glassy.

"For a very long time I've gone into places with orders to eliminate whatever threat my superiors deemed dangerous to national security."

Aubrey moved closer, sitting on the edge of the desk so at least their knees touched. "I was always proud of your service. Not many people reach your level, and even fewer know a woman was behind the scope. All they know is the rules say the army would never put you in any combat situation."

"If that's another way of saying I'm one of the best killers out there, you're right." Wiley's eyes went to Aubrey's hand and her long, elegant fingers.

"When you say it like that, it makes me sound like I'm ashamed of you." Aubrey lifted her hand and caressed her cheek. "That has never and will never be true."

"Thanks, and I was trying to make a point. I served with as much honor as our dads, and it cost me so much. Now I want to use my skills to protect you and Tanith." She laid her hand over Aubrey's. "By doing that maybe I'll be blessed this time around instead of cursed."

"We can stay locked in here or run away, but I'm not letting you go. Bravery isn't the price you have to pay, my love. Not again."

"I'm not very good at running or hiding." She kissed Aubrey's palm. "Looking over her shoulder for the rest of her life isn't something I want for Tanith either."

Aubrey nodded and slowly moved into her lap. It'd take much more time before they regained the naturalness of their relationship. If Wiley didn't want to get back to the point where they interacted with each other without the slight hesitation that hinted at the fear, now was the time to push Aubrey away.

She couldn't, though. Having Aubrey this close dispelled every lie she'd tried to tell herself of how well she was doing alone. She not only needed Aubrey, she wanted her. Wanted her more than anything she'd ever accomplished or had. The years hadn't dulled her love for Aubrey, and she was through hiding and running from it. When she kissed Aubrey, that's what she tried to convey as she held her.

"You know what I want when this is done?" Aubrey said.

"What?" She threaded her fingers with Aubrey's and enjoyed Aubrey's perfume. In a way it was like she was nineteen again and life was full of possibilities that had nothing to do with killing.

"I want to drive out and see if that old tree is still standing so we can show it to Tanith."

"Think it still has any magic left in it?"

"I look at your painting and say yes."

Wiley pressed her fingers to the underside of Aubrey's chin so she could see her eyes. "That piece is yours. Even if we'd never seen each other again, I'd made arrangements to have it delivered to you." She kissed Aubrey when she didn't say anything.

"Is it the sunrise or sunset?"

"It's a painting for the beautiful girl who always greeted me at sunrise, whispering in my ear of all the wonders the day would hold for me. Those promises were what kept me from getting swept away in the darkness. You, and the memory of you, kept me sane."

"I want that to be my lifetime job."

❖

"Have you decided?" the waitress asked, appearing bored and tired.

"A burger and a beer. Whatever you have on tap is good."

Walter handed her the menu and rested his head on the back of the booth in the diner outside New Orleans. After his meeting with Carter in Mexico, he'd used an alias to get back into the States. Orvik had done him a favor by not taking him into custody right then. He wouldn't be that lucky again.

It galled him that Wiley was off-limits to him. Carter had explained in his own circular way that he'd pushed too far and the military had pushed back when he'd tried to exploit their precious asset.

Wiley was beyond his reach, so he had to concentrate on something else to get himself out of this bind. Roth Pombo. In hindsight, he should've left Roth Pombo to his fate. Roth's new home would eventually bury him as efficiently as a kill shot.

"What proof does the fucker have? It's his word against mine as to what happened," he muttered as he watched his waitress lumber over with his beer.

Yeah, he'd figure out something to not only fuck Orvik over, but Wiley as well. If the bitch had done the job and not whined so much about it, it'd still be business as usual.

"What?" he barked into his phone. "Just do what I told you and keep it simple."

He laughed when he disconnected. Everyone was about to find out what he could do even without CIA backing.

"Fuckers."

CHAPTER NINETEEN

Wiley transferred the results of her searches to her phone before strapping on the double shoulder holster. In her jacket pocket was the leather case Don had given her as a gift, with its syringes and special bottle, and she repacked the rifle she'd used that afternoon. Anything else she'd need was in the Suburban.

Her search yielded two addresses for Natalie, and she intended to visit the one listed in the Garden District. The address and the satellite photo of the house didn't compute to the salary of a bar manager. Well, what she considered a bar manager's salary to be.

"You sure are heavily armed for someone who's only doing recon," Aubrey said as she entered the office. "Or did I misunderstand?"

"After seeing all the players and how they problem-solve, I don't want to head out with only a slingshot." She stood still as Aubrey ran her hands under her jacket along the leather of her holster.

"I don't need to tell you to be careful, right? The thought of something happening to you makes me crazy."

"Here." She handed over a new cell phone. "I'm not planning to be out too late, but I'll call if it goes much past one."

"Do you buy these things by the case or something?"

"Actually Uncle Sam keeps me in phones."

Aubrey pressed a few buttons, and Wiley's phone buzzed in her pocket. "Just checking."

"My number's the only one in the contacts."

"Do you trust your bosses not to tamper with these so they can track you?"

"They did, but hopefully they're smart enough to know I'm going to tamper right back. Anything in there meant to gather intel on me is gone, and I shred them when I'm done."

"Your mom and dad were on the money when they named you."

"I'm only wily when someone else tries it first." She kissed Aubrey's hand, then her lips. "Try not to wait up."

"You can't have forgotten that much about me."

"It was worth a shot," she said as she zipped her jacket shut. For this job, she had dressed completely in black.

Wiley wasn't that far from the house she was going to check out, but habit made her head in the opposite direction to flush out anyone trying to tail her. The heat had driven almost everyone inside, it seemed, since a few of the bars she passed were full.

After ten minutes of wandering she turned toward the Garden District. Natalie's house was off St. Charles Avenue, where none of the dwellings were small and almost all of them had a high wrought-iron fence with a shrub liner planted in the yard for added privacy.

Wiley parked on the opposite side of St. Charles and walked a block over before crossing the wide avenue. That one-block detour made a world of difference since the real estate was mixed. Some smaller homes sat dwarfed by their neighbors, but here too the sidewalks had few people on them. As she neared the hundred block she needed, she found two houses with For Sale signs in the yard, and one of them was dark.

She slowed her pace and discreetly looked around to make sure no one saw her enter the yard. Luckily it was cloudy, without much moonlight, and as she walked along the small space between houses wearing her dark clothing, she didn't raise any alarms.

"Where are you?" Don asked when she answered his call.

"Closing in on Natalie Naquin, hopefully." The yard had no tall trees, and the house it butted up to was a two-story monstrosity. No way could she get a clear shot of the street from here. "Any luck at the hotel?"

"The bar's still closed and empty, and I didn't see any sign of the two guys you showed me."

She gave him the location of her car and where she was as she watched someone standing in the window of the house across from her. The woman was on the phone, but she wasn't facing the yard. The rest of the house appeared to be fairly dark, as if she was either alone or there weren't many others there.

"Park and call me when you get here."

Wiley walked forward slowly, studying the two-story house. The best vantage point for what she had in mind was high, and the back porch near where the owner was standing was her way up.

She secured the pack to her back and tried to be quiet as she climbed, using the iron-work support at the corner away from the window with the light on. When she was close enough to hear, she thought she heard an argument, and from the cursing, the woman was pissed. That was helpful since anger always distracted people. Even if she stood in the window she doubted the homeowner would've noticed.

The roof would be better, but it didn't have enough footholds for her to get up without breaking through the woman's rage, so she carefully walked along the wraparound porch. The beautiful outdoor space was common to some of the larger homes in New Orleans, but so were termites. If she stepped through a weak spot a broken leg would be a major inconvenience.

The large oak in the front and the one in the neighbor's yard were huge, but also severely trimmed back—a common sight around the city after the storm. With only the major branches still left, she had a good view of not only Natalie's house, but a block down from it in each direction.

She spotted fake cop four houses down from Natalie's, sitting low behind the wheel of a new car as if not to be seen. Next to him was Mitch Surpass. Wiley adjusted her night-vision binoculars, not believing her luck.

"Don, I need you to drive down the street and park when I tell you to."

"Found something?" he asked, breathing hard as if running back to his car.

"Two somethings, and I don't want the healthy one to get away." She put her rifle together, switching out the scope and screwing on the silencer.

"What's wrong with the other guy?"

She saw Don's headlights, glad he was driving slowly. "Turn into the driveway on your right and kill your lights, but not the engine." She aimed toward fake cop's car and got comfortable on her stomach. "To answer your question, the other guy's going to need surgery on his right upper arm to repair the damage from the gunshot."

With the windshield there was a chance the bullet wouldn't stay true, but she'd taken enough of these shots to feel good that she wouldn't kill him. The scare would maybe encourage a career change.

"Mitch is in the passenger seat, so if he runs I need you to make sure he's available for a chat."

"I'm ready."

She took a deep breath and held it for a few seconds. Her crosshairs fixed on the spot right above fake cop's bicep. With the breeze she'd hit directly between his shoulder and bicep. Not a debilitating blow after months of physical therapy. Fake cop would live, but rainy or cold days would remind him of tonight.

She exhaled as she released the safety. Because fake cop was busy watching Natalie's house, he was still and in quiet conversation with Mitch. In Wiley's world that meant easy target, so she pulled the trigger.

The howl caused a slew of lights to flick on nearby, so Wiley crept to the corner, slung her rifle across her back, and threw the pack into the yard. It grew quiet again so she guessed fake cop had either passed out or Mitch had shoved something in his mouth.

She felt around with her foot, hoping that the same decorative iron work held up the front porch. Once she was back on the ground, she headed for the shadows and dismantled the gun.

"Have they moved?" she asked Don.

"They're both in the car, but I only see Mitch's head. He might be waiting for curious neighbors to go back to their televisions."

"I'm taking a walk." She reached for one of the flat black pistols meant for night operations. They were black holes for light, and the small silencers attached made them sound like puffs of air when shot. She carried hers at her side as she walked toward Mitch without a problem. If Natalie and her boyfriend had heard the scream, they hadn't been worried enough to check it out.

Mitch was still in the car when she got closer, with his hand clamped over fake cop's mouth. The shock seemed to have paralyzed him into indecisiveness, so she took advantage. In one quick move she opened the back passenger door and pressed the gun into the back of Mitch's head.

"You did this shit?" Mitch said loudly.

"Don't complain. He's alive, isn't he?" She pressed harder. This was an exercise she'd experienced in training. When an instructor was able to slip past her defenses and get the drop on a head shot, the barrel had always been cold, as if it flaunted its ability to cause your death with a quick squeeze of its trigger.

"Think how much luckier he is than Maria Ross."

"Who?" He squirted out the predictable answer faster than she imagined, and it was loud enough for Don to hear and laugh at.

"You weren't there, but he was, and after they brought out all those body bags he went running to you. All your goons with the chain saw died, and your friend here acted like he was next."

"How do you know all that?" Mitch sat with his head straight as if she'd shoot if he moved too much. "What's your connection to Maria?"

"Mitch, when you're holding a gun to my head, you'll get to ask whatever questions you want, but right now, answer. Don't ask questions. Correct answers are the only way to get yourself out of here. Understand?"

"What do you want to know?" he said, ignoring or missing that she knew his name.

"Who do you work for?"

"Emray Gillis." Mitch spoke so fast, he stuttered the last name.

"He was Maria's boss too?"

"No, but the stupid bitch was planning something and avoiding her phone."

"Planning what?"

"I don't know," Mitch said, letting his head fall forward, as if realizing the answer would cost him. "It was like she was trying to run out on her life and start over without giving Emray a chance to get what he wanted."

"I thought you didn't know? Are you sure it was Emray she was holding out on?"

"Everybody in the business knew the score at the bar, but word was she was trying to sell. Maria didn't advertise, but she was ready to leave. She was willing to give anyone but my boss a shot."

"Why are you here?" Fake cop's moans were starting to give her a headache.

"Emray wanted us to watch and see where the bitch in there goes. That's all he said."

"Don, what clearance do I have?"

"Officially you have none," he said softly, "but personally, the fewer people that can find their way back to Aubrey and Tanith, the better off you'll be." The line went dead.

"Where do I find Emray?"

"I'm dead if I tell you that. He's not the kind you mess with or turn on."

"You're dead later, or you're dead now, pick."

Mitch gave up the address as easily as he had everything else. "That's all I know."

"I doubt that, but there is something else I want to ask you." There was a bullet chambered so she lowered the barrel to the back of his neck. This was why she'd killed the call with Don. He had nothing to do with the next part. "Do you remember Tammy Culver?"

"Who the fuck is that?"

"A young girl from Brownsville, Texas. Her father's the sheriff."

Mitch made the mistake of laughing. "You're a cop? Man, you ain't ever getting away with this, and you're not gonna make anything stick from this conversation." Just like Dr. Jerry, another legal expert.

"Tammy Culver's father's a cop, but he loves being a father more than upholding the law against scum, so he asked me to do him a favor."

"Wait," Mitch screamed.

"You remember her now?"

"Yeah, and it wasn't my fault she took too much. I told her not to do it, but she didn't listen."

"You'll have plenty of time to explain it to her." Fake cop moaned louder when she pulled the trigger and Mitch's throat hit the dash before his head. She'd intended to leave fake cop alive, but he'd obviously seen something else in her expression and he clumsily reached for something in his lap. "If you have a gun in your lap, drop it out the window or I'll paint the steering wheel with your brains."

"Please don't kill—"

She hit him with the butt of her gun, not wanting to waste any more time. "Meet me back at the house," she said to Don as she made her way up the street. Her gait was so controlled, anyone watching would think she was out for an evening stroll.

"You making any stops?"

"I doubt I'll find him, but I have to try this guy Gillis's address before he finds out about his crew. There's no way he's the top guy with this caliber of help, but I have to keep working my way up until I find who ordered those guys to kill Maria."

"You're not going alone, so don't start complaining. I'll give you ten minutes to make it to your car before I follow you."

"Let's check out his house before we call the cops about our friends back there. Unless someone takes their dog out, they should be fine for another hour or so."

The address Mitch had given them appeared to belong more to a user than a dealer, but Wiley walked the entire perimeter carefully. Thankfully there weren't any trip wires, like some of the stash houses in South America and Mexico, but the surveillance cameras outside were worth more than the house. Whoever Emray was, he knew his stuff.

Every window was covered, but she doubted anyone was inside since both the front and back entrances had their iron gate doors chained and padlocked with the locks facing out. This wasn't Emray's home, it was his office.

"Anything?" Don asked. He was parked down the street acting as her lookout.

"I'd say his local Radio Shack loves him, but these cameras are high-end," she said as she climbed a tree to cut one down. "They're all wireless, so I'm going to have to walk around inside to see where the signal is going to."

"Don't hang up."

She dropped the camera by the back-door steps and picked the lock after she checked every inch of the door for nasty surprises. The outer door was clean, but the inner door was unlocked, a major red flag, so she went back for the camera and used it to smash out the glass top half of the door.

The army-issue land mine was set up with a wire across the bottom of the door. Anyone who made it through the lock would've stepped about an inch inside before taking out every windowpane in the neighborhood as well as themselves. "Interesting security system," she said as she carefully climbed in.

"What is it?"

"Land mine rigged to blow by swinging open the door." The rest of the house was fairly empty, and the front door was free of booby traps. "You're going to have to come disarm this thing. I don't want to leave it."

"Where'd he get a land mine?"

"It's drab green. Is that enough of a hint?"

"If it's army issue, there's a serial number on the firing mechanism. That won't tell us who, but we can narrow down the location where it was taken from."

She finished her sweep as Don was talking, finding no other explosives. The computer on the kitchen-counter screen was split into ten boxes, each displaying a section of the yard except the middle top. That was gray static from the camera she'd taken down. She didn't find any saved footage on the hard drive, so she assumed the feed was being stored off-site via the Internet.

Everything she saw added up to Emray not being your average dealer.

"Head to the front and cover me," Don said as he climbed in. "Hand me the toolbox I borrowed from your car."

"Want me to hold the flashlight?"

"I work better on these without an audience, so go and make sure no one surprises me into blowing myself up."

It didn't take Don long to join her with the disk under his arm and the firing pin in his hand. "Do you need to make any more stops?" he asked.

"Just one, why?"

"I don't want to drive around with this thing any longer than I have to, but one more stop won't kill us."

"Interesting choice of words." She took her tools back and opened the trunk of Don's rental.

"Where to?"

"Back to where we started, at Natalie's, but this time we knock."

❖

Emray watched from two blocks away, laughing when the black-dressed person headed to the back of the house. His only regret now was he hadn't made it a remote detonator. He was too far away to see whoever it was clearly, but if he took out whoever this new player was, it'd be worth the loss of the house.

"Mitch, when I find you, I'm going to shove my phone down the hole I'm going to make in your forehead," he said when Mitch didn't answer his cell. Since Freddie wasn't answering either, the two morons were probably together. Mitch had shown promise but couldn't handle the pressure of the big leagues, so it was time for a performance evaluation before Emray moved on.

The competition was getting in the way, and the cops were getting better organized, so he was ready to head back to his place in Colombia. There wasn't as much money in the plants and production, but it was much lower profile than this. If he left now, no one would ever know who Emray Gillis was, especially Hector Delarosa's people. When he found the cash and the kilos Roth had brought in, it'd take him less than a year to reach his goal.

While people like Nunzio and Hector ran around posturing, he'd been working on the easiest part of the business to take over—the land and the crops. With the wages he paid the grunts harvesting his fields, a majority of the field hands that worked for him had abandoned Hector's agricultural efforts for the reality of bigger paychecks.

No one paid attention because nothing had changed as far as who they supplied it to, but with the money Maria hid, that'd change in a day. Then Hector, Nunzio, and every other loser who wanted the hassle of the streets could have that part of the business. To get it to the streets, though, they'd have to start with him. Ultimately he wanted to control the supply. The demand would work itself out then.

"But I still want the money." He punched the seat next to him. "I'm not leaving without it, and I'll be goddamned if I'll let that little bitch walk away with it."

Whatever Maria had done with it had kept it buried successfully, but he was getting close. When he saw what the guy was carrying, he punched the seat again. "Fuck."

Though, he thought when his anger cleared, if Mitch couldn't find the duffels, these people could. He just had to find a way to them and explain the consequences of failure.

❖

"You see it?" Don asked.

"Peel off from me and see what happens." She'd spotted the car too and was impressed with the distance they were able to maintain without losing them. "Where are you dropping your package?"

"I'm headed to the airbase on the west bank of the river for the disk, but I'll let Carl run down the numbers. You still want to head over for your visit?"

"Not tonight, so run your errand and call me when you get to your room."

Don made a U-turn when he could, but their tail stayed with her. At the next traffic light she slowed so she'd catch the light, but whoever was driving pulled to the side way back. She wouldn't be able to see the driver's face.

Wiley waited until the signal changed before turning toward the zoo, which was still closed. She wanted to see how brave her new friend was, so she turned into the parking lot and swiveled back around to face the oncoming car. The idiot behind the wheel gunned the engine like a juvenile, making the car jerk forward a few feet.

"Buckston Gremillion taught me a long time ago that attitude is everything," she said as she put her SUV in drive.

She stomped the accelerator to the floor and headed right for the sedan. In this game you were either a chicken or chickenshit, and the macho behind the wheel was the latter. She still hadn't seen his face, but no woman she knew would taunt someone by revving her engine. Before she got anywhere near the car, the driver put it in reverse and did a decent job of driving backward at a high rate of speed.

"I don't really have time for this, but I have loner tendencies, asshole," she said as she chased the car down and bumped fenders with him. "I detest anyone following me." The black Camaro with black-tinted windows screamed muscle car, but the Suburban outweighed and outgunned it. She flipped her bright lights on and disengaged her air bags so she could smash the hell out of him. The advantage was hers now.

She wasn't interested in seeing the driver's face. Her priority was making it to the end of the street without hitting any oncoming traffic. The massive levee along the river was her goal, so she put it in low gear and four-wheel drive to push the sedan up the embankment. She could hear the squeal of his brakes, and the back of the car was fishtailing as the driver cut the wheel to break away, but she refused to let up.

"You'd better pray that pretty car likes water," she said as the car reached the top and started down the incline. Wiley braked when her front wheels dipped down, and she waited to see what the driver would decide. This was his only chance at surrender.

As if reading her mind the driver cut his tires, turned his lights off, and turned sharply so he could drive along the embankment, as if trying to put as much distance between them as he could manage. She watched, deciding to let him go. She'd had her fill of killing for one night. Whoever Emray was, his people were determined to follow every lead until he got his money, because whoever was in the Camaro had to have been sitting on the house waiting. That strategy showed patience and cunning, whereas Maria's death was sloppy and cruel. Wiley was no profiler, but the vastly different approaches were, in her mind, psychotic.

She drove back to the zoo parking lot so she could survey the damage and to center her emotions. This situation was like a hydra. She cut off a couple of heads and another one popped up ready to either expose her secrets or take her down.

"Did I wake you?"

"No, I'm in your studio looking at the ocean piece," Aubrey said. "It's beautiful."

"It's the coast off Big Sur."

"You know what it reminds me of?"

"I couldn't guess," she said as she buckled her seat belt. "We never went to California together."

"It reminds me of how you touched me. You were meticulous in your detail, and your technique always made me feel beautiful. You always knew every nuance of what I wanted, and you gave it to me."

"Now might not be a good time to talk about that." The words made her want to go home, but her desire to destroy the threat won out—for now at least.

"Probably not, but I need you to know how much I missed you."

"A lifetime of apologies won't be enough, will it?" She headed back toward St. Charles and any one of the abandoned buildings along the side streets.

"Did what you feel for me die when you walked away?"

"No."

"Did it when you found out about Maria and Tanith?" Aubrey asked, her voice soft and seductive.

"No."

"Then you don't ever need to apologize for something you saw as necessary. I do want you to come home."

"One stop, then I'm done for the night."

"Maybe done, but not for the night."

❖

Natalie stood at the French doors that led to the large backyard and stared at the faint outline of trees she could make out at the fence line. The floodlights made it appear like noontime when they were lit, but it would've also marked them as different, and she wanted desperately to blend. Being different was an invitation for the animals who wanted her dead to knock her door off its hinges.

"What's wrong? Did you hear or see something?" her brother Brian asked. Both their lives had become an endless road of eggshells where every step could lead to disaster.

"No, I couldn't sleep." She studied Brian's reflection and for the hundredth time cursed herself for involving him. "I'm fine, so go to bed. No sense in both of us being tired tomorrow."

"Come on." Brian came close enough to take her hand. "I'll make you some of that tea you like."

She allowed him to lead her away, even though her gut said to stay vigilant. It was time to get the hell out of here and enjoy everything her time with Roth had brought her. The morning couldn't come soon enough.

Wiley waited for Natalie to move before she left her position by the magnolia tree in the corner of the yard. She'd already disabled the alarm system on her way to the back, so she'd spent her time leaning against the thick trunk and watched Natalie staring out at the darkness. Not a smart move on Natalie's slash Willow's part.

The man coming out in his boxers saved her from finding another way in, because while she could prevent them from calling for help, she couldn't keep them from shooting at her. Their phone lines had gone with the alarm, but there was no telling how many weapons Roth's girlfriend had stashed around the house.

She couldn't hear the conversation in the kitchen, but she could see both of them as she unlocked the door. As soon as she felt the click, she took one of her guns from her holster and moved fast. The man she'd met earlier stood motionless with a mug in one hand and teapot in the other.

"I hate to come in uninvited, but I need a few more answers," she said as she drew out the other gun and pointed at Natalie. "If you think you can make a move on me, don't go there. All I want is for you to be honest, but if you can't, you can't."

"You're going to kill us?" the man said, obviously being brave enough to put down everything he held.

"You shouldn't waste time wondering if I'll kill you or if it'll bother me."

"What do you want?" Natalie asked.

"Why lie about your name?"

"Ever since Roth was arrested, we haven't been safe. I promised him we'd stay long enough to hand over the information he had, then I'd take off. Roth thought it was the only way to shake the vultures who'd come to feed on his dead carcass, as he put it."

"Get down on your belly and put your hands away from your body," she said to the guy.

"No."

She laughed, since that most probably would've been her answer. "Are you fond of those cute kneecaps?" He dropped like a docile puppy that'd been spanked. "Sit," she said to Natalie.

"The guns aren't necessary. We're just trying to get out of here, not hurt you."

"Let's start with who is *we*? Roth is lying around nights staring into the fluorescent lights crying over you, and you're entertaining Rambo over there." She moved behind Natalie and dropped her hands so the guns rested against her thighs. She wasn't as accurate with fast aiming, but neither one of them would leave the room alive if it came to that.

"Brian is my brother, not my lover," Natalie said, and kept her head forward. "How do you know my name?"

"Maria Ross, remember her?"

"Maria's dead," Brian blurted out, and Natalie's shoulders hitched. "You killed her?"

"No, but I'm interested in who did." It took iron control not to lift a gun over Natalie's head when she heard the noise.

"Mama."

The little boy wasn't steady on his feet and dropped down to his butt after he called for Natalie. If Wiley had to guess, he was perhaps one.

"What are you doing up, little man?" Natalie glanced back at her before she stood to get him. The baby immediately put his head on her shoulder. "I swear nothing will happen if we sit and talk, but if you can't relax I need to put him down again."

"Come on, Uncle Brian, have a seat," Wiley said. She didn't holster her weapons, but kept them out of sight. "He's Roth's?"

"I know it's probably not my right to ask, but how do you know Maria?" Natalie asked as she gently patted the baby's back. "And yes, he's Roth's son...our son."

"Maria lived with a friend of mine, and she left her in a bind by supposedly stealing from someone who'd like his money back."

"Do you know who?" Brian asked.

"Who she stole from or who has the money?" The question was rhetorical, she realized. Natalie did, and she'd gotten it from Maria.

"Who thinks the money is theirs?" Natalie asked.

"Emray Gillis," she said. These things were so frustrating. Why couldn't people ever make it easy by spitting out what needed to be said? This was why she was never interested in interrogations. Her job was dark, but it was easier than the cat-and-mouse game everyone tried to play when they'd been caught. "But Maria gave it to you." With the baby faced away from her, she raised a gun. "So let's review our options."

"The money belongs to my sister," Brian said in a loud voice. Wiley could tell he was pissed, but he also wasn't stupid. "Emray's full of shit if he thinks he has rights to it."

"As long as my friend is being hunted, that's not set in stone, so shut up." She flicked the pistol's safety off and he complied. "Two men were outside tonight watching your house. Why?" she asked Natalie.

"Were?" Natalie asked.

"They're gone, and once this Gillis guy figures that out, there'll be more, so here's your chance to make a clean break from all this."

Natalie and Brian exchanged looks and Natalie nodded. "Maria had been in business with Roth for years, but nothing big and never any direct dealing. Last year she opened a place in Cabo San Lucas so there'd be a reason to ship from one place to the other."

"Ship what? The feds are hypersensitive to anything like that."

"Maria was importing tequila, and all her paperwork was in order.

After a few months the shipments had become so routine, the port people didn't even open any of the crates. Only it wasn't tequila in the bottles, but liquefied coke. Maria would hold every shipment until Roth's people could collect it here. Everything was working fine until Emray Gillis was forced on him."

"Have you met Gillis?" If Natalie kept talking, Wiley was sure she'd get all the answers that had eluded her so far.

"Emray doesn't exist, it's only a street name."

"Have you met him?" she repeated, and the siblings looked at each other again. "I don't think I have to explain the fastest way to help my friend is to turn over the money, so answer the question."

"I don't know his real name, but he was in a lot of the pictures I gave you."

"Can you be more specific?" she asked calmly, but her head was about to explode.

"He brought the guy to Roth's boat for that last big meeting before they took Roth down. He was the white guy."

"Walter Robinson is Emray Gillis?" As she spoke, a whole slew of things snapped into place.

"Roth told me he worked for the CIA, but he kept his name from me to protect me. Emray was using Roth to build his own business, but betrayed him when he said no to the guy Emray brought to the boat. I was in Cabo when they picked Roth up, so I did everything we talked about if that were to happen. We just wanted to keep our son safe." Natalie sounded both scared and resolute. "Maria did give me the money, but you'll have to kill me to get it back. I need it to leave and start over. Besides, my brother's right. You might not like how Roth made it, but it's his to do with as he pleases. With Roth out of the way, Emray figures it'll be an easy score."

"Who was Maria to you besides your boss?"

"We hooked up occasionally, but she wanted more. I finally said yes a week ago when she agreed to come with us to help keep my son from harm."

"Hooking up with women who didn't really want her was a bad habit of hers," Wiley said, more for her own benefit.

"Maria was in my life before Roth," Natalie said defensively. "I met Roth on a trip to set up the new place. He was fun and persistent, and unlike Maria, he didn't have someone else holding him back. We partied until it became something deeper, then I got pregnant. I thought he'd freak, but he tried to get out of that life instead. He said no to Emray because of the baby."

"And Maria?"

"She was pissed when I stayed with Roth, and I didn't hear from her until I came running back. Roth got to her first and made her promise all the cash from the sale would come to me. Maria never shared with me who Roth sold to or what went down, but she set up the buys and then she was dead."

"A few million doesn't seem to be worth the effort Walter's put into this."

"Maria gave us the last three million the day before she was killed. Roth knew, though, that to make a clean break from here with enough money to start over would take everything he had. It took me about three weeks to finish with the attorneys, but in total, we had over fifty million." Natalie handed her son to Brian. "If your friend is Aubrey, all I can tell you is that Emray ordered Maria's death, and he won't stop until he gets everything from all of us."

"What makes you think I won't do the same?"

"Because if you know Aubrey, you know Tanith. What Aubrey would do for her daughter is no different than what I would for my son. Please let me get him out of here."

"Do you have any idea who the guy on the boat with Walter was?"

"The only person I recognized was Emray, or Walter, as you keep saying."

She couldn't kill this woman and her child, and more importantly, Natalie knew that. Letting her walk, though, meant Aubrey had no way out of this other than the death of all the hunters, starting with Walter.

"Where are you going after this?" Wiley asked.

"Like we'd tell you," Brian said, and laughed.

It'd been a long night and she wasn't in the mood for sarcasm, and she also didn't care that he held the little boy in his arms. "Let's try this again," she said, having moved so fast Brian stopped breathing as she pressed the gun to his temple. "This isn't some game, asshole, and you aren't good enough to hide from me. They could drop you in the middle of a jungle covered in pig shit and I'd still find you, put a bullet in your head, and be home in time for dinner. Do you understand me?" She pulled his head back by his hair so he'd look at her. "Do you understand?"

"Yes," he rasped.

"We have an older sister who lives in Jersey, so we're headed there," Natalie said.

"Don't make it easy for them," she said as she took her phone out. "If you're set on running, go in the opposite direction. Take this and I'll call you when it's over." She slid the phone toward Natalie.

"Thank you," Natalie said.

"The two guys outside were alone, so if you're ready, leave now. Drive and use cash."

"Roth said the same thing."

Wiley let Brian go and put her gun away. "I'm sure he did, but one last thing. If you lied about anything, I will find you and take everything from you." She purposely let her eyes drop to Natalie's son. "I realize why you're fighting for what you love, but Aubrey means more to me than that. Did you leave anything out?"

"No, but I'll call you if I remember something." Natalie held up the phone and, from her expression, Wiley knew she was telling the truth.

"If you fail to answer the phone, I'll be on my way, but not for another talk. As long as you help me, I won't be a threat to you, but don't try to screw me."

The guilt that swamped her as she left through the same door she came in should've been because of the threat to Natalie's child, but it wasn't. It haunted her that she was allowing Aubrey's best chance at peace to run with enough money to vanish. She stopped at the side of the house and contemplated going back. Her hands shook from the urge to take the easy way out.

If she did, though, Walter won.

"Not this time."

CHAPTER TWENTY

Hector Delarosa sat by the pool of his new home in New Orleans and listened to the men who led his crews on the street update him on their progress. His real home was back in Colombia, but spending time in the States was necessary if he wanted to take over the cartel. Expansion took time, but by meeting with what was essentially the last stop of his supply chain, he was building loyalty as well as market share. Loyalty was the foundation of power.

So while his competition was locked behind their tall barbed-wire walls enjoying the posh homes the narcotics business had built for them, he was keeping his hands in the game. Eventually he'd unleash men like this on the old guard with no vision and claim the top spot. Once he did, he'd give his daughter, Marisol, her chance to run things. Of all his children, she was the only one interested in continuing what was important to him.

"Things won't always be this easy, sir, but with the police spread so thin, our numbers are way up," the young man to his left said.

"Good, give your men a bonus this month," he said, and slapped his hands together. Some of them hadn't gotten a turn, but he saw Miguel on the back patio with Tracy Stegal. Hopefully Miguel brought good news about the thorn that'd bothered him for months. Hector wanted the annoyance gone.

"Tracy, good to see you again." Hector kissed both her cheeks. "Come inside."

The storm had caused some wind damage to the house, but the work crew he'd flown in from Colombia was almost done. They'd completed his study first, and that's where he led them. Pictures of his wife and family stood in the numerous teak bookcases, but only a picture of Marisol sat on his desk.

"I haven't heard from you in days, Miguel," he said in an even tone, not wanting to scold him in front of Tracy. "Anything new with Gillis?"

"Not yet, but Nunzio has come sniffing around. He wants to deal, and he's interested in large buys every month."

Hector nodded but kept his attention on Tracy. She was still an unknown variable, thus he didn't trust her. "How's he taking your sudden disappearance?" he asked Tracy.

"Nunzio doesn't cry over anyone. I was with him long enough to find out what you wanted, but knowing he was responsible for Kim's death made the days long." Tracy spoke in heavily accented Spanish, but her pronunciation was good. "Nunzio is lost after his father's death, and his drive for validation is making him sloppy. He might be good as one of your managers, but he'll never run his own crew, not for long anyway."

"Nothing about Gillis, though?" He asked Miguel but kept his eyes on Tracy.

"He's cleaning up his messes here and trying to take over for Roth Pombo. If he gets to the woman, he'll control the money. It won't touch us, but it'll buy him enough willing mercenaries in Mexico to alter the balance of things," Miguel said.

"Did he set Pombo up?"

"I don't know that for sure."

"What's your opinion?" he asked Tracy.

"Whoever Emray Gillis is, he's shy. As desperate as Nunzio is to make a buy, Emray refused to meet with him even though Nunzio wouldn't hand over the money without a face-to-face. We dealt with his man Mitch." Tracy crossed her legs and didn't sound nervous. "Nunzio and I agreed that Emray was somehow involved with the alphabet soup."

"What is this alphabet soup?" Hector laughed. This girl's brilliance was starting to bubble up.

"FBI, DEA, ICE, CIA," she ticked off. "It doesn't matter which one, their objectives are always the same."

"And if Emray gets the money?"

"It's not as simple as getting the money, Señor Delarosa," Tracy said clearly over Miguel's sigh, a sure sign he was starting to get aggravated. "The product the money paid for is still in play as well. From what my sister's old contacts tell me, it hasn't hit the streets yet."

"Pombo got the last shipment out?"

"It's huge and it's here somewhere. The buyers really don't have anyone to retaliate against since Roth's gone and his middle person is dead. If Emray finds the money and the product, he'll be able to entice twice the number of willing men to join his cause."

"What do you think his cause is?"

"To not only control the Mexican cartel, but build one here that'll severely limit anyone who wants a thriving business in the States. It's why he got rid of Roth without bloodshed. Since he was arrested, no one loyal to him can blame Emray because no one can prove the federales got the incriminating information from him."

"You have no proof of that," Miguel said, his hand coming off the armrest. He was moments away from literally slapping her down.

"He's right. It'd be hard to collect enough evidence to prove that to me."

"Has someone told me that?" Tracy said, with her hands up. "No, but Roth Pombo was as insulated as you are in Colombia. The size of his operations not only guaranteed that, it bought him even more influence in Mexico. Only Roth started small and, with smart decisions, rose quickly in the ranks. Emray will do the same, only he'll skip paying his dues so he'll have no respect. That means he'll never acknowledge you and your authority, so when he has the chance, he'll eliminate everything and everyone he sees as a challenge. Then he'll acknowledge you, only because you're a threat that needs killing."

Hector leaned back in his chair and finally turned his eyes toward Miguel. His old friend had made a huge tactical error in bringing Tracy along. In a short conversation she'd proved herself worthy, so she wouldn't be leaving with Miguel. Tracy would spend her time, including her nights, with him. Miguel could either accept it, or not. He'd made up his mind.

"Miguel, the others are waiting to talk to you," he said, and held his finger up to Tracy. "Please stay, so we can finish."

"Hector, come on," Miguel said.

"We're done," he said softly. "Do we understand each other?"

Miguel left without another word or glance at Tracy. "You were brilliant until the end," he said to Tracy once they were alone.

"If you mean making an enemy of Miguel, I couldn't help it. I've been waiting to talk to you, so if I'd sat here and pretended to be the dumb blonde, my chance might never have come again."

"Let's hear your price, then."

"I'll do whatever you need, if eventually you promise me revenge for my sister."

"That might or might not happen, but my terms are simple. I'm not Nunzio or Miguel, so don't think you're free to leave. You're here until I say otherwise. First, I want you to find what I don't know about Emray Gillis."

"That'll take time."

"You have two days."

❖

Wiley slept until noon and woke up alone. Aubrey and Tanith had both been in her bed when she'd gotten home, and even though she'd been quiet, Aubrey rolled toward her as soon as she joined them. She tried to distance herself, but ended up holding Aubrey until she fell asleep.

She thought out her next step as she stared at the ceiling. The only viable option was to take Walter out. She'd handle whatever repercussions came of that, but Walter wanted what Aubrey didn't have to give. She needed to decide whether to share the details with Aubrey, since it wasn't fair to give her anything else to worry about.

"What in the world are you thinking about?" Aubrey said. She'd made it to the bed silently enough that Wiley hadn't noticed her until she spoke. "You still look exhausted."

"Last night was more involved than I thought it'd be, but it was productive." She accepted the cup Aubrey handed over and stared at her when she sat facing her on the bed. For a fleeting moment she was transported back in time to one of the mornings she'd woken up with Aubrey. If she was a religious person, she'd think Aubrey was God's gift to her—the one beauty in her life that absolved every sin she'd ever committed.

She tried not to overthink her actions when she put her coffee cup down and ran her fingers along Aubrey's cheek. Like her dreams through the years, Aubrey's smile never changed, and she'd committed it to memory so long ago.

"Do you want to talk about it?" Aubrey asked, breaking the spell.

Telling a half truth wasn't in her, so she shared with Aubrey everything that had happened, including the fate of Mitch and fake cop. Perhaps these reminders of what she was capable of would make Aubrey give up the notion of a happy reunion. She was clinical about what she'd done, having often reported her actions in debriefings sessions, but Aubrey wasn't a superior.

"They're both dead?" Aubrey asked, and didn't flinch.

"The news will probably cover it today, but no, I left one alive."

"And Natalie was here with a child?"

"A little boy she had with Roth. Her brother is with her, helping her along." She hesitated briefly and mentally prepared for Aubrey's anger. "She has the money these guys want. Maria brokered the deal that gave her the last of Roth's fortune."

"Maria was leaving with her, wasn't she?" Wiley nodded, not expecting this. "God, what a fool you must think I am."

"You tried to make a life for yourself. When I had to go I physically ached, not only because I was walking away, but because I knew you would never spend your life alone. The thought of someone else touching what was—" Her teeth hurt from clicking them together so quickly.

"Mine," Aubrey said softly. "Is that what you were going to say?"

"I have no right to that word, and I'll never judge you for your choices."

"When are you going to forgive yourself?" Aubrey moved slowly until she was lying practically on top of her. "You aren't a monster, you never were. The service you took up made you incredibly good at eliminating targets, but have you ever enjoyed the kill? I mean really relished it?"

"No."

Wiley's short answer was forced and raspy, so Aubrey was glad she'd locked the door on the way in. Their interactions had been hesitant so far, but she thought the odds had improved when Wiley had come to bed the night before. Wiley had made that decision, no one had made it for her; she'd chosen to stay with her and Tanith.

"Then you're the same person I fell in love with." She sat up and straddled Wiley's waist. She'd habitually done that when they'd been together. Teasing Wiley, she'd pin her until she touched her. Wiley always did, gently at first, then in a way that drove her mad. From the way Wiley's nipples hardened, she was remembering those times as well.

"You can sulk and push me away, Wiley, but your heart knows me. It knows you're not only safe with me, but you belong to me." She reached for Wiley's hands and threaded their fingers together. "For once do what you want, not what's expected of you. Whatever you want, take it."

"How can you let so much time go?" Wiley asked, her eyes hiding nothing from her. It was the first time since their bizarre reunion that she had unlocked the gates to the walls she'd erected inside.

"I can choose to be as angry as I've been since the numbness wore off, or I can live in the moment. And since you're looking at me the way you did back then when we were in this position, I pick now." Aubrey went willingly when Wiley pulled her down and kissed her. The joy of knowing how much Wiley wanted her erased the terror that'd started when Wiley left her. Her fear of never truly belonging shriveled in that instant.

"Are you sure?" Wiley asked when she rolled them over.

The people on the other side of the door faded from her mind.

"The door's locked, honey, I'm sure."

Wiley stripped her T-shirt off, and she rolled them over again. Wiley had so many more scars than the last time, proof she'd suffered more than just heartache. Aubrey started with what she knew was a bullet wound on Wiley's right side by pressing her lips to it. There was a need in her to kiss every part of Wiley to prove this wasn't a dream.

She got as far as the spot over her heart before her tears started, and she cursed herself for not having more control. The last thing she wanted was to give Wiley an excuse to stop, and when Wiley moved off, that's what she knew was coming.

When Wiley tugged her sleep pants down it surprised her and made her cry harder. Wiley took things slowly as she stripped her of everything she was wearing, as well as every bit of apprehension. All that was left was Wiley's boxers, but a quick lift of her hips and they were gone.

The moment Wiley lay against her was surreal, because while

she'd never given up the hope of being with Wiley like this again, she'd never been totally sure. All of Wiley's scars had proved all the reasons why, but they'd survived. Both of them.

"You are my greatest wish," Wiley said before she touched her and found her wet.

"Can you tell me first." A small part of her thought it a foolish question, but it was important to know this wouldn't end after the passion had burnt out.

"I love you, Aubrey." Wiley said it as if she savored each word.

To hear them again with Wiley naked beside her was like receiving a full pardon from the governor a minute before execution. It'd been so long since she'd been this desperate. She not only needed Wiley to touch her, she craved it, and almost as if Wiley read her mind she started moving her fingers.

"Yes," she said as she gripped Wiley's shoulder so hard she was sure it hurt. Wiley never stopped, though, slipping her fingers through her wetness and never leaving her clitoris, making it hard with every stroke. Her legs spread farther apart and her tears started again when Wiley lowered her head and kissed her. The act saved her from the abyss her life had become.

"Go inside," she said, thinking she'd come apart into a thousand small pieces if Wiley didn't, and once Wiley did, Aubrey knew in that instant she was home. She opened her eyes and watched the muscles in Wiley's biceps flex as she moved her hand, but the expression of wonder on Wiley's face made her want to drag it out. The walls of her sex clenched around Wiley's fingers and she couldn't run back. She was going to come in Wiley's arms, and no matter all the hell they'd been through, it'd been worth it for this.

Her hips rose to meet Wiley's hand until her orgasm made her stop and enjoy the peak. She was found, and the joy made her cry harder.

"No matter what, promise me you won't sacrifice this…us. I can't and won't go through that again," Aubrey said when her emotions calmed.

Wiley left her fingers inside since Aubrey had grabbed her wrist when she'd tried to pull out. "As long as you know I'll do whatever it takes to keep you safe." Aubrey nodded and lost a bit of her smile. "I promise we'll do whatever it takes to not repeat my rash decisions. You weren't here physically, but I never stopped needing you."

For Wiley, the admission was painful but freeing. She'd been trained not to need anyone. Self-reliance was key to survival, but every dogma, rule, and belief had to have exceptions. Aubrey was hers, and had been from the moment she'd fallen in love.

"You're safe with me," Aubrey said as she traced her eyebrows with the tips of her index fingers. "There's so much I want to give, share, and experience with you that it'll take a lifetime to get through."

"I want to believe you more than anything," Wiley said slowly, and pulled her fingers out. "You have to know that."

"As long as you don't say it's too late for us."

"No, not that, but we have to get through all this before we make permanent plans."

Aubrey nodded as she moved on top and pinned Wiley to the bed. "Right now I'm not interested in tomorrow." Aubrey sat up a little so she could run her hands down her chest. "I need to touch you." Her hands moved lower, stopping at the small nicks she'd amassed in the field. "Can I touch you, Wiley?"

"Yes," she said, and kept her eyes open. She wanted to see Aubrey as she touched her. This wasn't a dream where the illusion would pop like a soap bubble when the slightest noise woke her from a light sleep.

Aubrey followed her hands with her lips, kissing her way down Wiley's abdomen until her mouth was between her legs. There her obvious resolve to go slow snapped as her lips sucked her in as if Aubrey too thought this was a dream she had to rush through before reality stole the joy of finally getting what she desired most.

The pressure and the way Aubrey's hands tightened on Wiley's thighs made her control nonexistent. She welcomed the orgasm that rushed through her like the intense current of the Mississippi River. Her entire body tightened as Aubrey sucked every bit of bliss from her. Her body remembered this, and the thought of losing it again momentarily swamped the pleasure.

"You're mine, and nothing will keep us apart again," Aubrey whispered in her ear as she held her.

Aubrey smiled as Wiley wiped her tears with the corner of the sheet. She hadn't cried in front of anyone in a long while, not wanting to show weakness or vulnerability, but Aubrey was different. She'd always said the truly strong were the ones who didn't hide what they felt from those who loved them. From the start, Aubrey had greedily wanted all of her—the Black Dragon, her darkness, weaknesses, and her love. She'd demanded it as well as her honesty because it was the only way Aubrey knew how to love. Completely and with total abandon.

"I love you," she said quietly as she put her arms around Aubrey. Her cell phone rang, and she picked it up when she saw Walter's name on the display. "Sorry," she said to Aubrey as she answered the call.

"You've been a busy girl," he said. The traffic noise in the background wasn't enough of a clue for her to narrow down where he was.

"So have you, starting with the loss of your job. I'm sure you'll more than make up for your paycheck and pension with your other job." Aubrey pressed against her back when she sat up and grabbed a pen to take notes.

"Don't be a fucking chump who believes idle gossip."

"Does Emray Gillis sound familiar to you?"

"I've been hunting him for a while, so yeah, the name's familiar. It's all I've done for the last ten years."

"One thing I like about you is your consistency." She concentrated on what was happening around Walter, hoping for the one nugget of information that'd flush him out. Once that happened he'd be in her sights—literally.

"How do you mean that?"

"You've been bullshitting me from the beginning and you're still at it." The background noise changed and she got what she was waiting for.

"Large mochasippi, up," a woman said loudly. Walter was in a CC's Coffeehouse, a strictly Louisiana chain. She wasn't sure how far outside New Orleans they'd ventured, but it didn't matter. Walter was in the city.

And as if he'd realized his mistake, the traffic noise reappeared. "I'm not your problem, so don't make the mistake of trying to cross me. I'm calling to warn you."

"About?" She laughed, thinking Walter's balls would probably break a wood chipper.

"Aubrey Tarver," he said, and left the name hanging for dramatic effect, she was sure. "I know you have her, but you've got to know that a lot of people are interested in talking to her. Don't let that tight ass and pretty face fool you. She knows more than she's saying, and she's keeping something that rightfully doesn't belong to her."

"Don't be so simpleminded," she said as she covered Aubrey's hand with hers. "I never make threats. I simply come up with solutions to whatever problem I was ordered to take care of."

"But you're willing to make an exception in my case," Walter said, and laughed.

"You didn't let me finish, Walter. You're simply a problem, and I already have a solution. You need to understand that you're after someone and something that doesn't belong to *you*. Wherever Aubrey Tarver is, she doesn't have what you want, and more important, she belongs to me." She heard Aubrey's quick intake of air and tightened her hold. "When a problem is so personal to me, I'm relentless until I put it behind me."

"You've been relentlessly stupid from the beginning of this, so try to let it register that you have very limited options here. If you don't start to cooperate, don't blame anyone but yourself when people start dying."

The line went dead and she was grateful and frustrated. "That was Walter, the guy who brought the FBI to our door."

"Sounds like he wants you to gift-wrap me and have me delivered along with Maria's money."

"He's getting a gift from me, but it won't have anything to do with you."

❖

Nunzio stared at University Hospital and questioned himself again as to whether he wanted to go in. The phone call he'd taken had forced him to rush over, but now he wondered if this was another trap. Memories of Kim's slashed throat had made him forever skittish.

"Sir, do you want us to come with you?" one of his guards asked.

"Wait here and I'll call if I need you." He crossed the street, glancing at every spot around him for anyone out of the ordinary. It didn't seem like even the feds were watching him.

The room he was searching for was on the third floor, so he didn't need to stop for directions, figuring the fewer people he dealt with, the better. Someone was in the bed by the window, but the patient he'd come for was lying shirtless with a huge bandage from his elbow up along his shoulder and down his chest. Even in sleep the guy appeared to be in pain.

"What happened?" he asked after he'd shaken the guy awake.

"Mr. Luca, you came."

"Yeah, so tell me your name and what the fuck I'm doing here."

Freddie told him about Mitch and how he'd died, but couldn't tell him who the woman with the gun was, or why she'd left him alive. He just knew they'd lost contact with Emray and he was the only one left that he knew of. But he couldn't be sure about either since Emray didn't share very much with them, only things he'd ordered them to do.

"What's that got to do with me?" Nunzio figured this was a waste of time that'd make him late for his meeting with Miguel Gonzalez.

"Mitch and me were going to go on our own, but he's dead. I got nowhere else to go, and I don't know no other life, so I want to work for you."

Nunzio had to stoop to be able to hear him, but once Freddie finished he glanced around the curtain to make sure they didn't have a captive audience listening in. The elderly man had his leg in traction and appeared to be asleep. It didn't matter, though. Coming here was a mistake. He really had become pathetic if he was chasing down flunkies on a whim, because that's what this guy was. He'd been Emray's flunky and knew nothing that could help him.

"Why me?"

"You're the only number Mitch had in his phone besides Emray's."

He had to laugh at the guy's honesty. "Kid, lie back and try to heal. I'm sure something will come to you, but don't call me again. Wasting my time like this would be a mistake that'll set back your recovery."

"You're going to need me." Freddie reached out to stop his retreat. "But you gotta swear you'll protect me," Freddie said, obviously taking a chance by squeezing his hand as he spoke, as if they were old friends.

"Again, why would I do that?" He pulled his hand loose and wiped it on a tissue from the box next to the bed. "If your loyalties lie with Emray, you're no use to me."

"My loyalties were to Mitch. We came up together and he took care of me." Without his hand to hold, Freddie rubbed the large scar on his face, making Nunzio almost turn away in disgust. "The way I feel about it, Emray sent us to die like a pair of bitches he had no use for anymore."

"It's a sad story, but I got no time for this." He was in the hallway when Freddie yelled for him to wait.

"If you sneak me out of here I can show you how Mitch and me were going to start our own crew. We was tired of taking orders, and I wanted to get back at Emray for this." Freddie pointed to his face.

"There's nothing you got that'll make me want to take you anywhere."

"What if I cut you in on the pile you were looking to buy. You got the operation, and I can get the stuff. All I want is to get out of here if you won't give me a job."

"Where are you going to get the money to finance that?" He laughed at the gutsy play. "You're sitting in a charity hospital, for fuck sake."

"Mitch and me know where Pombo's last shipment is, and it's big."

"Who's Pombo?" He was starting to not find this funny anymore.

"He's been moving kilos from Mexico for years, and Emray was trying to jack into his business. The shit Emray offered to sell you belonged to Roth Pombo."

"I'm not starting over by stealing from someone else. Shit like that gets you killed."

"Roth's in jail and no one he was in business with is alive to claim it. Trust me, everyone who touched the shit is dead."

Nunzio looked around the curtain again, but the old man was still sleeping. "Where does Emray fit into all this? If you know about it then he does too."

"Emray wasn't really looking for product—he was after Roth's money. Killed a bunch of people to try and find it, but he didn't." Freddie grimaced when he slightly shifted. "Get me out and I promise you a cut."

This was too good to truly believe, but maybe after the hundred miles of shit he'd had to swim through to get to this point, fate had cut him a break. "And you don't know the woman who shot you?" He was still too weak to cross the bitches who ran this town.

"She asked Mitch about some kid who OD'd, but no."

"You bring anything with you?" He threw a gown over Freddie's chest and grabbed the old man's wheelchair.

Once Freddie was seated, he pushed him out toward the service elevator away from the nurses' station. "This is your last chance to tell me you're full of shit."

"As long as we have a deal, you'll be happy with what I can get for you."

"Now what?" Nunzio asked once he had Freddie in the car.

"We have to wait until tonight, then I'll take you where the stuff is." Freddie was so pale he looked like a bottle of Elmer's Glue, and his face was slick with sweat. "What kind of insurance you gonna give me that you ain't fuck me over once I deliver?"

"Let's start with the truth. I think you're using me, and that's not too smart. If this Roth guy brought in the amounts you're talking about successfully, half the dealers in town would've found it by now." He tapped the driver's headrest so his guy would start driving. "The guarantee I can give you is I won't fucking kill you once I figure out you played me."

"But what if the stuff's real?"

"We'll talk price once I see how much is still left, but I promise fifty grand if it's more than five kilos. How about that?"

"If you don't give me a job that'll be enough for me to get out of here."

"You okay?" Freddie was so wet with sweat, his gown was painted to his body.

"I'm better than Mitch, so my luck's still holding."

CHAPTER TWENTY-ONE

Wiley and Aubrey came out to a quiet house, with only Tanith sitting at the kitchen island with her gaming device. From her closed-off expression, Wiley knew, despite her age, she'd figured out how close she and Aubrey had gotten that morning. So far she hadn't made eye contact.

"Where is everyone?" Aubrey asked as she stepped behind Tanith and kissed the top of her head.

"Granddad and Granny are in their room, and Mr. Buck and Miss Danielle are on the roof taking a look around."

"Can I talk to you, then?" Wiley asked, cocking her head once to give Aubrey the hint to leave.

"Sure, whatever." Tanith shrugged as she spoke.

Wiley took the milk out, along with two glasses, before she sat down. The gaming device was still on, but Tanith's thumbs were still. "Did your mom ever mention me before the night we met?"

"Yeah, when I was little," Tanith said, and shrugged again.

"How'd you feel about that?" Wiley sipped her milk, willing to wait the kid out.

"I was four, I didn't care."

"You're not four now."

"I didn't ask about you, if that's what you mean, but if you liked Mom, didn't it matter to you that she was miserable? Who cares what I think, but she wasn't happy. Not like other people's parents."

"She probably wasn't because she missed me as much as I did her. It won't be like that anymore, but before I try to make things right with her, I want to know what you think." Tanith hadn't raised her head, and her jaws were clenched. "If it was me I'd worry about two things. Is this stranger going to hurt my mom, and where do I fit in now?"

"Yeah, probably," Tanith said, slightly above a whisper.

"I'm not going to hurt your mom. I've done that already by leaving, but I've learned from my mistakes. There's no more running in my future." She let go of her glass and placed her hands toward the middle of the space between them. "You know why you and Maria maybe didn't get along?"

"She didn't like me. There wasn't that much to figure out."

"But do you know why?" Tanith shook her head, but this time she kept her eyes up. "When you meet someone you really like, but they don't feel the same, it makes you want to hurt them. You do it because you feel bad and you want the same for them. When Maria met you and your mom, you both already belonged to someone else, and I think Maria knew that."

"But you didn't know anything about me. Don't lie. I saw your face."

"You're right, I didn't, but you're a gift to me from the one person in my life I've loved. To me you were born the second I saw you in that attic, but you're mine, Tanith." She moved her hands closer. "I love you, and I'll always love you because you're mine. The only way I'll leave is if you can't or won't share your mom with me."

"What took you so long?" Tanith asked with a child's honesty as she jumped from the stool and wrapped her arms around her.

"I'm sorry, kid." The way Tanith embraced her made her eyes water, and some of the Black Dragon's darkness fell away. That part of her would never truly die, but now it'd know peace.

❖

"This is some shit," Don said.

It was late, but Peter, Buckston, and Don all sat in Wiley's home office staring at the updated wall. The information that Walter led a double life made this personal for Wiley. They were waiting for the phone to ring with orders from General Greenwald.

"How could his superiors not have known?" Peter said, both his hands around his coffee mug.

"He was smart, and he was getting results. Roth Pombo was a big fish, and the arrest went over well here and in Mexico." Wiley forced herself to concentrate and not think about Tanith and Aubrey. "It's genius if you really consider it. He brought down a major player, but only after he was ready to fill the void. Top that with the surrogate he put up as his front man, and he became invisible. If it hadn't been for Roth Pombo's need for great record keeping, he'd still be at it."

"It's a good lesson in greed," Buckston said as the phone rang.

"General," Wiley said, since it was the secure line.

"The particulars are in your in-box, Wiley. It didn't take long for the council to see the national-security issues. Their main concern is location, so call me if you can't keep this quiet."

"Any other fallout?" She'd uncovered this, but Washington would've taken her information and expanded on it.

"Not yet, but you know stuff like that has a tendency to springboard into something no one's expecting. Right now, start with your green light and I'll communicate through Don if there's anything else."

"Thank you, sir."

"We'll leave you to it," her dad said as he stood.

Don retrieved the papers from the fax and dropped them on the desk. Every bit of Walter's life was outlined in the document, from his education to his lines of credit. The house where they'd found the land mine wasn't on here, but she gave him more credit in separating his dual life.

"It's great wc can eliminate the problem, but for once there's no map to the target," Don said as he read over her shoulder.

"Walter's going to provide that."

Don laughed. "He has to know how the Agency's going to handle this."

"We're going to override his fear of bullets and jail by giving him what he desires most."

"And that would be?" Don held his hands up and away from his body.

"The money he's already killed to get."

"He's not falling for that."

"You bait a trap with enough honey, and a bear will come out in the dead of winter to get it. Walter's hibernating but he can't go back to the life he had, so he can go only in one direction." She glanced at her board again, trying to find the angle Walter would more likely go for. "He can't run back to his job, so he has to embrace Emray Gillis. Without a bankroll, though, he'll be dead outside two months."

"So you're betting he'll believe you?"

"I don't usually put this much into the front end of any operation. You know better than anyone that I'm the exclamation point the government uses after whatever statement they're trying to make." The only way to get to Walter was to use Natalie Naquin. If she reversed herself and hung Aubrey up as fair game, he'd know she was lying. Natalie was the answer, and not that she wanted her and her family harmed, but if it played out correctly, they wouldn't come close to danger.

"You were here the day Walter first dropped into our lives like a sack of horseshit. Does he strike you as the kind of person who works to get what he wants?" she asked as she stood and pushed the paperwork aside. The only pertinent thing in there was the green light to kill Walter. "He likes to cut corners more than a miter saw, so Roth's hidden treasure trove will draw him out."

She dialed Walter's number and waited. "What will it take to get you out of my life and, more important, out of Aubrey Tarver's life?"

"You're dramatically overrated if you think I'm falling for this shit."

"You've got one shot at this, so try to pay attention. Whatever you did to incarcerate Pombo is your business, but I've got my priorities. To ensure what's important to me stays safe, I'm willing to give up what's not."

"I see an acting job in your future."

"Okay, you've made up your mind, so don't contact me again."

"Wait, you can't take a fucking joke?" This time, wherever Walter was it was quiet. "What can you tell me that'll close Roth's case for good?"

"Maria Ross was a middleman for Roth, but the woman he entrusted all the money to was his lover, Natalie Naquin." Wiley's eyes went from Natalie's picture to Maria's.

"Natalie was involved, but not with Roth," Walter said.

"If you mean Maria again, they only planned to take off when Roth went down. Maria sold the merchandise Roth brought in, but she gave the profits to *her* lover, Natalie. If you'd broken Maria, that's who she'd have given up. Not Aubrey."

"Sad fucking story, but what does it mean?"

"You're interested in talking to whoever has the money, and I know where Natalie is. Do you see the benefit of meeting now?" In her mind she saw the bait hit the water.

"When and where?" Walter asked after a long pause.

"Same place as before. The bar in the W Hotel, and we don't need to go through all the particulars of coming alone, do we?"

"Ten o'clock," Walter said, and disconnected.

"What happens if he shows?" Don asked.

"I'm counting on him showing up, but that's only the first part."

"What's the second?"

"Walter will come, that I'm sure about, but such a public killing where I'm planning to live isn't a good idea. Once he sees me, he'll know I'm not bluffing, but I need him to know it's a trap." She moved Roth Pombo's mug shot down next to Walter's picture. "I need Walter to run for his life."

❖

Nunzio stretched out his fingers before making another fist. After they'd left the hospital, Freddie had asked to be let out close to the French Quarter so he could finalize that night's events. That he'd agreed, and actually believed what Freddie said, made Nunzio question his sanity. His grandfather would doubt his IQ once he found out.

"There he is," Nunzio said to the two guards with him. "Wait here."

He adjusted the pistol tucked into the back of his waistband and walked slowly to where Freddie stood outside the Hilton. The bar was the only logical conclusion, which made him a sucker. The police had to have collected anything of value.

"Thanks for coming," Freddie said as he led him into the building.

"That police crime-scene tape means there's nothing in there," he said, and pointed to the still-dark bar.

"Maria didn't mix Pombo's shipments with her regular inventory, but Mitch didn't figure that out until she was dead. We went through the stockroom before the cops. There wasn't anything, and according to word on the pavement she hadn't moved a speck, so we went looking after we found this." Freddie held up a room key out of Nunzio's reach.

"You really found it?"

"Come on," Freddie said, talking slow, he guessed, because of the pain.

The tenth-floor room was a simple setup with two queen beds, but you could only see the foot of both. Stacked on them, between and around, were boxes of tequila. Dozens of them.

"I don't know how you turn all this shit back to powder, but this is what a lot of fucking coke looks like," Freddie said as he lifted a bottle up. "Never met this guy Pombo, but Emray fucked him. Since he was this smart, I can't believe Emray even got the chance, but this was the last shipment he got in."

Nunzio had heard of liquid cocaine, but only in doctors' offices. He had never heard of Roth Pombo, but Freddie was right. He was a fucking genius. He took the bottle Freddie held out to him and studied the top. It was sealed and marked like a real bottle of booze. The port authority or customs wouldn't have any reason to think it wasn't.

"The bar took a shipment about once a month, from what Mitch said Emray told him. That's a lot of money, and Emray spent a shitload of his own trying to find it," Freddie said.

"Did he?"

"The night Mitch first met with you, he'd hired some guys to hack up the bitch who owned the place downstairs."

"And?" Nunzio asked, quickly losing his patience.

"A whole lot of body bags came out of there, and Emray never got shit. It drove him crazy, and he kept threatening us cause we didn't find Pombo's stash." Freddie leaned against a stack of boxes and held the bottle by the neck. "That's when Mitch decided we needed to split, using this as our way out."

"How long is the room paid for?"

"Mitch checked, and we got it until the weekend. Maria paid for it by the month."

"You want the job or your cut more?" Nunzio asked. He had no way of knowing exactly how much all this was worth or how much powder it'd yield, but it was what he needed at the moment.

With this he could blow off Hector, Emray, and any other arrogant asshole who wanted him to beg for his cut. Finally his luck had turned. Not only had fate dropped this in his lap but given him an idea that'd assure a profitable future. This simpleton had in a way provided him something tangible to work toward. If he could set up the same operation Roth Pombo had, he'd be bigger than his father ever dreamed of.

"You offering now?" Freddie said. He'd had to put the bottle down so he could place his hand over his wound. From the grimace, his pain was back full force.

"If you're willing to come to New York with me. New Orleans will be our starting point like this Pombo guy's, but I don't want to live in this hot hellhole."

"I don't know nothing about New York."

He took his phone and ordered his guys to get a rental truck and some dollies. He had to get this out before anyone else knew it existed. "We got to start with this, but not here. Let Emray waste time with the money, but he's not the only one trying to do business in the city. The longer this sits, the more we have to worry about someone trying to take it away from us. You get that?"

"Who'd be whacked enough to try that?"

"Ever hear of Hector Delarosa?"

"If you're leaving, I'm coming. The job's more important." Freddie moved closer and held his good hand out. "I got your back, Mr. Luca."

"Good," Nunzio said, and shook his hand. "We'll be back eventually, and when we do, we'll own this town. That means I'll be able to settle every score, even if I got to blow this place to hell to make it happen."

CHAPTER TWENTY-TWO

A re you sure about this?" Aubrey asked as Wiley put on a bulletproof vest under her T-shirt.

"The vest or the plan?" When the last Velcro strap tightened over her shoulder, Wiley's breath quickened from the sense of claustrophobia. She rarely used a vest even in the worst of situations because she thought it threw her aim off. Tonight it was just another prop in the charade she was trying to run on Walter.

"Are you sure this guy doesn't recognize our fathers?"

"I really wanted your dad to stay here, but he refused." She opened her arms to Aubrey and cursed the vest again. Not only did it stop bullets, but it blunted the warmth of Aubrey as she pressed against her. "I promise this won't take long."

"Please don't think I asked because I don't trust you." Aubrey leaned back so she could see her face. "In so many ways I believe I don't deserve you."

"Why say that?"

"Because even if you haven't said anything, I know, like you do, that Maria was a huge betrayal to what we had. I should've waited since I knew you'd come back."

"You don't owe me anything now, and you didn't back then."

Aubrey shook her head and shut her eyes tight. "Don't be so self-sacrificing, Wiley. It's okay to be honest. Every time you go out to try to get me out of this mess, it scares the shit out of me that I'll lose you. I can't let that happen without saying anything."

"You want the truth?" She put her hand at the back of Aubrey's neck and gently brought her head toward her shoulder. No matter how many medals for valor and bravery the military had awarded her, they'd never make up for the cowardice of walking away from Aubrey. In time she'd realized it was the easiest solution, but not the right one. Walking away had been a mistake that she had compounded over the years by not coming back. There was no forgiveness for that.

"Maria wasn't a betrayal, but a gift." Aubrey tried to look her in the face again, but she held her in place. "I walked away to keep you safe, that was true, but I'd convinced myself that I had no choice. In reality I panicked because I didn't know what to do. Leaving was the last thing I should've done."

Aubrey relaxed against her, but she'd have to let her go eventually. If she walked because she was finally being honest, she'd have to beg to make her stay. "Now, though, I'm getting another chance to get it right, and what you see as a betrayal isn't the way I see it. If you'd loved Maria, if she'd been perfect for you and Tanith, I would've always had to live with the regret of what I'd done. I can't blame you for finding someone to fill the void I dug for us, and I sure as hell won't ever hold it against you. Because Maria wasn't the right fit, and because she made you miserable, I get another shot."

"But there are mistakes, and then there's this mistake. I couldn't have gone out of my way to make it bigger than this."

"Did Maria tell you she dealt on the side?"

Aubrey laughed and shook her head. "Give me more credit than that."

"I'll be happy to if you'll do the same. Maria was a convenience, I know that, so forgive yourself. I never met her, but she strikes me as the kind who would've acted any way and said anything to get what she wanted. And she obviously wanted you." She kissed Aubrey's lips lightly. "The drugs weren't smart, but I can't fault her for wanting you."

"You're a generous grader." Aubrey hugged her and laid her head on her shoulder. "Be careful tonight, and keep an eye on my dad. My mom's starting to really like you, so I don't want anything to derail that," she said, and laughed.

"No problem." She rested her head against Aubrey's. "If this works we might see the end of this soon. I'm sure you're tired of being cooped up in here."

"Being inside has its advantages."

"I talked with Tanith." She didn't mean to change the subject from Aubrey's flirting, but it was almost time to go.

"She told me."

"I know it might take time, but I'd like to try for a future that includes all three of us."

"You may not realize it, but you won Tanith over from the very beginning. I think she's been starved for someone other than me and my parents in her life, and you showed a genuine interest in filling that gap." Aubrey lifted her head and looked at her. "She's gravitated to you because you want a relationship with her, not pretending because you want one with me. Does that make sense?"

"It does," she said, and kissed Aubrey again. "We'll try not to be too late, but no phone calls tonight, so don't worry that something's wrong if you don't hear from us."

"You are coming back though, right?"

"Yeah, no more disappearing acts. I promised Tanith my running days are over."

"Good," Aubrey said, dropping her hands to her chest. "And the reason you need this is?" she asked about the vest.

"Walter wants two things right now," she held up two fingers, "the money and his freedom. As important as the cash is, his freedom is paramount since he figures as Emray he can make more. Getting caught, considering what he did for Uncle Sam, doesn't necessarily mean jail time. If his superiors fear what he knows, and what he can do with that knowledge, they'll clean up their mess."

"Okay." Aubrey dragged out the word.

"The vest is part of my cleaning costume. At least that's what I want Walter to think."

"You're planning to kill him?" Aubrey asked, but didn't appear disgusted.

"Not tonight."

❖

"Where'd they find him?" Tracy asked the patrol officer that her contact in the police department had led her to. From the moment the guy sat down he'd looked at her chest and the fan of hundreds under her hand. One of Miguel's men sat close by but feigned disinterest. When she snapped her fingers the guy broke out of his titty trance.

"Here's the report." He handed over an envelope. "It gives a few addresses because he was parked on the street with someone named Fred Buhl. Freddie got shot too, but before we could question him he vanished from the hospital."

"The department didn't have him under surveillance?"

"We don't have enough guys for that."

"What else is in here?" she asked as she tapped the envelope against the top of her hand.

"The detectives who worked the call said the weird thing was Freddie got shot through the windshield, but his buddy Mitch bought it at close range from the backseat. They thought different at first, but the trajectory indicates shots from two different directions. Whoever ordered this sent a killing team."

She slid over five bills and kept five. "Nothing on Emray Gillis?"

"We've picked up some punks in the last few months who mentioned that name, but no one's ID'd him yet. I'm beginning to think he's like Bigfoot. Plenty of people claim to have seen him, but there's no proof he's real." The guy put the money she'd given him in his breast pocket and laughed, obviously at the analogy he'd made. "Stop wasting time chasing this guy down. He doesn't exist."

"Mitch Surpass was his front man, and someone killed him. Because you didn't think Freddie was important, you lost the only link you know of to this guy you don't think is real." She folded the remainder of the money and pocketed it. "Brilliant."

"How much is Freddie worth to you?"

"You'd be surprised," she said as she stood. This guy was a dead end.

Even if Hector had given her a year, her time would have been up. Emray Gillis was in the wind after someone made a move on his organization. Tracy figured he'd disappear until his house was in order again. Who was the new player? The storm might have decimated the city's population, but it was getting crowded with gunslingers trying to mark their territory.

But that was something for Hector to worry about. Her problem was staying alive when she told her new boss she couldn't give him what he wanted. Not yet anyway. Keeping Hector happy was key to getting what she wanted in return. It was the only way she'd share all the training and wisdom her sister Kim had given her before she was murdered.

Tracy closed her eyes on the ride back to the house, using the time to organize her thoughts. When the car stopped and the driver opened the door, the first thing she saw was Miguel's vehicle. He was another, not unexpected, surprise she'd have to deal with.

The conversation stopped when she was escorted into Hector's study. Miguel sat there, along with the woman she recognized from all the family photos. This had to be Marisol Delarosa.

"Well?" Hector asked. "Where is my trophy?"

"Mitch Surpass, Emray's front man, is dead." She handed over the police report. "I just found out, so give me a few days to discover why he was killed in his car parked in the vicinity mapped on there."

"Mitch was your only lead," Marisol asked.

"Mitch was anyone's only lead. He represented Emray's interest, but someone else was in the car with him." She told them about Freddie and rushed through the part about him being missing. "We find him, and with some creative incentive, you'll have Emray."

"Disappointing," Hector said as he swiveled his chair away from her.

"I apologize, but you can't have expected me to find someone none of your people have been able to in such a short period of time." She was being disrespectful, which could bring her closer to Hector or to him ordering her killed. Strength was all these guys understood, Kim had told her.

"Listen, you bitch," Miguel said as he got on his feet.

"Enough," Hector said loudly. "With all this complaining you're starting to remind me of an old woman." He returned his attention to her. "Forget Gillis for now, and tell me what you haven't about Nunzio."

"I got everything from him you asked for."

"Then why did he just call and tell Hector and me to fuck ourselves?" Miguel screamed.

"That's unexpected," she said, and kept her eyes on Hector.

"Let me explain something to you, Tracy," Hector said, and waved her into a chair close to his daughter. "When I was a young man, I knew I wanted more than hustling a few dollars on the streets of Bogotá. My first step in getting here," he pointed his index fingers down, "was to make a big play. I stole the biggest shipment I could pull off from someone higher than me. I did that numerous times until I could afford to kill the enemies I'd made. That sent a message to anyone who tried to take away what I'd gotten for myself."

Tracy nodded and clamped her jaw shut. This wasn't the time to interject anything. "Roth Pombo's business was essential to what I want most. Only before I could take what I needed, someone cut his legs out from under him, and what was left was easy to deal with except for Emray Gillis. He wants the same things I do, but in this game there can be only one winner."

"I understand that, sir."

"Do you? Do you realize how big Pombo was getting? Actually he reminds me a lot of you. He was smart, and because he thought he was the smartest boy in the playground, he forgot that at times the most savage is the only one left alive."

Marisol smiled and nodded when her father spoke. "Miguel and I have tried to find how he was able to move such a large amount of product in without any problem. The only thing we found in the last shipment makes two things possible. Either it can bring someone enough power to put our family in danger, or it can make my father the head of the cartel. I don't think when you and Nunzio met with Mitch, you realized this. Pombo's last shipment is a bomb ready to explode, with devastating consequences."

"And you think Nunzio has it?" Tracy asked.

"He has it," Hector said, as if expecting everyone to agree with him. "And what you said about respect will come into play here. How do you think he feels about me? Now that he has the prize, will he forget your betrayal and how we treated him?"

"What would you like me to do?" she asked. Sitting here was suddenly like having been dropped into a viper pit. The fear of danger was licking every part of her body like the forked tongues of a thousand deadly snakes ready to strike.

"I could use you as bait for Nunzio." Hector smiled as he said it. "But I believe you to still be of value to me, so don't worry. You know Nunzio better than all of us, so find him so I can show him my savage side. Unlike those who he crossed before, I won't leave him alive."

"We need to start with the story of what has happened up to now," Tracy said to no one in particular. "Why would Pombo have sent another shipment when he was already out of the game, as you say? If the federales have him, what could he hope to get from that?"

"It's in your best interest to find out," Marisol said. Hector might not have threatened her directly, but his daughter didn't seem to mind.

"It's in all our best interests," she answered.

❖

The Whiskey Blue Bar in the W Hotel downtown was surprisingly full, with what seemed like young professionals from the surrounding buildings trying either to blow off steam or to not go home to a long list of renovations. Wiley sat in the darkest corner she could find and watched Walter literally sweat as his head swiveled around enough to give him an ache. The cocky manner in which he'd always conducted himself seemed to have vanished, along with the money and drugs he was searching for.

"Do you all see him?" Wiley spoke into the mike attached to the top button of her shirt.

"Yeah," her father answered. "You ready for us to move?"

"Wait until we're about two minutes into our talk, then try to coordinate it so you each take a door. We're going for a take-flight response from our boy."

She moved across the room, trying to stay out of Walter's line of sight until the last possible moment. The way he jumped when she put her hand on his shoulder made her almost laugh out loud. Walter's whole life had changed in a very short period of time, and he didn't act like he was taking it well.

"Fuck," Walter said, pressing his hands to the bar as if to hide that they were shaking.

"No, thank you. You're not my type." She waved the bartender off and sat on the stool next to Walter's. It took him a few seconds to look at her, and as she watched his eyes zero in on the vest, she could almost see his brain cells slamming together, trying to come up with a reason for the change in her tactics. "Do you want to try to lie to me some more about what you're planning to do or not do, or can we get this over with?"

"You don't want guarantees I'll stay away from Aubrey?" As he spoke his smile began to come back, but it was short-lived. The way she'd asked her backup group to dress had captured Walter's attention completely. He had to recognize Don, but her father and Peter weren't familiar, and from his expression he had no idea who they were but guessed why they were there. "You fucking bitch," he said as he grabbed Wiley's arm and squeezed hard.

"Give me who you're working with and this all ends with you

walking out of here." She didn't try to get out of the hold Walter had on her, but he didn't notice her moving her other hand. Under the bar she pressed a pistol hard enough into his crotch that he stopped fidgeting immediately. "I'm not interested in you facing a jury or giving up what you've already made, using whatever name you want. I'm here because I want Aubrey and her family taken out of the line of fire and out of the mind of everyone who's interested in asking questions she has no answers for."

"I'm not this Emray Gillis, don't make that mistake," Walter said, and sounded almost sincere. "You can shoot me, but that's not going to do shit for what you want."

She turned toward Don for a second and nodded. "Not what I wanted to hear."

"Wait," Walter said when Don started toward them. "Emray Gillis was someone a guy named Hector Delarosa made up to keep everyone occupied with trying to figure out who he was while he moved in on Pombo's business. I'm trying to do my job by finding both the money and the drugs."

"You've been burned, Walter. I'm not that stupid."

"I'm telling you the truth. Maria worked for Pombo, and together with Natalie they planned to rip him off. When Pombo got taken down they tried to move up their timeline to leave with the cash. Hector wanted it all, though, so he took out Maria, trying to find out where all the shit was, and when that happened, Natalie went underground." He spoke fast, like he only had a small window before he really had nothing but a small window in the cell she was fixing to put him in.

"Hector Delarosa is behind this? That's the best you got? Walter, it wasn't this Delarosa guy who showed up with a warrant at my house looking for the Tarvers and acting as if they were fugitives. That was you, and that makes Natalie's story on Emray trump yours."

"I'm not fucking with you. I went to your house because I was after the same thing you are, keeping the Tarvers safe."

"What I see is a simple solution," she said, putting her gun away and preparing herself for Walter's response.

"What, turn me in to these goons? I haven't done anything wrong that anyone can prove, so you're fucked if that's your answer."

"No, Walter, I'm going to do what I've spent my whole career doing. When I was sent into the field, everyone I answered to wanted the job done however I needed to do it without any ramifications." She leaned a little away from him, prompting Don and her father to take a step in. "You just gave me the easiest out to a situation the Tarvers and I want no part of."

"What the hell are you talking about?"

"If Hector Delarosa really wants Emray Gillis, I'm going to hand him over. I don't know the man, but I'm sure his reach is longer than mine."

"Weren't you listening? Gillis doesn't exist. It's a name Hector made up."

"I'm willing to test that theory. Are you?"

That's all it took. Walter's expression closed off as the fear grew, and from what she could tell it was the kind of fear that spread faster than a virus. Like her, Walter knew how to play the government they both worked for, but men like Delarosa didn't bother with rules of engagement. You screwed someone like that and you ended up tied to a showerhead getting cut to pieces by some animal who'd go out to dinner after he finished.

She put her hand on the back of Walter's neck and squeezed. "I'm going to return the favor of sending unwanted guests to your door, and then, unlike you and your need to control me, you'll never cross my mind again."

If she hadn't been expecting it, Walter would've knocked her to the ground as he tackled his way past Don. She followed him as far as the lobby and watched him speed off in the back of a cab.

"Now what?" Don asked.

"We have to call General Greenwald since I don't want to deal with the FBI directly."

"For?"

"I want Delarosa's background and contact information. After I get in touch with him, we'll deal with Walter."

"How are you going to do that? Your whole supposed team was in there," Peter said.

"Walter can stand in a shower for the next month and he won't wash off what came off my fingers." She walked them to her vehicle and started her evasive route home. "Our target is painted, so don't worry about how far he runs. Once you wake a sleeping dragon, there's nowhere to hide."

❖

Nunzio stared at the moving van they were following. With his men dividing the driving time, they'd be in New York in a day. Freddie sat next to him, asleep after taking three pain pills at once. How long he'd let him stick around was something he'd worry about later, after he'd gotten all the information Freddie had.

He smiled when he thought of Tracy, Miguel, and Hector. The gift Freddie had led him to had helped him get over any humiliation they'd made him suffer. For the first time in a long while, he was invincible, and eventually he'd prove it to the world.

"We've got a guy waiting that can help us make this street-ready, Mr. Luca," the driver said after he put his phone down.

"Who recommended him?"

"Your grandfather. His man said he's been working on it since you called. He also sent word that he'll be waiting when we arrive."

Finally he'd proved himself worthy of his name. He'd lived his whole life to hear either his dad or grandfather say that.

That time was now.

CHAPTER TWENTY-THREE

General Greenwald had come through the next morning, so Wiley ate breakfast with everyone before she left alone. At the elevator Tanith hugged her, tentatively at first, but after Wiley wrapped her arms around her, she tightened her hold. To get to know Tanith, and help Aubrey raise her, gave her life much more meaning than her duties as the Black Dragon ever could.

"Will you come back?" Tanith asked her when the three of them rode down together.

"It might be late, but yes. I have only a few things left to do so you can get back to school and your friends."

She was willing to keep that promise by perhaps making a deal with the type of man she'd battled for so long. Granted, her superiors had given her their blessing, but that she was taking a shortcut twisted the sense of justice that burned in her into a knot.

When she arrived at her destination, she parked the big Harley she'd chosen for the trip where she imagined the surveillance van usually sat always watching, always listening. That the watchers were gone seemed to put the men patrolling the grounds on edge, since they stopped and stared as she removed her helmet. When she unbuckled her leather saddlebag, more than a couple of them put their hands on their weapons.

Judging by the number of guards, the size of the house, and the cars parked outside, Hector Delarosa was a successful man. He was at the top of the food chain, and in her experience, no amount of surveillance ever brought these guys down. Roth Pombo was the anomaly, but Walter had destroyed him for his own selfish reasons. A blow for the greater good was the last thing on his agenda.

"Get lost," the man at the gate said with a heavy Spanish accent.

"Tell Señor Delarosa I'm here to give him Emray Gillis, if he's interested. You have two minutes. Then I ride away after calling him and telling him *you* refused the offer," she said in decent Spanish. After the guy had a brief conversation on the phone close to the gate, it swung open.

She walked the length of the long drive, keeping her eyes on the front door. She wasn't here for reconnaissance, and General Greenwald had called off the agents out front for only the morning. As the door started to open, the tingle in her scalp that was part fear and part adrenaline made her lips curl slightly upward. She'd stayed in the field so long because of this rush. Nothing but having Aubrey love her had duplicated it.

The young woman waiting was truly stunning, even though her face was an expressionless mask. "I'm Marisol Delarosa," the woman said, turning as if expecting her to follow.

She walked with her eyes glued to the back of Marisol's head. She didn't intend to spook a group of paranoid and highly armed people. Marisol led her to a study where three people waited, and she recognized the handsome man behind the desk as Hector from the intel packet she'd received. He and Marisol had the same facial structure.

"Who are you?" the man sitting with a blond woman across the big desk asked.

"I'm no one." Her response made Hector laugh.

"I've stayed safe all my life by not trusting no one," Hector said.

"In my life I stay safe by being no one, and if you want what's in here," she touched the folder under her arm, "you'll acknowledge that I'm no one you want to remember."

"The other thing I rarely trust are gifts that simply drop into my lap." Hector spread his hands out. "Especially if no one takes credit."

She opened the folder and started laying the pictures out on his desk. The first group she put out for him were the ones Natalie had given her. The next set showed Maria's mutilated body and the men sent to kill her.

The other man in the room and Marisol moved to stand behind Hector. "I'm not sure how social you are with your competitors, but the man on the yacht is Roth Pombo," she said, and pointed to the first picture she'd laid down. "This is Maria Ross." She indicated the bloody mess. "Maria worked with Pombo to get his stuff into this country from Mexico."

"How do you know this for sure?" Marisol asked.

Wiley gave the briefest synopsis of the history Maria, Roth, and Natalie shared. "When Roth was taken into custody, Maria tried to negotiate their last deal so she could leave with Natalie. She did this with Roth's blessing."

"I know of Roth Pombo," Hector said. "I've never personally met him, but he's more known for his viciousness than his charity."

"Natalie gifted him with what no one else ever could, a son. She took their baby and the money Roth gave her, so she won't be a problem for you or anyone. Her concern is strictly for her child."

"Understandable," Hector said. "But it doesn't explain why no one would come to my house to share their tale."

"Weren't you ever curious how Roth was taken down? He had to have had the same level of insulation you enjoy from the regular policeman on the street." She removed one of the two pictures she had left. "How could some beat cop take someone like you down? Because that's what happened." The picture she'd shown him was of Roth sitting on his yacht with the supposed Tajr member.

When Hector glanced down she noticed the slight reaction. The flare of his nose and the widening of his eyes meant Hector knew this guy, terrorist or not.

"When was this?" Hector put his hand over the photo.

"About a week before Roth was sent to Almoloya de Juárez."

"This fool brought him down?"

"No, this one did." The last photo showed Walter's face clearly as he maneuvered the speed boat next to Roth's vehicle. "If you wanted Emray Gillis, there he is."

"He did business with Roth, then set him up?"

"Actually, he was sent to Mexico to find out how Roth's business ran. He was assigned to figure out how he moved product and who was working for him. Emray is really Walter Robinson of the CIA."

Hector sat back and cut his eyes up to the man behind him. Whatever the silent communication was, the guy paled considerably. "Where is he now?" Hector said, his voice now controlled and his face neutral again.

"That I don't know."

"How convenient that you don't have an ending to your story," Hector said, and smiled. His upturned lips in a way marred his good looks.

"Like you said, you have no reason to trust me, but I truthfully don't know where Walter is at this moment." She wasn't lying since she didn't have a tracking device in her hand. "That's not why I'm here."

Hector picked up Walter's picture and handed it to Marisol, who then left the room with it. "No one wants credit but perhaps is interested in a reward for this because I'm grateful for the visit."

"I simply want one reward." She placed the folder on his desk and folded her hands together at her front, not wanting to appear threatening in any manner. "I need you to understand that I don't know where Roth's last shipment is and if Natalie left with the money. Perhaps Maria Ross gave up that secret before she died, or perhaps it died with her and the men she might've told it to."

"I believe you, so what do you want?"

"Only your understanding that neither I nor anyone close to me knows where this stuff is, and that we're not interested in finding out. Walter could never accept that message."

"That's all you want?" Hector picked up everything she'd brought and placed it in the folder. "All this is worth more to me than that."

"It's not worth more than my family. My price is for them to be able to stop looking over their shoulders for something they have no clue about."

"Why me?" Hector placed the folder in the drawer to his left. "Why bring this to me?"

"Walter blamed you for Maria and for Pombo, and he swore he had proof."

"And still you're here."

"It's simple," she said, and noticed the time. They had fifteen minutes before the watchers were back on post. "Walter's a lying scum, and you're going to take the fall for him if he can orchestrate it. That means if you catch up to him, he'll reverse himself and blame me or the people I care about."

"Can you at least tell me if you're FBI or DEA?"

"I'm retired, but not from either of those agencies. You have nothing to fear from me, and after today we'll never meet again unless by chance."

"The hunters outside, though, left before you arrived. Obviously you are not just anyone."

"I've done enough for people to owe me a few favors. Believe me, I'm not powerful enough to make them disappear from your life permanently. They'll be back shortly, so I've got to go. Do we have a deal?"

"We do, and thank you," Hector said as he stood and shook her hand.

Another woman led her all the way to the gate and smiled at her as she locked it. She'd started Walter running the day before, and this would ensure he'd go as far as he could get. That's what she wanted, along with wiping Aubrey and Tanith off anyone else's hit list. She hadn't wanted to push, but she wondered who Walter's terrorist was. From Hector's response, he knew and so did his man.

"Enjoy your freedom, Walter. It'll be short-lived."

❖

"Explain this to me," Hector said as he held up one of the pictures the woman had brought.

"He's my brother and a bastard. I'm not responsible for him or anyone else in my family," Miguel said defensively. "I'm loyal only to you."

"Tracy, leave us," Hector said as he glared at Miguel. It was hard not to lash out for what he took as a lie. "What the hell is this on his chest, and what's he doing with a CIA agent?"

"I don't know. Diego has always been one for easy money. Give me time and I'll find out, but you're taking the word of some nameless bitch you met today over mine."

"A picture is worth more to me than words, Miguel." The door opened again and Marisol entered with four men. "I love you like a brother, but this is more than coincidence. I've given you months to find this asshole who's trying to gut us all, and he's with Diego. Do you honestly want me to believe you had no idea this was happening?"

"Yes, I want you to think about what I've done for you, then believe me when I say I had no idea."

"How many fucking trips did you make to Mexico to find out what I wanted? In all those trips you had to have run into Diego at some point. You never mentioned that. Either you're planning to betray me, or you've gotten lazy."

"Hector, come on. I deserve your consideration."

"Like the woman said, it's about family and keeping them safe."

"For the love of God, I'd kill myself before I'd betray you."

"Thanks for the offer." He nodded once. It was time to promote from within, so he called Tracy back in. "What's your advice?"

"It depends on what will happen with Miguel."

"Miguel is moving on."

"Then he should take his brother with him, since there's no way he didn't tell Miguel who Emray Gillis is."

"And this strange tattoo?"

"It looks Arab to me, and something easily dangled up for the Mexican and American authorities to distract them. No wonder they took Pombo down if they thought he was helping a terrorist."

"Will you be as loyal to me as Miguel has been?"

"Miguel has proven disloyal," Tracy said as she crossed her legs. Her skirt hiked up her thigh, but he didn't take it as a come-on. "Think of my loyalty as a lifetime commitment, like my sister gave to Nunzio."

"According to you he led her to her death."

"He did, and eventually he'll pay for that. What's important is Kim's visit with you before that day."

"She was ready to throw Nunzio over, so that's the example you want to use to convince me to open my door to you?"

"If that's true Nunzio would've been dead, then left like garbage. She went with him because she loved him, but her visit here was to tie my future to you. She didn't want me to repeat her mistakes." Tracy stood and took the two steps to touch his desk. "I was your gift from her, so it's time to accept or let me go."

"Was she telling the truth about the money?" He pointed to the door as he got up as well.

"Yes, and I'd guess more people than Maria Ross knew where Roth's stash was."

"Where is it?" He walked around and held his hand out to her.

"The only way Nunzio had the cojones to blow you off is if he found it."

"That'll give us a place to start, then," he said as he watched his men carry Miguel out. His longtime friend was slumped between the two larger men, and Marisol followed them out. "Perhaps my future lies in new alliances."

❖

Wiley started the bike and took the shortest route home, secure that no one was following. The meeting pleased her because of how it'd gone, but it disgusted her to have to go to someone like Hector. He'd throw everyone on his payroll at Walter, but she missed the anonymity of her scope. Problems were so much easier to solve with a quick squeeze of the trigger.

The first floor of her place was empty, so she took her time putting her helmet away and used the phone. "Thank you for the window, sir."

"Anything of value?" General Greenwald asked.

"You can tell anyone who got spooked by the terrorist Walter photographed with Roth that it's probably a false alarm. Delarosa didn't say anything, but I believe he recognized him. If you find him I'm sure the tattoo is paint-by-numbers." She kept her eyes on the stairs and the elevator as she spoke. It didn't shock her to see Aubrey on her way down the steps.

When she put her finger up, Aubrey sat and smiled at her. "This started as a fluke, but we stumbled into a shakeup in the cartels' hierarchy."

"Would you be opposed to helping us defuse the situation?"

"I'll take the shortest solution."

Greenwald laughed. "Sure, but finding Walter might take time."

"If you give me a ride to and from work when I ask, I don't think that'll be a problem."

She gently put the phone down and looked at Aubrey. Something in her eyes must've scared Aubrey because she got up and came closer.

"Don't do that," Aubrey said as she put her hands on Wiley's cheeks. "It's like you can't help giving in to the fear, but if you do, there'll be no room for me."

"Doesn't it ever scare you?" She closed her eyes and rested her head against Aubrey's chest. Though years had passed since that van exploded right before her, she hadn't forgotten even the smallest detail of the scene. The memory of the mix of smells at times made her nauseous still, but she'd fought hard not to forget. Forgetting meant she could relax and try to gain her life back. It'd been an unacceptable reality for so long.

"The moment I became a mother, I swore I'd do anything and everything to keep Tanith safe. No sacrifice, no amount of misery I had to live through would be too great as long as my daughter was safe." Aubrey lifted her head and kissed both of Wiley's eyelids, as if to get them to flutter open. "It'll always be my goal, but by trying to do the right thing for her, I ended up hurting her more than anything. I've learned that I could forgo my own happiness to make her whole, but truthfully that ended up hurting her as much as my staying away from you did me. Maria did everything to put her in harm's way, and I wasn't happy with her."

"You believe me that I'll do everything to keep her safe, right?"

"I believe that with everything I am. I know that as well as I know you'll do whatever you can to give her and me the love and attention that'll end up making the difference in how Tanith looks back at this time." Aubrey kissed her and crawled to straddle her lap. "I want her to see what it is to love someone and how the intensity of it should take your breath away. That's worth everything, and I'll take a chance on having it even if it's for only a short time. It'll be worth it."

"You might have to say that more than once to bring my paranoia down a few notches over the next months."

"I'll tell you as often as you need to hear it," Aubrey said, then kissed her again. The way Aubrey held her with such fierceness made Wiley want her right there, to hell with whoever else was in the house. Her body burned and ached at the same time. "How did today go?"

"It won't matter now how long it takes to catch up to Walter. I gave him plenty to worry about and more incentive to run."

"Why not confront him here?"

"Because here is where I plan to live with you, Tanith, and your parents, since they lost their house in all this, and I don't like to make messes where I live. Right now that's not the government's agenda anyway." She touched from the bottom of Aubrey's neck to the top button of her jeans. "They want Walter to run to whoever helped him put this together, sort of like putting bait out and waiting for the ants to take it back to the nest. Once you have them all in sight you take care of the bunch."

"Do you know how much I want you right now?"

Warmth spread from her chest downward to her crotch. As it inched forward as if spreading tentacles of desire and passion through her, she felt like she was thawing after a deep freeze. "I do, but right now I want to go up and let Tanith pick a bedroom so she can change whatever she wants to make it feel like hers. Your parents can do the same."

"How about me?" Aubrey asked with a smile so big it shattered the last of her doubts.

"You have a room," she said, and stood with Aubrey still wrapped around her. "You can change whatever you like, except the woman in the bed next to you. Tonight will be the first time of many that we lock the door and put a bullet through old fears. You're mine, and I want to show you how lucky I believe I am that you're finally back here with me."

CHAPTER TWENTY-FOUR

A week later Wiley left Aubrey sleeping as she put her uniform on, waiting until she was in the den to put her boots on. They'd said their good-byes, like they had in the beginning, the night before because Aubrey didn't like crying in front of her—never had.

Tanith wasn't used to that custom, so Wiley sat next to her on the sofa and watched her tie up the green laces in silence. A week of her paying special attention to Tanith had erased the worry lines no one under ten should have, and the night before she'd sat on her bed and explained mission timelines and how many days she could be gone. Tanith hadn't gotten hysterical but she wasn't happy either.

"Did Mom tell you to be careful?"

"More than once, but you can say it again. I don't mind."

"Can I see them again before you leave?" Wiley tossed her jacket aside and stripped her T-shirt off. As she'd done often since Wiley had first shown them to her, Tanith ran her finger along her and her mother's names on the Tanith tattoo. "Do you think Mom would let me have one of these?"

"Maybe one day when you have a partner and child you want to carry around with you always. Once you have that, I'm sure she won't mind." She put her shirt back on and buttoned up the jacket with only her rank insignias on it. Once she was on the ground she'd strip even those away. She'd become the Black Dragon, or *no one* with a big gun. If Hector saw her like that he'd understand what she meant when she went to see him that day.

"Take care, okay? Keep an eye on your mom for me."

"Here." Tanith held her arm out rigidly. Clutched in her fingers was a picture of her and Aubrey, both smiling wide for the camera somewhere outside; a perfect blue sky outlined their heads. "So you won't forget us."

"Thanks." She took her cap off and tucked it inside. "I love you."

Tanith's face was wet with tears when she left, but the picture and the fact that she cared had smoothed Wiley's guilt for leaving them behind so soon. She looked at the picture as the transport plane she'd boarded in Mobile, Alabama, flew over the Gulf. They were landing in Cartagena in four hours after a couple of stops, where she'd have a ride waiting.

The unit heading into the rivers and jungles west of the Nukak Natural Reserve in the Guaviare Province of Colombia could take her within fifteen miles of her destination. Guaviare was one of the three leading places in the country for coca plants and was where Walter had picked to hide. A spread outside a city with less than fifty thousand residents was a perfect place: big enough to blend in, but remote enough to climb the ladder in the drug trade.

The tracking dot she'd glued to Walter's neck had stopped working two days ago, which meant the heat had to be brutal, but she was confident Walter was still hiding there. He'd made a smart move since Hector's farmers weren't that far away. They'd never get close to Hector's top lieutenants to report a suspicious American harvesting plants and making cocaine.

She didn't know who Walter had morphed into now. He'd probably buried Emray in New Orleans, and Operative Robinson was long dead as well. She was curious but not concerned as the plane landed and she was escorted to one of the sparse barracks on the remote military base. The U.S. military personnel were there as guests of the Colombian government, so she nodded at the hour the staff sergeant said she had. That's when the scheduled American and Colombian patrol would leave. Wiley had to be in position before they rolled out.

She took her duffel and removed the kit at the top. It didn't take long to apply the paint that'd make it impossible to spot her in thick foliage. She then changed uniforms and strapped a smaller pack to her back, along with her sniper rifle. It'd take her two days tops to get back, wash all this shit off, and return to her life.

As she crawled under the truck that'd bring up the rear, she started a mission carrying something personal for the first time. She had the picture Tanith had given her in her breast pocket, and she took one last look before they started rolling.

Her handheld GPS had a blinking target in the upper right-hand corner. From her current position she'd have to suffer the bad roads and mud for thirty-eight miles before she could drop and immediately roll before the lead vehicle made the turn and noticed her. It was two in the afternoon by the time that happened. Once she was clear she pushed herself to get to her perch with some daylight left.

The overcast skies made that impossible, but at midnight, with night-vision goggles and patience, she stopped at the tree line next to a cleared field near a grouping of buildings. For security she backtracked about five hundred yards before she started her climb, wearing a leaf-covered cape she'd removed from her pack.

"I hope you're having a good night, Walter. Tomorrow morning will be memorable."

❖

Walter stared at the food put out by the woman he'd hired, but he hadn't had an appetite since he'd run from New Orleans. Years of work and one flaw at the end had knocked him down as he reached for the last rung to total success. Greed had made him stupid, but he wasn't giving up.

Major Gremillion might've thought she'd gained the upper hand, but she and the group of misfits she'd collected through this process weren't important enough to waste energy on yet. Hector Delarosa and his goons, though, were. Hiding in Hector's backyard was brilliant, especially since he knew Hector's men were plastering New Orleans with money trying to find him. No matter how much money Hector had made, he was like any other thug he'd met in his job. They were rich with no imagination.

"We'll be ready to mix in two weeks tops, Mr. Clyde," said the man he'd put in charge of his fields. The guy was young but hungry, which he needed right now. The guy actually reminded him of Mitch when they'd first met—eager to please and never saying no. If he could find a few more like this he might make a comeback.

"Good," he said as he pushed his plate away. The potent aroma of garlic and cumin was making his stomach queasy. "You'll get a bonus if you find some good people who can produce around the clock."

"I do that for nothing. You gave me a job and a chance to show what I can do. Don't worry, I'm taking care of everything."

That was the problem, though. Something was eating away at his gut and his confidence. Something seemed to be bearing down on him that he couldn't stop or reason with. He waved the man off and walked out to the patio that ran the length of the back, hoping for a breeze to drive back the humidity a bit. He leaned against the railing and lit a cigarette.

"Fuck this," he said, inhaling and feeling the smoke rush along the back of his throat.

"Come on, Walter, there's no such thing as the boogey man."

The sun came up behind Wiley, and she got a clearer look at the group leaving one of the buildings and heading toward her. Each man had a rough cloth bag strapped across his shoulder that she figured contained lunch and the tools he'd need to work the grove of coca plants she'd walked through to get here.

She sat quietly, not worried they'd see her as they talked and laughed their way through their walk to work. Only one of them scanned the area, as if he expected to see something he could run and report. Who he'd tell was still a mystery since she saw no armed guards or protectors. That was highly unusual, but made sense to her. Walter had either learned subtlety or partnered with someone who'd mastered it.

In forty minutes the voices completely faded behind her and she'd stretched out on the large wide branch. The compound was still, but she knew she was right, so she took the bullet she'd shown Walter and chambered it. An hour later, there he was.

Walter walked out with a mug and cigarette pack in hand and stood looking out toward his investment with only a pair of boxers on. As she fine-tuned her focus, she saw how haggard and tired he appeared, as if being the prey instead of the hunter had taken its toll.

He set his mug down and cupped his hands around his mouth to light a smoke. "That's really bad for your health, Walter," she whispered as she set her sights.

The first inhale was deep, and he closed his eyes like he was enjoying his vice and the sun on his face. He held his breath momentarily, and as he opened his mouth to exhale, she pulled the trigger.

The bullet hit as the smoke trickled out, but Wiley only saw a little of it since the force of the shot threw Walter back. She could see the pool of blood fanning out from under his head like a grotesque halo. No one screamed or became alarmed as Walter lay dead.

She took a long look before she started back to her family. Not that they wouldn't face other problems, but for Aubrey, Tanith, and her, this one was resolved. Walter would haunt them no more.

One Year Later

"Don't stop." Aubrey panted as Wiley buried her fingers deep in her sex. The sun wasn't up yet, but every few days they woke with the need to connect. Touching Aubrey like this, watching the ecstasy flush through her entire body was a gift Wiley had never taken for granted from the moment she'd gotten her back.

Starting over hadn't been as difficult as trying to quiet her demons, though they'd had to work at assuring Tanith of her place in their new life. Some nights she held Aubrey as she cried for the scars her time with Maria had left on her daughter's soul. Those times were becoming more infrequent as she taught Tanith to draw and perform martial-arts maneuvers.

Aubrey groaned and pressed her legs together, trapping her hand to still it. "I love you," she said as Wiley stroked her hard clit with her thumb. "And I can't get enough of you."

"That makes me a lucky bastard." She stared, moving her hand slowly as she rolled closer to see Aubrey's eyes. The passion she always saw there had reignited her art as well as her heart.

Aubrey arched into her as she came and immediately moved to lie over her. Their position reminded Wiley of waking up that morning with Aubrey kissing her way down her body until she'd wrapped her lips around her, making her instantly hard and ready.

"Will you be back before I leave for work?" Aubrey asked, since she now took Tanith to school every morning and picked her up in the afternoon.

As soon as their lives had regained some normalcy, Aubrey had returned to work in the mayor's office. She had accepted the opportunity because it gave Wiley time with Tanith. Both of them had blossomed because of it.

"No, but I'm free for lunch if you are."

After a shared shower they took their time dressing, and Aubrey didn't make any comments about her slacks and dress shirt, a change from her usual shorts and T-shirt. Tanith was in the kitchen already, so they had bowls of cereal before they left.

"You aren't leaving, are you?" Tanith asked when the car doors closed and they were alone.

"No, and to prove it I was planning to take you with me this morning, unless you don't want to be late for school."

They sat together in the back of the courtroom and stayed silent as a shackled prisoner was brought in wearing an orange-and-white-striped jumpsuit. The trial hadn't taken long, and the pile of evidence had made deliberations easy on the jury, considering they took less than an hour to reach a verdict. They'd agreed on thirty-nine counts of aggravated rape, assault, and the other assorted charges the district attorney had tacked on.

"Mr. Jerry Dupre, having been found guilty by a jury of your peers, I sentence you to the maximum penalty. You are to spend the rest of your natural life in the state penitentiary." The judge stopped and removed his glasses, as if to better glare at Jerry. "I find it amazing that after working so diligently to make it through years of schooling and training to receive your medical degree, you would indulge in these depraved acts. You tried taking the coward's way out to stop, but failed. Rest assured, though, you'll never have the opportunity to harm another person as long as you draw breath."

Jerry stood as the judge had his say. Wiley had monitored the trial, not surprised when no one took seriously Jerry's claim that a crazed woman had kidnapped and mutilated him, then set him up. He'd gained weight and had a blank expression, but he wasn't fooling her. His need to dominate would never disappear, even if he was caged. No one could cut off that part of Jerry's makeup and drop it into a chipper.

"Perhaps you'll use your time to try to give your victims, including your family, some kind of peace and healing," the judge said.

As the proceedings ended she stared until Jerry was led out. Watching him shuffle away gave her the same satisfaction as calling Sheriff Wilbert Culver and telling him that his daughter's killer was dead.

"He sounds like a really bad man," Tanith said.

"He is, but today was his day with Tanit, goddess of justice and vengeance. He can't hurt anyone else."

"Will that always happen?" Tanith asked as she took Wiley's hand to walk to the car. She didn't seem interested in why Wiley had brought her along, only happy to be included.

"I hope so, especially when I can help out."

With what she'd regained she welcomed any challenge to end the need of people like Jerry to do harm, no matter how difficult, especially if she could keep those she loved safe.

Not that long ago Wiley was emotionally dead, but now she knew the Black Dragon had a lot more flights to make.

About the Author

Originally from Cuba, Ali Vali has retained much of her family's traditions and language and uses them frequently in her stories. Having her father read her stories and poetry before bed every night as a child infused her with a love of reading that carries till today. In 2000, Ali decided to embark on a new path and started writing.

Ali now lives in the suburbs of New Orleans with her partner of twenty-eight years, and finds that living in such a history-rich area provides plenty of material to draw from in creating her novels and short stories. Mixing imagination with different life experiences makes it easier to create a slew of different characters that are engaging to the reader on many levels. Ali states that "The feedback from readers encourages me to continue to hone my skills as a writer."

Books Available From Bold Strokes Books

Silver Collar by Gill McKnight. Werewolf Luc Garoul is outlawed and out of control, but can her family track her down before a sinister predator gets there first? Fourth in the Garoul series. (978-1-60282-764-6)

The Dragon Tree Legacy by Ali Vali. For Aubrey Tarver time hasn't dulled the pain of losing her first love Wiley Gremillion, but she has to set that aside when her choices put her life and her family's lives in real danger. (978-1-60282-765-3)

The Midnight Room by Ronica Black. After a chance encounter with the mysterious and brooding Lillian Gray in the "midnight room" of The Griffin, a local lesbian bar, confident and gorgeous Audrey McCarthy learns that her bad-girl behavior isn't bulletproof. (978-1-60282-766-0)

Dirty Sex by Ashley Bartlett. Vivian Cooper and twins Reese and Ryan DiGiovanni stole a lot of money and the guy they took it from wants it back. Like now. (978-1-60282-767-7)

Raising Hell: Demonic Gay Erotica, edited by Todd Gregory. Hot stories of gay erotica featuring demons. (978-1-60282-768-4)

Pursued by Joel Gomez-Dossi. Openly gay college student Jamie Bradford becomes romantically involved with two men at the same time, and his hell begins when one of his boyfriends becomes intent on killing him. (978-1-60282-769-1)

The Storm by Shelley Thrasher. Rural East Texas. 1918. War-weary Jaq Bergeron and marriage-scarred musician Molly Russell try to salvage love from the devastation of the war abroad and natural disasters at home. (978-1-60282-780-6)

Crossroads by Radclyffe. Dr. Hollis Monroe specializes in short-term relationships but when she meets pregnant mother-to-be Annie Colfax, fate brings them together at a crossroads that will change their lives forever. (978-1-60282-756-1)

Beyond Innocence by Carsen Taite. When a life is on the line, love has to wait. Doesn't it? (978-1-60282-757-8)

Heart Block by Melissa Brayden. Socialite Emory Owen and struggling single mom Sarah Matamoros are perfectly suited for each other but face a difficult time when trying to merge their contrasting worlds and the people in them. If love truly exists, can it find a way? (978-1-60282-758-5)

Pride and Joy by M.L. Rice. Perfect Bryce Montgomery is her parents' pride and joy, but when they discover that their daughter is a lesbian, her world changes forever. (978-1-60282-759-2)

Timothy by Greg Herren. Timothy is a romantic suspense thriller from award-winning mystery writer Greg Herren set in the fabulous Hamptons. (978-1-60282-760-8)

In Stone by Jeremy Jordan King. A young New Yorker is rescued from a hate crime by a mysterious someone who turns out to be more of a something. (978-1-60282-761-5)

The Jesus Injection by Eric Andrews-Katz. Murderous statues, demented drag queens, political bombings, ex-gay ministries, espionage, and romance are all in a day's work for a top secret agent. But the gloves are off when Agent Buck 98 comes up against the Jesus Injection. (978-1-60282-762-2)

Combustion by Daniel W. Kelly. Bearish detective Deck Waxer comes to the city of Kremfort Cove to investigate why the hottest men in town are bursting into flames in broad daylight. (978-1-60282-763-9)

Ladyfish by Andrea Bramhill. Finn's escape to the Florida Keys leads her straight into the arms of scuba diving instructor Oz as she fights for her freedom, their blossoming love...and her life! (978-1-60282-747-9)

Spanish Heart by Rachel Spangler. While on a mission to find herself in Spain, Ren Molson runs the risk of losing her heart to her tour guide, Lina Montero. (978-1-60282-748-6)